OBSIDIAN MASK

SCARLETT DAWN

CHAPTER 1

November 15, 2014
The day after the charity event...

I had lied to Daniil.

I knew nothing good would come from the fabrication.

No one gets away with lying to the Russian mafia without repercussions.

But I hadn't liked his backhanded ways, nor had I enjoyed the fact I had been duped. It took me too long to catch on about the alcohol here at the resort, and I wanted to verify it by saying I was on my period.

I wasn't. No bleeding for me yet.

I was bloated though, so it was on its way.

I would deal with Daniil on that issue when my monthly friend really came.

With the shadow of Least Ugly following me from Daniil's room to mine, I waved to Zane as he came out of his room. He scratched his head full of messy curls, wearing only his boxers. *In the resort's hallway*. I vaguely wondered if their group had rented the entire floor.

Zane stared at my hair as I hit the elevator button before he banged on the door opposite his. "Stash, you bastard. Open up!" He *banged* louder. "I know you stole my boots." He paused. "And my fucking alarm clock." He grinned as the elevator opened, saying more softly, "Nice hair."

"Same to you," I replied. My red curls were a disaster of their own. I needed a shower and caffeine to wake up. Our flight wasn't until later today, well after the last farewell outing Mrs. Donovan had scheduled for this fun-filled event. She had scheduled The Ernest Hemmingway Home & Museum, a quiet affair. I merely thanked God it didn't involve blood. She had taken mercy on the worn out contenders and the snobs donating to her charity.

I blinked when a blonde open Stash's door from inside. I paused halfway in the elevator, my shadow still...well, my shadow guard. I gawked. She had a blue dress shirt on that wasn't buttoned up. And that was all —bare under underneath and showing it blatantly.

Zane glanced down at her as she leaned against the doorframe, his gaze darting over her voluminous curves. He peered back over her head, shouting, "Stash! I want my shit! Now!"

"Is Cara awake yet?" the blonde asked.

Zane nodded. "She's finishing getting dressed."

Another blonde exited. But it was from Zane's room.

She looked just like the other one. Although, she was clothed. Twins.

Nope. *Scratch that.*

Another blonde peeked around the naked blonde's head from inside Stash's room, asking, "Cara, I think you took my purse last night." She looked just like the other two. Triplets. "Does that one have a toothbrush in it?"

The elevator started buzzing, and I jumped.

The triplets and Zane turned their attention to me…

A fourth blonde came out of Zane's room. *Where did they find them?*

My jaw was hanging wide, but my reporter instinct came to the fore. I had to ask, "Quadruplets?"

The fourth blonde shook her head. "No. We're all each a year apart." She waved her hand when I blinked. "We get that all the time, though. You're not the first to ask."

"Hmm," I hummed, staring at Zane's hair. Now I got it. So I replayed our previous greeting but reversed, "Nice hair."

He chuckled, playing along. "Same to you."

I waved—my hair always looked like this after sleeping—and pressed the button for my floor as he started shouting at Stash again. My shadow slipped into the elevator with me. I needed to hurry.

Getting out on the green floor I noticed a quiet, smallish man resting against a wall. His eyes were closed, but when I stepped out of the elevator, they

3

opened. He surveyed Least Ugly, his gaze instantly darting to me, his eyes assessing. My eyebrows came together as he and Least Ugly did a little nod toward each other as if they knew one another.

After walking past him, I asked my shadow quietly, "Who was that?"

"Ruslan."

"Who's Ruslan?"

"Ms. Lerrus' bodyguard."

"She has a bodyguard?"

He snorted. "Not happily."

Then Ruslan wasn't hers.

It didn't take a brain surgeon to figure out who had stuck a guard on her.

My lovely lover had been busy.

My attention altered, and I stared at the other site in front of me in the hallway. Brent and Cole were sleeping on the floor outside a door. They still wore their competitor's attire from the event yesterday—winning, of course.

And Ember had taken a room next to mine after breaking it off with them.

Giddy with reporter's delight, I quickened my strides. They started to stir, their brows puckering in my haste past them, so I opened my clutch and yanked my keycard out. Camera. I needed my fucking camera. While I had burned the truth about one story, I wasn't against this one. It was a beautiful moment. To be caught on film.

I charged inside my room, going straight for my

duffle and yanked my camera out. I turned back toward the door. And stopped. Staring at the adjoining door opened on my side, but not Ember's room. I blinked at the room. There wasn't anything else to be had in here. She had already bargained—and taken—the photo of true value.

Glancing at my bed, I gawked.

Ember was in my fucking bed. Under the covers. The bitch's fire engine long red hair spilling over my damn pillow. Sleeping. *And* snoring very softly.

What the hell?

Christ. *Later.* I had a reporter's delight to take care of.

I raced back across my room and threw open the door, it banging loudly with camera in hand…and they were gone! I glanced up and down the hallway frantically and saw them at the elevator, rubbing their faces and running their hands through their hair…just before they got in after the doors opened. *Shit!*

I slammed my door shut, hopefully waking sleeping beauty.

It did. I walked back over to the bed.

She was stretching, looking pretty damn comfortable and rested.

"What the hell are you doing in here?" I was trying for calm. It wasn't working so much.

She pointed to her room, yawning. "I came back to my room to get some seclusion and rest after the gun control event, and I did for a little while…" her lips thinned, "well, it got a little loud in there later in the evening, so I came in here to get some sleep since I figured you wouldn't be coming back." She scratched her nose with a languid hand. "You bang around a lot when you're getting ready, you know? Lots of hostility from the sounds of it." She glanced at my hair. "Although I can see why."

No way was I going to tell her she was right. I stated dryly, "Brent and Cole left. You can go back to your room now." I paused. "And stay there. Unless you want me to run an article on you hiding from them."

She yawned again and rolled out of bed, wearing a huge red thermal that read *DEATH COMES* and a pair of black gym shorts that were ten times too large. She had to hold up the shorts to keep them on.

"Do you not know your own size?" I gestured at her clothes.

She looked down and picked at the shirt. "I like these."

I walked to her adjoining door, opened it, and motioned for her to leave. She did after grabbing her cell phone, the gun, and the knife under my pillow. She bumped my shoulder hard as she walked into her room.

These people were all fucking crazy. At least Daniil made up for it in other ways.

I locked my adjoining door and shoved a chair behind it.

There. That might help.

I went into motion, hurrying to shower. And… banged around again afterward because it was no use. My hair was just inhuman bizarre, but luckily, my face was back to normal coloring. Dressing in a long white, soft cotton sundress that floated around my ankles, and a white scarf I tied once around my neck and let hang down my bare back, I slipped on a pair of pearl-jeweled flip-flops and grabbed my purse so I could store my camera and recorder. I was ready to go.

CHAPTER 2

I entered the lobby fifteen minutes later where I was supposed to meet the group heading to the Hemmingway Home. There were muffins, Danishes, and juice waiting on a courtesy table for the milling group. I made a beeline to the table, grabbing two muffins and juice. My stomach growled in appreciation.

Scanning the back of the lobby, since that was where Lion Security would be, I spotted them. They were like a blob of black paint against all the light and airy colors in the lobby. I mean seriously people, it was going to be over a hundred degrees today and they were wearing all black. Yes, some wore shorts and t-shirts, but the only one wearing any color was Ember —from the red skulls on her shirt. But this was Key West! Live a little.

Daniil stood next to his only daughter, Eva— who was staring at me with hostility. He wore a pair of wide legged black linen pants that were rolled casually at the bottom, black flip-flops, and a black and silver island shirt with short sleeves that button down the front. It had an open V-neck neck, showing his muscular chest. A pair of black shades sat on top of his head, pulling his hair back from his face. He looked damn good.

He followed Eva's gaze, his eyebrows together after staring at her face. His perusal stopped when his eyes landed on me, and his eyes went to my hair first—*come on!*—and then down my frame, quickly hooding. *Hmm.* Guess I had chosen a decent outfit.

Deciding to take my chances—since Daniil and I weren't public (too many enemies on his side)—I headed their way, finishing off one of the muffins and tossing the wrapper before beginning on the other one. It was strawberry. My favorite. Sipping on my drink, I went up to my nemesis. "Morning, Ember. You're looking refreshed this morning. Sleep well?"

She had scowled for a second before Brent and Cole looked her way, quickly altering her expression to remote coolness. "Yes, fine. Thank you for asking, Elizabeth." She glanced around, discerning how most of Daniil's children were watching me with not-so-friendly expressions. "How did you sleep? I didn't hear you come in last night."

Bitch. "Fine." I shouldn't have baited her in the first place. Daniil's kids were still in hate mode after finding out about us last night. "Thank you for asking."

Daniil's lips were twitching, and he quickly looked away and began speaking to Carl and Anna. Grigori, on the other hand, was decidedly blank faced, although he was staring at both Ember and me. I went to nibble at my muffin, but it had a large chunk taken out of it.

What?

Glancing to my right, Ember munched on a piece of strawberry muffin, holding it delicately between her fingers.

Oh. My. Shit-fuck-hate-her. "I'm hungry! Get your own!"

A few of her colleagues were chuckling, watching us. Again. Snooping damn group.

The sad thing was I kind of fit right in being a reporter.

"Mmm," she murmured. "It's good."

"I know that—" I stopped abruptly.

My head cocked. I listened…and slowly froze.

Growing up, there are certain noises you become accustomed to—like the ringing of a bell in high school. You know when you hear it you need to get to class. Or the sound of a whistle blowing in a swimming pool. When you hear that, you know to look at the lifeguards and hope they didn't just catch you doing something wrong. Or, in my father's case, it was his feet. When you heard my father's stomping footfalls, you knew you were in trouble and you needed to straighten up, shut up, and take the ass chewing he was about to give.

And…listening…those same clicking footfalls were on the tile behind me.

It couldn't be. There was no way. I had ignored

his and my mother's calls. I hadn't known what to say to them, so I now had thirty-eight missed phone calls on my cell. And just as many messages on my voicemail I hadn't bothered to listen to.

Perhaps I should have answered just one.

My face drained of color and my vision blurred.

I didn't want to look back.

I reviewed that thought.

No. Curiosity wasn't even strong enough in this reporter.

I said a small prayer that I was hallucinating.

"Christ," Ember muttered, staring as her eyebrows formed a harsh line. "Maybe I shouldn't have taken your food. You look like you're going to faint." She stilled. "Are you diabetic or something?"

The group went silent, staring at me.

Daniil's gaze snapped in my direction, probably at the actual *worry* in Ember's tone. His eyes darted over my features, and he literally started moving toward me...but then, I heard it.

My father's voice. Moving closer. He shouted, "Elizabeth! Is that you?"

Daniil halted, and his gaze snapped toward my father, his eyes narrowing.

Apparently, he didn't know what Dad looked like.

Embarrassingly, I whimpered, but I quickly bit my lip to stop the sound.

Ember whistled low and started chuckling softly. "Oh. This is too good." *Evil bitch.*

"Elizabeth!" my mother stated. Lord help me. My

mom was with him. They were getting real close. "I know you can hear us, young lady!"

Another whine left me, and I didn't look anywhere even close to Daniil as I slowly turned around. I licked my lips nervously and peered up from the floor. My parents stopped right in front of me. *And* my aunt Susan and my cousin Katie.

It was a real family affair.

I croaked, "Mom. Dad. What are you doing here?"

Zane started choking off to my right, and I even heard Grigori clear his throat a few times. From the corner of my eye, I noticed Daniil freeze. Perfect.

Dad's gaze darted all over the group I was standing with, and he muttered under his breath, "*No wonder.*" His regard landed directly behind me where Grigori stood. There was instant disapproval in his eyes…and his perusal continued as he grabbed my bicep, yanking me next to him, damn protectively. His inspection stopped on the bodyguards, and he sucked in a breath…and when they landed on Daniil…it was like instant hate hardened his stare. Slowly, he finished his scan, and I kept silent. Nothing said was better than babbling right now. He didn't seem to like Zane or Roman much, either. And then they landed on Ember.

She stiffened under his attention.

Dad asked, "Are you Ember Lerrus? The one my daughter," he shook me by the arm, "was fighting with?"

My mouth bobbed. "It wasn't Ember. It was Chrissy."

"She was in the photo with you."

Her eyes were huge and she nudged my arm but continued to stare at my dad. "Have you given him the check?" When I shook my head, she nudged me again, saying quickly, "Give him the damn check."

My father wasn't a big man in stature. He was only about five foot, nine inches and lean. But when he looks at you…you know he means business. It was one of the reasons why he was such a great preacher. People instantly knew he believed in what he was speaking about. I didn't blame Ember for being nervous around him.

I handed her my muffin and drink, then lifted my purse, digging through it and pulling out her money order. "Dad, Ember donated this." I held the check out, and he took it with his free hand.

He stopped, staring down at the numbers on it.

Ember's shoulders relaxed. She even started eating my muffin.

He cleared his throat and pocketed the check, stating calmly, "Thank you for your generosity, Ms. Lerrus. God, the church, and I thank you." Then, he clamped a hand down on her shoulder, startling her enough that she spilled my juice. "Now, my wife and I would like to have a word with you two."

"Huh?" Ember mumbled around a mouthful of muffin, her gaze frantic.

"An intervention, of sorts." He started hauling us away from the group.

"Dad!" I hissed, tugging on my arm. "Don't bring her into this." Christ, my editor was going to kill me if word of this got out.

"Elizabeth! Not. One. Word," Dad growled low.

I still opened my mouth.

Mom interrupted, "Elizabeth, so help me!"

Oh. I shut my mouth. That wasn't a tone that boded well if I argued.

Zane started choking hard.

The rest of the group watched us being pulled away, with gaping mouths.

"Sir, this really isn't necessary," Ember pled with Dad loudly, trying to get his attention as he hauled us toward the side of the room. "Elizabeth and I weren't fighting then. We're friends now." She glanced at me frantically for help.

I kept my mouth shut. I knew better. When Dad and Mom got it into their heads—which they obviously had, traveling all the way down here—to do something, they did it. With passion. There was no stopping them.

"Sure you are," Dad stated dryly, depositing us in two seats in the corner of the lobby—unfortunately, not too far away from where he had yanked us away. Everyone was staring, and I sunk back into the chair and rested my forehead on my hand. My stomach rolled, now decidedly queasy. This was mortifying.

"Now, would you two care to explain why my

daughter was fighting?" Mom asked calmly, crossing her arms. "Maybe, we can help work this issue out."

Ember stabbed a finger in my direction. "She started it." Good God. My parents did it to everyone. Gone was the strong, deadly woman I knew her to be. That woman had been replaced by a naughty child standing before a scary-ass principal.

I stayed silent, rubbing my forehead and staring at my lap.

"I didn't ask who started it. I asked what the issue was about," my mother said slowly as if she were talking to a halfwit.

Ember's mouth shut, finally following my cue.

This would go a lot smoother if Ember kept it up.

A half minute passed in silence, and then my father dropped to his haunches, staring up at us since we were both looking down. "I know this is embarrassing, but we're just trying to help. From what we saw on that video… That type of hostility and hate isn't good for the mind, body, and soul…" And he was off. Lecturing and teaching all at the same time.

We took it silently. All fifteen minutes of it. I had heard this all before, but he directed as much of his sermon to Ember as he did me. He spoke calmly and patiently, but I knew he wasn't because he kept running his hand through his graying blond hair and fiddling with his gold cross necklace hanging over his white button up shirt.

My mother bent down when my father stood,

and spoke to us of the dangerous hazards of letting violence, hatred, and prejudice enter your heart and mind. This went on for at least ten more minutes. I knew the tour bus was going to be arriving soon, so I kept that in mind as my salvation as she droned on. Her voice powerful and commanding made it hard to ignore. But after twenty-eight years of hearing it, she only sounded like Mom to me and I could tune her out with the best of them.

When she stood, I breathed a tiny sigh of relief, still picking at my dress and started rubbing my forehead again. Then Dad stated, "Your mother and I will be staying here for the next few days, so if either of you want to come and speak to us privately about anything we just discussed, our door is open."

I instantly flinched. They were going to be here for a few days?

Thank the Lord above we were leaving tonight.

"We won't interfere with your work, sweetie. And we know your flight is scheduled for tomorrow." My old flight had been scheduled for then. I had canceled it, taking Daniil's private jet home tonight. I was fucked. Mom mistook my reaction and patted the air. "We're just taking a small vacation with the added benefit of being here for you if you need us."

Sure they were.

"Ms. Lerrus, we're done here. You can go." Dad paused. "And again, thank you for your incredible generosity."

Ember popped up from her seat even faster than

I had seen her move in the ring, nodding and quickly darting away to her group. I stared after her in envy. The group had started to quietly talk again, but when they saw Ember coming toward them, they all shut-up and watched her arrive, then started speaking to her. Ember's face was blank, kind of shell-shocked, and it didn't look like she replied to any of them. Yeah, I got that.

Dad said, "What are your plans for today?"

I looked at him directly for the first time in almost a half-hour. "I'm working. Going to the Hemingway House to see if I can get a story." Not really the story bit, but it would keep them from tagging along with—

My mother's face lit up. "Wonderful! I've always wanted to visit there."

I groaned, my head falling back onto my palm. And then a thought occurred. "It's a reserved event."

She waved her hand. "We'll drive ourselves. And we won't bother you."

This was bad.

A tour guide walked into the lobby. "The bus to The Hemingway House & Museum is waiting outside for anyone who's attending."

I jumped up, putting my purse over my shoulder. "Gotta go."

"We'll see you there." Dad grabbed my hand and stopped me. His eyes glanced at the Lion Security group that was beginning to make its way to the entrance—Daniil was covertly watching me, along with most of his children, and Ember and Zane. "Are those the type of people you're hanging around now? Because I can tell you, sweetie, those are not the type to bring anything good into your life." He was watching me closely.

"They're the story I hope to get," I stated. I really hated lying to my parents.

His eyes flicked to my fading hickey, and I had to mentally stop myself from covering it with my hand. "If you say so." He smiled, and it was…something…I wasn't sure, but it wasn't one he normally gave me. "We'll see you there."

I rushed off, flying out the doors of the resort as fast as I could. I climbed the stairs to the bus and glanced around for a seat, more than embarrassed for my parents' interaction. Daniil sat in the back of the bus with a seat empty next to him. There were others closer to the front, and I really debated sitting in one… until Daniil's eyebrows rose in a mocking gesture when I glanced at him again.

Fine. I wouldn't wuss out from shame. Trekking my way down the aisle, a few teasing comments pinged in my direction from Lion Security's group. But when I started to pass Ember, she threw her right arm out, stopping me. Staring at the back of the seat where her arm was a barrier in front of me, she stated quietly, "I don't owe you any longer."

No. She didn't owe me shit after that. She near killing me was now forgotten.

I nodded and moved to Daniil, ignoring his

children's gazes. Daniil had sat in the aisle seat, and I squeezed between him and the seat in front of him. His guards were sitting in the seat across from us, and Zane and Brent were in front of us. He was in no mood for secrecy right now his hands landing on my hips and helping me get past him.

I sat and stared out the window while the tour guide gave a small spiel.

Daniil's left hand slid around the back my neck under my hair. He just left it there, gripping my neck possessively. I turned my attention to him as the bus began moving and met his brown eyes. He stared at me, not saying anything.

He bent and cupped my cheeks, kissing me softly.

His mouth felt like heaven and fireworks exploded. It was what I needed right now. No condemnation. No lecture. No questions. Nothing but kindness and contact. It was a small act a lover gave another when they were having a bad day. I moaned against his mouth, taking his offering.

At the sound, he pressed harder.

From the seat in front of Zane and Brent, Eva muttered, "They had better not be doing anything back there."

"I don't even want to think about it, so shut up," Artur grumbled.

Daniil paused, and we both opened our eyes, staring at one another.

Zane chuckled, hearing my moan only a moment before.

Daniil gently kissed me once more, rubbing his thumbs over my temples, then whispered quietly in my ear, "It's probably best to wait on this until they're not around. They need time to adjust."

No shit.

"That's fine," I whispered just as softly. "And thank you for not commenting…on that."

He grinned against my ear, kissing softly right behind it, his lips soft and warm.

I shivered, making him grin again against my skin before he pulled back. But he did put his arm behind me and wrapped it around my waist, tugging me against him. Letting my head fall against his shoulder, I stared out the window and played with his fingers, watching the scenery pass by.

"My parents, aunt, and cousin will be staying for a few days," I stated. "I won't be able to leave tonight with you."

He placed his chin on top of my head, watching out the window with me. "I figured as much." He raised his voice louder. "We'll wait it out with you and take my plane home when you're ready."

Answering groans erupted from the Lion Security group.

"Thank you." That helped. I played with his pinkie, twisting the small onyx ring he wore there in steady circles. "They embarrass me."

"Because they love you."

"To death."

"That's what parents do."

I sighed. I would just have to take his word on that since I had no personal viewpoint. "It's still humiliating."

"I would imagine so."

"Did your parents ever do anything like this to you?"

He chuckled softly. "It's safe to say Papa kept me in line growing up. And not always privately."

"What about when you were my age? Did he still do it then?"

"Even then. He's never stopped. He's a force to be reckoned with."

"Parents are a pain in the ass," I muttered darkly.

He laughed outright. "Yes. They are. But they're also a necessary evil."

I went silent. He was showing his age again. He knew things that I didn't, and was talking about things I didn't understand. To me, my parents needed to butt the fuck out. I had no clue why it was a necessary evil. I didn't like not understanding things like reasoning. It made me feel stupid.

A few moments later, I felt him still before he slowly took his chin off the top of my head and whispered in my ear, "You'll understand in time. It's not something I can explain. You have to experience and feel it to fully comprehend what I mean." He kissed my neck and then sighed. "This is difficult. Even for me. Don't think it's not." He kissed my neck again. "But I believe it's worth it." He bit down gently on my neck, making me sink back against him, completely relaxing.

SCARLETT DAWN

Yeah. We may have an age-language issue, but it was definitely worth it.

CHAPTER 3

The tour had been dreadful. Not because of the location—that was amazing since Hemingway was one of my all-time favorite authors—but because my family had actually beaten us there. They had been waiting, my mom and dad watching from the parking lot. It was only luck that I had noticed them, and I had quickly exited my seat and shot forward down the aisle, being one of the first to exit the bus. And Lion Security's group found it pretty damn amusing that my family had tagged behind, silently taking the tour with us.

They weren't finding it as amusing now, where we sat in a restaurant that overlooked the ocean—with my family coming right for us after my dad somehow managed to coax an invite out of Anna before we loaded back onto the bus. Lion Security's group was glaring at her, and her cheeks were pink while Carl kept an arm around her protectively, scowling at the group. She hadn't meant to. I knew that. I *really* knew that.

Dad just had a way of getting what he wanted. No one was safe when he was on a mission.

And, like clockwork, as soon as Dad stepped up to the table, everyone seated at our table sat up straight, as if a drill sergeant had just bellowed, even though Dad hadn't even spoken and was only perusing everyone. Daniil sat across from me, fully knowing my dad was showing up. I wasn't sure what that was about, but I kept my gaze firmly off him.

My cousin Katie, who looked a lot like me but with blonde inhuman hair, sat on my left and my aunt Susan, who looked like an older version of her daughter, also with inhuman blonde hair, quickly sat on my right. My mom, who appeared like an older version of me with the same crazy hair—but with white streaks in her strawberry blonde curls—sat next to my aunt while my dad instantly went to the far end of the table. Away from me. He sat between Roman and Torrez.

I blinked at him.

Then at the empty chair next to Katie.

Back to him.

Now the empty chair.

What the hell was he doing?

Picking up my water glass, I whispered to Susan, "What's Dad doing?" She was my cool aunt. My mom's sister. They couldn't be any more different in personalities.

She didn't even glance at my dad. "He's trying to figure out who you've been having sex with, dear."

Water spewed from my mouth. *Like a broken fire*

hydrant. It landed all over my plate. The flower arrangement in the middle of the table. Daniil's plate. And on his black shirt.

The table fell silent. Staring.

Daniil's lips had twitched for a second at my aunt's quiet pronouncement, but he had quickly pinched them, so it looked perfect for my undignified blunder. He gradually picked up his napkin and started drying off his shirt, his gaze down on his task.

"Elizabeth, what in the world?" my mother sputtered, her attention turning to Daniil, and although she was shocked, she watched him warily. She glanced at me quickly. "Apologize. Now." My mom was actually fearful of Daniil.

"I'm sorry," I murmured quietly, wiping my mouth.

Zane and Stash start speaking to Dad, distracting him.

The conversation around the table slowly picked up.

But they were all multitasking, listening in.

Daniil's hair hung down around his face as he soaked the water from his shirt into his napkin, saying quietly and evenly, "That's all right, Beth. I'm sure it was an accident."

I froze.

So did my mom, aunt, and cousin.

Mom got over her fright in a hurry because, from her frozen state, she asked—this wasn't a good thing— delicately, "What did you call her?"

Just barely, Daniil's head tilted up, his eyes lifting as he held the napkin to his shirt. His dark gaze darted to each of us under hooded lids. I should have warned him earlier. But I hadn't even thought about it. It hadn't even entered my damn mind. And now I was going to faint because I had forgotten one very simple detail.

Daniil's eyes landed on my mom, and he finished lifting his head. He casually placed his napkin on the table, his accent *heavy*, answering in a bored quiet tone, "Her name. Why do you ask?" He relaxed back in his chair, his arms comfortably in his lap, his expression serene.

"No, you didn't. Her name's Elizabeth, so why did you call her Beth?" My mom kept her voice very soft as she zeroed in on him.

I bit my cheek. This wasn't going to end well.

Daniil's eyebrows pulled together, his expression turning thoughtful. When he spoke again, his accent was heavy. "Beth is a..." His right hand waved in the air. "...short name of Elizabeth, correct? Like Jon for Jonathan or Joe for Joseph?"

My mom stared for all of a heartbeat. Her expression unfroze, and her shoulders lowered, easing. Same as my aunt and cousin.

My God.

He was playing dumb with our language. I blinked, utterly astonished. Somehow, I was betting he very rarely played stupid for anyone. Carl, who was sitting next to him, even stared at him for a moment before grabbing his coffee and sipping at it. His gaze darted to me, thoughtful...then stunned...before quickly cooling to steel.

Well, Carl had figured it out.

Mom nodded. "Yes. It's a *nickname*. But Elizabeth doesn't allow anyone to call her that. I imagine my daughter..." She glanced at me. I quickly looked down and started drying off my plate. "I imagine she was a little intimidated to inform you of this. I'm sure she would appreciate it if, from now on, you would call her Elizabeth instead of Beth."

Setting my napkin down, I gradually peered up.

Daniil was staring at me, his eyebrows unfurling. He continued speaking with the heavy accent. "My apologies...Elizabeth. I did not realize this."

I bit my lip. Hard.

Christ.

I wanted to laugh my ass off. I lowered my gaze so no one would see my expression since I evidently suck at keeping a blank face. "It's all right. No harm done."

He grunted deep in reply.

I almost lost it, kicking his leg under the table. If I started laughing, it would give it all away. He needed to cut it out. He was just being mean now.

Carl was choking on his coffee.

Anna rubbed his back, evaluating him with worry.

But Carl kept his gaze away from us.

Probably a good thing since I was close to busting up.

Artur took his seat next to his father, returning

from the bathroom. He blinked from my mom to my aunt to me to my cousin. He stared only at our hair. "It comes in fours."

I lost it then and chuckled loudly.

And…that's when Mom honed in on him.

Poor Artur didn't know what hit him. He stared at her in rising confusion and shock as she asked him who he was—his age, his profession, his hobbies, his views on politics…that was when Daniil cut in, saving his son from further inquisition, since Artur was utterly baffled and ready to bash his head against the table.

Mom no longer looked at Daniil with worry. In fact, she spoke slowly to him—making Artur even more muddled—when he asked her what she would recommend from the menu. She must have felt damn brave because she…she pulled out pamphlets from her purse.

"Mom!" I groaned. I didn't have a problem with the statists of rising violence, but I was pretty sure this group was going to give me hell for this later. "Not now."

She shook her head and passed them out while the waitress took our orders. "This is the perfect crowd for this, sweetie."

"Not really," I muttered, sinking back into my chair.

Katie nudged me and leaned over, whispering, "Mom tried to stop your parents from coming down here, but they were dead set on it. We decided to rescue you by tagging along." She glanced at my dad and then came back to my ear. "Your dad made your mom drive here from Hemingway House because he wanted to get started on a list of possible men—from this group— that has to be responsible for your sudden downfall." My eyes bulged. "He put them all in order from hair color and age since he didn't know everyone's names. You should see it. It's fucking hilarious."

I groaned, nodding. "Good to know."

She grinned. "Uh-huh. I thought so."

I rolled my eyes, ignoring how everyone was either staring at my mother—or at the pamphlet in their hands—wide-eyed. "You're enjoying this and you know it."

She shrugged, still smirking. "I'm no longer the black sheep of the family." She raised her right hand, holding it there. "You hold that title now."

Sighing, I gave her a weak high five. Yeah. She might be the wild child of our family, but apparently, I had even surpassed her colorful lifestyle. I covertly glanced at Daniil. He had the pamphlet closed on top of his plate; he hadn't touched it other than to accept it. He was speaking to a—now—cool and composed Carl. And as if he could feel me looking at him, his gaze darted to mine and his lips twitched before continuing his conversation, accent ever so slowly getting lighter.

He was coaxing the memory-sound out of my mother's mind.

Damn cunning is what it was.

My aunt casually asked against my curls in an extremely soft voice, "You do realize if your father or mother finds out you're having sex with the head of the Russian Mafia, they will ship you off to another country, don't you?" I sucked in a harsh breath, and Daniil's speech faltered with Carl before continuing, and she snickered. "Don't worry, dear. Your secret's safe with me. Although, I will say, aside from the obvious danger and stupidity of your choice, he is a little old for you. Now me, on the other hand…" She tilted back and fluttered her eyelashes at me…and I started having a coughing fit.

Two glasses of downed water later, demanded by my mother that I drink, I recovered. I trusted my aunt to keep quiet. She was a wild woman herself, but it was still unnerving knowing she had been observant enough to catch on and…well, just that she knew. Daniil understood she knew too, from the way he had assessed her when she wasn't watching. Probably trying to make sure she wasn't going to snitch on me. Because the truth was, she wasn't too far off about what my parents would do if they found out. I was pretty sure neither Daniil nor I was ready to give each other up yet. Our time was definitely not finished with each other.

Once again, Daniil's plate was far more appetizing than mine was, but I didn't see any way to get around stealing his food. The man had a sixth sense and ordered what I wanted, even when I didn't know. I picked at my food, staring at his, watching as he twirled his fork in his spicy Cajun pasta. Glancing down at my burger, it just looked like a dead cow smashed inside a bun. I felt a little nauseous even looking at it.

Sometimes, my pickiness in food annoyed even me.

Daniil rubbed his chest. "I forgot. This will give me heartburn." He sat his fork down with frustration. "I'll have to order something else."

Artur glanced up from his plate. "That'll take forever, Papa."

I blurted, "I'll trade you." I paused when Mom's gaze shot up in surprise. "I haven't touched mine yet, same as him. Plus his," I pointed at his plate, "looks really good."

"Deal." Daniil reached over and swapped out our plates. "Thank you."

"You're welcome," I mumbled, staring down at my new plate. *Mmm.* I grabbed the fork he had left on the plate and chowed down.

God, it was good.

The table sat in companionable silence as we all enjoyed our first few bites.

With a mouth full of food, I almost choked when Mom said, "Elizabeth, your father and I went ahead and set up a date for you and Don to meet. He's the young man we were telling you about. His schedule is just as hectic as yours so we had to schedule it in advance."

Everyone paused in mid-motion—at least those in the know that I was sleeping with Daniil—as I grabbed my water, taking a hefty gulp, firmly keeping my eyes off my lover. When I had full control of myself, I glanced up. "Mom, I told you I wasn't interested in any more of your blind dates."

Mom waved her hand. "I know you said that, but it's already scheduled."

I felt my features harden as irritation took hold. "Unscheduled it."

Mom leaned forward, peering past her sister to me. She smiled. It was hard and determined. "No. I don't think so." Staring into my eyes, she stated firmly, "It would be rude to cancel now. You're going." She paused. "And besides, you really do have quite a bit in common. And he's very handsome. We think you'll get along with him perfectly."

She stared me down as the table stayed silent. Those that weren't in the know, finally catching on there was something amiss, so *everyone* began to stare at us.

And…I was pissed.

She was doing this on purpose. My parents' intuition skills had led them to believe I was sleeping with someone in this group. Correctly. And she was trying to ruin it. Humiliating me even more in the process.

If I said anything to dispute this further, they would make today's antics look like child's play with this group. I knew this from past experience. I hadn't lived with them for eighteen years of my life without learning their ways. And their *ways* could be ten times worse than what they were doing right now.

Looking out for my best interests, they always called it.

Overbearing parents was what I called it.

I stayed silent until I felt I could speak without yelling. I turned my attention back to my plate. "I understand. I'll go on the date with him." A quick glance at her and away. "One date. That's all."

"I promise you'll really like him. It won't be a hardship by any stretch of the imagination." She paused. "We even set the date up at that new club Crimson City. We know you love to dance."

I felt my eyes close. Kirill owned that club, one of the Russian men sitting at our table. My parents didn't know that though, since they didn't keep up on things like that. It had been just dumb luck on their part. I muttered, "Perfect."

Mom stated cheerfully, "We thought so."

The silence didn't last too long because Zane and Stash—I was really beginning to feel like I owed them —started up the conversation at the table.

Katie said quietly, "He really is a hottie. I've seen him." Waggling her eyebrows, she offered—what she so obviously thought was helpful, "He's a cop. And he has these green eyes that are so clear…"

Half the table went silent again, apparently multitasking even better than I sometimes did. Ember asked slowly, "Would Don's last name happen to be Phillips?"

My mom's face lit, and she nodded. "Yes. Do you know him?"

Ember's eyes widened and her jaw gaped for a moment. Her eyes began to travel to Daniil, who I hadn't glanced at yet, but they slammed back to my mom and her mouth snapped shut. She nodded, her lips twitching. "Yeah. I actually went on a few dates with him at one point in my life." She glanced at me, her gaze utterly amused. "Elizabeth, your mom's right. It won't be a hardship for you."

Grigori started chuckling softly and quickly cleared his throat even as my aunt grabbed my leg under the table. Brutally. Her fingers digging into my inner thigh.

Wincing, I tried prying her fingers off as Mom began a conversation with Ember about this Don Phillips guy. But my aunt only gripped my leg tighter, and I glanced at her. Her eyes were huge, and she was staring directly across the table. At Daniil.

After peeking over at my dad, I ventured a glance at Daniil. And froze.

He was…upset.

Very, *very* upset. Or furious.

Maybe in a killing mood would be a better way to phrase it.

Apparently, Mom, Ember, and Katie weren't lying. And he knew it, too.

My gut was telling me he had seen Don—who must be fucking gorgeous from Daniil's reaction—at some point, and most definitely didn't like me going on this date.

He stared. At me. Blatantly. His eyes on *fire*.

Furious. Possessive. Carnal. Ruthless.

It was all there. In dark brown, uncompromising orbs.

Aimed. At. Me.

Unhurried, he set his cup of coffee down and then moved his hand under the table.

When it appeared again, there was a cell phone in his grasp.

His nostrils flared, and he mouthed, "*Not. A. Fucking. Chance.*"

Licking my dry lips, I sucked in a breath when I realized I hadn't breathed since turning toward him. I watched as he—finally—looked away from me, dropping his head slightly, and focused on his cell. My aunt shivered, apparently no longer trapped by him, and her head snapped toward me as his fingers flew across his touch screen.

She squeezed my thigh even harder, putting her mouth directly against my ear. "Are you sure you know what you're doing?"

Licking my lips again, I nodded. Yeah. I knew what I was doing.

I kicked him under the table.

His response? A slight eyebrow lift.

I kicked harder.

A tiny puff of air left his lips.

I kicked him as hard as I could right in his shin.

The response? I shouted when it felt like I broke my foot.

His hand immediately went under the table,

grabbing his gun, which I perceived the briefest flash of when I jumped up, shaking my foot. Everyone watched me hobble about. I felt tears spring to my eyes, and they burned, but I pushed them back and leaned heavily over the table.

No. I was not sneaky. But it was no less effective when I was able to distract everyone with my foot waving antics and snatch Daniil's cell from his hand without many noticing. The important ones were my family, and they didn't see a damn thing because they were too busy standing and evaluating my swollen red foot. In hindsight, it was better not to kick someone made of steel with only flip-flops on.

Half of the table was looking at me like I was crazy.

The other half were snickering or flat out laughing.

And one lone man glared.

With my family squatting down, seeing to my foot, I mouthed, *"Not. A. Fucking. Chance."* Then I smiled. Sweetly. Right before I dumped his cell into my water glass.

It made an odd *burzp* sound and then the screen flashed off under water.

He scowled harder, his gaze downright scary, but I just beamed at him as the table really started hooting. That was until my dad's head shot up, and he leveled them with a look. He didn't find it funny that I was hurt. And neither would anyone else as their snickering cut off abruptly, pretty much all of them sheepish in the face at my dad's displeasure.

All except Daniil, who took my water glass after Dad turned back to my injury. He stuck two long fingers into the glass, pulled his phone out, and dried it with his napkin calmly. All while staring at me. His expression had turned…to nothing. Calm and quiet.

Somehow, I didn't think that was a good thing.

"I still don't see how you did that," Mom griped as we walked out of the restaurant.

Two ice bags later, I was able to walk normally even if my foot was still red. It wasn't broken, but it was sore. Trying not to let it show, I complained, "I told you I was popping my foot, and it bent too far." I wiggled it, keeping the grimace at bay. "See, it's fine."

She bent down, evaluating it one more time before sighing and standing. "Are you sure you don't want to ride with us instead of going up the bus stairs?" She eyed me skeptically before turning her attention to half the men in the group who she and Dad had pestered all throughout the rest of our meal. Even through dessert. I was never going to live this down.

"I'm sure. I'll see you later. I have work to do." Not completely a lie. I was going to have to deal with

Daniil, who had been decidedly mute the rest of the time at the table.

"Fine." She kissed my cheek. "We'll see you later, then."

Dad hugged me.

Aunt Susan winked at me.

And Katie alternated staring between Torrez, Lev, and Artur.

When they were out of eyeshot, I walked slowly —my foot seriously killing me—to the group, dreading this, but it needed to be done. Daniil waited until we were halfway through the aisle of the bus, back where only Lion Security could see us, before his hand shot out, gripping the back of my neck where he walked behind me. Yep, he was pissed.

I didn't fight him because I wanted to keep this conversation private, away from the competitors in the front of the bus. So I waited until we were seated to start whacking at his arm. "Let me go, Daniil." I whacked his arm again. "You're acting like a barbarian." Another solid whack—doing no good. "You can't just go around killing everyone who hits on me! Or hasn't even hit on me, but might. That's pure lunacy."

A split second later, his mouth pounded down on mine.

My head slammed back against the window where he held me, kissing the shit out of me. Sadly, after the shock wore off, it turned me the hell on. I knew I should probably be upset with him, but knowing and actually doing are two very different things. Instead, all I felt were the damn fireworks. And it felt like the Fourth of July erupted between us.

Somehow, I was suddenly flat on my back on the two seats with him on top of me. I knew everyone in his group was listening since the back half of the bus was quiet. I shook my head, whispering, "Daniil. Stop." His mouth went to my hickey where he bit me solidly, gripping me. I hissed, "Your kids, Daniil!"

"Yes." Grigori's voice could be heard, his tone dry. "Your kids, Papa."

Eva groaned, sounding like she was getting sick.

Artur hushed her.

Roman was the only silent one.

I guess one out of four wasn't bad. It could have been worse.

Daniil stiffened over me, and then licked over his fading mark, being silent. Honestly, I wasn't sure how silent we had been before. When the explosions went off, the world disappeared around us. He lifted his head, his black hair blanketing down around us as he whispered harshly, "I will kill him if you go on this date." He was serious.

I shook my head, his hair tickling the sides of my face, leaning up and whispering just as brutally, "You will not! If you keep this shit up, I'm going to walk." I paused, letting him see that I was serious. "I may not agree with violence, but I do understand protection. I get your mentality on that fact. Protect your family. Your loved ones. Your colleagues. I can only hope with words, not with fists or guns. But you killing him is not about protection. It would be flat out murder. He has done nothing to you, and you're acting like a spoiled executioner, getting your way with only a few taps on your cell phone." I stared hard. "Is that what you are, Daniil? A murderer? A monster?"

He was silent as he stared down at me with a crazy look in his eye. "I have been called that. But only to those who attack me first or threaten my family." He paused, his head cocking. "Did you call me a spoiled executioner?" Another pause and he nodded. "Yes. You did. Maybe I have become a little lax on how I take care of business. Perhaps I should handle this one personally." He grinned. "That would be amusing."

My head fell back against the seat, and I thumped him on the forehead a few times lightly with my knuckles. "Are you listening to me? I will walk if you hurt someone else because you're jealous. Do. You. Understand. Me?" We would work on the whole issue of what he thought was a 'threat' instigating him with the need to be a 'monster' later.

He stared, still smiling. "You think you can just walk away from me?"

I stilled as crazy stared down. "Is that a threat?"

He paused, his smile slowly fading. Sanity emerged in his brown eyes. "No. I would never really threaten you."

I nodded bit-by-bit. I must be the cracked one because I believed him. "Good. Now are you going to go after this Don guy? Do I need to walk away now?"

His jaw clenched. "You haven't seen him."

I shook my head. "Not what I asked."

"He's as good looking as Lev. Maybe better. And he's young. Like you." He paused. "And he can dance well from what I'm told." He appeared thoughtful and shook his head. "No. You're not going out with him."

I smiled. It probably looked a lot like my mom's had earlier. "That is not your call." I hushed him when he scowled. "Going on one date to appease my overbearing parents does not equal sex. A date can be just a simple date to keep Mom and Dad off my back. And yours, since they're on the fucking hunt right now."

"You haven't seen him." He was furious.

Fuck, Don had to be something special.

Reaching up, I placed my hands on his cheeks and gently rubbed his stubbles that were already showing from his morning shave. "I'm not going to have sex with him. I promise. This is for my parents. Now calm down." My eyebrows crinkled as I realized how much effort I had to put into something as simple as being lovers with this man. "You know, when guys normally get jealous, it's kind of cute. You don't fit that category very well."

He leaned his cheek more into my right hand as I caressed him. "I never said I was an easy lover." His eyebrows snapped together. "When you're with me, I consider you mine."

Absently, I rubbed where his eyebrows met. "I'm not *yours*, Daniil. So back off just a little."

His jaw clenched again. And he stayed mute, his gaze darting all over my face. He really didn't like that answer, but it appeared he was trying to contain his frustration. Very sluggishly, he whispered, "This is not easy for me."

Ah. "Me either." I had just figured out his issues with me. He was of a different generation. One where the women weren't quite so liberal. And from the sound of it, he was used to no one arguing with him in the first place. Those were his problems, whereas mine were that he was so much more experienced than me— in life—and his reigning violent 'tendencies.' "It's a good thing the sex is so extraordinary; otherwise, I think we'd both wise the fuck up."

He chuckled but cut it off when all four of his children groaned. Biting his bottom lip, he asked gently, "Can I at least bust one of his knee caps? He won't dance so well then."

I started laughing because, fuck, he was serious. I snorted. "No. You can't." I pulled his head down, breathing right against his ear, "If you're good, I promise to be in your bed that night."

Downhearted, he muttered, "I suppose that's better than nothing."

My jaw dropped, and I pinched his ear. "That was not very flattering, smooth talker."

He paused, and his nose crinkled. "Shit. That didn't come out right." He leaned down, pressing more of his body on me, kissing my neck lightly. "I'll dance with you that night when you arrive. Out of bed. And in bed."

I grinned, squirming under him, brushing against all his hard muscles. "That's much better."

"Thank you." He nibbled on my earlobe. "Only one date with him. Right?"

Rolling my eyes. "Yes. That was the deal."

He nibbled up my jawline, pressing his rapidly hardening cock against my thigh. "You were right earlier. Your parents are a pain in the ass." He paused. "Try not to make any more deals with them like that if you can." He actually asked it nicely.

I nodded. "I don't plan to." Utter truth.

"Hmm…" He kissed me silently, and slowly, his tongue hot and warm. Against my lips, he murmured, "I suppose I don't have to hurt Mr. Phillips this time."

I bit his bottom lip, keeping it between my teeth. "Daniil."

He stared down at me even as he moved forward, kissing me, eyes open. His heated breath blew into my mouth. "That's the best I can do."

I growled but nodded. We would work on that.

CHAPTER 4

Katie strolled out of the stairwell at the end of the hallway. She waved and ambled toward me. Her computer bag hung over her arm, and she was carrying pajamas in her hand. Grinning, I threw my arms wide, hollering, "Are we going to have a slumber party?"

She laughed. "You know it! Since you're officially the black sheep of the family, it deserves a little celebration." She glanced over my shoulder, most definitely taking in Least Ugly as he trailed behind me. Her smile grew even wider. "*So* the black sheep, baby!" She hooted, punching the air with her fist. "I don't have to listen to anyone bitch anymore!"

I unlocked my door, opening it slightly and stalled. "At least I'm not the one running an escort business as my profession." She crossed her arms, raising her eyebrows. I winked. "How are the girls, anyway?"

"I'm going to check on them if we can get inside your damn room." She nodded toward my room.

"Come on. I'm exhausted. I had to listen to your parents all the way back from the restaurant. It was… stimulating."

I snickered and let her into my lit room. I locked my door—Least Ugly keeping guard outside—and took all of three steps, and stopped, remembering I hadn't left my lights on this morning. Staring, I growled at the opened adjoining door—where the chair was knocked on its back—where Katie was peeking through. She pointed, asking, "Whose room is that?"

"The wicked redheaded bitch," I hissed, tossing my bag on the bed. I stormed around my room, checking my things. She hadn't gotten into any of my bags, so I went into the bathroom.

"You mean Ember Lerrus?" Katie asked.

"Who else?"

"Well, you are a redhead. And a bitch…"

I hissed, picking up the mousse I hadn't used this morning. It was on my bathroom counter. "Strawberry blonde!" I waved the bottle outside the door. "She broke in to use my fucking hair products!" I had no clue how she had even managed that.

Katie was already snickering. "So you two really don't get along, huh?"

I tossed the mousse in the sink and stomped back into the room. "No. We don't." I stared into Ember's room, my hands on my hips. I grinned and darted into her room, grabbing the *Death Comes* thermal shirt hanging over a chair. "Gotcha, bitch."

I stole it, going back into my room and slamming

her door, then mine, locking it—whatever good that did. I pointed at the dresser. "Help me." Dropping my *new* shirt on the bed next to my purse, I went around to the other side of the dresser as Katie picked up the front. We grunted, pushing the dresser in front of the door. When it was firmly moved, we both dropped onto the bed, out of breath. The damn resort didn't go cheap. That dresser weighed a ton.

Panting, Katie muttered, "So you're fucking the father, hun?"

"Dammit!" I grumbled, turning my head to stare. "Your mom told you?"

"Of course." She grinned. "For an old guy, he's pretty hot. He doesn't look as old as he'd have to be to have four kids their age."

"He's only forty-nine," I clarified. "He and his wife had their kids young." I grinned. "And yeah, he's fucking hot." An image of him lying on his back—beautifully naked—came to mind. "His body is better than most men our ages."

Katie pushed up on her elbows. "Okay, give the deets. With that look on your face, it's got to be good." When I smirked, her eyebrows rose. "Better than good?" I stared, and she hissed, "Do not say he's the best you've ever had."

I laughed. "I don't kiss and tell. So no details. You know this. But I will say yes, he is the absolute very best I've ever had." Turning my attention the ceiling, I quieted and asked her softly, "Have you ever kissed someone, and everything else just disappears around you? All you feel and hear and see is him?"

I heard her suck in a harsh breath, and she stood. "Jesus…"

"What? Is that crazy or something?" I had wondered that myself.

She was silent for a few moments, walking over to the window and staring outside. When she spoke, it was quiet. "No. It's not crazy." She cleared her throat. "I know what you're talking about. I've experienced it before…" She trailed off, her head dropping against the window.

Eyes wide in surprise, I asked, "Who was it?"

She banged her head once against the window. "The asshole who put you in the hospital for two weeks."

I stared. I didn't know what to say to that.

Slowly, she turned around. "You knew I was seeing him and tried to talk some sense into me. And I even knew he was all wrong…but…but when we…" she interlocked her fingers in front of her face, "…came together, it was something else entirely." She dropped her hands. "Though none of that mattered after he beat you damn near to death for doing your job. He wasn't even a cockroach to me after that. He wasn't anything but the man who had hurt you." She brushed her hair behind her ears, staring at the floor. "I'm not going to try to talk you out of seeing Daniil. You're smart. You'll know when to walk away. I just hope it's not after it's too late." Her eyes were gleaming when she looked up at me. "Just don't let it be too late, Elizabeth. The guilt will haunt you."

My heart twisting, seeing for the first time that she truly still hurt from what had happened to me. I knew she felt guilty, but not…this. I jumped to my feet and wrapped my arms around her. "Don't you fucking cry. I'm stronger than what he did to me. It's the danger of the job. I knew it when I started as a reporter. And I haven't backed away yet." I kissed her forehead. "Seriously, I don't stop because some jerk decided to use his fists instead of his feet—like he should have done and run far away, when he knew he was going to be exposed."

Katie snorted, hugging me back. "He wasn't the running away type."

Chuckling, I nodded. "Yeah. I got that."

"You're such a bitch."

"I know." I kissed her forehead once more and then released her. I pulled my laptop out of my duffle. "I've got a few things I need to do before we get down with our partying."

"So do I." She sighed, pulling her own laptop out of her bag. "And this little party tonight just consists of dinner and a movie here in the room. Did you know the place is out of alcohol?"

I stared. Daniil didn't believe me. "Yeah. It sucks." I jerked my head at the TV. "But there are some awesome new releases on the television."

"It'll do, I guess," she grumbled, signing on to her computer. "You let him call you Beth." She stared.

Keeping my gaze on my computer as I sat on the bed, pulling my camera and tape recorder and earphones out, I nodded. "Yeah. It kind of came out in the heat of the moment."

She started typing. "You haven't let anyone call you Beth since my brother died."

I stilled...and instantly burst into tears.

I had no clue where the fuck it came from, but suddenly, I was a sobbing mess.

Katie didn't know what to do at first, but she quickly got up and folded me into her arms, sitting down next to me on the bed and murmuring softly, "I'm sorry. I'm sorry. Hush. It's all right." She chuckled a little harshly. "Fuck. What a party this is turning out to be."

I rubbed at my eyes and hiccupped. "Sorry. I'll stop in a second." I choked as a fresh wave of tears hit. "I don't even mind Daniil calling me Beth. It doesn't bother me at all. I actually like it."

She nodded, rocking me in her arms. "It's hard, letting go of the past. Lord knows I have issues as you saw just a second ago. But my brother wouldn't want you hanging on to his memory like this." She nodded. "It's a good thing Daniil's calling you Beth. It'll help you get past this."

I sucked in a shaky breath, my lips trembling. "I won't ever get past those fucking parents lying. People deserved to know the truth. And they did, but not before we were all hurt by it." A good fucking reporter discovered the real reason why Justin had died. He didn't just run his car into a guardrail, killing himself. He and another boy, Mike Glass, had been playing Chicken. And my best friend, my cousin Justin, died because of it.

Katie patted my head, and I heard her sigh before she returned the gesture I had given her earlier, kissing my forehead and standing. She stared down at me. "Listen. I'm telling you this because you seriously need to hear it. Mike and his parents came to our house before any of what really happened was exposed. They told Mom what Mike and Justin had been doing. They asked Mom what she wanted to do. They gave her the option even though it was obvious they wanted to protect their son from any charges. Justin and Mike were young. And did a stupid thing. Mom knew this. And even though she was furious, she wouldn't condemn their son, take him away from the life he had. It was an accident."

I stared and then screamed, "You fucking knew?" I choked, grabbing my throat. "And you didn't tell me before?" It had taken a year for the truth to come out.

She shook her head. "No. Mom knew. Only after the papers did she tell me when she was called in to testify privately. She probably wouldn't have even told me if I hadn't overheard her phone call. She was still protecting Mike. One son had been lost, she told me, and another didn't need to be taken too, for an act of adolescent stupidity." She paused, slowly sitting back down on the bed as I stared at the ground. "I know a lot of what you do now is because of what happened to Justin. You believe the truth should always be known…but…sometimes the truth is better kept quiet when the people who really need to know already do. It only hurts those who didn't know when it comes out." She stared hard, her implication clear.

"I deserved to know the truth about what happened to him," I ground out.

She stayed silent, staring at me and then licked her lips before saying, "What was better for you? Knowing he was killed in just a simple car accident? Or him dying because of a fatal game he was playing against another kid? What would have really been better for you? Or for me?" She shook her head, standing and walking back over to her seat and sitting down. "Some days, I wished all I ever knew was he died from not paying attention behind the wheel. Not that he intentionally took his life into his own hands by playing a stupid game, deciding to take that chance to leave Mom and me." She paused, staring at her laptop screen. "Sometimes the truth is best kept quiet. Too many innocents get hurt when it rears its fatal head."

I stared at her mutely as she began typing, probably checking on all of her girls.

Could she be right? Would I have been better off not knowing?

Knowing is what had driven me so hard my entire adult life.

Always striving for the truth.

Because the truth needed to be known, no matter the cost.

Didn't it?

Not always. I *had* burned the truth about Cole.

I turned my attention to the black surface of the television screen. Thinking. Debating inside my own mind. If I hadn't known, would I have been a happier person now? Would I be less of a bitch? I was smart enough to know even if I hadn't known the truth, Justin would have been dead anyway. Nothing could change that. My best friend. Dead, no matter if the way he died had changed. He would still be only a memory and a gravestone now.

I felt tears trickle down my cheeks again and didn't bother wiping them away…ever so slowly realizing I probably would have been a better person if I hadn't known. I wouldn't hate Mike Glass with a vengeance to rival any warlord throughout history. I wouldn't have this heaping hole in my heart knowing Justin took his chances—with me and the rest of our family. And I wouldn't be so cruel and merciless against those who tried to hide the truth.

Even though I already knew the answer, I asked, "You really believe that, don't you?"

"I do," she stated instantly. "Because that, my dear inexperienced cousin, *is* the truth."

I snorted. "You know, that's my biggest concern with Daniil. My inexperience compared to him in life. Sometimes he says things I just don't comprehend, and yet, I see the truth of what he's saying in his eyes." I shook my head. "I can even handle the violence over feeling stupid."

"You're the smartest person I know, Elizabeth. Don't ever let anyone make you think you're not." Her tone was pissed, and I knew she was staring at me.

"No. You're taking it the wrong way. He doesn't do it intentionally. And when he does do it, he realizes he has and tries to explain the best way he can." I glanced at her, seeing the shock on her face. "He isn't just a heartless monster. He has a softer side when he chooses to show it." I shook my head, turning my attention back to the black television screen. "He has his own issues with me, too. He can't stand being told no. And how I'm not like all the other women he's taken as lovers. I don't just bow down and do what he tells me to. It drives him crazy."

"Sounds…interesting." She chuckled. "Good thing you said the sex was good. Otherwise, you'd both probably be running away from one another."

I nodded. "I actually said something like that to him."

"Oh, for fucks sake," a female's irritated voice muttered from the window area.

Both of our gazes darted to the voice.

Brown hair began peeking out from behind the large side curtain on the windows.

Katie and I *screamed*.

Until a head fully popped out. It was Eva.

I stopped screaming, in shock, same as Katie.

We both stared as Artur glided out from behind the other side curtain.

Grigori and Roman came out of the closet, all of them staring at us.

I instantly stood and grabbed Katie's arm. Daniil's children had been lying in wait for me. I yanked Katie toward the door. Closer to the door. An escape route. They could only be here for one reason.

"Katie. Why don't you go get that nice gentleman outside for me?" I whispered. Least Ugly sounded like a pretty rainbow right now compared to the alternative.

She stilled for all of a heartbeat, her face no longer shocked as she stared at the people in my room. She turned, and started to race toward the door, but Artur was already moving and grabbed her around the waist, yanking her back against him again. He instantly placed a hand over her mouth as he restrained her.

I held my hands up, saying, "Let her go. Please."

Roman muttered, "Let her go, Artur. Unless you don't want to for other reasons."

Artur glared at his brother but turned his attention to his captive. "I'll let you go if you don't try to run again. We don't want trouble. We were just here to talk to Elizabeth, but then we realized she had company, so we hid." He shrugged, glancing down at her. "Then we eavesdropped." He paused. "If I let you go, will you run? Or be smart?"

"Smart," she mumbled instantly from behind his hand, her voice muffled.

"Perfect," he murmured but held her a moment longer. Staring. Then he released her, watching her carefully as she zipped over to me, grabbing my hand.

His gaze moved to our hair, and he blinked a few times before shaking his head and turning back to his brothers and sister. "I honestly don't have a damn thing to say to her anymore. Not after what I heard."

Katie's grip was brutal, but I held on. Artur had freaked her out.

"Me, either." Eva shrugged. When she peered at me, she no longer scowled like she had done all day. "I'm good with her for Papa. Just wish she was a little older."

I choked off a laugh, quickly swallowing it down. Christ, the whole family was loony.

Roman stared hard, walking silently to me. He bent down, and I tried not to cringe when he looked me straight in the eyes. He had much of his dad in him with that scary gaze thing going on. "You hurt him, and I will kill you." Simple. And to the point.

Since I had thought this was what they were here to do in the first place, instead of just scare-talk me, I nodded amicably. "I won't hurt him. We're just lovers. Nothing more."

His eyes fell to the floor, and he snorted. He walked away from Katie and me. Silent.

Yep, all loony so far.

It was Grigori's turn now to intimidate me if he was game like Roman had been. It was silent for a full minute before he asked softly, "Why do you hate Ember so much?" That...wasn't where I thought this was going.

I opened my mouth but quickly snapped it shut.

He loved her. Like love loved her. I couldn't say too much without angering him.

Grigori stiffened, not missing my blunder. He slowly inhaled and exhaled. "Papa has a large mouth to be speaking to a reporter." And if I thought Roman was scary…well, Grigori was the spitting image of Daniil doing scary-crazy.

"No. He doesn't," I stated instantly, even taking a step toward him until Katie yanked me back. "He didn't tell me shit. I'm a good reporter. I find where the truth lies." I paused, seeing him get even more furious. "You and your dad could use some anger management classes. You know that, right?"

Katie's breath caught, and she yanked me behind her a little, saying quickly, "Ignore her. Oddly, she's just trying to be helpful." She stared at cracked-eyed Grigori, who had wrenched his neck on both sides, popping it. "You're fine just how you are." Katie kept a straight face while saying that doozy of a fib.

I tried to be courteous and do the same.

There was silence until Artur snickered quietly, and everyone looked at him. He was holding up the *Death Comes* thermal shirt. Glancing at me, he looked positively furious even as he laughed. "Where did you get this?"

Grigori moved and yanked it out of his hands, staring at it…then at me. Before I could even speak, he shouted, *"Have you been in our fucking house?"* Christ. Least Ugly was bound to have heard that—a man's voice inside my room—but maybe not. My door didn't bust open.

I bit my lip, feeling my gut talking to me again. "Is that your shirt?"

"Yes. My favorite," he ground out, shaking it. "It's been missing for two weeks. How the hell do you have it?"

Roman rested against the wall and grumbled, "I told you I didn't take the damn thing."

My lips trembled I wanted to laugh so badly. Maybe I was as irrational as they were.

Katie saved me, stating in a calm tone, "Elizabeth took that shirt from Ember's room when we first came in."

I added, "She was wearing it this morning when I found her in my bed. I thought it was an odd choice. She also paired it with these huge black athletic shorts. She said she liked them when I commented on her clothing." This was fucking sweet. Ember had stolen his shirt—probably his shorts, too—right out of his own house. And only two weeks ago. Good thing I'd had a change of heart about reporting piddly shit like this. Otherwise, I would be typing up an article tonight.

Everyone stared at me silently.

Grigori's grip on the shirt was white-knuckled.

Slowly, he asked, "Ember had this?"

I nodded. If he wanted to be pissed, let it be aimed at the bitch.

"She was in your bed?" Eva asked.

Grigori blinked, and suddenly, he was charging me.

Artur and Roman grabbed him, even as Katie and I stumbled into the closet doors.

Eva said quickly, "Explain, Elizabeth."

Grigori was staring at me like the devil's own was seeing through his eyes as he struggled with his brothers. I quickly sputtered, "Brent and Cole were sleeping outside her door. She came in here to get away from their racket. I spent the night...elsewhere...so I didn't find her until the next morning." There. Dammit. Calm down, bucko.

Roman shook his brother. "She was hiding, not having sex with Elizabeth!"

Grigori stopped struggling, dazed where they had fallen on my bed.

My door made a clicking sound...and in stormed a breathless Daniil.

He wore only his black linen pants from earlier. He sucked in air, his large bare pecs rising with the motion and abs constricting, slamming the door shut behind him as his gaze darted all around the room, his children suddenly frozen. When he strode past Katie and me, I had a full view of the silver handgun in the back waistline of his pant. His gaze took in Grigori, Artur, and Roman on the bed, obviously from a struggle. Eva was standing off to the side. In a soft voice, he asked, "Who made her cry?"

"Katie," Eva stated immediately. "They were talking about how Elizabeth doesn't let anyone call her

Beth because of her cousin—Katie's brother—who died. I'm assuming he used to call her that. And when they started talking about him, she started bawling."

I gaped and swiped at my cheeks, feeling the dried, salty tears there.

Total tattletale.

Daniil's eyes darted to mine for a few seconds, his gaze unreadable, before going back to his children. "Did Grigori attack her?"

"No," I stated instantly before they could say anything. Fuck, I didn't want anyone in trouble. They hadn't really done anything. "There was a slight miscommunication about Ember staying the night in here. Once it was explained, he calmed down." At least, it had looked like he was about to.

Daniil hummed. He didn't look convinced, staring hard at his children. He jerked his head at the door. "Get fuck out of here and up to my room. Now." When it appeared they weren't moving fast enough for his liking, he started speaking harshly in Russian.

Eva and Roman darted out of the room.

Artur paused to stare down at Katie for a moment before walking out calmly.

And Grigori stood...staring down at the red thermal in his hand...then at the adjoining door, his mind somewhere not nice again from the look in his eye.

Daniil rolled his shoulders and crossed his arms. He spoke calmly to Grigori—still in Russian. Grigori flinched, his gaze going to his dad for a heartbeat before he stared down at the shirt and started answering him—also in Russian.

I whispered, "I need to get one of those Russian/English books."

Katie nodded as she stared wide-eyed at Daniil. "He doesn't look like any father I've ever seen." Her eyes moved down his body. I scowled and elbowed her in the gut before walking over and blatantly pulling up Daniil's pants that were starting to slip to dangerous levels. Daniil looked down at me, and for the barest heartbeat, his gaze flicked to Katie. His attention held amusement, but he kept talking to his son.

Even as he helped adjust his waistline to appropriate levels.

I let him move the gun.

Grigori spoke, and Daniil's attention went to the shirt. He blinked. He hid a smile before he started speaking again. Grigori shook his head and tossed the shirt to me, stating in English, "You'll put that back where you found it." He then went to the dresser and shoved it back to its original starting point. Easily.

I stared. That thing was fucking heavy.

He opened the door, staring into her room before gesturing for me to enter. "Now. Exactly where she had it."

"Grigori…" Daniil's voice was a low growl. A warning to be nice.

Grigori flicked him an irritated glance but didn't say anything else.

I ground my teeth together but placed the shirt

back over her chair. I probably shouldn't have taken it in the first place. That was what I got for acting on impulse.

Back into my room, Grigori shut the door and mine. But he didn't lock it. "If you seriously think putting a dresser in front of a locked door will keep her out, you're delusional." He almost looked proud of her B&E skills.

Daniil growled something low in Russian.

Grigori clenched his jaw, but he stalked out of my room. My door slammed shut.

Daniil sighed, taking a hand off his hips and rubbed in the center of his bare chest.

The side of his pants he had released lowered.

I grabbed it, pulling it back up. I glared at his pants. Maybe I would splurge on my charge card and purchase a pair of pants for him that didn't look so fucking sexy. Flannel maybe. Or cartoon characters. And ones that didn't ride so damn low, showing every *sexified* part of his body.

He chuckled softly, deep and slow.

"What is so damn funny about all of this?" I tried getting that side to stay, but it just kept falling back to fuck me level.

"Nothing," he murmured, kissing the top of my head as I tried to get it to stay put one last time. I growled and gave up when it was obvious it was no use, going to my suitcase and pulling out a large yellow shirt I wore to bed sometimes. I tossed it to him.

He caught it, his lips twitching. "You want me to wear this?"

I crossed my arms, irritated. "What do you think?" I scowled at his chest. And then lower. "Put it on."

I ignored his low snickering, watching as he put the shirt on. It had been huge on me but fit him perfectly. And covered everything that needed to be covered. I nodded, satisfied. "Better." Now he wouldn't be walking down the halls flashing everyone his fucking perfect body.

He was still chuckling, but he bent, his hands sliding over my hips. "If you don't want me calling you Beth anymore, I'll understand."

Biting my lip, I mumbled, "No. I kinda like you doing it." Yeah. I really did.

He kissed my neck. "Then I need to say goodnight…Beth. I have some unruly children to attend to."

"They really didn't do anything too bad."

He nodded. "Yes, but they were still in here in the first place. And I need to deal with that." Delicately, he kissed my lips, his warm and soft…and damn perfect… then turned toward Katie. He moved through the room while he asked her. "Are you single, Katie?"

She blinked, then asked baffled, "Excuse me?" Her gaze was huge as she banged back against the closet door. He was just that intimating.

My eyebrows snapped together as he asked her slowly, "Are. You. Single?"

Her eyes darted between him and me.

I shrugged. I had no clue where he was going with this.

Her attention returned to him, and she sputtered, "Yes. Why?"

Running a hand through his hair, he stared at the door. "No reason." He opened said door, then started speaking harshly in Russian to Least Ugly—who must have called Daniil earlier when the noise levels rose—as he shut the door behind him.

Katie stared at the shut door. "What the fuck have you gotten yourself into?" A glance at me, before staring back at the door. "And why the hell did he want to know if I was single?"

"I have no clue to both questions," I murmured. "It's not a party of the newly minted black sheep of the family without intruders, threats, and the Mafia. Right?"

She laughed outright. "Christ. You really have taken over the roll."

"Yes. I would have to agree with you." I gestured at the dresser. "Let's get this shit cleaned up, so we can both relax and watch a movie." Plus, I just remembered I did have a photo I could send off to my editor. The doctored photo of Daniil and Zoya kissing. That one everybody already knew about. No harm there.

CHAPTER 5

"Would someone answer the fucking phone, already?" The feminine voice came from my right, next to where I lay, waking me. "Whoever it is, has already called twice. In a row."

The voice belonged to Ember.

The ringing phone on the nightstand was just a bonus.

I jerked to a sitting position as Katie groaned on my left, rolling over onto my pillow. "What the hell are you doing in here?" Ember was sleeping on my right side, snuggled up tight under the covers, her red hair barely visible from beneath.

"My bed's lumpy," she grumbled. "Answer the damn phone before I get pissed."

Irritated beyond belief, I reached over her to the phone as Katie woke. She blinked and stared at Ember's visible hair. I barked into the receiver, "Hello?"

"Good morning, sweetie!" Mom's overly perky

voice sung over the line. And it was barely dawn outside. "Meet us for breakfast."

Like hell I would. Katie and I had been up all night watching movies. "Not this morning. Katie and I had a late night. Thanks anyway." I hung up, ending the call the official way a pissed off daughter did with her mom. Enough of that shit. I was sure Mom was going to ruin my day. I didn't want her doing it to my morning, too.

Katie was up on one elbow, staring wide-eyed at Ember.

I shoved the intruding redhead. "Get out of here."

"No," she griped, bringing a red thermal covered arm out from under the covers and shoving me back. Not-so-lightly. I fell back against Katie as she continued. "I had a late night, too. Leave me alone." She paused and then snickered. "If you shut up and let me sleep here, I'll let you in on a secret you can publish when we wake up. When it's daylight."

I stopped in the act of pushing her, my reporter's instinct coming to the fore. "Is it good?"

"Let's just say Zoya hasn't been exactly truthful with everyone." She paused. "I'll let you know more when I'm really up." Not even a second later, she was snoring softly.

I scowled, but damn if I wasn't curious. That part of me would never back down. It was too deeply ingrained. Grumbling, I laid back on my—soft, not lumpy—mattress, squished between two people.

Katie was still frozen in place. "You're going to let her stay?" She was completely disbelieving. "She could be lying."

"She may be a bitch, but she hasn't lied to me yet." And she hadn't. Not from what I understood. "Now, hush. I'm tired."

Katie blinked a few times and shook her head before falling back down onto the bed. "You're living a very interesting life lately, cousin."

"Whatever," I grumbled. Like I didn't know this. I tossed and finally managed to get comfortable when I, grudgingly, threw an arm over Ember since I couldn't push it under my pillow—because of her own arm. Then I fell back asleep.

We all woke two hours later to a loud ass shriek. Startled, the three of us shot up to sitting positions. Albeit, Katie and I didn't hold a gun like Ember did, aiming it at...my mom and dad and aunt. She blinked when Mom shrieked again—it had been her before—and quickly hid it under the blanket.

I rubbed my eyes, muttering, "How did you get in?"

Did everyone have a damn key?

And was I really getting so used to seeing a weapon unholstered that I didn't freak?

"The maid let us in," my aunt stated quickly. She shoved my gawking parents toward the door. Or, at least tried, but my parents dug in their heels. "We'll come back later…when you're alone." Her stunned mien was stuck on Ember.

Ember stayed mute, blinking sleepily.

My family had a very wrong impression. "No. No. It's not what you guys think." I'd had my fucking arm over Ember. No wonder they thought the worst. "She just slept in here because her bed's lumpy."

Mom was holding her throat. "You weren't…"

Dad asked point blank, "You're not having sex with a woman, are you?"

I gawked, even as Katie started snickering.

Ember stated slowly, "We are not sleeping together. I wouldn't do anything with her if I was stuck on a deserted island with only her." She paused, her eyebrows coming together. "And I'm bi, so that's clearly saying something."

I gaped at her now—because I didn't know that.

"Same to you," I muttered, agreeing wholeheartedly.

Dad straightened to his full height, staring at Ember. "I think you, and I need to have another chat, young lady."

Ember's face was priceless as she fully remembered who she had let that little bit of information slip in front of. She almost appeared to panic, glancing at me for help. I just shrugged, at least trying not to laugh at her. In the end, it was my mother who saved her when she asked, "Sweetie, that bruise is horrible. It looks like you were strangled." Then I heard her gasp as I still stared at Ember, her face slowly shutting down, probably fully expecting me to rat her out. "You were choked, weren't you? Who did it?" She sounded like she wanted to strangle whoever had strangled me.

Winking at Ember so my parents couldn't see, I said, "It was Chrissy. The woman who attacked me." I turned back toward my parents after seeing Ember not react at all. Like she was a block of cool nothing. She was fucking good at hiding her emotions when she tried hard enough. "Don't worry. It doesn't hurt anymore." Last night, I gave the same story to Katie when she saw the bruise, once I changed into my pajamas. I was going to keep Ember's deal and not tell anyone. No reason to go back on it since I hadn't gotten my interview from her yet. "Now. What are you doing in here?"

Mom still stared at my throat.

Dad cleared his. "We thought we'd take you on one of those day cruises. Your flight isn't until later, so we reserved a spot for all of us. But we need to leave," he glanced at his watch, "in a half hour to get there on time."

"I changed my flight, so don't worry about it anymore." I sighed. I knew I wasn't getting out of this. And honestly, it was better than being caught around here with them pestering each one of Lion Security's group. "All right. Out you go. I need to get ready."

Katie, Ember, and I started to climb out of bed.

My dad watched—probably to make sure we had clothes on—and nodded, before they left the room, telling us to meet them in the lobby.

I turned to Ember. "Spill it. I let you sleep."

"Is the preacher really going to try to talk to me?" Ember asked slowly, holding up the black athletic shorts.

Katie was taking in her attire, trying—badly—to keep a grin off her face.

I nodded. "Probably. But you set yourself up for that one. Now give me what you have on Zoya."

Ember cleared her throat, and her eyes gleamed with an unholy light. "You can't say in your article how you got the information. I want to be anonymous in this." She paused, letting the suspense build, then said quietly, "Zoya was married five months ago. Her husband only thought she was visiting old friends here in the States. None of the pictures ever showed her cheating, so apparently, he believed whatever lie she was telling him." She grinned as I gawked. "Make sure you're back for the party tonight. We'll be having dinner at the Rock Restaurant. It's supposed to be reserved privately for us like we normally do for dinner. You can get the first shots of Zoya and her husband's happy reunion then. You see, her husband received a photo. One showing that she had been lying." She yawned even as she grinned. "I stayed up most of the night making sure he did as I expected and hopped on a flight. My contact over there said he made it just fine."

"Christ," I hissed, starting to pace. Daniil wasn't

going to be happy with me on this one. "I sent that picture of him and Zoya kissing to my editor last night. I'm sure it's in the paper today."

Ember's grin dropped instantly, and her face hardened. "I guess I can only be happy you waited this long, but I think it would be a good idea for you to follow up on this story, clearly explaining that Grigori didn't know she was married. Which he didn't. He already looks bad enough in the press. There's no reason to hurt Lion Security or him by being branded a homewrecker, too."

"Why didn't you tell him?" I complained, knowing I was going to have to write this piece. My new—annoying—conscious telling me it was the right thing to do.

"Because I only found out a week ago. I didn't expect them to…" She waved her hand at her mouth, her eyes like ice. "The only thing that stopped me from kicking her fucking ass then was the fact you had proof I could send to her husband. I'd been trying to figure that out anyway, and you provided." She bowed her head. "Thank you ever so much."

She waved with her free hand, still holding her pants up as she opened our doors, stepping into her room. "I want that bitch shown for what she really is— a lying, selfish gold-digging, cheater. No one fucks with my partner like that and gets away with it. Remember to be at dinner." She slammed her door shut.

Katie and I both stared at her door.

Katie whispered, "I don't think she even knows she's in love with Grigori."

I shook my head, completely struck dumb. "Nope. Me, either." I couldn't tell Katie she had said she would never be 'in love' again. But it was painfully obvious she was head over heels for Grigori. "You better get ready. We've got a fun filled day out on the sea planned."

"Yeah us!" Katie mumbled sarcastically, rolling her pointed fingers in the air in mock celebration. "Sounds like a blast."

"Yes, ma'am. Sure does."

And it sure…had not been. Walking to the restaurant dressed in jeans, a t-shirt, and sneakers with my duffle and purse slung over my shoulder, I knew I was underdressed. I just wanted to get this story and go to bed. I zigzagged as I walked, still feeling the rolling sea under my landed feet. I swallowed hard. I didn't puke on board, but I had spent the entire time occupying one of the bathrooms just in case. It was awful. My parents even felt bad for me.

Only about half of the group was sitting at a large table inside an emptied out restaurant. Ember said they ate privately for dinner, but I hadn't expected the black-tie affair. I *really* was underdressed. Must be nice to have that kind of cash flow to order everyone else the fuck out so they weren't bothered. I didn't even have to give my name to the guard at the door. I'd not seen this one before, but after one glance at my hair, he opened the glass door for me. I slipped inside, Least Ugly following a few minutes later.

He had gone on the cruise too since it was a public cruise. It was more than weird to see him out of his black fatigues and in a pair of shorts and Bermuda shirt trying to fit in. Honestly, he did somehow, my parents not even giving him a second glance on the crowded boat. It was mind-boggling though.

Brent, Cole, Zane, Stash, Peter, Lev, and Ember were already seated, sipping on what looked like red wine—nonalcoholic, of course—and I swallowed hard again, feeling the bile rise. The nonalcoholic wine was fucking gross, and the thought of it made my stomach twist even more. They paused, dressed in their finest. All of them in black, of course, since they didn't realize there were other colors in this world. They watched me wobble my way to the table.

Ember's eyebrows snapped together. "Have you been drinking?"

I snorted, plopping down next to her and pushing my bags under the table. I let my head thump down on the table. "I wish." I lifted a hand, and put my pointer and thumb an inch apart. "Little boat." I waved my hand grandly. "Big ocean." Then I made my hand and arm do the wave. "Makes for a bumpy ride."

Stash chuckled, setting his glass down. "Not a sailor, I take it."

I moaned and my stomach turned. "It's safe to say the ocean and I do not agree with one another."

Zane mumbled, "Why aren't you resting? I'm sure your editor gives you sick time."

"No, he doesn't." Best to keep it at that. "Just nudge me when everyone else gets here." I shut my eyes. And groaned.

I felt like shit.

"You mean Daniil, right?" Brent asked, sounding amused.

I waved my hand blindly. "Whatever."

They snickered, but I concentrated on my feet and butt and the side of my face, where they were firmly planted on non-moving objects. It helped. But only a little. When a hand landed on my forehead, I moaned, "Are they really here already?" It had only been a minute.

"I was already here," Daniil murmured softly. "I was in the restroom."

I wrinkled my forehead under his touch. "I hope you washed your hands."

The conversations at the table cut off, and then they started chortling.

"Of course, I did." Daniil petted my hair back from my face. It felt good soothing a few of the wrinkles from my forehead, so I kept my eyes closed and let him continue. He sat down in the chair next to me, still stroking me. He asked softly, "What's wrong?"

"I got sea sick on the boat my demonic parents dragged me on." I hadn't told him what I was doing today, figuring Least Ugly had probably already done that. Plus, when I had paused to actually call him, I stopped myself since it seemed a little off to have to check in with someone who was just my lover. It was even more bizarre that I had thought to do it in the first place since I had never done that before.

Gently, he started massaging the back of my neck. "Why aren't you in bed, then?"

I groaned, not wanting to talk anymore.

Zane helpfully supplied, "She said her boss doesn't give her sick time."

"Really," Daniil clipped in an irritated tone, his hand stopping its caress. I waggled my shoulders, letting him know to keep going. He did, his touch soft and gentle, but he was clearly pissed when he asked, "What kind of fucking asshole doesn't give his employees time off when their ill?"

Ember murmured softly, "Probably not the best time to be having this conversation when she's not feeling well." Thank you, Ember, for saving my ass since my editor did, in fact, give me time off. "Plus, everyone else is arriving." She nudged me as I had asked. But much harder than she needed to in my ribs.

"Bitch," I mumbled, pushing up off the table and swallowing hard. I wiped the sweat from my forehead. She almost pushed the puke up. "You're so not sleeping in my bed tonight."

She smirked even as the table went mute,

gawking, the others just coming through the door. "We'll see about that. You didn't even know I slipped in with you and Katie last night. I could sleep there and be out without you even knowing." She patted my cheek cheerfully.

"Evil bitch," I griped, taking a large drink of my water. I glanced down as Daniil wrapped an arm around my back, pulling me in closer. He placed a long, red colored velvet box in front of me with his other hand.

"I got you a little something," he whispered in my ear.

I stared. And slowly picked up the box. It was heavy. "What is it?"

Daniil brushed my hair behind my ear. "Open it and see."

The group entering was loud and rowdy, no one actually—for once—paying attention to us. Except for Ember next to me. She had gone mute, blatantly staring at the box, her hand at her throat where she wore an interesting necklace that probably cost a fortune, but the silver was shaped like skulls, the eyes diamonds— large ones. Not really my cup of tea, but morbidly beautiful nonetheless.

Slowly, I opened it, and…just about fainted. Inside was the most beautiful black and white pearl necklace I had ever seen. Fumbling the gift, as I literally slumped, Daniil tightened his hold on me. He caught my hands under the box, keeping both it and me steady. The pearls were enormous and it would wrap around my throat a few times over.

"I can't accept this," I murmured. It was too much.

"Nonsense. It's yours," Daniil stated calmly. "I know you like jewelry, and I made sure not to get you earrings."

Ember nudged me—softly—whispering fiercely, "Take it. It's fucking gorgeous. Light and dark. Like the two of you."

Yeah. Like I hadn't already understood that.

"Butt out," I mumbled, closing the lid before anyone else could see. I peered at Daniil straight on, ready to argue with him. I stopped and stared. Groaned. "Jesus. It's not fair." I let my head fall against his suit jacket covered shoulder. "You look amazing. And I look like shit." Understatement.

He had tied his hair back from his face, and all of those sharp angles were on full display, his eyes even more intense than normal. His suit was tailored to fit his large body perfectly. He looked like a million bucks while I sat here looking like a pile of dog poo.

A sweaty, disgusting pile of dog poo.

He kissed my damp forehead, brushing my hair back. "Is that a thank you?" His next words were hesitant. "Or do you not like the necklace?"

I clutched the box to my chest, suddenly wanting them as I had never wanted any other materialistic item before. "No, I love it. I'll keep it. Thank you."

"Running a little hot and cold tonight, aren't you?" Ember asked.

"Butt. Out," I griped loudly, feeling very much irritable. Thank you, boat ride.

She held her hands up, a small look of surprise on her face, which she quickly banished, glancing out toward the door. Her mouth dropped open, asking in a hushed whisper, "Is that your parents coming in?"

"What?" I squeaked, pushing off Daniil.

But...no one was there.

Ember snorted with amusement. My stomach rolled.

I was very tempted to puke on her.

She scooted her chair closer to Stash, watching me closely, no longer laughing.

"Leave her alone, Ember," Daniil stated gruffly, pulling me back against him as the rowdy group took their seats. He leaned over my head. "And I wouldn't suggest coming into her room tonight unless you'd like to sleep in a bed with Beth and me."

Ember's face turned ashen before she quickly looked away, playing with her necklace.

I patted Daniil's leg with my free hand, still gripping the necklace box with the other. "Thank you."

"That was mean of her when you're not feeling well," he griped quietly, practically pulling me off my chair into his lap. "Are you sure you can't go lie down?" His expression turned brutal. "I think I should talk to your boss."

I stared. "You do that and I'm going to shave off your hair in the middle of the night." He may be one scary motherfucker, but he was very much vain. His feet, perfect hair, and grooming proved that.

Grigori snickered across from me where he was sitting.

I glared at him, not in the mood for everyone fucking eavesdropping.

I blinked, though. Staring. "Jesus, you two are fucking identical."

Ember snorted but didn't say anything, keeping her trap shut.

Grigori was dressed exactly like his dad, his hair slicked back and in a tie, too. I doubt they had planned it that way, but the only difference between them was a few more laugh lines around Daniil's eyes when he smiled, and Grigori's sporadic braids and hot pink streaks. Other than that, they could be damn near twins.

Grigori's lips twitched, and I swear, he glanced Ember's way before he started to turn toward Roman—oddly, ignoring Zoya on his other side. But he stalled in the movement, his gaze slamming back to Ember. He stared. At her throat...or...I glanced at her...the necklace. He was staring at the skull necklace. He cleared his throat, saying quietly, "I like your necklace." Honestly, I think those were the first nice words I had heard him say to her. And it was like half the table heard it, too, and started leaning in toward them. N-O-S-Y G-R-O-U-P.

She touched it, glancing down like she could see it even though it hugged her neck like a choker. Her voice was soft and faltering. "Thank you." Grigori stared at it a moment longer before turning his attention to Roman—away from her—just as Ember looked up, her mouth open to say more...but she closed it gently, seeing he was no longer paying attention and her gaze fell to the table. Her hands landed on her lap where it looked like she was gripping them in a vicious hold. And, I swear, she looked like she was about to cry for a heartbeat before she sucked in a breath, and her face turned cold.

Remote, no emotion showing.

Scary in itself how closed off she became within one heartbeat and the next.

I felt Daniil stiffen against me, and he muttered something under his breath in Russian, turning from Ember to glare at his oldest son. And while he did that, a little bit of the bitch fell off Ember in my mind, seeing her vulnerable and hurting. My gut started talking to me again—and I began to put everything I had heard together like I did a story.

They had been lovers. Brent and Cole came back from the dead. Their relationship had obviously ended by Brent and Cole's return. Grigori said he had given her what she wanted...but...maybe she didn't want it. What woman doesn't want a man to fight for her when she cares for him? And what man wants to be dumped for someone else when he cares for the woman? Grigori was cold and furious toward her.

My gut instinct was telling me I knew why now.

And sadly, for them, Brent and Cole hadn't missed that little exchange, finally catching on that

Ember had been with Grigori before their return. Their eyes flashed as they stared, seeing what I had seen. They were now staring at Grigori, completely ignoring Carl and Anna's attempts to distract them. Zane and Stash were sitting mutely, their expressions neutral as they looked at their best friends. Obviously, all four of those individuals knew what was going on.

A looked passed behind their eyes that had me silently sucking in a breath.

Daniil felt it, glancing down at me, and then followed my gaze. His entire frame turned rigid, and he reached behind his back—for a gun—just as Brent and Cole, with that same death-like expression in their eyes, started to stand.

I wasn't sure what possessed me to do it, but I was a sucker just like anyone else when it comes to love. Ember's heart didn't belong to these two. Her heart belonged to someone else. Even if she was going about getting her love back in extremely weird ways—ways she didn't even understand. I blurted, "Cole! Didn't I see you in the Ocean Restaurant the other day?" Half the table went quiet. I sounded a little frantic. My *burned* story was going to work for this situation.

Grigori got a decent view at what he had been missing behind his back before Brent and Cole froze, their deadly gazes turning toward me.

Understandable shock rocked Cole for a second, but he quickly covered it with believable confusion. "What are you talking about?" They were both standing, but they hadn't moved yet.

I waved my hand, the simple motion making me feel ill. I swallowed. "I'm pretty sure you were in there. I was picking up some silverware from the hostess area in the corner, and I could have sworn I spotted you."

Brent's expression didn't change as he glanced at Cole, his brows furrowing.

Perfectly. Played. Perfectly played, Mr. Terrance.

"Ah." I waved my hand again. "Maybe it was someone else." I glanced behind them, seeing the waitress coming out of the backroom. "Cole, you should probably sit down and not intimidate that poor waitress. She looks the timid sort." Luckily, she really did.

Brent sat, staring at me. "You're very observant." Contradictory, since the argument was that I hadn't actually seen Cole in the restaurant, but I could work with it. Cole, on the other hand, just picked up his glass and sipped, watching me.

"Yes. I am. And I have a perfect memory of events. It's what makes me so good at what I do." I paused and forced a tiny laugh. "What do you think, Cole? You've seen my work. It's usually front page material, yes?" He didn't need to know if I still had the photos and audio. He just needed to not kick Grigori's ass for something that happened while they were dead to the world.

Cole sat and took a hefty gulp of his drink. The only indicator anything was amiss. "Yes, it normally is, Ms. Forter." He said no more to me but turned, giving his order to the waitress. Ignoring everyone as if he hadn't just been threatened to have his picture posted on the front page of a paper. Tonguing his best friend.

No one knew. Only me.

War heroes. Brent and Cole.

It would ruin them.

Ember's eyebrows were together. "Did I just miss something?" She was utterly baffled at the possibility.

I snorted quietly.

Daniil kissed my forehead, a silent thank you for stopping the gunfight.

I whispered right back, "Only that you and Grigori's past love life is no longer a secret."

Her whole body stilled, and she breathed shallowly. "For some reason, I think I owe you a thank you."

My lips twitched as much as they would in actual humor. I wanted to ralph in her face. "You're welcome."

She nodded once curtly and went back to conversing with Zane next to her as if nothing was wrong…except her shoulders were extremely stiff.

Daniil ordered his food, and I ordered a chicken noodle soup and some crackers. That seemed like a safe bet to me. I closed my eyes and didn't care if I was rude. I was waiting for a story to fix the one I had done the night before, and that was all. The conversation continued around me, Daniil speaking to Artur about Black City, the club he ran and owned. Artur asked him about issues he needed some advice on. I learned through their dialogue Daniil might be fierce-scary, but he was extremely business savvy. Hell, I didn't even understand some of the financial aspects that he spoke of, or the employment laws here in the United States he referenced.

When the food arrived, the scent of Grigori's crab wafted through the air.

I just about puked in my mouth. "Jesus. That smells awful." I was being ill-mannered, but it just blurted out. And his food smelled like the boat did I had rocked on all day.

"Smells awful?" Ember asked, taking a big bite of her pasta that didn't look so bad.

"Yeah." I breathed softly, focusing on my soup. My chair felt like it moved under me, even though I knew it wasn't. I was never going on a damn boat again.

Daniil started rubbing my back, and I slurped at my soup—until I spied the big piece of wheat bread on his plate. I didn't even ask. I just took it and bit into it with relish. I swallowed it down with the Sprite he ordered for himself.

God, he did it again. His order was much better than mine.

"Papa…" Grigori spoke softly.

I swallowed hard as another waft of his salty crab came my way.

Daniil didn't seem to hear him, talking right over him. "Here. We'll switch again…since you've already eaten half of it, anyway." He switched the plates.

I sighed in relief, staring down at simple spaghetti and meatballs. "Thank you." Jesus, I sounded pathetic even to my own ears. I slapped a hand over my mouth, my gaze darting to Grigori's plate, bile rising further. Fucking disgusting is what was on his plate. And the damn air conditioning was blowing its stench my way.

"You know…" Grigori stated slowly, obviously seeing my distress, "I'm not really that hungry." I didn't look at him because I was a little embarrassed, but I heard him call the waitress over. His plate blessedly disappeared. I was betting Daniil must have given him some sort of scowl because Grigori didn't seem the kind type to me.

I tried not to pay attention to the quietness of the conversation around me, everyone probably staring. I was here to right what was going to become a wrong very shortly. I didn't know what time hubby was supposed to show, but I just had to make it until then. After that, I could go and quickly write my article and pass out. Tomorrow I had better be able to walk right. Otherwise, I was going to the fucking doctor. The bathroom I spent most of my day in hadn't looked particularly sanitary.

I ate the spaghetti while Daniil rubbed on my back, his movements never faltering even as he ate my soup one handed. Feeling a little guilty, I tried to give him the rest of the delicious bread, but he wouldn't have it. He literally tore a piece off and placed it in my mouth when I started to argue. The waitress filled his coffee cup, and I sniffed the air experimentally.

Daniil stiffened next to me. Glancing my way, he paused with the cup in the air, halfway to his mouth.

"Does the coffee bother you? I can have her take it back if it does."

It was like the whole table shut up. I glanced at the tables occupants as they all stared at Daniil. I seriously never met another group quite like this one. "No. It actually smells pretty good." I pointed down the table weakly at Torrez's plate—lobster. "It's overriding the seafood smell from his plate."

Daniil's eyes unfocused. He asked, "You can smell his plate from down there?"

I nodded slowly, glancing around as everyone still stared at us. My eyebrows snapped together in irritation. "Yes. I was on a boat all day with that shit. It's disgusting." I raised my hands, completely fed up, and asked the entire table, "Seriously! Is our fucking conversation any of your damn business?"

I glared at anyone who didn't look away immediately.

Stash stated not so quietly, "Somebodies PMSing."

"No..." I stopped and considered that. Yeah, I probably was. "It's just rude to stare at someone while they're having a private convo. If you're going to eavesdrop, at least do it with some damn skill." I slammed my mouth shut, sitting back on my seat quickly, realizing I was being a major bitch. I bit my lip and moved my attention back to my plate. It was probably best to keep quiet.

That way they wouldn't do their 'thing.' And I wouldn't yell at them when they did.

Ember held up her glass of gross non-alcoholic wine, actually being kind. "You know, when I have an upset stomach," she twirled the red liquid around in her glass, "this helps settle it. Do you want some?" She stared at me hard. Odd.

Even before I could say no thank you, Daniil told her quickly, "Ember, if she wanted that in the first place, she would have ordered it. Just let her eat in peace."

Placing my hand on Daniil's leg, I gazed back at Ember, where she stared at Daniil over my head with that horrible dead coolness in her eyes. "Thank you. But he's right. I don't want that right now."

Her gaze flew to me, nodding even as her eyes went all freaky as she…looked me up and down from head to toe. "You're welcome. It doesn't work for everyone, anyway."

I ate again. I was determined not to yell at anyone anymore tonight…

And that went beautifully until the bitch went and elbowed me.

Right in the fucking boob.

"*Ow!*" I yelped, putting my left arm over it protectively. "What the hell, Ember?"

No one was paying attention to us, except for Daniil and Grigori, who both stared at what I was protecting from her. Ember glared for a second, not saying anything but her eyes darted to the door, where almost the entire table was already staring, which I might have noticed if I wasn't so focused on trying to ignore them in the first place. There was a man, a nice looking man, right outside the glass door in jeans and a button down shirt, staring inside and arguing with the bodyguard. Ah. Showtime.

When Grigori looked away, I hissed, "Watch what you're fucking doing next time."

Ember shrugged but kicked me under the table, pushing my duffle with her foot against my leg. She wanted this more than I did, it seemed. I sucked in a breath and scooted my chair back as Zoya started freaking out. I needed my damn camera and recorder. Digging through my bag, I placed the recorder on the table next to my plate, turning it on, barely even noticing as the guy barged through the door, and Zoya jumped from her chair. Grabbing my camera, I immediately started snapping shots as hubby stormed up to the table—making sure I didn't get any with the guns being drawn, and then he and Zoya started speaking quickly. In Russian.

"This isn't going to fucking work. I can't understand them," I muttered.

How the hell was I supposed to get this if I couldn't use Ember's name? She wanted to be anonymous so it had to come from the damn source. And the source needed to speak my language. Shit!

Daniil was looking back and forth between the arguing couple and me with his eyebrows raised—his gun was drawn—and he halted. He focused completely on Zoya, asking quickly in clear English, "Zoya, what is this about?"

It wasn't her who reciprocated in kind. It was hubby. He pointed at Grigori, shouting, "Your fucking son has been trying to steal my wife!"

Zoya's pretty face strained even further.

Grigori stilled, asking slowly, "Your wife?"

"Yes, you ass. Zoya is my wife!" He tried to charge Grigori. Stupid, stupid move.

Grigori stopped him easily, slamming his face down on the table where his plate had previously been. I sat there across from them, putting a hand on the tape recorder so it didn't go flying, but that was all the quick movement I could do. Unless I wanted to add to the scene with my spew.

Grigori hissed, clearly, "I had no clue she was married. She never told me." He paused, sighing as he stared down at the struggling man while Zoya sobbed behind him. "Nothing happened other than a kiss. All right?"

"I saw the damn photo!" hubby shouted.

"Everyone saw the photo," Grigori explained, clearly thinking he had seen the paper online from my article.

Well, that was all I needed. I got the initial shot of Zoya and her husband's confrontation. And I had the story on my recorder. Picking said recorder off the table, I stopped it and tossed it in my duffle even as Grigori continued calming the man down, alternating between looking at the guy with irritated sympathy, and glancing over his shoulder with an expression of stunned fury at Zoya. He absolutely had not known.

That much was evident as I carefully put my camera away, making sure to tuck Daniil's gift in my bag where the red velvet wouldn't get ruined, and zipped it up.

Daniil was staring at me. He knew now why I had come to this dinner when I didn't feel so good. He knew I had known this was going to happen. He looked a little pissed and surprised all at once. "Going somewhere, my sweet?" Ah. That was a new tone. A sarcastic, yet ticked off one. Good to know he didn't just use the endearment in bed.

"Yeah. To write an article so your son doesn't look like a homewrecker tomorrow, since that picture of him and Zoya was in the paper this morning. Then I'm going to sleep," I stated bluntly, not telling him how I knew this was going to happen. I would probably tell him later, but not now around everyone else.

He blinked at me for a moment, and then stood when I did, grabbing my arm, and helping me up. "I need to stay here a bit longer." He chuckled, shaking his head because that was obvious. "Then, I'll come to you." He pressed his mouth against my ear, both of us ignoring the racket just across the table. "You will explain."

I nodded wearily. "If I'm not asleep." I patted his chest after putting my duffle and purse over my shoulder. "I probably won't be good company tonight. If you want, we can wait until tomorrow to talk."

He kissed my lips softly, right in front of his kids, if they were paying attention. Which Roman was. He spoke against them, "I'm sleeping with you tonight."

"Okay." *Dumb-dumb-dumb-dumb*—that was me when I was sick. Brilliant phrase extraordinaire. I was really going to have to concentrate while writing the damn article. "Make sure Least Ugly knows to keep my family out then. They dropped in this morning unannounced and uninvited."

Daniil's nose crinkled and his jaw seesawed. "Maybe my room's the better choice for us. It would be too obvious if he tried to stop them from entering your room."

I nodded, agreeing immediately. "Thanks. I'm not thinking straight right now. There's too much icky going on inside." I swallowed hard, getting another whiff of Torrez's plate. "I'm gonna go." I started stumbling off, but Daniil grabbed my arm. He snapped his fingers at Least Ugly, who came up immediately, taking over Daniil's place, holding my arm.

Daniil growled something to him in Russian.

The guard's expression cooled.

I asked, "What did you just say to him?"

Daniil was looking back where Zoya was shrieking. "He should have called me when he saw you were this ill. He won't make the same mistake twice."

I patted Least Ugly's arm as he helped me walk out of the restaurant. "I'm sure he meant that in a nice way."

Least Ugly grunted, his lips twitching. "No. He didn't." He glanced down at me, herding my person toward the elevator. "Do you want some more Sprite for your stomach?"

"You saw what I was drinking?"

His lips twitched again. "It was tasted before it was set on the table."

I blinked. "Huh?"

"All of the food is tested when he's out in public. If Stepan—the tester—dies or passes out, then we know the food has been poisoned."

I walked...until I muttered, "I think I need to have a talk with him about the threat of him being killed."

"Your food was tested, too."

Yep. Definite talk.

"He seriously pays an employee to test the food?" I paused, realizing the obvious. "Some idiot actually took the job?"

"Yes. Stepan is paid very well for his services. And if he does pass on while on duty, his family will be taken care of. It is a job that is coveted."

"Maybe I should have a talk with this Stepan, too."

Least Ugly chortled.

I asked, "What's your name?"

"My name is Trofim, Ms. Forter."

"Call me Elizabeth. Please."

He shook his large head. "Thank you. But, no."

Okay. Must be a bodyguard thing.

"Do you want that Sprite, Ms. Forter?"

"No. Just the room. I want to get my work done, and then pass out."

He nodded. "That boat was something else today. I almost got sick it was so horrible."

"I know, right?"

He glanced down at me. "I just said it was."

His comprehension wasn't as good as Daniil's. "Yes. You did. Sorry." I stayed silent until I got upstairs to Daniil's room, having to stop by mine for my laptop first. When I started down Daniil's hallway to his room, I said, "Good night, Trofim."

"Good night, Ms. Forter," he said softly.

That was the last of the bodyguards I saw that evening.

In fact, that was the last of anyone I saw that evening.

I wrote my article, reading through it four times before sending it, making sure it portrayed the correct person—Zoya—in the limelight as the evil-doer of the love triangle. It was tricky making Grigori and hubby still sound manly, and not like idiot boys who had been duped by a pretty woman. But, I made it work. I attached the photo, sent it on to my editor after making a quick call to him, and then stripped down and got under the covers. The bed seesawed for a few minutes, and then blessedly, I passed out.

CHAPTER 6

The next two days flew by in a hurry. Other than being a little tired, I recovered from my boating experience without major mishap, like a visit to the toilet. Although the damn smell of seafood—which I had never liked to begin with—was still a major distraction at any meal. After my embarrassing bitchfest with the Lion Security group, they never ordered it again when I ate with them, and my parents were polite enough to not do so either after I told them they had scarred me for life.

The morning the Zoya article ran, I woke to Daniil, reading—on my laptop—and nodding his head in approval. But his mood had changed quickly, turning completely somber. He pulled me on top of him, holding my hair back from my face as I stared down at him. Then he proceeded to gently and specifically explain his dangerous life and what that meant for someone he was with. And let me tell you, he hadn't skimped on any of the details—for some reason ignoring what my profession was and giving me all of the dirty, low details of what his life entailed and what people would do to usurp his...empire...for lack of a better word.

And there was...a lot. Daniil dabbled in just about everything. The only thing his 'organization' didn't have a hand in was drugs. Apparently, he drew the line there. His Papa hadn't, and when Daniil took over five years ago as the boss, he cut that part out, causing a slight conflict that only recently had been resolved between himself and his dad. *After* Daniil proved they weren't hurting for profits from their other businesses, which included respectful businesses, such as construction and property management, to not so respectful businesses, such as extremely risqué nightclubs providing anything sexual a person could want and *somewhat* legal arms stores. There was a plethora in between too since it took him a half-hour explaining all of his assets that were, as he put it, *run with a firmer hand than most genteel businesses.*

I stayed mute. And it would be a lie to say I hadn't been a little freaked that he was so easily giving up the information on the inner working of the Russian Mafia. I wasn't a fool to believe he was spilling all of it, but he was giving more than he should have to a reporter, even one who was his exclusive lover.

He explained the attacks that were taken against him so far and what could happen to me. He said it was too vast to list all of the attempts on his life, but explained the most significant times.

He began with the attack on him and his late wife. He hadn't shown any emotion when speaking of her, which made me wonder. She died in a fire after she was drugged at one of the clubs, at the same time Daniil was beaten almost to death. The result was he was in a coma for almost six months, his children fled —he showed emotion there—and his wife died. All at the hands of his brother who wanted to take over the family business. It hadn't worked out so well for the brother though in the end—*somehow* being slaughtered and Daniil's dad taking back over.

He then explained the seven other attempts at his life in the past five years, none as deadly as the first, but still very serious nonetheless. He hadn't really needed to say what the hazards would be for me after all that, but he did. In explicit detail.

And it utterly and completely scared the shit out of me.

He wasn't surprised by my reaction, almost accepting of it. So, when I fled his room, telling him I needed time to think, he let me go without a word, just watching me with a hooded gaze…but he had stolen a quick, succulent kiss before I raced out.

Shaking and freaked, that was when Brent and Cole stopped me, managing to get me in the elevator alone…Trofim was lagging behind since Daniil had poked his head out the door, calling him back for a moment to speak to him. Right as the elevator opened, Cole and Brent stepped out of the room the maid had been cleaning and followed me into the elevator—leaving Daniil shouting down the hallway.

I knew a bad situation when I saw it. I tried to get out, but before I could even scream, Brent wrapped an arm around my waist and a hand over my mouth just as Cole pressed the close button, also hitting the button for my floor.

Cole stated quickly and quietly when I started struggling, "We only want to speak with you privately." All three of us could hear the racing footsteps out in the hallway, coming fast at the elevator. Cole thumped the close button again. "We aren't stupid enough to harm you publicly like this, so calm down before you do it to yourself."

The door had closed before anyone became visible, but the three of us still heard Daniil's furious uproar through the doors as the elevator began to travel down. It was more than unnerving that Cole said 'harm you publicly' so I kept up the struggle for a few beats. Pretty much until I completely wore myself out. The previous day had taken a toll on my body. I wasn't sure what it was with the Lion Security's group, but it was like they were all made of steel and couldn't be hurt because, no matter how hard I fought in Brent's arms, he didn't even flinch or break a sweat while keeping me restrained.

Cole hit the button to stop the elevator. We came to a halt between floors. He asked, "Are you done so we can speak?"

I nodded, exhausted.

Brent released me, and I slumped against the wall. I crossed my arms and glared at these two men. No one enjoys being cornered in an elevator to 'talk.'

"What were you trying to imply last night at dinner?" Cole questioned.

In return, I rolled my eyes, not wanting to play this game right now and be stuck in an elevator all day with them. "I wasn't *implying* anything. What I *meant* was that if you go and pick a fight with Grigori for something that happened while you two were supposedly dead, I will write an article," *no, I won't*, "about the two of you... experimenting... complete with photos of your tongues down each other's throats."

I shrugged as they glared. "Be fucking men about this. You two were gone. Life moves on after death. She did. He did. You can't hurt him for that. For them making each other happy."

I sucked in a breath, noticing they were actually listening to me. "What happened when you were gone you can't erase. Or blame them because they decided to live after tragedy. That would be selfish as hell, and the two of you are very far from that." I believed that wholeheartedly. In the armed forces, which we all knew they had been a part of, most of the time you're put in situations that require sacrifice. And they figuratively sacrificed their lives for their country. So, no, they weren't selfish. They made the ultimate sacrifice. And they may have lost the most important part of their life because of their selflessness.

Brent cleared his throat, and his fierce eyes moved over my shoulder where he stared at the wall. "We get that now. Last night, we were reacting off emotion. We'd only just realized…" He cleared his throat again. "We won't harm him for what he did in the past." *If he does it again, though, it's a different ballgame*—I heard him even though he didn't say it.

Cole stared, his eyes ice as he hovered over me. "What are you going to do with the information you have?"

In other words—are you going to write the article about us smooching?

"Nothing. I wouldn't ruin you two just to ruin you." Not after my new—annoying conscience—kept bugging me. "For now, anyway." Best to keep them on a leash if need be.

Cole's eyes flashed. "Blackmail?"

I shook my head. "No. Just insurance." In case they ever get stupid again. "Now, can we get the elevator going? And if you don't want to be shot, I would stay back until I exit. Daniil didn't sound very happy." Those words really shouldn't have rolled off my tongue as easily as they did, and my eyebrows snapped together. Daniil wasn't going to be shooting anyone today.

Brent grinned a crooked smile, and it was adorable with his blond curls falling around his face. "I think we'll be fine." He turned toward the panel of buttons, popped open the small door after he removed two quick screws with a small kit he pulled out of his pants pocket. Only fifteen seconds of messing with the wires, and the button for my floor went dark and the floor we had come from—theirs—lit. The elevator started moving again. Up this time, while Brent put the panel back on, just as the doors opened.

Cole pushed my floor's button again.

They both exited into a quiet hallway.

The doors closed.

I blinked.

It was good to know Brent knew a thing or two about wiring.

When those doors opened to my floor, I gawked.

At a mess full of bodyguards and Daniil and his children.

They were all standing in front of the elevator door with their guns aimed into the elevator—which only held me. And it didn't go over well.

Predictably, I fainted.

That had been the particularly low point of my past few days, even over awakening in Daniil's arms and having to convince Daniil—and crew—that nothing had happened in the elevator other than a private convo, and then still having to practically plead for Brent and Cole's lives.

Yeah, that first morning after the Zoya dinner wasn't fun. I'd been ready to split from Daniil…until I observed my family sitting next to him in the lobby of the resort, amazingly being charmed by the mafia king. That was been odd. And endearing since he knew I was ready to run.

He didn't want me to and had gone to the one place he knew was an enormous sore spot for us. And delighted the hell out of them. My dad talked about the possibility of having Daniil in church the following Sunday, and honestly, I think my mom had a little crush on him since he kept smiling at her when she would give him pamphlets on gun control. My aunt and cousin found it all very amusing.

When they left for their own flight, I had decided to stay with Daniil.

Though they didn't know that. Hell no.

Waiting on the Lion Security team for breakfast, I yawned and let my head fall on the table. I had seen my family off before going there—their flight was at the buttcrack of dawn, so I was early. Daniil and I hadn't spent the night together because my mom dragged me out to dinner with them, and then I had to get up early to see them off. I hated getting up early, and I was a bit crabby. In fact, I was tempted to get back into bed. Our flight was scheduled for nine o'clock tonight.

What seemed like only a few heartbeats later, I yawned and…toxic fumes hit me.

I choked, hearing voices all around. Blinking and coughing hard, I stared at a…

Christ, what was that?

Some sort of swordfish? I shot up in my seat, gagging and scowling at the dead piece of sea-crap on Ember's plate. The bitch had been sleeping in my bed every night—half the time with me in it—and she knew I hated that seafood shit, and yet she still brought it to the table. Belatedly, I realized the table was full. And I had slept right through it. I could sleep some more even.

Still choking, I glared.

She smirked, taking a hefty bite of her fish-stink-meat. She hummed in delight, and I felt the color drain from my face. That just wasn't nice. Not at all.

"Ember," Grigori stated casually across the table. I scanned for Daniil but didn't see him anywhere. "I don't think that's a great idea."

"Whatever do you mean?" she asked cheerfully, stabbing her fork into the flesh. I burped, placing a hand over my mouth as she lifted her fork with the meat dangling from it. "It was a great idea. I haven't had a good piece of fish all week." She turned her attention from Grigori to me. "Besides, Elizabeth here had her boating experience days ago. This shouldn't faze her at all now. Right?" Her eyes were hooded as she smiled, placing the fork right under my nose. "Wanna bite, Elizabeth?"

"Ember…" Grigori stated in warning.

"Fuck off, Grigori," Ember spewed, her expression hardening. "I'm just helping her find the truth. And she does love her truth, even if she's getting a little soft."

I stared cross-eyed at the meat. I had no chance. I held my breath as long as I could, and even tried to swat her hand away, but she was stubborn. I had to breathe…and, well…I got a big whiff of the fishy ocean on a fork. And it just came.

Out.

All over Ember's lap.

Ember shrieked, her hands flying in the air and hovering over me as I heaved up my guts on her. I gripped the back of her chair and the table, my head beneath, so luckily only the people next to us saw me puking. But everyone most definitely heard me after the place went silent from Ember's initial shout. The girl had a fucking pair of lungs on her.

Ember was whining, no real words coming out of her mouth. Except this high-pitched, disgusted whimper as I sucked in air, everything emptied on her bare legs and shorts, and a little on her black shirt, too. I groaned, "You're a fucking bitch."

Ember moaned again.

Daniil's voice came from somewhere to my right. "What the hell's going on?"

I froze but really wanted to pull my face away from the smelly puke. Ember made that funny noise again, starting to lightly swat at the back of my head.

Stash spoke, sounding awed and fascinated, "Man, Daniil. I haven't seen puking like that since Brent and Ember. But I'd have to say Elizabeth just beat them on that front. It was loud and long and full of body motion. A definite ten. Especially, with Ember's freak out." He paused. "Fuck, I wished I'd had a camera for that."

Staring at my puke while he spoke—something I never did—the 'truth' Ember so helpfully said she wanted me to find, dawned on me. I screamed, "Oh,

Jesus Christ!" I jumped up, grabbing a napkin from the table, wiping my mouth as I backed away from a rapidly approaching worried Daniil, pointing a finger at him. "Don't you come near me. Jesus…"

I swore harshly, walking backward in circles around the table, Daniil following. I didn't even have the common sense to take the conversation elsewhere, pretty much forgetting anyone else was around but him. "You've already done enough. Stay back."

My period should have come…yesterday. "Oh. Oh. Oh. Fuck!" Puking, smells, the tender breasts, not to mention the unprotected sex. I pointed at him again, shouting, "You asshole!" I was pissed and scared, and Christ, he was the fucking head of the Russian Mafia. I would have a little mafia heir. "I think I'm gonna puke again." I felt it rising. Especially, as I passed Ember where she sat, staring at her lap with her hands in the air.

Grigori was spouting off harshly to the bodyguards in Russian.

"Beth," Daniil spoke softly, holding his hands up, trying to look innocent. Too bad it lifted his black shirt up to show his abs a little…and also showed the holster he wore under his shirt. I whimpered, turning the table, using Eva's chair—God, she was going to have a new little brother or sister soon—to steady me. Daniil kept pace with me, moving slowly even as I moved fast, the bodyguards herding everyone out of the restaurant. "Calm down. Everything's all right."

"Don't give me that bullshit!" I shouted,

stumbling. Grigori caught me somehow, and I pushed away from him quickly and started moving again. God, this was awful. My life was over as I knew it. My youth was gone in the blink of one drunken night. Not to mention my parents were going to disown me. No matter how much charming Daniil had done—it was nowhere near enough for me to have his baby.

"Papa, what's going on?" Eva asked quietly, startling me since the place had gone silent like a crypt. Like my life.

I whimpered. One day my child was going to call a gun-wielding crazy *Papa*.

"Not the time," Zane grumbled quietly. But we all heard it.

My attention snapped to him. "You fucking know? How the hell was that possible when I didn't?"

Zane's mouth closed. He glanced off to the side, not wanting to enter this.

My jaw clenched, and I looked back to Daniil… and shrieked. He was right in front of me. Moving so quickly, I didn't even see him. He wrapped his arms around me, smashing me against his chest, saying quickly, "It'll be all right. You just need to calm down. We can talk about this."

And…I started bawling.

Ember stomped by, walking like her legs were made of solid wood. "Congratulations." She banged through the bodyguards and out the restaurant's door.

I sobbed harder while Daniil held me in an unbreakable embrace.

A half hour later, I was peeing on a white stick proffered by a bodyguard to the head of the Russian Mafia. While said head of the Russian Mafia and his heirs, plus a few stranglers of the United States best security company and New York's favorite nightclubs, waited outside the bathroom door for the verdict.

Not exactly how I had envisioned taking my first pregnancy test.

These people did nothing privately.

When Daniil and I had gone to my room, hoping for solitude, he explained that he already suspected I was. He had noticed—snooped—that there had been no feminine wrappers in the trash after I had said I was on my period. Then the whole damn gang just barged in through the door—via a magical keycard everyone seemed to have—or through the adjoining door I had locked to Ember's room. I didn't even try to get them out. I just kept hiccupping and staring out the window while Daniil consoled me, and ordering one of his guards to buy a test. To say this group didn't know everything about the other and weren't involved in everyone else's business would be only a hopeful dream.

I set the now yellowed stick on the edge of the bathroom sink, pulled my pants up, and flushed. I slammed the toilet lid down before thumping down on it and choked, "Start timing."

I heard Artur say, "Fuck. It won't work."

"Give me the damn thing," Chloe griped loudly.

I let my head fall into my hands and started counting in my head as they all started arguing outside the door. I was on a minute-twenty when I felt a hand on the back of my head. It didn't scare me. I knew it was him. The father of my possible child.

Squatting in front of me, he lifted my chin and stared me in the eye. And I lost count. He stayed that way on his haunches, his hands going to my cheeks, wiping away the last few tears I had shed. And while that last minute-forty passed by, his eyes told me that he wasn't going anywhere. If I were pregnant. Or even if I wasn't. He wanted more than to be just lovers.

That calmed me. Knowing he wanted me. Just me.

Somehow, he had seriously come to have feelings for me.

And...I liked that idea.

My lips twitched as I took in my first deep breath since the restaurant. "You and I couldn't be any more fucking different."

His lips curled. "And that's the beautiful irony of it."

"You're crazy, you know?"

He grinned. "Yes."

"I think I find it a little attractive like all those other women you spoke of."

"That's a good thing. There aren't going to be any other women for me."

"You sound so sure. How do you know this will last?"

"You already said why. Because you and I couldn't be any more fucking different." When I just stared, he explained, "We won't get bored with one another."

My eyebrows came together. "Is that supposed to be flattering?"

"Yes. It is. Because I find your differences oddly attractive, even if aggravating."

I thought about that. "I don't find your violence attractive."

"I know," he stated simply. Nothing more.

"Think we can work on that?"

"No." He brushed my hair behind my ear. "It keeps everyone safe."

"We're gonna talk about that."

He just smiled.

Then…his watch started beeping loudly.

I stilled. Everyone behind the closed door stopped arguing.

Daniil turned off his watch's alarm. Again, he brushed my curls behind my other ear. "Do you want to check? Or do you want me to?"

I cleared my throat and shook my hands out beside my legs. "Me. I want to look first."

"All right." He sat on the edge of the tub, his elbows on his knees, his hands loose.

Simply watching me.

I sucked in a big breath, mumbling, "Just stay cool. It's helping me."

He nodded, his black hair moving with the motion, his eyes on mine.

Silently, I stood and turned toward the mirror.

In a gradual movement, I let my eyes fall toward the test.

I blinked.

Stared.

Picked up the test, and slowly pivoted toward Daniil, handing it to him.

He held the test, staring down at the clear plus sign.

I barely manage to breathe. "You're going to be a papa again." I sucked in air. "And I'm going to be a mom."

Gently, Daniil placed the test on the edge of the tub, and then reached out, grabbing my hand. His gaze found mine as he slowly pulled me to him, tucking my legs between his. His brown eyes were open to me as he began to unbutton and unzip, opening them. He leaned forward and placed his lips above my panty line. And I almost started bawling again, seeing the tenderness in his gaze as he kissed where his child was growing.

He smiled softly against my skin. "I bet it's a boy."

I choked. God save us all from another one like his brood. "I bet it's a pacifist."

Daniil chuckled, kissing my stomach again.

Banging erupted against the door, interrupting our privacy.

Artur hollered, "What's the damn verdict?"

"I already said she's pregnant," Ember stated loudly.

Daniil sighed, zipping and buttoning my pants.

Lev argued, "You can't know that just because she puked."

"I'm not taking your word for this. I want to see the fucking test," Eva griped loudly. "If I'm going to have to put up with another damn brother, I need to know so I can shoot myself now."

"Fuck you," Artur griped. "We're not that bad."

Daniil rested his head against my stomach, sighing again.

Roman griped, "At least we don't leave tampons and bras everywhere. We're fucking men. We don't want to see that shit from our sister."

"My point exactly," Eva muttered dryly.

Running my hands through his hair, I pulled his head back. "Let's get this over with, so I can eat. I'm hungry." Now that I knew the complete truth and was oddly calm, I was starving.

Daniil grinned as he stood, his chest puffing up a bit. "Definitely a boy."

I rolled my eyes. "Or I just puked my guts up and have nothing left in my stomach."

He smirked. Then he rolled his shoulders, almost moving in front of me protectively as he opened the door. Everyone backed up, stumbling over themselves, some even falling back on the bed or dresser or even plastering themselves against the windows as he walked into the room. He must have one hell of a look on his face for everyone to be reacting like that. Even the owners of Lion Security backed up.

Daniil went immediately to Ember where she sat cross-legged on top the dresser as she played with her ponytail, apparently going for a bored look. I know he had seen what she ordered on our tours around the table earlier, but I had already puked on her in revenge. I mean, after all, I could have aimed it somewhere else. He didn't need to yell at her for it.

Even though Grigori and Ember weren't getting along—at all—Grigori was suddenly in front of her, standing there with his hands in his back pockets, also with a calm look on his face. But still standing there protectively as Daniil stepped toe-to-toe with his son.

Ember stood on the desk, her hands landing on Grigori's shoulders as she leaned over him, staring down at Daniil. "I won't do it again. But she needed to know."

There was a silent pause as Daniil raised his head to her. Still, I couldn't see what kind of look he gave her, but I did see her hands tighten on Grigori's shoulders, and his hands moved from his pockets and back, wrapping around her legs, holding her against him. Brent and Cole didn't seem to like that much from where they stood, and actually started to move forward, but Roman and Artur smoothly slid in front of them, completely blocking their way.

This was ridiculous, and I was getting a little irritated with all of the testosterone flying around. Daniil was just supposed to come out here and tell his kids, and the rest of the nosy group, the news. Not start a brawl in my room. I clapped my hands loudly, ending this shit, stating clearly, "I'm pregnant. Everyone, be happy and tell me congratulations or get the fuck out." I kicked Daniil in the back of his right leg while he still stared at Ember. "You too, Papa."

There was a silent pause, and then Daniil turned swiftly from his son and Ember, pulling me against him. And in the process managed to bump his son hard, Grigori and Ember falling back onto the dresser in a tangle of body parts and limbs. Everyone started talking around the room about my pregnancy. I scowled up at him asking, "Is that how you treat your children?"

Whispering in my ear, he said, "Take another look."

Even as Roman, Artur, and Eva walked up to us first, I glanced around Daniil's shoulder, seeing Ember and Grigori untangling themselves. Their eyes were still cold and remote, but both of their cheeks were flushed and they were even breathing a little heavily. Oh. Guess Papa did know best on that one.

"Nice," I murmured, nodding with appreciation.

I would like to actually see the bitch end up with Grigori.

"Thank you," he said, kissing my neck before looking up to his children. "Well, you're going to have another brother. And Eva, no more theatrics."

I blinked and sputtered, "Wishful thinking on his part. I have no clue what it is." I waited to see what they would say. They were really quiet now.

It had to be weird. Hell, it was weird for me.

Instantly, Eva bent, stunning me, and kissed both my cheeks and pulled me into a hug. "Congratulations. And I'll keep my fingers crossed for a sister."

Artur yanked me away from her, repeating the kisses and hug process. "And I'll cross my fingers and toes for a brother."

I stood blinking at them, shocked. It was peculiar. I felt better when Roman did the same thing but whispered in my ear, "What I said to you that one night still stands." After threatening me, he leaned back, smiling. "Congratulations."

Artur was maneuvering his body so Brent and Cole couldn't move up when Grigori lifted Ember from the desk…slowly sliding her against his body as he set her down…then quickly moved away from her, his expression turning pissed and hers doing the same. They were so screwed up. He reached down, even with that pissed off look and grabbed me around the waist, lifting me off my feet.

I squeaked at the sudden movement, instinctively wrapping my arms around his throat, as he hugged me tight, whispering, "I'm sorry I didn't try harder to stop her with the food. But honestly, I agreed with her. You needed to figure it out." *Had everyone known but me?* He leaned back grinning, his eyes a mixture of anger and amusement, like the two sides were at war with each other. He bounced me, glancing at his dad. "A baby brother, huh? Think he'll have her family's hair?"

Daniil's hands had just landed on my hips, beginning to pull me out of Grigori's embrace, but everyone in the room went quiet at that statement. Staring at my hair. And it didn't please me. Not at all. Scowling, I grumbled into the quiet, "If anyone makes one more crack about my hair, or even stares at it wrong, I'll puke on you next." My curls were huge. We all knew this. Time to get over it.

The rooms' occupants immediately shuddered, looked away, and started talking.

Daniil chuckled and tugged me out of Grigori's hold. He petted my hair, kissing the top of my head. I growled a little at him, making him smile even wider. I pointed a finger against his chest. "I'm hungry. Get this moving along."

He laughed louder. "It's a boy."

CHAPTER 7

Racing into my room, I dumped my equipment down on the bed. I needed to hurry and pack. Luckily, the sucky car rental agency was going to pick up my keys at the front desk so I didn't have to return it. I would be riding with the Lion Security group to the airport.

I jumped in the shower since I was a disgusting, sweaty mess after today's heat, and quickly changed into a cool brown strapless cotton dress that flattered my complexion and hair, and slipped on a pair of white flip-flops. I *tried* doing something with my hair. It was a mess. I raked through my curls with a large toothed comb and dumped that in my bag, then went to grab my mousse. It wasn't there.

Christ, the bitch had struck again.

Growling, I went through the adjoining doors that were still open, and glanced around her room, but didn't see it. Checking the bathroom proved victorious, though. I snatched it up—this product cost me a fortune—and started stomping out. And then instinct had me stilling.

A muffled male's voice came from outside, and the door clicked.

Shit. I was in her damn room. She may be used to entering someone else's private abode, but I wasn't. The door handle started to turn, and I panicked. I dove into the closet, closing the slatted door just as the room's door opened. I couldn't see up because the slats were facing down. A man entered, slamming the door behind him. He wore black athletic shorts and a pair of black flip-flops, and oddly, his legs looked familiar.

I stilled, completely silent when I realized those were Daniil's pedicured feet.

What the hell was he doing in Ember's room?

He walked past the closet, and he shut the adjoining door.

I froze even further.

What was he doing?

Did…him and Ember…

No. No way.

Which meant he was probably here to threaten her for the food mishap.

I sucked in a breath, reaching for the closet door…but stopped when the door to the room opened. A woman walked in from how small the legs were and how tiny her feet size was. About my size.

Ember.

She closed the door behind her.

I stilled when her top hit the floor.

Maybe I was wrong?

My stomach churned. And I wobbled in a daze. If Daniil was having a secret love affair with Ember...I didn't know what I would do. My heart was in my throat, and I decided to be silent. I started sweating, hating this...him with her...but if it were true, I needed to know.

Ember walked into the bathroom, kicking her shoes off, grumbling under her breath a few curse words. Daniil's feet moved into my line of vision and he stopped right in front of the bathroom door. Ember's feet halted, and slowly turned toward Daniil.

"What the hell are you doing in here?" she asked quietly, her tone furious.

There was quiet, and Daniil said, "We need to talk..." That voice. It was *Grigori*. Relief rushed through my veins, cooling my heated skin. But his tone was violent. "You stole my shirt and you wore my necklace. Why is that?"

Oh. Crap.

Silence.

Grigori's feet crossed, and he moved as he leaned against the doorframe. "Would you please care to explain this to me? You broke our arrangement when *they* came back." He growled. "I gave you want you wanted. And you're still mad at me. Stealing my shit and wearing that damn necklace to taunt me." He shouted, *"What the fuck, Ember?"*

I held my breath in the extended silence. If I were still writing about this kind of shit, it would be so prime. I still felt a little giddy inside. I wasn't sure the ruthless part of me that yearned for the insider's information would ever go away.

When Ember didn't respond, Grigori lunged.

Ember didn't move out of his way.

They stood toe-to-toe.

I was betting Grigori had her by the shoulders with the way her legs shook back and forth, with him yelling, "Goddammit, answer me!"

And...Ember came out of her mute state. She started struggling as she shouted, "I took the damn shirt because it reminds me of you! And I wore the necklace because you gave it to me!" She kicked him, but Grigori must have pushed her because he suddenly had her against the sink. "It's *you*. And I've missed you, you fucking asshole." Her shouting voice cracked. "You didn't try, Grigori. I may have been confused, and I did screw up, but you didn't even try."

Instant. Grigori shouted right back, "You did screw up! They fucking lied to you worse than anyone ever could, and you still decided to be with them. What the hell was I supposed to do? Beg? Plead?" It looked like he shook her again. "I couldn't do that. I wouldn't do that. It was *them*!"

Silence, except for their harsh breathing.

"*I know*," she breathed, her voice strangled. "I...I screwed up." Her tone altered to venomous. "*But so did you*. I didn't expect you to beg. I didn't expect you to plead. But, I did—pathetically—expect you to fight for me. And you didn't."

Grigori was just as furious as he spoke, his voice slowly rising, "What. Do. You. Want. From. Me?" He growled, and she shook again. "Do you want an apology? Fine. You have it. I never should have let you leave me. I know that now. But again, it was *them*." She shook again, and he repeated, "What. Do. You. Want. From. Me?"

"I...I..." she stuttered.

"You...You... *What?*" Grigori shouted. A pause. "Is this what you want?" There was a pause, and I heard Ember gasp. But it was quickly muffled. It sounded like one hell of kiss ensued. Breathless, Grigori asked, "Is that it?"

It sounded like Ember was panting when she said, "No. That's not all." She cleared her throat, and her voice was quiet. "I've missed you so damn much. I want us. The way we were. I want my partner back."

"I don't know if I can give that to you. A quick fuck? Yes. What we had before? I don't know." He growled so gently. "Ember, you hurt me."

"And. You. Hurt. Me," she punctuated each word in a hiss. "I may have started this fucking mess we're in, but you sure as hell ended it."

A minute of silence. I couldn't even hear them breathing this time.

"Fuck, Ember," he rumbled. "I don't ever want to feel like I have been since they came back. This isn't me. I don't understand it."

"I know," she whispered. Her arms fell and dangled at her sides. "I feel the same. It's tearing me up inside and I don't...I don't get it. But I do know the only time I feel even halfway normal is when I'm around you."

It was quiet. "I'm so mad at you."

"Back at you."

"Fine. We'll try this, but so help me, Ember, if I find out they've, or anyone else, touches you, I'm fucking gone." He paused and asked slowly, "Have you been with them?"

"No. I never even let them kiss me." Her fists clenched. "What about you?"

"Other than that shot for the photo, I never touched her. Or anyone else." He backed up a space. "I don't know if I can be gentle the first time. I'm too upset."

"I understand," she murmured softly.

"Good," he stated harshly. In a sudden movement, I could see them. Because she was lying flat on her back on the bathroom floor with a furious Grigori on top of her. She had squealed, her hands gripping his shoulders, but his mouth landed on hers, kissing her. Brutal. She groaned, her hands going to his hair and pulled him tighter to her, even though he was kissing her hard enough to bruise. He pulled back, staring down at her. "Take your bra off."

She panted, arching up, doing as told. He moved down her body, yanking her shorts and panties off in one motion. But she still said, "We don't have time for this right now. The flight leaves in an hour."

"We've got time," Grigori growled, pulling his

shirt over his head and tossing it aside. He leaned and took his shorts off. And, oh goodness, he looked identical to his father everywhere. I averted my gaze quickly—ahem—from his nether regions. Somehow, it just seemed wrong to be seeing him that way. He was Daniil's son. I really shouldn't be here for this, but Lord help me if I was going to expose myself. Not after eavesdropping on that intimate conversation.

Grigori dropped on top of her, lifting one of her legs, his hand immediately going between her thighs. She gasped, her eyes huge. His mouth landed on hers, biting her lips and saying, "I told you I'm not going to be gentle. I can't. Not this time." And he kissed her again. Just as hard as before, even as Ember started trembling under him.

Them coming together was damn violent.

Grigori was pissed, his movement jerky and harsh.

And Ember…her fury was quickly melting away. Especially, when two minutes later, he lifted his hand from between her thighs, grabbing her knees and pushing them apart. He held her that way, spreading her, and ordered gruffly, "Put me where I need to be."

Ember hesitated, staring up at him. I couldn't see his face, but she was beginning to look decidedly nervous.

"Ah, kitten. Backing down now?" he taunted in a dangerous purr.

Her jaw clenched, and her hand darted between them. She wiggled some… and right before he slammed his hips down into her, a harsh grunt coming from him, their bodies flush to one another. Her mouth flew open on a choke, and she lifted her hands, slamming them onto his shoulders, her face only showing pain. Not pleasure, at all.

"I can't," Grigori groaned, staring down at her and shaking his head, and then pulling back and slamming into her again with the same force.

"I know," she whimpered.

"You hurt me," he whispered, thrusting into her repeatedly, pushing her tiny body down into the unforgiving tile. "You fucking left me."

"I'm sorry," she choked, and tears started spilling down her temples. "I'm so, so sorry." She shook her head, crying. "I'm sorry, Grigori. *So sorry.*" She was pulling at him now, instead of the obvious reflex she'd initially had when she was pushing him away, even though she still looked like she was in pain.

He thrust harder, saying viscously, "I shouldn't have let you go." He drove into her repeatedly, groaning, "Fucking mine. Shouldn't have let you go."

"Yours." She nodded. "All yours. Just yours."

His fists clenched in her hair, his movements not slowing, only picking up in pace. "I'm sorry, kitten. I should have fought for you. Christ, I'm sorry. I've missed you so damn much."

"Not as much as I've missed you," she sobbed.

"You have no clue how bad it's been for me." He ground against her differently, and her pained expression turned surprised through her tears. "Don't cry, kitten. I'll make it good for you."

"It's all right. I'm not crying because it hurts. If you did to me what I did to you…" She shook her head. "Just keep going. I understand."

He moved again, pushing her legs open more, and started thrusting and grinding against her, making her features turn to complete bliss. "Hush. No more tears." He drove into her again, cupping her cheeks as she groaned his name. "You're mine, Ember." He moved against her again. "No fucking others. No running from me. I don't want to miss you anymore. You aren't leaving me again."

"No. I won't," she whimpered, wrapping her arms around his neck and legs around his waist. And said fiercely, "And you're fucking mine. I know that now."

"As much as we can be," Grigori whispered, kissing her forehead.

Ember nodded. "Yes. As much as we can be."

And…it suddenly struck me that they weren't professing their love to one another.

Ember had said she would never be 'in love' again.

And apparently, Grigori had the same holdup.

My, God. They truly believed it.

Even though, as they made hard love to one another, they stared at each other like they were one another's air. The part that kept them alive. Screwed up didn't even begin to explain them.

And this supposed 'quick' tryst turned into a much longer ordeal.

Grigori obviously felt he needed to prove something and had much of his dad's stamina because, after Ember's third orgasm—the girl had lungs fit for a Queen—I was beginning to lose feeling in my feet from standing still for so long. They needed to hurry the hell up. Or I was going to end up toppling out next to them. And wouldn't that be fun?

Ember's head was thrashing back and forth, as she came down from her last orgasm and whispered hoarsely, "Grigori, I can't. No more." He must have been doing something I couldn't see—his hand had disappeared between them. She shivered, and he started kissing her neck, and then she screamed his name, her body bucking as he started sucking on her earlobe.

"One more," he spoke gutturally. "Just one more. It's been too long." When she started trembling again, he stated possessively, his accent so damn heavy, "*My kitten.*" And his mouth went to her throat, his hair falling over Ember's cheek and shoulder as he started pounding into her. Her mouth opened, her eyes open wide in shock as she rocked under him, a slow keening sound—thank you, God, she wasn't screaming again—coming from her.

Grigori groaned long and hard and then shouted her name against her neck, slamming into her jerkily. She gripped his ass, digging her black fingernails in as they both went over the edge, their bodies quaking.

Thank you, Lord. I rotated my ankles. They were

seriously sore. And I would hardly have time to finish packing once they both got the hell out of here. Glancing around, I didn't see any clothes, so Ember wouldn't—hopefully—open these doors.

And then…they lay there for like ten more minutes.

Are they fucking serious? Get up, people!

Post bliss, and all that, I understood, but I needed to get out of there.

I was really getting dizzy.

I unlocked my legs, wiggling them. Passing out in here wasn't an option.

Ember ran her hands through Grigori's hair, turning her head and kissing his temple. He groaned a contented sound and wrapped his arms around her, holding her tight as she ran her fingers lightly up and down his bare muscled back. She asked slowly, "Did you seriously just give me a hickey on my neck?"

Grigori twitched, and then raised his head to stare down at her neck. "Um…yes. It's big, too." He flipped his hair so it wasn't hanging in his face, tilting his head and staring at her. And I could clearly see his face that way. His cheeks were flushed and his lips were swollen—I firmly ignored any familial resemblance—and his lips twitched. He smiled full out, something I never saw him do unless he was with her or her kids. But this one was a bit different. It was a little devilish. "You're mine. I don't want anyone else coming near you."

Ember tapped her nails on his back, eyeing him.

It took her a bit to comment since her gaze seemed stuck on his mouth. "So were going public with this? We've never done that before."

Grigori sucked in a breath, and then shrugged casually. "Just about everyone knew we were having sex before. It seems pointless to hide it again. They're all fucking peeping toms, anyway. Half of them have actually seen us together." *You can add me to those numbers.* He kissed her when she gasped at this info, but his face had hardened when he lifted it back. "Especially, now."

"You mean because Brent and Cole are back," Ember clarified. "You want everyone to know because of them."

Grigori stared her down, his cheeks turning even pinker as he became upset. "I hate worrying or being jealous… Can you blame me?"

Ember studied him and lifted her hand, running a finger over his pinched lips. "No. I can't blame you. And I understand. I'm good with it. Plus you took care of anyone who would come after us in Moscow. We won't have that to worry about."

His eyebrows snapped together. "You never know about that. You'll still need to be careful."

Tilting her head more, she kissed his lips. "We're public then."

He nodded against her lips, licking her bottom lip, his tongue ring glistening in the bathroom light. "Yeah. We're public."

CHAPTER 8

I hurried down the hallways with my luggage over my arm—my hair was a damn mess since I was never able to use the mousse when my hair was wet—and I glanced at my watch. I was seriously running behind. Daniil had called the room to check on me when I finally made my way back into after Grigori left and Ember jumped into the shower. I praised God she had done that. Otherwise, I'd probably still be in there where I had heard her opening and closing drawers, packing her stuff.

I hit the lobby. The group was waiting in the back like normal. There had been only a few minutes before our ride was supposed to be here, so I quickly checked out, giving my rental keys to the guy behind the counter. The same guy as the time before, and the time before that. I smirked at him, saying, "Still out of alcohol?"

He glanced at—yep—my hair, and nodded. "Yes, ma'am."

"Boy, that just sucks," I said cheerfully. Walking over to the group, I sat down next to Daniil, unsure of how we were supposed to behave in public. I didn't lean into him, but I did turn my head and whisper, "You're going to see some fireworks shortly."

He tilted his head down, his hair hiding his expression from everyone else and his eyebrows rose. "What do you know that I don't?"

My lips twitched, and I jerked my head softly to where Grigori was entering the lobby. "Just watch."

His eyes darted all over my face, and then his attention snapped to his son, his gaze assessing. Grigori didn't look any different, so it wasn't obvious. But Daniil took my word for it and kept his attention on his son, who sat down on the arm of a chair that Artur was sitting in, starting a conversation with him.

Ember entered. She was dressed like normal. She wore her usual drab colors of gray cargo pants, a gray thermal with a tight black t-shirt over it with boots. Her socks were her only color and they were bright yellow, only showing over her boots about an inch. Her hair was down, and when she made her way over to us, Grigori stood and walked straight toward her.

She stalled, her eyes widening. Grigori stalked like he was ready to consume her, his gaze intense. I, on the other hand, picked my camera up—I had it out ready for this—and put it to my eye. They were going public and my editor would kill me if I didn't get this. I had to take the shot.

I heard Daniil suck in a breath as Grigori stopped

right in front of her and said something softly. Though she still appeared somewhat frightened, her eyes were huge, she softly smiled at him and said something back. Grigori's hands lifted and he touched her cheeks. He ran his fingers through her hair, pushing it back.

Vividly putting her hickey on display for everyone.

The group stilled when he moved, but they were blatantly staring now.

And…Grigori…bent down and kissed her. Right in front of everyone.

I snapped my photo and put my camera away. Even though I knew there would be more to come. I didn't have to get this next part. I actually felt a little bad for Brent and Cole.

Ember and Grigori were a little stiff in the kiss at first—their first public kiss—but it swiftly turned into one hell of a tongue twister. Ember clenched her fists in his hair, and Grigori wrapped his arms around her, lifting her off the floor and standing straight as her feet dangled. She wrapped her legs around his waist when he stuck his tongue down her throat.

I had seen this all before. I glanced at Brent and Cole, who were standing shocked in place. Instead of charging Grigori like I thought they would do, Cole ran a hand through his hair, his face turning to ice, and rested back on his chair and started flicking through a magazine. Brent dropped his head for a few moments before turning from them and started speaking with Stash, who instantly responded in a soothing tone, filling in when Brent stayed quiet when he should have responded.

Well, not what I would have expected.

I wasn't sure if they had really given up or if they were just biding their time.

Daniil leaned back onto the couch, placing his arms on the back of it, his arm brushing the back of my head. Quietly, looking very pleased, he asked, "How did you know that was going to happen?" He was staring at them while Grigori put Ember back on her feet, even as reporters were starting to swarm them, the bodyguards doing their thing to keep them away.

"Let's just say, unfortunately, I was caught in a certain situation and saw a lot more than that." I didn't say anything else. I was going to try to erase the image of Daniil's son getting it on with Ember. It just didn't seem right.

Daniil paused and then chuckled. "You saw him give her that hickey."

Rubbing my eyes, I grumbled, "And a lot more."

He laughed outright, deep and booming, turning and dipping his head down to where I stared at my lap. "Are you going to be all right?"

I sighed, rubbing my eyes again before looking at his shoulder, mumbling, "The family resemblance is uncanny." I paused and my own nose wrinkled. "Disturbing, really."

He laughed again, softer this time, starting to say something, but a flash blinded us.

Startled, I jumped.

Daniil stilled, then relaxed back against the couch, looking out at the person who had just taken our picture. I mimicked him, turning to see Micah Olson standing a few feet away lowering his camera. One of my biggest rivals in New York. I smiled—all fake. "Micah, I think you're missing the action over there." I jerked my head toward Ember and Grigori, who were answering questions.

He smiled, imitating me now, and shook his head slowly. "You know, Slugger, I don't think I am." He glanced in Grigori and Ember's direction. "Moreover, I already got the shot. I followed your lead and raised my camera when you did." He smiled again and winked, nodded in farewell to Daniil, then walked away.

I sat not saying a word. That picture was going to end up in some paper.

"Shit," Daniil grumbled under his breath. "I should take care of him."

"Take care of him?" I asked slowly. "Do not tell me that means what I think it does."

He waved a hand, and then leaned his elbow against the arm of the chair, covering his mouth as he watched Micah walk away. "Not kill him, if that's what you mean. I don't always go the extreme route, especially where reporters are involved. They usually leave a fucking paper trail behind. It's too much trouble." I stared at him in shock as he glanced at Ugly Duckling and gave a tiny nudge of his head in Micah's direction. The guard instantly moved toward Micah but stayed back, keeping an eye on him.

"What are you going to do?" I asked slowly.

Daniil sighed and straightened his pants, really relaxing as he stretched his legs. "The photo will be gone before he even goes to view it on his computer."

I kept my mouth shut. I didn't agree with that. I knew what it was like to have a prime photo destroyed mysteriously. For a reporter, there was nothing worse, and sometimes, it only ticked them off more. I knew my lips were pinched and my eyebrows were glued together, so I kept my face averted from any reporters and Daniil. It wouldn't be good to show emotion again when the press was around.

Deciding quickly that it would also be best not to be seen leaving the lobby with them, I stood and grabbed my bags. Without a backward glance, I went outside to wait for everyone. Daniil didn't try to stop me. He wouldn't with so many people around. But Trofim was hot on my heels, not really helping the situation with Micah, who watched me leave.

In fact, Micah followed me outside. I covertly gave Trofim a look, and he disappeared somehow before Micah saw him standing a few feet away. I blinked, glancing around, and decided he had slipped into one of the little nooks in the architectural design.

Micah leaned back against the wall next to me and lit a cigarette, inhaling deeply before turning his attention to me. "You going to tell me the truth now?"

"The truth about what?" I asked, staying out of his billowing smoke.

"You and Daniil. He was laughing awfully loud at

something you said. Looked pretty cozy for just screaming at him this morning." He flicked his ashes, his eyes never leaving my face.

"I had just told him I puked on Ember on purpose." I shrugged, playing with my hair. "He found it amusing. Since he's not someone I want to piss off—especially after being stupid enough this morning to yell at him—I gave him the full details. A little ass-kissing, you know?"

"Hmm." He took another drag. "You've become awfully chummy with their group when most of your work involves bashing them."

I leaned back against the wall, staring out at the cars being loaded with baggage. "You know the saying…keep your enemies closer." I shrugged.

"Dangerous enemies to be playing that game with."

"All in a day's work."

He flicked his cigarette behind a chauffeur lifting a suitcase into a trunk. "Well, good luck with that, Slugger." He smiled at me. And I knew instantly he wasn't done with Daniil and me. He hadn't believed a word I said. "See you in New York." He waved and walked away, heading back into the lobby.

"Perfect," I muttered, kicking the wall.

"Problem, Ms. Forter?" Trofim asked, appearing at my side, staring where Micah had been walking. "Do you need me to handle him?"

I glared at the sidewalk. "No. There will be no

'handling him' just because he's smarter than the other reporters here."

"It would be no trouble," Trofim said softly. Honestly.

"Look, Trofim, I don't like violence. I don't like shooting." I interrupted him when he started to open his mouth. "Or stabbings, drowning, strangling, poisonings, or pushing him off a tall building…or anything else that I missed. I don't want him killed. Understood?"

His mouth pinched, but he nodded slowly.

"Good." My tummy rumbled. Trofim and I both glanced down at it since it had been louder than a jet engine starting. "Maybe you could get me something to eat, though."

Trofim grinned. "It's a boy."

I glared, placing my hands on my hips. "Food! Not commentary."

His ugly smile only increased. "A definite boy." He dug his cell phone out and started dialing. "What do you want?"

I thought about that while he talked to someone inside since he wasn't going to leave my side to get the food. "Maybe pasta, no meat on it. Some bread, no butter. Fries with a side of ranch. Some bacon with syrup." I tapped my stomach. "A slice of chocolate pie with cherries on top. Oh!" I pointed a finger in the air. "And some Twizzlers."

He stared at me, then at my stomach, slowly repeating everything I'd said. I snapped my mouth shut because I had been ready to add a strawberry shake to that, but as he listed everything I wanted, it did sound a little off. Probably best to not gain too many pounds in the beginning.

Driving to the private airport we would be flying out of, I tried not to be too embarrassed with the box of food in front of me. Daniil, his kids, and Ember sat in the limo with us, and they were all studiously trying to ignore me as I finished off the pasta, grabbing for the fries next. Daniil hadn't said a word only smiled a little when the food was brought out at the last minute before the limo left the resort.

Well, all except Ember, who grinned. "You know, when I was pregnant, I ate everything in sight, too." Her eyebrows snapped together. "Well, at least until the twins got really big, then I just ate smaller portions, but all the time."

Eva, Artur, and Roman snickered, and then quickly cleared their throats. I was too busy stuffing my face with fries dipped in ranch to say anything, but Grigori pulled her in closer to his side, wrapping his arms around her stomach, murmuring, "I remember you had a thing for pickled eggs. Never in my life have I ever smelled something so foul. You ate them non-stop."

Ember's cheeks pinked. "Funny thing is, I didn't like them before, and I don't like them now. It was only then." She shuddered.

Daniil's hand snuck into my line of site and went for my food. I growled a little, and he quickly took his hand back without the goods. I cut it off, my eyes enormous.

What the hell?

"Papa, you should know better than that," Grigori chided, staring at me and holding Ember close, like a content kitty cat.

"It's been a while," Daniil murmured softly. He glanced at me, sheepish. "Sorry. I'll get something later."

"No," I squeaked, completely embarrassed, shoving the box of fries in his hand. "Go ahead. I've got plenty." I dug out the bacon, ignoring how much I wanted those damn fries. Pulling out the bacon next, I turned my back on him a little so I didn't take the gifted food back. "I ordered half the menu. I'm good."

Ember was chuckling. "It doesn't get any easier."

"Wonderful. I'll be a bottomless pit, crankier than shit, and I'll get fat on top of it. I don't know why more women don't do it." Then, I stuffed my mouth full of bacon slathered in syrup. Mmm.

Daniil started rubbing my back, but I scooted farther away from him because I could hear him munching on those fries. Ember laughed in an uproar, her head falling back on Grigori's chest. She said, "There's all that, but the end result is worth it. When the doctor lays that baby in your arms, there's nothing in the world better."

Grigori smiled softly. "I remember when Beth and Nikki cried for the first time. There really is nothing more precious than that."

I paused in my munching—briefly. "You were in the room when the twins were born?"

They both nodded.

Artur snorted, saying, "She had to have them by C-Section. Only one person was allowed in the room with her. It was a no-brainer who was going in there, but they didn't let him in immediately while they got her ready. He was like a caged lion roaming back and forth in front of the door... wearing pink scrubs. It was hilarious."

"I didn't think so," Grigori growled.

"You were awfully cute in those scrubs," Ember teased, patting his leg. "I think my doctor had a thing for you."

Daniil and I stopped eating when his kids went silent.

I stared as Ember's red brows puckered.

Grigori quickly said, "You obviously weren't interested at the time. And you know I wasn't a monk."

Ember's jaw clenched, and she stayed silent.

I chewed on a piece of bacon slowly.

This was the first time I had ever seen Grigori frantic. It was kind of amusing.

"Honey, it wasn't while he was your doctor." I damn near choked realizing Grigori was also bi. All of this information was gold. "It was afterward. He came into Blitz Club one night while I was DJing. It was only once."

Eva delicately cleared her throat.

Grigori stopped and then amended, "Twice. I meant twice. That's all." He paused. "You and I were only friends then."

"Mmm," Ember said through her teeth. "He was very pretty if I remember correctly."

Grigori's mouth opened, and then snapped shut.

He outwardly decided it was best to keep quiet.

I kept eating in the silence. Daniil did the same.

Ember sighed, breaking the silence. "Elizabeth, a word of advice. Make sure you have an ugly doctor."

It was in the early hours of the morning when I stirred from Daniil lying me down. I yawned and stretched, glancing around. "Where are we?"

"My bedroom." He began undressing.

I only remembered being on the plane. Not the landing. Or leaving the plane. Or the car ride. I must have been out completely. "I should really be back at my apartment. I have to go to church in a few hours."

Unbuckling his belt, Daniil paused. "What time do you need to be there?"

"Ten o'clock," I grumbled, and rolled, staring

around the room. The bedroom itself wasn't large. The four-poster King size bed took up most of the darkly colored room done in mauves and deep blue hues. The woodwork was dark, but the woodwork along the ceiling was intricately carved with swirls and loops. There was a dresser in the same dark wood. A flat screen TV hung above it on the wall. There were two nightstands, with lamps on each with dark blue lampshades. Off to the right, there was a bathroom, to the left was probably a closet, and through the open door next to the dresser there was a large area resembling a living room done in the same deep shades. It appeared he had an apartment of sorts. Like back in the 1800s in England. Very posh.

Daniil sat down next to me on the bed and set the alarm clock for eight. "I'll be attending with you."

I grinned. "Dad'll love that." I paused, yawning. "I guess I can wear something from the trip. Did someone bring in my luggage?"

"Yes," Daniil kissed my forehead. "Go back to sleep."

The next morning, my stomach churned as the alarm clock blared. I rolled out of bed, disoriented for a second, holding my mouth and glancing around, trying to remember where the hell I was. Daniil shot up in bed

—I felt a little relief seeing him—took one look at my face, and jumped out of bed. He rounded it, opening a door, and ushered me inside. It was the bathroom, thank God, because almost as soon as my knees hit the tile, I started puking into the toilet.

He held my hair back with one hand, crooning to me softly and wetting a washrag with his other hand. I didn't even have time to feel embarrassed. All I felt was sicker than shit. I groaned and felt it coming again even as he set the cool, damp washrag on the back of my neck. And it did come again, even as I repeatedly flushed the toilet.

Puking was so not my thing.

Hugging the toilet when I was done, Daniil left me for a moment. I heard him turn the alarm clock off that was still beeping annoyingly. I didn't move when he came back in, but he unzipped the back of my dress I was still wearing, and gently undressed me—and himself—then picked me up and carried me into the shower. He proceeded to wash himself and me with the gentlest hands imaginable.

By the time the shower was done, I was feeling much better...and starving.

Go figure.

Daniil found it amusing. I didn't. Nope. Not so much.

There wasn't much time for any fooling around, and honestly, since we were going to church, I felt a little funny about that anyway, so we quickly readied ourselves, and made it downstairs to the dining room. Oddly, everyone was already there.

Fucking early birds. All of them.

I hadn't known that Chloe lived with Kirill, but I found out soon enough when she was eating pancakes compared to everyone else's…gruel…or some such. I stopped next to a chair that Daniil held out for me and then slapped a hand over my mouth, staring at their crap-on-a-plate. If it had just been the look of it, it probably would have been all right because I could have kept my attention averted. But it was the *smell*.

Chloe said around a mouthful of pancake, "I think she likes your food as much as I do."

That was all I had heard before I dashed back out the room, darting to a bathroom I had seen on my way downstairs inside this fucking mansion. The place was so damn big, I barely made it there. Daniil was there, holding my hair back as I lost whatever was left in my stomach. He asked for someone to get a toothbrush and toothpaste for me as I lost my cookies and then dry heaved. I couldn't believe I had eaten that much yesterday.

After brushing my teeth—Daniil told Trofim to keep the toothbrush and toothpaste on him at all times —we made our way back to the dining room. I was a little nervous about going back in there, but when we entered, the windows had been opened, and everyone was eating pancakes now. Albeit, a little unhappily, but their stinky food was gone.

Chloe grinned. "I'm going to like having you around."

I smiled weakly, feeling a little sick still. "Um, I'm not sure what for. But, thanks."

Chloe just chuckled, her gorgeous face clearly happy. Guess I had done something right.

When I sat down, I realized Grigori wasn't at the table. And I didn't think he was before. "Where's Grigori? Doesn't he eat with you guys?"

Daniil glanced at Artur, his eyebrows raised.

Artur explained, "He spent the night with Ember. I think they were going to talk to the girls this morning."

"Ah." Daniil nodded, smiling. He looked damn pleased. "That's good."

"I can't believe they finally got over their rift *and* went public." Chloe wagged her shoulders. "Think we'll hear wedding bells soon?"

I snorted.

And probably shouldn't have because everyone's attention turned toward me.

I bit my lip. Oops.

Daniil leaned in close. "Is that just an opinion or do you know something we don't?"

My lips pinched as I glanced at everyone.

They were staring at me intently. Like they had frozen except for their intensity.

"You know I saw more than I wanted to," I stated. "I also heard too much."

"And?" Daniil asked, his eyes darting all over my face.

I sighed and put my fork down. "Don't take this the wrong way, but they're seriously screwed up. They believe they belong to one another, but they don't think they're in love with each other. They said exactly, 'As much as we can be.' They're holding themselves back." I rested on my chair, taking in everyone's expressions. Nope. They didn't like that news one bit.

Daniil leaned back in his chair as they grumbled about how idiotic Grigori and Ember were behaving. He mumbled, "Those damn stubborn fools." He sighed, rubbing his chest, and then glanced at me. He indicated with his hand for me to eat. "They're public, at least. They've taken the first step, even if they don't realize it."

The table's occupants agreed with him, and we all started eating.

That was when Daniil dropped the bomb. "You're all going to church today with us." There were a few forks that clanged down onto their plates, but other than that, the table went silent. "It will seem odd if we go there together, just the two of us." He pointed with his fork. "You're all going. No arguments."

"I think I've got something—" Chloe felt brave enough to say in the face of Daniil's fierce expression. But Kirill glanced at her and she shut her mouth slowly, nodding. "Okay. What can one Sunday service hurt?"

Daniil shook his head. "Every Sunday. We'll all be attending." He lips pursed and he glanced at Roman.

"Call Grigori. Make sure he's back here. Tell him to bring Ember. And Nikki and Beth too, if she wants. Mr. Forter told me they have a wonderful children's church."

Everyone continued staring at him.

I offered, "It's potluck Sunday." Everyone liked to eat.

Artur asked, "Potluck?"

Oh. "Everyone brings a dish of food, and after service we sit down and eat together."

Daniil started barking something in Russian to a servant standing in the corner.

Roman muttered, "Wonderful."

After Daniil, grudgingly, dropped me off at the end of the block from my church, I made my way there. It wouldn't look right if I showed up with them, and Daniil wasn't happy about it but did as I had asked. Honestly, it was kind of funny because Trofim followed me. As if I hadn't known that, but Daniil tried to be sneaky about it, so I didn't let on that I knew.

Making my way inside the church, Daniil and crew were just pulling up at the front doors, giving me enough time to make it there 'alone.' I walked up to my family, and my mom immediately hugged me, along with the rest of my family. Like I was a long lost relative. It was normal for Sunday service.

We all chatted amicably for a minute.

Until my Aunt Susan stilled, staring over my head. "Oh, my. Frankie," my mom, "look who just walked in. James," my dad, "will be thrilled." Her gaze darted to me and away, a small smile playing on her lips.

Everyone stared over my head.

I turned around as my Aunt Ella said, "They look like the Mafia or something. Who are they?"

My aunt and mom both chuckled, Mom saying, "They are the Mafia." Aunt Ella gasped, and Mom helpfully supplied, "The Russian Mafia, to be exact." She glanced around at their group all dressed in black—albeit in suits and dresses—amidst the sea of colorful outfits worn by others. "And some of Lion Security's company, also."

Aunt Ella and Aunt Rebecca actually took a few steps backward, and Aunt Rebecca asked in a hushed whisper, "What are they doing here?" And she stilled, saying through lips that didn't move, "I think they're coming this way!"

My mom turned a little, her curls hiding her face as she whispered fiercely, "Be nice. They're obviously here for church service. James talked to Daniil all week long. He's very excited to have him here." She smiled great big. "Now smile and greet them properly."

Nervously, I watched as they came forward, everyone parting around them, unconsciously and some consciously moving out of their way, people slowly starting to stare. I'm not sure why I was nervous, but I was. Having them all here in a place that was normally a safe haven for me was…different. And then, I finally glanced at Daniil where he walked in the center of the group, leading them. And his gaze flicked to mine, and I relaxed instantly. That quick look was somehow soothing. It was as if he knew I needed calming and had given me what I needed.

I stop the soft smile that wanted to make its way to my lips. It wouldn't do to show I was overly happy to see him here. I had to play it cool—which wasn't hard because all of my aunts and mom practically shoved me out of the way, moving forward a few steps to greet them all head on.

And…Daniil charmed them like normal. It was truly amazing to see him soothe any worries they might have had, and at the same time, compliment them on what a wonderful church this was. He even stated who the architect must have been, and my mom beamed, nodding. Either he had done his research or he was an architectural buff. I wasn't sure which.

Katie came and stood next to me, moving away from the pew where her girls were sitting, appearing glum-faced like normal on Sundays being forced to come. "So. It didn't end in Key West, huh?"

I shook my head slightly. "No. Not at all." I hesitated, then whispered to her, "Keep this to yourself, but I'm pregnant."

"*What?*" Katie shouted.

And…the place went silent. Maybe it wasn't the best time to tell her.

She cleared her throat, and waved at the masses, and turned her back to them, staring at me as slowly the conversation picked back up. She asked in a whisper, "What are you going to do?"

"Deal. Like I have been," I said quietly. Daniil and Artur strode up behind her. "It's not as bad as you think."

I nodded and said, "Hello, Daniil. Artur."

Katie stilled, and slowly turned. Her hooded gaze had stayed on Artur for a second before she turned her attention on Daniil. And, swear to God, she bared her teeth at him when she smiled. "Daniil."

"Katie," he inclined his head toward her, overlooking her hostility. "It's lovely to see you again. This is my son, Artur." He was playing as if we hadn't had that big get together in my room at the resort. Smart since my aunts were watching.

She glared at him a moment longer—going all protective cousin on me—before turning her attention to Artur. She stuck her hand out slowly, saying, "It's nice to meet you, Artur."

He switched the large bowl he held to his left arm, and shook her hand—holding it a smidge longer than necessary, and said, "It's lovely to meet you, too, Katie." And…then…he went mute.

Daniil stared at him for a moment, looking perplexed before his lips twitched, and he turned to Katie and me, breaking the awkward silence. "You're

151

mothers said you could show us where to put our pasta salad for the potluck."

Katie nodded, her eyebrows clearing of confusion as she looked back at Daniil. "Sure. We can do that." She motioned for them to follow us, muttering, "It'll give us a chance to talk." She glanced at Daniil, who in turn smiled at her charmingly.

When we went through a side door and started progressing down the hallway toward the kitchen, Katie started walking slowly and Daniil did the same, Artur and I moving ahead. I blinked, glancing back, and Katie was talking quietly to Daniil, who stared down at her—respectfully—while she spoke, and nodded, saying something to her in return. Katie sighed and started speaking again, which Daniil shook his head and spoke again. And Katie glanced at me, looking somewhat calmer than what she had before.

I was guessing she was giving him the dressing down his kids had given me, and Daniil was amiable with her just as he had been with our parents. I wished I had that gift. I spoke more in fact. Bluntly. Not everyone appreciated that.

"Where to?" Artur asked, glancing to the left and right as we came to a fork in the hallway.

"This way," I motioned to the left. "So, you like Katie, huh?"

He sucked in a harsh breath—yep, not everyone liked my blunt ways. Continuing to walk with a casual swagger slash stalk that all of Daniil's kids seemed to have, he said quietly, "I don't even know her."

I smiled. He liked her.

The service was…a bit educational and a lot humorous. After Ember and Grigori had taken the girls to the children's area, the whole group sat in the pew behind my family. Before service Mom must have rushed off to tell Dad they were all here, because he hadn't looked surprised when he came out. It fact, he welcomed them specifically. His sermon was about forgiving yourself and your past, asking forgiveness to God, and moving on to a brighter future of love and happiness through God's will.

I was pretty sure he had made two sermons available for today. One for if Daniil attended, and another if he didn't, because this sermon was perfectly tailored for those with dark pasts. It hit home pretty hard for myself. What I had been thinking of for a full week. The things I had done in my past work history. Never showing any type of mercy. Always striving for the truth, and then putting it in print no matter the cost to anyone else. Letting go of how horrid I had been was a hard thing to do, and I wasn't sure I could do it so easily. I felt like I had a lot of penances to do, and I wasn't honestly sure I could change my ways so easily… because I truly enjoyed it. I would have to think more on it and come up with a middle ground, or I was going to start messing up work wise.

Right about the time I had figured that out, there was a light snore behind me. After covertly glancing back—as much as I could—I saw Zane was asleep, right along with Grigori. Ember was sitting between them. She elbowed both of them hard, waking them with a jolt. And honestly, most of their group looked pained to be sitting there, not hiding their emotions very well.

It tickled me from my own sour musings; especially since I knew they would have to keep coming back every Sunday if Daniil had anything to say about it...and they knew it, too.

After the service had concluded, we went into the large dining and rec room area where folding picnic tables had been placed and a buffet style lunch set up with all of the goodies brought in for the potluck. And I was in hog heaven. All of the comfort foods of my past were on display, and I filled my plate to the brim, and then made my way next to a few of my cousins, since I couldn't make it too obvious Daniil and I was together.

"So, who are the newbies?" my cousin Mary asked. She was nineteen and my Aunt Ella's daughter. She also had strawberry blonde hair like me, but hers was long and naturally curly—in the pretty way. Not inhuman hair. Just very normal. She pushed her pink glasses up on her nose, brown eyes staring at Daniil and crew as they loaded their plates. She reminded me of a butterfly today with wisps of different material that looked a lot like scarves mismatched together to make a dress. She was the artist of the family now that Katie no longer danced. An introvert and weird were what others sometimes called her, but she was sweet and smart, and I loved her despite her oddities.

Katie bit into some macaroni. "The Russian Mafia and some employees from Lion Security."

"Oh," Mary stated calmly, her gaze even more curious and not at all scared like most would be. "That part time job I got a month ago is right under Lion Security. I ride the elevator with some of them."

Surprised that she had gotten a normal job, I asked, "Who are you working for?" My Aunt Ella paid for most of Mary's expenses right now, so I didn't think she needed cash.

"Jericho Advertising." Mary shrugged. "I'm just a filing clerk. But it's helping pay for some of my school tuition since I didn't get a full grant."

Katie and I nodded, stunned. I couldn't imagine Mary…well, keeping anything organized much less a busy advertising agency's workload. Her small apartment always looked like a tornado went through it.

She grinned, glancing at us. "I've color coded everything in tie-dye. My boss loves it."

Tie-dyeing and color coding didn't really go

together in my opinion, but I lost track of that thought when Grigori, Ember, Nikki, and Beth sat down at the end of our table with Daniil sitting next to his oldest directly across from us, the rest quickly following. Daniil glanced at my plate, and his eyes hooded, but a small smile lifted his lips. Scanning his plate, I realized I had twice as much as he did...or anyone else at the table. And pathetically, I had already eaten some off it, so that was really saying something.

Katie didn't miss the interaction, and she stared at my plate, really taking it in for the first time, and she started chuckling...which she quickly cut off when Artur sat next to his dad. She and he both went oddly mute. Hell, they both were interested in each other.

Zane sat across from Mary, and she leaned forward, her head cocked. "You work at Lion Security, don't you?"

Zane actually appeared a little startled since he had been ready to bite into his roast beef sandwich, but he politely put it down, looking up at her. Mary and I have the same tendency to get glued on a subject when our minds were on something. It was like all we saw was what in front of us. A one-track mind, my mom usually said. Zane assessed her, nodding. "Yes. I do."

Mary smiled, nodding back. "I think I've seen you in the building. I work for Jericho Advertising. It's right under your office." She nodded down the table where Grigori and Ember sat. "I'm pretty sure I've seen them, too."

Mary also has a tendency to make people feel

welcomed—again, a trait I wished I had, and Zane and she started up a conversation about a 'wonderfully adorable' café across the street where Mary had eaten lunch at. Zane actually laughed a few times, all of us staring as they hit it off instantly, quickly becoming fast friends. An odd duo to say the least. Zane had to be in his early thirties and was harsh and scary looking—still extremely handsome—while my cousin was still in her teens—almost out, and looked innocent of ever doing any wrong even though Lord knew she wasn't so innocent.

I think we all blinked at their easy interaction.

Mary pushed her glasses up on her nose, grinning like the evil imp she could be. "You were sleeping in service today."

Zane choked on his drink. "Hopefully, the preacher didn't see."

"Uncle James wouldn't care…too much."

Everyone's attention went to her hair.

I barely bit back a curse.

Not everyone in my family was cursed with my god-awful hair. Example—hers was very pretty whereas mine was…not.

"The red hair makes since," Zane mumbled.

"Strawberry blonde," Mary and I both stated curtly at the same time.

That got a chuckle out of everyone, and I glanced at Daniil, who was watching me eat with relish. He was going to have to cut that shit out or everyone would know. Kicking him lightly under the table, he

grinned but went back to eating. And I glanced up…
and damn near growled.

In every parish, there was one woman who was
known as the 'steeple slut.' The woman who would fuck
anyone, including the preacher, if she could. And like
every other church, we had our very own. I like to call
her a cougar instead of a steeple slut since it was more
polite, but today, the cougar was checking out the
newbies, and her gaze had landed on Daniil.

Marissa was in her late forties, a brunette, big-
boobed—which she flaunted in simple silk dresses that
draped prettily over her voluptuous figure, big brown
eyes—I was pretty sure she had some Hispanic blood in
her, and big red lips. And today she looked as good as
she normally did, every article of clothing and hair
perfectly in place. She was also headed our way.

Ember was opening Nikki's milk box, but she
must have seen my expression because she glanced over
her shoulder. Her gaze was instantly caught on Marissa,
and Ember glanced back at me, eyebrows raised. My
eyes narrowed, and Ember started to grin, but Nikki
grabbed her attention back.

"Steeple slut alert," Mary murmured quietly, also
seeing what I was.

"What?" Zane asked.

"Guard the family jewels, gentlemen, unless you
want them gripped in red talons," Mary told him quietly
before taking a sip of her root beer.

Artur, Daniil, and Zane all stared at her…a little

in shock. Probably because she looked so sweet, and this was a church. They hadn't seen anything yet.

Marissa was almost on them from behind, and I instantly looked around the room, catching Aunt Susan's eye from where she sat clear across the room. My aunt must have been watching our table because she raised her eyebrows at me, and I nodded slightly. Reinforcements were going to be needed, but it would take her a while to get over here. Dammit.

"Hello," Marissa purred from behind Zane, Artur, and Daniil. Slowly, they turned after scanning Katie, Mary, and my faces. Daniil's eyebrows were pinched, but he quickly cleared his expression before turning. They all stared. Normal reaction. She was that pretty. She continued, holding her hand out that didn't hold her plate. "I'm Marissa Vasquez. I understand today's your first day here."

Zane shook her hand, his gaze going to her red painted nails, and his lips twitched before releasing her hand. "Yes. Today's our first day here."

Marissa gave him a winning smile, but she quickly shook Artur's hand, her attention zeroing in on Daniil, who watched her with a relaxed air now that the initial shock of seeing someone like her here. She held her hand out to him. "It's a pleasure to meet you. I've heard so much about you." Dear Lord, she leaned over to his eye level, putting her tits right out there on display.

Ember wasn't hiding the fact that this amused her greatly, and Grigori even looked tickled, watching and missing the fact that Beth stole one of his cookies… and Nikki quickly stole the remaining one.

Daniil shook her hand, and it looked like he tried to take it back, but she gripped it, not releasing him. Daniil's eyebrows rose slightly in a bored manner, but Marissa wasn't to be put out and moved in closer.

Mary started laughing abruptly, and Marissa stalled glancing at her.

Me? Well, I was pissed beyond measure, these damn pregnancy hormones kicking in. I wanted to pummel her right here and now. Belatedly, I realized I was playing with my knife and quickly set it down before I did something too stupid.

Marissa raised a perfectly plucked eyebrow at Mary, slowly letting Daniil's hand slide out of hers. "What is so funny, sugar?" She let her eyes roam down Mary's butterfly dress, her mouth pinching in distaste. "That new boyfriend of yours that your mother was telling me about surely doesn't approve of that…that… *thing* you're wearing, does he?"

Mary grinned good-naturedly even as most stopped their conversation at the table to pay attention. I instantly started to spout off something just as rude, but Mary leaned over Katie, placing her small hand against my mouth, shutting me up, and saying herself, "Actually, he just enjoys me naked. All young and firm. But you've probably forgotten what that was like since it's been so long since you were…well, young and firm." She said this, all the while smiling sweetly at Marissa, who was starting to seethe. "But you're right.

He doesn't really care for my sense of style." She shrugged.

Marissa's teeth were clenched, and I started playing with my knife again. This was the Mary, who liked to come out and play sometimes. The fun one, instead of the Mary, who sometimes lost herself in her work becoming a true introvert. I smiled just as sweetly as Mary—as did Katie—at Marissa while the guys across from us stared. It was more than entertaining to see we had shocked these badasses.

"Sounds like a dick, if he actually told you he doesn't approve of your clothes," I murmured in a sweet tone, ignoring Marissa now in hopes she would slink away.

Mary pushed her glasses up on her nose. "He is."

"Doesn't sound like a good relationship to me." Katie's eyebrows came together, also focusing on Mary.

"It's not good. And it's not much of a relationship, either," Mary stated factually, but her eyes went a little unfocused behind her glasses, and her lips curled.

Zane chuckled, joining the conversation, saying, "The perks are that good?"

"Yeah," Mary stated. "He does this thing with his tongue…" She crooked her finger back and forth.

I gawked, having déjà vu. "Tell me his name isn't Tumas."

Mary snapped out of it, shaking her head. "His name isn't Tumas."

"Quit being word for word."

"No. Really. His name isn't Tumas."

I sighed. "Thank God."

My Aunt Susan arrived then, herding Marissa away.

All three of us—Katie, Mary, and I—gave a small wave with those same sweet smiles on our faces as she left, scowling at us. I glanced at the table that was eavesdropping very poorly and stated, "Welcome to my church, people."

CHAPTER 9

I wasn't sure how we had all gotten here. One minute we were all talking after stuffing our faces—me more so than anyone else—and then next, my dad and mom had somehow procured an invite to Daniil's house for a game of basketball, which my cousin Katie and cousin Mary had also come out for. I left the church with Katie and Mary, even though I could tell Daniil wasn't thrilled about that, and we went to each of our apartments and changed for a game of b-ball. I stuffed a few extra things in my bag, so if I stayed the night again, I would have clothes for tomorrow—Monday, a work day.

And now, I stood in front of a fairly furious Daniil, who was quietly arguing with me about playing while we stood in a freaking gymnasium that was built inside his house. He thought I should be sitting on the sidelines with Ember, Nikki, and Beth. Now, the girls looked damn cute in little cheerleader outfits, but I wasn't about to sit out. I loved basketball. It had been one of the few sports I ever played growing up, and I wasn't too bad at it. Katie and Mary were staring around the room wide-eyed—I had to let Mary in on the secret I was carrying since she wasn't blind or stupid —and they were pointedly ignoring us. My parents were going to be here at any minute, so we needed to end this conversation quickly.

I said, "I'm playing. Get over it."

Daniil's cheeks flushed, and he took a step in closer, his bare chest fairly vibrating. "I will not get over it." His hand landed on my stomach where I carried his child. "You're pregnant. You shouldn't be doing anything strenuous right now."

Katie and Mary came out of their shock of the room and its occupants, which held a shit load of handsome men, half wearing shirts and half not. They stared where Daniil's hand was, taking in his size, and Mary blurted, "You better hope for a C-Section. Any baby of his is bound to be huge." She cringed. "God, that's gonna hurt." She shivered visibly.

"Butt out," I countered, ignoring the fact that she was probably right and turned my attention back to Daniil. "No strenuous activity, huh?" I smirked. "Boy, that's going to suck for you…or not suck so much…" I let that hang out there. Our bedroom activities were more strenuous than a game of basketball.

Daniil stilled.

I heard Mary and Katie snickering off to the side.

"That's not fair," he said softly. "I can be gentle, unlike," he jerked his head toward the court, "out there.

They won't go easy on you. We play to win, so anyone out there's free game." He pulled me in close, his hands sliding around my waist, and like an addict, I pushed in against him, wanting more. "Beth, I don't want you to get hurt. Or our child." He was whispering against my neck, lightly kissing me.

"Oh, for shit's sake," Katie mumbled, and my eyes snapped open. I hadn't even realized they had closed. And God, he smelled good. Katie started yanking on my arm, but Daniil wasn't letting go. In fact, his head lifted slightly, and he stared at her. It was scary enough that she let go of me, but she cleared her throat, saying, "It's a proven fact that women who regularly exercise while their pregnant have easier child birthing experiences. Elizabeth has played basketball at least once a week since she was young. This is nothing new to her body. It'll be good for her."

"Did I ask for your opinion?" Daniil asked quietly. Damn violently.

"Daniil. Be nice," I hissed when Katie stood stalk still. I pushed out of his embrace. I couldn't think straight as he seduced me with words and his body. Cunning man. Damn him. "I'm playing. And I'm done talking about it."

"Beth, I don't want you doing this," Daniil all but ordered.

"I do it here, or I go and do it somewhere else," I said stubbornly. He wasn't going to start bossing me around. I was my own damn person. "Your choice, big boy." I patted his chest, which felt like heated steel. Mmm.

"I don't want you hurt," he tried again through clenched teeth, his hands in fists, looking pretty pissed off.

"I won't get hurt," I told him easily. "Come on. Let's warm up together."

He crossed his arms, standing there like a statue, his gaze furious.

I shrugged and glanced at Mary and Katie, who were staring at him wide-eyed. "Let's go warm up since it appears, I don't have a partner."

Daniil growled behind me, and suddenly, I was off my feet and he was carrying me like a baby toward the court, whispering in a hiss, "You know this isn't easy for me, and yet you continue to provoke me." He jaw clenched. "Why?"

I sucked in air and gripped his neck, staring over his shoulder where Katie and Mary were running to catch up with us, their expression startled. "I'm not trying to provoke you, but you aren't going to order me around. I don't want that kind of relationship. I'm not the sit back and do what I'm told kind of girl."

Daniil gripped me tighter, stopping where spare basketballs were placed. "I don't like this." That was all he said, but he really didn't need to say anymore.

It looked like he needed a little reassurance. Not because he was bossy, but because he was genuinely worried about my welfare. If it had been any other reason, I wouldn't have been so nice, but I offered, "I promise not to overdo it. I know when to stop. If I get tired, I'll take myself out of the game."

Daniil's eyebrows came together, and he puffed out a breath staring down at my face. "If anyone harms you, I can't say that I won't hurt them." He shrugged when I glared at him. "I'll deal with your differences, but you're going to have to deal with mine."

I glanced over his shoulder and saw half the group was his kids. He wouldn't harm them. The others —Zane, Bas, Brent, Cole, Peter, and Stash—all looked like they could take care of themselves just fine. I nodded. "All right. Deal."

Daniil's curled me, lifting me further, placing our noses an inch apart. "Don't get hurt."

I patted his cheek. "I won't. Now let me down."

His nose crinkled, and he stalled, but eventually, put me on my feet...and I instantly dumped my bag, grabbing a ball and raced around him, dribbling between Zane and Mary, who were laughing about something, twirling and barely missing Cole who was taking a shot, and jumped, shooting. Swoosh! Bea-u-tiful.

To say the game was physical and brutal would be something of an understatement. Brent and Cole weren't exactly nonchalant in their dirty playing against

Grigori—who, oddly, seemed to relish in it. And Chloe and Eva were damn violent too on the court on offense or defense. Luckily, Katie and I—who were always playing against them—knew a few tricks of our own. I was just blatant in my brutal plays while Katie was graceful like the dancer she used to be when she went on offense, hiding it better. Now, poor Mary got paired against Roman. I wasn't sure how that happened, but she was getting pissed being thrown around like she was. She played just as often as we did, but Roman was just as big as his dad and his other brothers, so she was getting the shit kicked out of her on the court. Daniil was paired against Zane, and Artur was paired against Stash while Bas and Kirill and Peter subbed in, each one of them fine players, going for this game as if the victory was a gold medal in the Olympics instead of just dinner.

My parents were sitting with Ember—who looked pained next to them—while they spoke to her between cheering us all on, seeming thrilled to be here. Daniil and everyone had greeted them warmly when they came in. Even though I knew my parents were still on the hunt to figure out who I had slept with from this group, they were relaxing back as they tormented Ember. I knew there would be revenge involved, and that thought stalled me, wondering if my bag was still where I had dropped it. My hair products were in there.

And I should never have gotten sidetracked. I was only slightly winded, and hardly even sweating even though the play was brutal when I was slammed into from behind. I grunted, seeing the ground coming fast, and threw my arms out…and felt a pair of arms wrap around my waist, whoever had rammed into me, going along for the ride. But, before we hit the ground, the guy—had to be a guy by the solid body—twisted in mid-air, taking the ground on his back with me on top of him.

The impact still jarred me, and I lay there for a second, staring at the ceiling as the play came to a halt, tennis shoes squeaking on the floor as everyone came to a sudden stop. I had enough sense to roll after that pause though and get off whoever had taken that cruel landing. I stared down at Roman, his eyes shut, and his body limp.

Oh…shit… I started shaking his shoulders as everyone came running over, their initial shock wearing off, making Daniil's rush to us look normal. "Roman! Roman! Shit!" I shook him harder, but I was pulled back—gently—by Artur, who took my place, both he and Daniil kneeling next to Roman and trying to wake him. I stared down at Daniil's unconscious son…and started bawling.

God. Damn. Fucking. Hormones!

Eva sighed, putting her arm around me and hugging me tight. "I hate pregnant women." She sighed but kept soothing me.

My mom's quiet, oh so quiet voice said from right next to us, "Why did you just say that to my daughter?"

I heard Roman groan from the floor, waking, even as Eva stilled with me in her arms. Apparently,

Mom had rushed over, too, which meant…Dad asked, "Elizabeth, what did she mean?"

I froze, and it felt like my tears froze, too, in sudden fear. *Oh, shit. Oh, shit. Oh, shit.*

And then… it was like I was the ping-pong ball during a vicious volley. Suddenly, I was ripped from Eva's embrace by my dad, and my mom—who hadn't done this in years—grabbed me by the ear, ignoring my shrieks as they both started hauling me away. One holding my arm, the other pinching my ear. And it hurt like hell.

I was the ping-pong ball again when, in mid-holler, I was torn from their hold and lifted into the air, and pressed back against Daniil's chest.

He yelled at my parents in Russian and held me around the ribs, but his other hand was feeling my arm where my dad had gripped me, bringing my arm up, and inspecting it. I could even see the bruise starting to form there, and Daniil growled, dropping my arm, pointing at them and slashing his hand through the air, still shouting at them in a language that neither they or I could understand.

I had seen the shock on their faces for only a brief second before a wall of Daniil's kids slammed in front of us, their backs to us, staring at my parents. Or glaring from what I could see from Eva's face at the end of the line. Hell, Roman was even there, apparently fine from our fall. Daniil brushed my hair back and started inspecting my ear, rubbing it and continuing to blast my parents with his language.

I dangled there with drying tears on a rollercoaster of emotions. I was scared my parents obviously knew I was pregnant, and if they hadn't gotten the hint that Daniil was papa…no point in even hoping for that with the way he kept carrying on. And hurt that they would treat me like a child, and actually hurt me in front of everyone…and stunned to go along with the nauseous from being jerked around like I had been.

Ember handed off Nikki and Beth to Cole and Brent, rushing over, holding her hands up when Daniil growled at her, backing up a few more steps with me in his hold. She stumbled to a stop a few feet away from us, her hands out to her sides, saying quickly, "Daniil, they can't understand you."

Her expression showed that she couldn't either as Daniil barked something at her in Russian, his grip tightening on me, and I started to feel real sick to my stomach being held like this. I tapped Daniil's arm, which he didn't seem to notice.

My lunch began to rise.

I swallowed hard, trying to keep it down.

Stash raced over, standing next to Ember, and spoke in a calm, monotone low voice…but it was also in Russian. I had no clue what he was saying, but Daniil stopped making the soft growl that was coming from deep within his chest and listened. He made an odd grunting sound then, shaking his head and I burped, groaning.

Daniil stilled, and then glanced down at me. Stash

kept speaking, and slowly, Daniil lowered me. I barely kept from puking, but I did manage somehow to keep some of my dignity intact. And even though Daniil lowered me to my feet, he kept not just the one arm around me but added his other, keeping me flush against him.

I felt his chest rise, and he nodded at Stash, before slowly speaking past his children, in an extremely accented voice, but thank God in English, "No one harms her."

The place was silent, and I felt Daniil all tight behind me, practically vibrating. I sighed, staying where I was—half because I wanted to and half because I really didn't think Daniil was going to let me go anytime soon. "Mom. Dad. Yes, I'm pregnant. And Daniil's the father if you hadn't already figured that out."

There was a pregnant pause, and then my dad shouted my mom's name, and Ember and Stash lunged toward them. I couldn't see what happened, but I guessed Mom fainted. I hadn't heard her hit the floor, so one of them must have caught her. And I was sure it was only going to get worse.

Daniil, Dad, Mom, and I were in a study that Daniil had led us to after Mom woke from her fainting spell. Daniil still had his arms around me—he hadn't let go yet—

and he still wasn't speaking very well in English, his accent very heavy. But, I got the gist that if I tried to move away from him it would probably end with me chained...inside a dungeon.

Hell, I wouldn't put it past him to have one here.

Stiffly, Daniil steered me toward a large black marble desk. He lifted me, sitting me on top of the desk and started examining my arm and ear again, his movements jerky and clearly agitated. Glancing at me, he asked, "Does it hurt?"

Yes. "No. I'm fine." Didn't want my parents being thrown in that dungeon, after all.

He scowled, stating quietly, "You lie horribly."

"She always has," my mom stated softly, staring at us wide-eyed while falling into a black leather chair just opposite the desk, her arms hanging over the arms of the chair, appearing completely shocked...and even a little scared.

Daniil stiffened even more, his muscles bulging, as he stood straight, turning to face my parents, but I interrupted, saying, "You think you can find a shirt to put on?" His body was going to be a distraction to everyone.

My dad snorted. "A little late for that, sweetie, don't you think?" He rubbed his face where he stood on the opposite side of the desk before placing his hands it, head down and eyes closed. "Elizabeth, how could you do something so foolish?"

Daniil started that little growly noise again, and I quickly put a hand on his chest, keeping him from doing anything to my dad. "It wasn't exactly planned, Dad."

"Let me guess. It just happened?" Dad asked sarcastically, not really looking for an answer, glancing up and giving his full penetrating glare to Daniil. "How could you let this occur? She's young and makes mistakes, but you're old enough to know better."

Daniil sucked in a large breath and took my hand from his chest, holding it at his side. "Yes. Of course, I know better, but Beth is right. We didn't plan this, but it did happen." He shook his head. "You don't really want to know the details, do you?" His eyebrows rose, as he seemed to get control over himself finally, resting his hip directly between my legs hanging over the table, showing blatantly that we were together now, even if we hadn't planned this.

My dad stared silently at our close positioning, and my mom snorted this time, waving a hand. "*Beth is a short name of Elizabeth…*," she shook her head. "You tricked me. And I should have known better."

Daniil nodded once. "I did trick you. Beth and I didn't want you knowing then." No apology.

"It's not as bad as you think," I tried placating them. "It's not like it's the end of the world." I might have thought that at first, but now…well, it wasn't so bad a thought. "It's a baby. Your grandchild."

"Elizabeth," Dad said softly. "You can't stay in this relationship."

Immediately, Daniil countered, his voice fierce

even if he wore a bored expression, "She can. And she will."

My mom stood, glaring now. "That's my daughter's decision. Not yours."

Quietly, into the tense silence I stated, "I want to be with him."

Mom crossed her arms, turning her rigid back to us, and dad's eyes closed even as he asked, "Sweetie. Do you love him," *I stilled*, "because as much as it pains me to say this, you shouldn't be with him just because he's the father of your baby? We can help you raise this child without him." His eyes opened, staring hard into mine. "His world is no place for you or a child."

Truth time. My parents deserved that at least. "I don't know him well enough to love him. We're only in the beginning stages of our relationship." Although, yes, I was already pregnant. We were doing things backward, but doing them nonetheless.

My mom turned around and opened her mouth, but Daniil cut over her, stating, "I agree with Beth. Our relationship is too new for love, but I do care a great deal for your daughter. I won't let anyone harm her… *including her parents*. She's stated that she wants to be with me. Let her be without the arguments. Let us get to know one another better. As you said, I'm old enough to know better, and I know as well as you that arguing with your child, who's an adult, gets you nowhere. They tend to do what they want, anyway."

I bit my lip because I agreed wholeheartedly and just about spouted something off very childish like

"*Duh. Like they could hold me back.*" I would do what I wanted. But, I got the feeling Daniil—even though he agreed with what he had said—found ways around that little flaw stubborn children tended to have. I didn't think there was much that he didn't get when he wanted it.

My dad shook his head. "I can't agree with her being with you." He walked a few steps, coming to stand next to us, staring up at Daniil, but somehow, Dad didn't seem so small with the intensity of his conviction so obvious on his face. "Put yourself in my shoes, Daniil. If you were me, with my beliefs and standing before a man like you in this situation, what would you do?"

Daniil's lips twitched. "Run."

Sighing, I slapped his chest lightly. He wasn't helping. "Daniil, stop it." Staring at my dad's furious face, I said, "Dad, Daniil has explained his world to me. I know the risks of being with him. And I still choose him."

Dad got right in my face, somehow maneuvering between Daniil and me. "Elizabeth, there's knowing and then there's *knowing*. You have never experienced his world. And Lord save you from ever doing that." He paused, his gaze straight on mine. He blinked slowly. "Oh, sweetie. You don't think you can actually change him, do you?"

I felt my irritation rise over being freaked that I was having this conversation with my parents. "Maybe." When my dad sighed, I stated, "What do you think you were doing today? Every day, every Sunday, you try to change people to God's ways. Educate them. You invited Daniil to service with that exactly in mind. What makes me different than you?"

Dad opened his mouth and shut it slowly, his lips pinching.

He leaned back, and I nodded. "See. We're not so different after all."

In a lazy, bored tone, Daniil drawled, "Beth, my sweet. I've already told you I'm not changing my ways."

I smiled at him sweetly, still irritated. "Yes, you did say that." *Didn't mean it wasn't going to happen.*

And Daniil actually chuckled, turning between my legs, staring down at me. Lightly, he gripped my cheeks as I scowled at him—damn man thought I was cute—and lightly kissed my lips while still laughing softly. "I adore your conviction, but you're not going to change me."

Ignoring how my parents went mute at our chaste kiss, I grumbled, "It's worth a shot." I paused, and then stated honestly, "You're worth a shot."

Smiling at me softly, he shook his head. "Your father is right about one thing. You don't really know my world. I've told you what you need to know to make an informed decision to be with me, but what I do… who I am…it's too much a part of me. It is me. I do what I do to keep my family safe, and that's not going to change."

I shook my head. "No. You tried talking to Ben instead of using force first. When I asked you to stop with Samuel, you did so, letting me handle it the legal way. You agreed not to hurt that Phillips guy even though you were overly upset. You didn't hurt Micah over that photo," I ignored the reasons behind it, "and you kept me from doing anything stupid like drinking when I was ignorant enough not to realize I might be pregnant." I pointed a finger at the tip of his nose. "There's good in there. I believe I can help you find it."

Daniil's grin broadened and he kissed the tip of my pointed finger. "You are adorable."

I sighed, rolling my eyes since the man wasn't listening. "And you're crazy."

"Uh-huh," Daniil murmured, tilting his head and brushing my finger away with his cheek. He bent lower and kissed me again...but this time it wasn't so chaste.

I damn near melted into him, but a few seconds —hopefully—later I was sane enough to remember my parents were in the room, and I pulled back. I smiled— it was damn cute—when Daniil followed with a small humming complaint, but I quickly put a stopping finger against his lips, saying, "Daniil, my parents."

His lids opened, and his brown eyes that had started to darken, blinked without comprehension before intelligent reasoning was reflected there, and he cleared his throat, straitening and pulling me back to a more upright position. He didn't turn to face my parents since I could feel the beginnings of his erection resting between my thighs, but he did turn his head to them, holding me close.

My parents were staring. My mom's gaze was

stunned, to say the least…but…oddly…a tiny smile lifted her lips. And my dad was resting right against the desk next to us, he hadn't moved, but he was staring at Daniil calmly. Very, very calmly. It was…peculiar.

Daniil cleared his throat again, running his hand through his hair and opening his mouth to say something.

But my dad lifted a hand, stopping him. "I can't condone this right now. But you're correct, Daniil. I can't stop it, either." He pushed off the desk and slowly paced behind the chair that my mom had sat in again at some point during our smooch. His gaze never left Daniil's face. "If this is going to continue, which it appears it's going to," his hand went to the cross necklace that was hidden under his shirt, "I would request that you continue going to church. And we'll all have dinner together at least twice a week, whether it's here or at our house, I don't care just so long as it happens."

He stopped pacing, and his expression turned pained when he spoke. "I don't suppose you two can stop your," his hand gestured between the two of us, "intimate relations while you get to know each other…" His voice trailed off as Daniil and I both stared. "Never mind, that was too much to hope for. Although, I might add that this pregnancy wouldn't be a problem if you would have followed His ways and waited until marriage." Neither Daniil nor I commented—*what was there to say?*—on that, and he scowled but continued talking. "I would prefer this be kept quiet also, for the sake of my daughter's safety, until you two get this figured out." His cheeks flushed with fury. He rarely got mad, so it shocked me enough to keep my mouth shut.

Daniil gently nodded. "I don't see an issue with what you requested. It will give you, your wife, and me a chance to get to know one another better since we will be linked through my child and your grandchild no matter the outcome. And I agree with the secrecy for now. Beth's safety should be our number one priority."

"Yes. It should be," my mother stated, rising from her chair again.

Daniil held up a finger. "But I have a few requests of my own."

I stayed quiet, wondering what he was going to say while my parents watched him with narrow eyes, appearing not to appreciate this.

"First. You will never lay a hand on her again," Daniil's voice was a soft growl, and he absently started rubbing my bruised arm. "Ever."

My parents stayed mute but nodded, their eyes still constricted, but amazingly looking sheepish. As they should. Sure, they spanked me growing up when I really misbehaved, but they had never really harmed me. I knew they felt bad about what they had done. Their expressions said it all.

"Second. You will never degrade her in front of anyone again. She is not a child and should not be treated at such."

My mom stiffened. "She will always be a child to us."

Daniil nodded. "I understand that. She is your child, and will always be so, but demeaning her in front of others is not healthy for her." He paused, staring them down. "If you have an issue with something she's doing, take her to a more private venue to discuss your issues. I'm sure Beth would appreciate this."

I nodded. Hell yes, I would.

"All right," my dad stated stiffly, clearly irritated at being told what to do, but understanding nonetheless. Otherwise, he wouldn't have agreed.

"And third." Daniil paused, his voice going to a deep and dark place inside him. "Since you know about us, you will cancel that date you've set up with Don Phillips. She won't be seeing anyone else."

Both of my parents' mouths thinned, and they glanced at me for confirmation. They really didn't like the command in his voice—I could tell, so they weren't going to just agree with him on this one. They wanted that 'request' coming from me. So, I nodded. "Daniil's right. Please cancel the date." I sure as hell didn't want to be seeing someone else when I was with him. The fewer people I had to save, the better off I was. And Don was.

"You may have more in common with Don than with Daniil," Mom stated hesitantly.

Daniil started to move away, clearly irritated if the sound of the small growl vibrating in his chest meant anything. I quickly wrapped my legs around his, grabbing his waist. "Mr. Phillips is not who I want to be with. Just cancel the date." I kept my legs tight around

Daniil, and when he saw my parents shoulders sag even as they nodded, he relaxed back into me.

Letting my feet fall from his legs, I placed a hand on his warm back. "Mom, do you know a good OBGYN? I would like to set up an appointment." I didn't want my parents too upset. They may be overbearing most of the time, but deep down, I loved them. They were mine, and I wouldn't trade them for anything.

Mom's mien changed instantly like I knew it would, going all mother-in-charge on me. "You haven't had an appointment yet to confirm the pregnancy?" She paused, looking a little hopeful. "How do you really know you're pregnant?"

"She's carrying my child," Daniil stated bluntly. He placed his hand on my lower stomach. His eyes gleamed with pride. "I'm almost positive it's a boy."

Rolling my eyes, I patted his back. "Mom, I took a pregnancy test after I missed my period. It was positive. I am pregnant." I shot Daniil a look. "And the sex is undetermined even though some wish for another little 'Daniil' running around."

Daniil grinned and shook his head, rubbing on my belly. He had that same look on his face, letting me know that I was being *cute* again.

My dad was watching our interaction carefully, staying silent, even as my mom nodded, grabbing her purse, and pulling out a black book. She stated, "Well, in that case, I do know of an excellent OBGYN. We send some of the single teen moms who come to the church to her. She has an excellent bedside manner and she's very skilled." She flipped through the pages of the black book.

A thought occurred, and I blurted, "Is she ugly?"

Mom was startled at my question even as Daniil laughed outright, pulling me in closer to him. He had remembered Ember's advice too. Whispering in my ear, he said, "You have nothing to worry about, my sweet. I choose you."

Since the conversation with my parents hadn't taken too long, we went back to the gymnasium with a little persuasion on my part to Daniil and both my parents. They even agreed that I shouldn't be playing, but I stayed firm in my belief that exercise was good for me.

Daniil grumbled the most. "If you're going to play then tell Mary to not trip my son into you again." I didn't know she had. I just thought he slammed into me because I hadn't been paying attention. Although it didn't surprise me since I knew Mary was getting ticked off while playing. She could hold her own if need be.

The game was a blast in the end.

We won.

I was in fine spirits, grinning like an idiot and taunting Daniil, who was decidedly a sore loser. I didn't have to hide our relationship from anyone here, so it was easy.

Daniil was free to be himself, even with my parents looking on, staying quiet through the game, their eyes never leaving the two of us. Assessing. Just waiting for me to say I had changed my mind. I wasn't going to. I wanted to get to know him better, and that wouldn't happen if I followed the path my parents wanted.

I smirked, the game only ending a few minutes earlier. "I told you I could play." I spun and bowed. "Tell me who just schooled you."

Daniil's lips pinched and he crossed his arms, miffed. "You did not just *school* me. We only lost by five points."

I laughed. "Ah. But, you still lost."

Daniil's nose crinkled. He stayed mute. Pouting.

I ran a finger over the top of his nose. "So…"

He grabbed my hand, pulling me closer to his glistening body. "How about we play one-on-one and see who the winner is?"

I stared at his chest, and then his neck. His jaw. His lips. All of a sudden, I very much wanted to play "one-on-one." Just of a different variety. "No. I don't think so." He would kick my ass if I went up against him by myself. "But, I think I deserve a treat for my current victory."

Daniil paused, obviously hearing the huskiness of my tone. He bent to face level with me, purring, "And what kind of a treat would you like, my sweet?"

I licked my lips. "You. Me. Tangled in sheets."

Daniil pulled me in closer, quietly talking against my cheek, and told me exactly what he had in mind to make those sheets tangled.

From right next to us, my mom said, "I think everyone's going to dinner now."

I jerked. Shit. I had almost forgotten about them.

Daniil stilled, stopping his intimate words but slowly standing straight, glancing around the room that was still completely full. His lips twitched, and he smiled down at my mom. It wasn't a very nice smile. "If we're going to get to know one another better, it will require some privacy every once in a while."

Mom scolded, "Yes. I agree. But that doesn't have to include," she gestured to us, "*that*." She paused. "In front of everyone else, no less." She shook her head, embarrassing me. I was positive she hadn't heard us, but I'm sure we looked pretty cozy. "Use a little discretion, sweetie. It'll go a long way."

Daniil actually chuckled. "She's pregnant with my child. *That*, as you so delicately put it, wasn't anything."

I gaped, taking a step back.

He had not just said that to my parents.

My parents and I stared.

None of us were happy with him.

His laughter cut off immediately, seeing my expression. His eyebrows pinched together as he gazed at me now. He reached for me, and I took another step back, crossing my arms. He was confused for a second.

God, he was arrogant. I waited for him to figure it out. Some things you just don't say to someone's parents.

Confusion and fury lit his eyes as I retreated again when he took a step forward, but slowly, his lips pinched. The arrogance fled him. Wearing a bit of a scowl since he didn't appear to want to say it, he informed my parents, "I'm sorry. That was rude." He didn't wait for their response, turning his attention back to me, holding his hand out. "There. Was that good enough?"

It was a start. I sighed and grumbled, "Just try not to do it again." I ignored his deepening scowl and placed my hand in his...to be jerked against him and held tight. He was too damn used to getting what he wanted. This was going to be interesting.

Dinner was a curious affair. There was a mixture of Russian and American dishes placed in the center of the table when our entire group sat down. Daniil put my parents at the end of the table, apparently a place of importance, reserved for honored guests, and placed me at his side where he sat at the head of the table. Grigori sat on his other side with Ember next to him— Nikki and Beth had conked out in the other room on a couch, already having their own dinner brown bag style during the game between cheering. The rest of Daniil's kids sat next to us. I almost laughed when Artur and Katie sat side-by-side, silent. I think Katie tried to sit somewhere else, but Daniil barked out where everyone was to sit. She didn't argue.

After my dad had said grace—no one acted surprised this time—dishes were passed around in a clockwise direction. And most smelled wonderful and looked great…except for a few of the Russian dishes. When Eva went to pass them to me, I grabbed them instinctively, and just about puked when the smell hit me. Daniil was quick on the ball, though, and every dish I reacted to that way—there were only about three—he quickly grabbed it from my hands and gave it to a cook, who stood behind him. And I swear she was staring at my plate and what I put on it, studying it like she was making a mental note of what I ate and what I didn't.

Smiling softly at Daniil, a little embarrassed, I said, "Thank you. I know what you're doing. And I do appreciate it, but I hope none of those were your favorites." I was betting they wouldn't be placed on his table again when I was around.

Daniil passed off some corn to Grigori and leaned over kissing my forehead. "You're welcome. And my favorite is this," he lifted his filled coffee cup, smiling at it, "and you already said you didn't have a problem with it." His eyes glanced at mine quickly, as if looking for confirmation that I hadn't changed my mind.

Chuckling, seeing that he seriously had a thing for coffee, I shook my head. "No. It smells nice. You smell like that sometimes." I had just realized that he did often smell of dark black coffee. He had to drink it a lot. "It's a good aroma."

Lightly, he grinned, taking a sip, his dark eyes on mine over the rim of his cup. "Eat, my sweet. I know you are starving."

My tummy grumbled right then, almost louder than the conversation around the table. And said conversation in my immediate vicinity stopped, and they all stared at my stomach. Instinctively, I covered my stomach, pushing a few stray curls back that had come loose from my short ponytail. That just added to my embarrassment.

Eva's eyebrows snapped together. "I thought you ate at lunch."

"She did. Leave her be," Daniil stated calmly, bending and placing his hand over mine on my stomach. Softly, he stated, "Ignore them. The food is delicious." He picked up my spoon and scooped some mashed potatoes and gravy on it, holding it up to my mouth.

I took the bite, and my eyes instantly hooded as the spices of the gravy and subtle texture of the potatoes hit my taste buds. Mmm. He wasn't kidding. Grabbing the spoon from him, I did ignore everyone and dug in. And I was in pregnancy heaven. The food was magnificent. So much so that my mom even asked from down the table if she could get the recipe for the chicken and whatever it was drizzled in.

Daniil answered any question given him, but his

eyes stayed glued on me as he ate. I could feel it. I took a breather between corn and the bread, glancing at him. He was smiling softly. He did that a lot.

That was until Cole stood abruptly from the end of the table, staring down at his own plate.

The bodyguards standing around the room, whom I had actually grown accustomed to, moved a tiny step his way as if they were all in sync, making me notice them.

The table went silent, and Daniil placed a hand on the back of my chair—which I was pretty sure he put there so he could toss me if need be, and stated casually, "Is there something wrong, Mr. Donovan?" He didn't call Brent or Cole by their names when he spoke to them, I had noticed.

Cole cleared his throat, and his attention went to Ember.

Ember and Grigori, I noticed had been almost respectful when they were around. Other than that initial kiss to show the world they were together, they kept their touches light and didn't moon over one another when Brent and Cole were around, like how they had acted yesterday in the limo ride to the airport. I wasn't sure who made that decision—heck, it may have been mutual—but, they were keeping it low-key in front of them, nevertheless.

Cole's eyes weren't ice like they normally were. There was true pain and heartache reflected in his gaze as he stared at her. As Ember's face turned stony, no emotion showing, she also lost all of her color, her face going white. It appeared she saw what I did through Cole's features. Cole ran a hand through his hair and said softly to her, "I'm sorry for what I did to you. I'm sorry I've made you into the person you are today." His eyes closed, and he sighed, shaking his head. "I did this to you, and I'm so very sorry." He opened his eyes and glanced down at Brent, who sat calmly next to him. "I can't sit here and watch this anymore." And then…he turned and walked out of the room.

I bit my lip, not understanding completely, but knowing from the conviction of his heartfelt apology, Cole believed what he was saying wholeheartedly.

In the silence, all of us hearing Cole's retreating footsteps in the hallway, Brent leaned forward, and casually wiped his mouth with his napkin. Laying it down gently on the table, he also stood, and bizarrely, he started chuckling. Everyone was silent, watching him as he turned furious and pain filled eyes on Ember, who looked a little faint. "You know, darl—" he stopped, shaking his head, "sorry, *Ember*. You know, Ember, the one thing that is so damn funny about all of this?"

Ember shook her head slightly, her breaths becoming a little shallow.

Brent ran a hand through his blond curls, still very casual even though his graze said differently. "The really fucking funny part of this is that I was once as you are right now. Once, I ran from you. Once, I was also a coward." He fiddled with the napkin on the table. "Cole's correct. We did this to you. We made you the coward you are today." He glanced up and stared at her hard, placing his hands on the table and leaning over it. "Sure, you're a fierce fighter. Sure, you kept on when we were supposed to be dead. You did the brave thing and didn't give up your life." He shook his head, watching as Ember's eyes hardened even further. "But, you did give up your heart. When we came back, instead of you giving us a real chance, the men that you gave your heart to, you ran to the only man who didn't have a heart to give. Like you."

He stood upright, turning his attention to Grigori, who was staring at him coldly. "Don't think even for a second that I, or Cole, don't know everything about your past. *Everything*. Including the fact that you lost someone you love too, and only have a coward's heart left." He shook his head, his eyes shutting like Cole's had. "And I'm still in love with a woman who has the same issues." He sucked in a deep breath and opened his eyes, saying casually to Ember, "You know I'll always love you. Always. We have too much history to change that, but," he faltered and cleared his throat, "...I can't sit back and just hurt waiting for you." He glanced away from her. "Cole and I won't be home tonight. The girls can stay here with you."

Ember's breathing faltered, and Brent glanced at her, stating, "It's time to move on." His eyes flicked to Grigori. "If you can do it, so can I. Or Cole." Ember's eyes went to her plate and stayed there, and Brent whispered, "You should have kissed us. Just once. But instead, you ran. You were a coward. You still are. And I wanted you to know that this was your choice."

There was silence.

Grigori was furious. It was all there in his dark expression. And he stood slowly, stating in a deeply accented voice, "You and Cole died to her. And she did move on. Picking up the pieces the best way she knew how to give the children that you left behind—heroic or not—a chance at a normal, healthy life." He leaned over the table, slashing his hand through the air. "You're right. You both did this to her. But, have you ever thought, for even one second, she didn't kiss you because she knew she belonged to someone else?"

Ember was practically trembling in her seat, and blinking rapidly at her cooling plate of food while Grigori and Brent stared one another down.

Brent's jaw clenched, and he hissed, "She may have chosen you to fuck, but has she ever said she loves you? Ever actually said the words?"

My mom and dad were mute—and by their expressions, they were keeping up, so they must have been reading my articles. That was a good thing they were letting this happen without intervening. Brent and Grigori looked ready to kill one another. Not the time to butt in and try to make peace.

Grigori sucked in a harsh breath and whispered fiercely, his voice trembling, he was so pissed, "No. She hasn't, and she doesn't need to." He paused and stated with an evil chuckle, "There is something you don't know. Something that would maybe help you to understand us together and leave her the fuck alone. Not even ten minutes after you and Cole walked out that door years ago, her and I were plastered together in your own damn hallway. You tell me if she ever really loved you if she was kissing me like that before you were even on the fucking plane."

The table occupants, who were already silent, completely stilled.

I didn't move a muscle as Brent also froze, staring at Grigori, and slowly, eyes on Grigori, he asked, "Ember, is that true?"

Ember looked positively deathly white, and she closed her eyes from their lowered position, whispering, "Yes."

Brent paused and then sucked in a breath, his eyes moving to stare at the wall behind Grigori and Ember. They went a little unfocused, and his hands clenched into fists. A few moments had gone by before he shook his head, murmuring calmly, almost to himself, "There's always been two. Always two. Never one." He shook his head harder, taking a step back from the table, turning to stare at Ember again. "You've always been a coward. I know that now. You and Grigori are perfect for one another."

Grigori stilled, and then shouted, "*Get the fuck out of my house!*"

Brent grinned, his eyes purely evil. "With pleasure."

Zane and Stash stood as Brent started walking out of the room, and Stash asked, "You need a DD?"

Brent paused, glancing at him and ignoring the enraged Grigori. "You won't want to see this, Stash."

When Stash's lips pinched, Zane slapped Stash's shoulders herding him toward Brent. "Stash can get drunk, too. I'll be the DD."

Brent shrugged stiff shoulders. "Sounds good."

When Brent exited, Zane and Stash paused, glancing at Grigori, and Zane stated calmly, "We're not leaving because we've picked sides."

Grigori nodded just as stiffly as Brent had been. "They're your friends."

Stash glanced at Ember, his eyebrows coming together. "So are you two, but they need us more now."

"I understand."

Zane and Stash nodded at us, and the table in general, and thanked Daniil for dinner before leaving and practically racing after Brent, and whatever he carnal exploits he had planned for the rest of the evening.

I glanced at Ember and she looked so damn frail sitting there. Her face was white, her breathing was still shallow, and she looked so vulnerable sitting there as Grigori still stood looking furious.

Oddly, it was my parents who broke the silence that descended on our table. Mom began asking mundane questions to the rest of the group, giving Ember and Grigori a chance to compose themselves. Although, I didn't think it was going to happen anytime soon.

Daniil leaned over and placed a hand on Grigori's arm, and Grigori jerked, glancing down at the hand on his arm. Daniil stared at his son, and I watched as

Grigori stared back, slowly coming down from his fury. Daniil patted his arm, then rested back on the seat, and reached over to hold my hand.

I hadn't started eating again yet. My stomach was in knots after seeing so much pain being expressed. The reporter's side of me was intrigued, but now that I had gotten to know these individuals better, I really didn't like seeing them hurting. Even the wicked redheaded bitch.

Grigori glanced at Ember as he slowly sat and paused, his teeth clenching seeing her as she was. He finished sitting, and slowly reached over, and took her hand like Daniil had taken mine. Ember's eyes closed slowly, and it looked like she flinched before gripping his hand in a white-knuckled grip. Grigori stared at their hands before leaning over and placing a kiss on her head, and she turned slightly toward him. They stayed like that for a few moments, his lips on her hair, both of their eyes closed before they both moved away from one another—barely—and started to slowly eat their food.

Daniil squeezed my hand and leaned over picking up my forgotten fork and stabbed a piece of chicken, placing it on my lips. I glanced at him. And my eyes stayed on his. Even though he appeared calm, his eyes told me something else. I realized then, the worry he owned bravely I would know myself eventually. That was a parent's worry. For a child they loved unconditionally and would do anything for. Daniil was a good 'papa' no matter what he did in life that I might not agree with. That much I knew right then and there. Our child would always be loved and cared for, just as he cared for his adult children now.

And…I smiled. At peace with that thought, taking the offered bite. His eyes darted all over my face and stayed at my mouth, and he gently used his thumb wiping away some of the pink sauce that I had at the corner of my mouth. He was distracted, I could tell that much, his mind elsewhere and yet he still made sure I ate and was happy with it.

After dinner was finished—albeit much more subdued than it had been in the beginning—I walked my cousins and my parents to the front door alone since Daniil hadn't seemed in the mood to be overly courteous, staying at the table and sipping his coffee with Grigori while Ember laid Nikki and Beth down in beds upstairs. I figured Daniil was going to stay there and let Grigori talk to him if he needed to.

My dad stayed mute since we left the dining room, but my mom asked, "Are you staying here tonight?"

The question was a little uncomfortable coming from my mom, but I nodded. "Yes. I am." I cleared my throat, ignoring her suddenly pinched lips. "I wanted to thank you for what you both did in there after the… confrontation. Grigori and Ember…well, they have a lot of problems, and you both helped keep the peace after…" I trailed off, not really knowing what to say other than what I had.

Dad hugged me, smiling softly. "We're not so

bad, are we?" I knew he was talking about our family dynamics and family drama.

I shook my head, glancing at my cousins and them. "No. We look like the Brady Bunch compared to his family." I rubbed my full stomach and yawned. I had finished all of my food and I was exhausted. Sleep sounded pretty good, but I knew I still needed to review the articles of my competitors before I went to bed.

Dad stared at me. "If you choose to be with him, they'll be your family, too."

Katie stayed silent, but Mary snorted. "You'll have four step-kids older than you." Her mouth snapped shut when we all glared at her. That seriously wasn't appreciated right now.

Katie glanced over my shoulder and said quietly, "We better go."

Dad glanced where she was looking, and he slowly nodded. "Yes, I believe so." He kissed my cheek, and suddenly, he was herding my mom out of the house, Mom waving a little startled as she went.

Mary glanced behind me, and her eyes went unfocused in that way she gets sometimes and she murmured quietly, "What I wouldn't give to paint him now as he stands." Her voice was soft and so much older than her nineteen years.

"Let's go," Katie mumbled, grabbing her arm, and herding her out the door even as Mary tried to stay, staring. "See ya later, Elizabeth."

I nodded, a little confused…until I shut the door

behind them and turned around. Daniil was resting against a wall beside the staircase, his head down, hair hanging around his face. His ankles were crossed, and he held a cup of coffee that he stared down into. He looked alone. Like alone in the world as he stood there, there world heavy on his shoulders.

I stood there staring, I wasn't sure for how long, but he twisted the coffee cup around in his hand repeatedly until he tilted his head, his gaze directly on me. And I realized he was waiting for me. Alone in the world…and waiting…for me.

The thought took my breath away, but my feet were moving before I even knew I was moving. Reaching him, I immediately grabbed his neck, pulling his face down to mine. I wanted to wipe that look off his face. It was helplessness in his eyes.

I kissed him.

His lips were soft and warm, and I licked them, tasting his coffee. He sucked in a breath and wrapped one arm around my waist pulling me in close even as he held his steaming cup away from us with his other hand, and he kissed me back, pressing on my lips like wanting entrance. I gave him what he wanted, and took what I wanted in return, holding him close and moaning against his mouth.

We stood there for some time just enjoying one another until we both heard Artur mutter, "Go to a damn room if you're going to do that."

Daniil broke our kiss, pulling back and glancing over my head, blinking at his son.

It sounded like Artur sighed as I stayed where I was, gripping Daniil. It was odd having his children around to catch us. I knew a thing or two about evading parents, but not children—even if they were adults. Artur grumbled, "I don't have a problem with you two together, but it doesn't mean I want to see it physically happening in the corridor, Papa."

Daniil cleared his throat, straightening to his full height, and I slowly let him go, turning so I wasn't really facing Artur or Daniil, but they were both in my peripheral site now. Daniil nodded, saying, "I understand it's…odd for you…but I can't guarantee you won't see this again."

Artur started to say something else, and I held up my hands. "You know, I have some work I need to do before bed, so I'll see you in a little while."

Daniil nodded, still staring at his son. "That's good because I have a few phone calls I need to make to my businesses in Moscow, too. I'll see you in a bit."

I left them to it as they both started speaking in Russian. They weren't arguing from the sound of their tone, but Artur was clearly trying to get a point across, making Daniil look even more alone and even a little tired. I barely stopped myself from glaring at Artur. They needed to give their dad a break.

Grabbing up my laptop from Daniil's room, I went to find some solace since I wasn't sure where Daniil would be making those phone calls. Even though he had a study, which was where I was headed, he also had a smaller desk in the living room area of his room.

And that desk was a mess, clearly indicating he used it more than the one in his study, which had been clean of debris.

Closing the door gently behind me, I went and lay down on a couch that was facing a black marble fireplace. I was tempted to light it since it appeared to be gas but decided against it since that seemed like taking too many liberties in this mansion I was only a guest in. Instead, I pulled a blanket over me and rested my laptop on my content stomach and began reading through the articles of my competitors, paying special attention to Micah's stories.

And nothing was there about Daniil and me, which I was grateful for. I guessed that Ugly Duckling had somehow taken care of that photo. Otherwise, he would have run it with the look he'd had in his eye. I yawned, and my lids drooped. I blinked a few times going to another paper's website…

…and suddenly, I was blinking myself awake, hearing music. Loud, obnoxious music. Staring blurrily at my black screen with the stars going off as a screen saver, I knew I had been asleep a little while. I closed it gently and rubbed at my eyes, wondering who the hell had come in here to play that god-awful crap.

I scooted up and peered over the back of the couch, still rubbing my eyes. I blinked. And then rolled said eyes. Go figure.

Ember lay in the middle of the floor, staring up at the ceiling. Of course, she would be the one to come in here and start listening to this junk. I sighed and started to roll off the couch. In her defense, she probably hadn't even known I was in there. She must have come in after I had fallen asleep.

But, mid-motion, I paused when I heard the door open. Again, my reporter's nosy intuitive nature coming to the fore. I didn't hear anything after the door shut, but a few moments later, the music was turned down.

And then Grigori's voice filled the air as he said, "I'm sorry I brought up our first kiss like that."

"I know," Ember said back after a pause. "I'm not mad at you." There was another pause, and she stated quietly, "He was right. About me and you."

"Yes, I know he was," Grigori stated calmly, and the music cut off abruptly and it sounded like he was shuffling through something. "But, he wasn't right about everything with us."

"I know that, too," Ember stated softly. "We fit. And not just because of what he said."

"Yes. We do," Grigori murmured just as softly, and I heard a mechanical sound, and suddenly *Chasing Cars* by Snow Patrol started playing over the speakers that were embedded in the ceiling. I heard him move across the room, and when there was silence for a few beats of this absolutely heart-wrenching song, I peeked over the couch again.

I stared. And just about started crying—damn hormones. Grigori had put this song on, then went and lay down directly next to Ember. They both stared at the ceiling not saying anything, but the back of Grigori's fingers were running up and down Ember's hand and she grabbed his. And they lay there, holding hands, both silent and staring at the ceiling. Silently loving the other.

Halfway through the song, Ember stood, and I ducked back down as she began hauling Grigori to his feet. I stayed there silent and realized I could see them in the reflective gleam off the marbles fireplace. They were slow dancing. Just holding the other, and moving together like they were made for one another. And I bit my lip, blinking hard to keep the tears at bay when Grigori lifted Ember's chin with one finger, and slowly bent down, kissing her right when the lyrics spoke of the words 'I love you' not being enough to express how they felt. And together they continued dancing even as they kissed each other just as slowly as their bodies moved together.

I stayed as still as possible, knowing if I could see them if they actually broke the kiss and turned their heads they would see me, too. And I didn't want that. I didn't want to break this moment. They needed this. Healing one another even though it was frustrating as hell to know they didn't realize it.

And then…I was caught in another moment I didn't want to be a part of—as *Chasing Cars* ended and Snow Patrol's *Crack the Shutters* began playing, they're kiss didn't stop. In fact, Grigori lifted Ember, and as they continued loving one another's mouths, he began walking with her wrapped around him to the marble desk. I closed my eyes knowing where this was leading.

And I really did try to just listen to the music as

items from the desk hit the floor. I even tried to go back to sleep, just picturing their soft moans and groans part of the lyrics to the songs that played. But it was no use. When you know people are having sex near you, it's like your body automatically picks up every little sound they make or their bodies—dear God, eventual—joining makes.

And even though the locale—the desk I would never look at the same way—was somewhat unromantic, it was obvious they were making love, not just fucking. Their words, when there were words, were soft and tender. Their loving unhurried and unselfish. The sounds of their breathing remarkable as one when —from the sound of it—they made slow love to one another.

I stayed silent and kept my eyes closed the whole time…through so many damn songs and dozens of freaking pleasure filled moans. I just prayed they didn't find me over here. There was only one door to this room, and it was too open an area to try to sneak out. So I was stuck.

I yawned quietly when it sounded like they were nearing the end. Their pace didn't sound like it picked up, but their breathing had become a bit erratic. At least, that's what I was hoping that was about. It would be a little awkward if one of them went into cardiac arrest because then I would probably have to show myself.

"I'm sorry I've never said it to you," Ember whimpered quietly. "Because I do."

"I know, kitten," Grigori groaned. "I know you do. You don't have to say it."

Ember sighed on a moan, "Yes. Yes, I do. I always had this stupid thought about those words…" She paused, gasping, and whimpered again. "But it was senseless and childish. I know that now." She gasped again and then murmured softly, "I love you, Grigori. I have for a very long time."

Grigori growled softly, almost sounding like a purr, and he breathed, "I love you, too, kitten." Both their moans became muffled, and his voice was a bare whisper when I heard him say, "We're both screwed up."

Ember chuckled, "Screwed up doesn't even begin to define us."

And then, she gasped his name, and he groaned hers, and soft murmurs ensued between their panting and moaning.

I was right, they were almost done, but I was still sitting there in shock realizing that two people could say they loved one another, and believe it, but not understand it wasn't just simple love for another human being. These two were so in love with each other, it was like a bright pink spotlight shone down on them when they were alone—at least, they thought so—and were able to be themselves. Their actions. Their words. It was all there…except for damn common sense.

Ember started whimpering Grigori's name, but that abruptly stopped and she began chanting a keening cry, "Love you. Love you. Love you. Love you."

Grigori picked up her mantra—and the pace from the sound of it—groaning with her, "Love you, too. Love you, too. Love you, too. Love you, too."

Suddenly, skin was slapping a lot harder, and Ember screamed—I tried not to flinch—Grigori's name. Their rhythm was hectic. Grigori was shouting Ember's name—I tried not to baulk again. Ember was whimpering brokenly and Grigori was groaning deep and long. Sounded like they were finally through.

I stayed quiet…and then, so did they, their breathing becoming steady and then rhythmic. Oh, they had not just done what I thought they had. I waited, praying they would make some noise of separation…

…and heard nothing.

Except for a slight snore starting up from each of them.

They had fallen asleep on the damn desk!

I tried not to groan. I was still stuck. They weren't the heavy sleeper types.

If I tried for the door, they would surely wake up.

So I did what I could do. I fell asleep.

Startled, I felt a sense of vertigo. I squawked, my arms flying out, but Daniil's voice murmured softly, "It's all right." It was him lifting me, his arms that held me tight. "Go back to sleep. They're gone. I've got you."

I groaned, resting my head against his shoulder as he started walking through the darkened study and out into the hall. "How did you know I was here?"

Daniil chuckled lightly. "I have eyes all over my house. I can see everything if I chose to."

I stilled, a little grossed out by that. "You know what happened in there?" *You watch your own kids get it on?*

Daniil kissed my forehead, walking up the stairs and laughing against my skin. "I said if I chose to see it. Not that I do. I have cameras all throughout the house for my own family's protection." He chuckled again. "And when I started looking through the footage to find you," his arms started shaking he was laughing so hard, and I hung on afraid he would drop me, "Ah, Beth, you know curiosity can get you into situations you don't want to be in, right?"

I grumbled, "You don't have to tell me that...but, I didn't want to interrupt them. They needed that."

Daniil held me tighter. "I didn't watch for any real period of time, just glanced at the screen to try to see if you were in the room. And, by the way, remind me tomorrow to show you a way out of there they might not have noticed." He hesitated, and then asked as he entered his room, "You said they needed that—was something said?"

I nodded, but I was thinking about what Daniil had said. There must be some kind of hidden door in that room. "Yeah, Ember said she loved him. He said he loved her." Daniil's face brightened in the room lit by lamps, so I shook my head. "Then they messed it up by saying they were screwed up. In essence still saying they weren't 'in love' with one another. Really fucking wrong, if you ask me."

Daniil shook his head in agitation but sighed, laying me down on the bed. "At least they said they loved one another."

"Yeah, and they both agree that they," I used finger quotes, "'*fit*' one another." I snorted and then yawned. "It sounded like they fit together perfectly in more than one way."

Daniil's lips quirked as I blinked sleepily at him. "It's probably a good thing you were hunkered down on the couch like a frightened doe." I scowled, because... well, that was just rude...and most likely true. And he had the nerve to grin, but he shook his head, pulling out my hair tie and set it on the table. "Those two together...let's just say I did a double take. At the distance of the camera, at first, I thought someone had dubbed in you and me together, and I was looking at a phony frame." His chuckled softly. "I understand why you found that all a little unnerving seeing them together before."

I nodded, and my eyelids closed, feeling more tired than I ever had in my whole life. "Yeah. Very weird." I snuggled down in the blanket. "I gotta be up at six o'clock for work."

His lips brushed mine, but I was too tired to even kiss him back. Sleep took me under again.

CHAPTER 10

A week later, I finally sat in Dr. Wisser's office dressed in a gown that opened in the front instead of the back. I tied it closed, but I still kept the tiny little blanket over my legs. Daniil sat in the room with me flipping through a magazine in irritation while my parents waited out in the lobby—probably also flipping through magazines in irritation.

It had been an absolute chore even getting to the doctor, who wasn't the woman my mom referenced a week ago. Daniil nixed that after running a search on the woman. Apparently, she had a black itty-bitty spot on her record for delivering a baby stillborn in her early years. Over dinner at my parents' house on Wednesday, Daniil adamantly refused to let his child be birthed by her. Actually, he wanted me to use a midwife. He believed a child coming into the word should be done more *naturally*. I just about smacked him that night at my parents' house.

Mom interceded and spoke of the risks that

could occur with using a midwife, and just because his late wife used one for all four of her children, it didn't mean that I was going to also. There had been a lot of growling and glares going on that night, but I finally just stood up at the table and stated, "I'm not doing a damn thing natural. So, find a doctor you do approve of. And quickly. I know I should be taking those pills…" I snapped my fingers, "prenatal pills or whatever they're called."

Daniil seemed taken aback to realize I was behind on what I should be doing for our child and he finally agreed. So, now I sat in a doctor's office posher than most millionaires' homes—I was pretty sure the cabinet handles were actually gold plated—who Dr. Benedict from Donovan Hospital had referred us. Apparently, Ember or Grigori—not sure which—had called her and asked for the best OBGYN she could think of here in New York.

And Daniil wasn't thrilled because, apparently, Dr. Wisser was a man…oh, no, the horror…and my parents weren't thrilled because of the doctors cost… which Daniil barely glanced at. My insurance at work would never cover the cost of this doc's fees, but apparently, he was the best. And since I wasn't doing the midwife thing, Daniil got me the best.

And Dr. Wisser wasn't late, either. I sure as hell hoped not with his fees. He strolled into the room— yes, strolled—looking very debonair in his white doctor's coat, reading over what had to be my file since I practically had to write a damn book in questions about my previous health history. He had black hair like Daniil, but it was shorter and slicked back. I was pretty sure I saw a flash of green eyes as they skimmed my paperwork, his body in prime physical shape. And his face was very pretty for a man of around fifty—I tried not to snicker—right around Daniil's own age. Though Daniil looked much younger than he did.

Daniil's jaw clenched, and he shut the magazine with a snap, his attention slamming to me. "He is not touching you." A blatant command, which had the doctor stopping in his tracks and glancing up, the door barely having time to close behind him.

"Daniil…" I murmured softly. "Remember, I chose you." God, he was a handful.

Daniil glanced at the doctor, glaring at him, making the doctor freeze in his tracks, and getting a good look at who he actually was. The doctor's jaw started to drop, obviously recognizing him, but Daniil didn't seem to give a shit about that and asked him harshly, "Are you married or gay?"

I snapped a hand over my mouth, trying to hold back the laugh that wanted to erupt.

The doctor sputtered, "No."

Daniil's gaze came back to me, eyebrows raised, and he stated calmly, "He's not touching you."

Clearing my throat, getting control over myself as my irritation started to peak. "He's the best. And that's what you wanted. That's what you get. So, if that means he has to put his hand up my crotch," I held up a quick stopping hand when Daniil's mouth flew open, "professionally, of course, then so be it. I don't want a midwife. You don't want to use the doctor my mom suggested. So here we are." I pointed at the doctor. "The best." I shrugged, lowering my arm. "He can't help the way he looks any more than you can."

The doctor cleared his throat, finally done composing himself and his obvious shock, also getting the gist of this conversation. "I assure you I am nothing but professional." He cocked his head. "If it helps you..." And he started in on all of his recommendations. We already knew this, but I let him continue because it gave Daniil time to accept the fact that I wasn't going to go through this all over again.

I kept my gaze on Daniil, letting him see I wasn't going to be pushed around again. Daniil so wasn't happy as he stared at me, then the doctor, and back and forth, his nose crinkling and his eyebrows together... but his eyes slowly went from spitfire mad to only slightly furious. That was an improvement. Finally, Daniil huffed out a breath, his voice deep, and asked me, "Are you sure you won't pull a Grigori?"

I coughed hard, glancing at the doctor, who stood there quietly, actually seeming amused by this now. "Yes. I already said I chose you."

Daniil crossed his arms, his tailored black jacket pulling at its seams as he glared at the entertained doctor. And then he stated bluntly, "I will watch everything you do. And if you so much as go near her clit, I will kill you."

I gawked, gasping, "Daniil..."

"Hush," he ordered me quietly, his eyes flicking toward mine, then back to the doctor. "Do you understand?" I was pretty sure I had never seen that look in his eye before. Even when he threatened me that very first morning. He was utterly serious, no smiles on his face right now.

Dr. Wisser's eyebrows rose, and he stated, "I normally order the partner outside when I perform a pelvic exam, but I can assure you I won't try to stimulate with Ms. Forter."

Daniil rested back in his chair, staring at the doctor. "I'll double your fee if you allow what I want." He reached inside his jacket, withdrawing his long black wallet, and pulling out so much damn money, I was in shock. Especially, when he put the wallet back in his coat and there was still some left in it.

Dr. Wisser eyed the money Daniil had placed on the counter and then used a pen to delicately spread the bills apart. "You do realize it's illegal to carry this much cash on you."

"And your point?" Daniil stretched his legs out when the doctor stayed mute. "Do we have a deal?"

Dr. Wisser's eyes were still on the cash— indicating he really wanted it, but he stated, "That's up to Ms. Forter. She's the patient."

"Do I seriously look like I care?" I asked exasperated by this. "I just want an actual doctor in an actual hospital. Just take the damn cash and keep me and our baby alive."

Dr. Wisser pocketed the money pretty damn quickly. "That shouldn't be an issue."

The exam started. First, there was a ton of questions that I had already answered in my book I wrote for him, making me even more irritated. But Daniil must have sensed this because he came over and sat on the edge of the table slash chair I was on and started massaging my shoulders lightly. The doctor ordered a nurse to come in and take some of my blood and left with her when it was done.

Exhausted just from that little bit, I rested against Daniil, grumbling into the quiet, "You can't just go around bribing people all the time."

Daniil shrugged against me. "He just wrecked his vintage Corvette a week ago. I knew he would take the cash."

Shaking my head, I asked, "What kind of investigation did you have done?"

"I hired Lion Security to see to it. I believe Stash and Torrez took care of it for me. It's fairly extensive."

"So, no little black dots in his history?"

"None. Otherwise, we wouldn't be here. He's as good as he says he is." Then Daniil grumbled, "Too bad he's so fucking pretty, though." He hummed. "Maybe I could fix that."

"Daniil, you won't touch the man. Just stop it," I hissed, and the door opened again, the pretty doctor walking inside. "Promise me or I go to my mom's choice."

Daniil grumbled a little but ended up kissing the side of my neck, and whispering, "Fine."

The doctor sat down, reading a blue piece of paper on top of my file. His jaw seesawed for a few seconds, and he flipped through the pages on my chart, reading again before lowering them, and staring at the blue paper.

Daniil kind of went predator-still behind me, and he asked softly, "Is there a problem?"

Dr. Wisser glanced up at me, asking calmly, "Are there any twins on your mother's side of the family?"

I blinked at him. "Um…" the question surprised me, but a thought occurred, "My grandmother has a twin on my mom's side."

He nodded, flipping through my paperwork again. "From the date of your last period I would put you at five weeks pregnant. Is the date correct that you indicated on the paperwork?"

"Yes."

He sat the folder aside and put his hands together, leaning on his knees. "The blood work shows you are indeed pregnant. Congratulations." He paused, and both Daniil and I nodded to him. "Although your blood work also shows that your HCG levels are very high."

Instantly, Daniil asked, "What does that mean?"

I listened carefully, wondering if I was somehow screwed up. High levels of whatever was never a good thing. At least, not in doctor lingo.

"It means she could be possibly carrying more than one fetus."

Daniil and I both stilled at that. Staring at him. *What?*

The doctor clapped his hands lightly and stood up. "I need to finish performing the exam to find out. We should know by the end of it."

Daniil and I both sat there, kind of shell-shocked by that little bomb he so lightly told us.

The doctor started moving a spotlight looking thing around. There was a small table next to it which he placed some really funky looking equipment. Yeah, and I started shaking a little. Almost absently, Daniil started rubbing my back, but a quick glance at him, and he was no longer looking like a strong protector. More like a man about ready to toss up his cookies.

"If you step aside for a moment, I need to start," Dr. Wisser said patiently to Daniil.

Daniil nodded quickly, and stood...but hardly moved from my side.

The doctor sighed, and gestured toward the other side of the table. "If you would be so kind as to stand over there, it would be helpful. You can see everything I'm doing from right there."

Again, a mute Daniil nodded and quickly made his way to the other side of the table as the doctor positioned me on the table. He had a wonderful bedside manner. Plus, I've got to hand it to the guy—even as he untied the knots I had put in my gown and began the breast examination, he didn't tremble or anything, even when Daniil stepped closer and hovered over the table a bit. Now, when he got to the actual pelvic exam part of it, I could tell he was a little hesitant—after all, Daniil had threatened to kill him if he touched my clit…and then there was the fact Daniil was standing right over his shoulder where he was sitting between my legs.

"You know, Daniil…" I started to say, thinking I really didn't want him down there seeing whatever the doc was going to do to me…but one glance at Daniil, and I realized the poor man was seriously worried the doc was going to do something he wasn't supposed to do. He didn't even seem interested in what I was flashing between my spread legs the way he was staring at whatever Dr. Weiser was doing. "Never mind." Let him get used to the guy. Trust him so he wouldn't try to harm him.

And, my goodness, did Daniil ever hover as Dr. Weiss began the pelvic exam. I have to admit, I probably didn't help the situation much because it was uncomfortable at first. He didn't hurt me, by any stretch of the imagination, but it was just…uncomfortable the way he pressed inside me and on my lower stomach.

I didn't exactly whimper, but a noise made its way past my throat and I tried pushing back in the stirrups.

Then, the doctor made a soft gasp, and Daniil said softly, "Get your fucking hands off her."

"Wait, wait," I mumbled. "I'm all right. It's just uncomfortable."

There was a pause, and Daniil looked up at me—

I couldn't see the doctor because of the sheet—and he asked, "He's not hurting you?"

"No. Not at all. It's just feels unusual."

Another pause and Daniil's gaze had darted all over my face before he glanced down at the doctor. "Try not to make it uncomfortable for her."

Dr. Wisser's voice was very soft as he said, "I won't be able to do that if you don't remove the knife from my throat."

I gaped, and then shrieked, "Daniil! Stop that right now!" No wonder the poor doc's hands were starting to shake inside and outside of me.

Daniil glared down at the doctor, then me. "If he hurts you, you tell me." His shoulders moved, and the doctor took a deep breath.

I glared right back at him as the doctor started to hesitantly do his job again. "Maybe you should come up here if you're just going to scare the doctor to death. He needs to be able to do his job without worrying about getting knifed in the back."

"I won't do anything to his back." Daniil shrugged.

"Or his front, Daniil. You're scaring him."

"If that scares him, then maybe he shouldn't be your doctor."

"Anyone would be scared with a knife to their throat."

"No. Not everyone."

"Oh. Excuse me. Only sane people would be scared."

"I know plenty of sane people who aren't frightened with a knife to their throat."

"And this coming from the least sane person I know."

"Then you don't know enough people."

The doc cleared his throat loudly. "I hate to interrupt, but I need to ask you a few questions." Daniil and I both shut up, he staring down and me staring at the blanket where the voice was coming from. "And he's also not insane. He knows what he's doing while he does it. That's not the actions of a technically insane individual."

I gritted my teeth. "What did you want to ask?"

"First, are you absolutely positive you could have gotten pregnant before your last period?"

Daniil stilled, and his gaze shot to mine. Oh, perfect. A medical professional asking me if I was having someone else's baby. "Yes. I'm sure. I hadn't had sex for six months before then." I wanted to give Daniil the finger. He appeared to have caught it and glanced away looking a little sheepish. Dick. But I knew that was the ever-present question of men when someone got pregnant outside of marriage. My dad was right about some things being easier. And I had to give Daniil credit that he hadn't actually ever asked that question.

"And you weren't taking any fertility drugs?" doc asked, pressing around inside me again.

I tried not to flinch and answered, "No. Just one night without a condom." Daniil and I hadn't even had sex since we got back from Key West. Half the time I was too exhausted and asleep as my head hit the pillow, and the other half of the time I stayed at my apartment, keeping some of my independence—albeit with a few grumbles from Daniil.

"Okay. Well, I need to finish up here, but you already measure too large for five weeks. You're showing all indications of a multiple pregnancy. I'll need to do a sonogram when I'm done to verify how many fetuses are in the womb."

I stared at Daniil, and I was pretty sure I looked about the same as him. Shocked. I almost forgot with the whole knife issue that the doctor had said my numbers were high. Although it appeared that Daniil might need to sit down, he was so stunned. He cleared his throat when I couldn't help the wince, his eyes going back down to the doctor and watching what he was doing. It appeared to help him.

Daniil froze when the doctor removed his fingers from me, and he hissed, "What did you do to make her bleed?" He was furious, and his arms moved again.

"Daniil, stop it." I knew from the doctor's gasp again that he had the knife back out.

Dr. Wisser wheezed, "It's a normal result of the exam because more blood flows to the cervix during pregnancy."

"Daniil!" I stated, completely vexed and sitting up on my elbows. "I swear to God, if you don't stop, I'll bring my parents in here."

That stopped him. Kind of.

"You think I'm scared of your parents?" Daniil asked softly, but his arms moved back. Which meant the knife had been removed without harm since I didn't hear the doctor hit the floor dead. "You really are adorable."

"And you're getting on my last nerve with the knife thing!"

Daniil chuckled, moving back as the doctor did and came around to table to look down at me. "I'm sorry. But what would you have done if you saw someone taking their hand from my cock and their hand had blood on it?"

That made me pause, but I said stubbornly, "I wouldn't pull a knife on them."

Daniil laughed, apparently seeing the pause I had tried to cover up, and said, "You're right. I'll have to train you to use a gun."

I scowled, halfway enjoying our banter because it helped me ignore the doctor pulling out a piece of the table and lowering my legs to it, laying me out straight for the sonogram. "My mom would have a heyday with you if she heard you say that."

Daniil brushed hair back from my face, brushing his thumb back and forth over my cheek. "You know most of the anti-gun coalition individuals know how to use a weapon better than others that don't have a problem with guns at all."

I snorted. "Mom so doesn't know how to use a gun."

Dr. Wisser interrupted, asking, "Your mother's part of an anti-gun coalition?"

"One of the largest anti-gun coalition companies in the US," Daniil murmured quietly, leaning down and kissing my forehead before glancing at the stunned doctor. "And her father's a preacher."

Dr. Wisser muttered, "You're kidding."

We both shook our head, and he murmured, "And I thought my Jewish ex-in-laws were bad."

Daniil snorted and started chuckling. I, on the other hand, glared at them both. My parents weren't so bad. Not all the time, at least.

Dr. Wisser seemed to get the drift when I smacked Daniil's head when he wouldn't shut up. He quickly went back to work, pulling over the sonogram machine, opening my gown at my stomach to squirt liquid on it, and placing a device on my stomach that he kept moving around after turning on the monitor to the machine.

Stupidly, I asked, "Will we be able to hear the heartbeat?" I'd heard that once before in a movie and it sounded really funky.

Daniil stilled from where he was leaning over me a little, staring in fascination at the screen.

His avid gaze darted to the doctor, waiting for his answer.

And he disappointed us both, murmuring, "Not yet. Maybe on your next visit." He kept pressing keys on the keyboard in front of the monitor, moving the sonogram device on my stomach at different angles. He cocked his head, pausing with his hand on my belly and hit a button on the keyboard. This kept up for some time and printed out pictures of the weird grayish black screen. It didn't make a lot of sense to me, but the doctor seemed pretty interested in it, along with Daniil, who was fairly vibrating with impatience above and next to me.

"Well?" Daniil asked, his eyebrows together.

"Just another moment," Dr. Wisser stated as he moved his hand again on my stomach and more pictures printed out.

Daniil's nose crinkled and I lifted my hand, rubbing a finger over it. He glanced down at me, his expression clearly worried and anxious. I smiled at him softly. He could be such a worrywart.

The doctor wasn't freaking out yelling "Twins!" He was calm and doing his job like it was a normal singleton pregnancy. I had high hopes.

Daniil stared down at my mouth and bent down, kissing me softly.

And I sighed against his mouth, barely feeling as the doctor started wiping my stomach off. Daniil's mouth was my own personal fireworks show. Beautiful and full of wonder. And he seemed to have the same opinion, grabbing my cheeks and deepening the kiss.

And, like so often recently, we were interrupted. This time, by Dr. Wisser clearing his throat loudly. We both stilled, blinking at each other before we both turned our heads to him. The doc wasn't looking at us, but staring down at the photos he had taken, giving us our privacy for a moment longer. Daniil glanced down at me, stealing another sweet, soft kiss before straightening by my side.

The doctor grabbed some scissors and quickly cut through the strip of photos. Daniil started to argue, apparently wanting all the shots, but the doctor held up a hand and lay a row of the photos on my stomach, pointing to the first, "One," he pointed to the second, "two", and he pointed to the third, "three." He smiled. "Congratulations. You're having triplets."

My jaw dropped. "*What?*"

"Triplets. Three babies. That's why you measure so far in advance and your HCG numbers are elevated."

Daniil made a noise in the back of his throat, and it was odd enough that it interrupted my shock. I glanced at his normally tan, now pale face…

…just in time to see him take a header into the floor.

"Daniil!" I screamed, scared to death seeing him faint. "Daniil!"

I started struggling to sit up, even as the doctor raced around the table, dropping down next to him. The door to my room banged open and six fucking bodyguards charged inside as I scrambled off the table. I hadn't seen all of these guards before, and I didn't even know they were here, but I was more than freaked, pushing them away so I could get to Daniil.

Ugly Duckling was yanking Dr. Wisser away, but I yelled for him to stop. Dr. Wisser was a fucking doctor. Not a gun-toting brute. He could help!

Amazingly, Ugly Duckling listened to me and let the doctor go. As I knelt down beside Daniil, Dr. Wisser started taking Daniil's vitals again. I heard the doctor mutter under his breath, "It's always the tough guys who hit the ground the fastest. I should have known better."

They moved the still passed out Daniil to the table, the doctor pronouncing him fine and just needing a few minutes to recover, and I'd had about a zillion blood tests done, and even had pamphlets and a book given to me about multiple births. I was fully dressed by the time Daniil woke up. I was in tears at this point, thinking he was never going to wake up, and ready to take the knife and probably gun, too, from him and demand they take him to the emergency room when he finally groaned from the table.

Throwing my arms around his neck, I sobbed, "You're not supposed to do that."

His arms were immediately around me like he was comforting me, running his hands up and down my back, but he asked, "What the hell happened?"

"You fainted," Dr. Wisser said helpfully, almost sounding cheerful, standing from where he was sitting patiently. "Can you sit up?"

"It's too early for that, don't you think?" I hissed, glaring up at the damn cheerful doctor, pressing down on Daniil when he tried to move. "He hit his head." He had a fucking bruise on his forehead.

"Beth," Daniil whispered, gripping my chin and

making me look at him. "I've had much worse. I'm fine."

Glaring at him now, I wiped away my tears. "You aren't fine. You fainted. And hit your head." I touched his bruise lightly to make him understand.

The damn man just raised his eyebrows. "Beth, my sweet, move and let me up, or I'll move you myself."

"No," I griped, glancing at his forehead. *Was there swelling there?* "Have the doctor check you from where you are."

Daniil sighed, and his arms instantly snaked under my arms, and I squeaked as his did a push-up… but holding me off the ground and setting me aside when he was sitting up.

I pointed at his nose. "That cannot be healthy after fainting."

"Pretty damn impressive, really," Dr. Wisser mumbled, grinning.

He took a light out and started shining it in Daniil eye's even as I stewed, and Daniil stated, "Thank you. I work out quite a bit."

Doc shut off the penlight, putting it back in his pocket and started taking Daniil's pulse. "I can tell. It took three of us to lift you on the table." His lips twitched when Daniil scowled, but he nodded and put a hand on Daniil's shoulder, almost looking like he was bracing him. "Do you remember what we were discussing before you fainted?"

Daniil's eyebrows snapped together, and he

glanced at the hand on his shoulder. "Why are you touching me like that?"

"Please answer the question."

Daniil turned his attention from his hand to the doc's face. I nibbled on my lip, evaluating his features. And I saw it. When his scowl disappeared, and his head snapped to me, and then to my stomach. His cheeks paled again and his eyelids drooped.

"Stay awake," the doctor barked, adding another hand to Daniil's other shoulder. "Open your eyes! Look at me!"

Daniil's eyes snapped open, and he gasped when the doctor shook him lightly, instinct apparently had him moving his arms and snapping the doctors hold off him, but he started falling even as the doctor stumbled back a step. I grabbed his suit jacket and shook him hard. "Don't you faint again. Otherwise, I'm taking you to the damn hospital no matter what anyone says!"

Daniil's eyes snapped open again at the sound of my voice, and even though his face stayed pale, he caught himself, sitting up straight. "I'm all right, Beth." His gaze went to my stomach, and he immediately placed his hand there. "Are you all right?" He swayed a little, his gaze trapped on my stomach. "Should you be standing with…with…three babies in there?"

I snorted, trying to keep him steady. I hadn't even had time to freak out properly with having to look after him. But, this much I knew—I had to put my foot down immediately before that thought took hold in his mind. "I'll be standing until the doctor tells me no more." I knew bedrest was probably a real possibility, but not before the doctor deemed it necessary was I going to become an invalid.

Daniil's wide eyes went to the doctor. "Should she be standing? Doing anything?" He gulped. "Sex?"

I couldn't help but chuckle. Of course, he would add that to the end.

He glanced at me, his free hand not on my stomach going to my face, cupping my cheek, staring at me even as he listened avidly to the doctor. He proceeded to tell us I was fine for mild exercise and work, and yes, we could continue sex for a short period of time—as long as it was gentle—until he told us otherwise. He then went through the risks of multiple pregnancies to the mother and babies, and Daniil's face turned ashen again and stayed that way. He didn't ask me about reduction, thank God, because I would never choose to do that, and apparently, he wouldn't either when he flicked a quick glare at the doctor, who quickly changed the subject seeing we weren't interested.

To say I was scared shitless by the end of his speech was an understatement, but I was pretty sure, by the look in Daniil's eyes, he was even more frightened than I was. After the doc wrote out a prescription for those prenatal vitamins I mentioned during dinner on Wednesday, and scheduled another appointment in two weeks to have another sonogram to check for heartbeats, we left the room silent and gripping each other's hands.

I knew I didn't look so good, but Daniil was barely able to walk a straight line. It probably appeared that we were drunk the way we stumbled out into the waiting room with his bodyguards following. Daniil had entered separately when we walked into the office, so as not to show that we were together. However, we had both forgotten about this. At this point, we didn't really give a shit because when we exited, both of my parents looked up from whatever they were reading, took one look at us, and jumped to their feet.

My dad grabbed Daniil's other arm and my mom grabbed my free arm, and while neither said a word, they both herded us out of the office. Silently, we walked down a hallway, down an elevator, and out to a limo waiting for us. I had driven separately and so had my parents, but no one said anything about separate vehicles. We just all piled into Daniil's 'armored' limo and shut the door, the six bodyguards sliding into vehicles behind us.

I hunkered down next to Daniil, letting my head fall against his shoulder. He immediately enveloped me in his arms, kissing my head and resting his forehead on the top of my curls. My parents sat side-by-side, their expressions carefully even, watching us.

And finally, my mom asked, "What's wrong?" Her face was calm, but her voice was hard as if she were walking a tightrope.

"Whatever it is, we're here for you." My dad didn't sound much better.

Daniil didn't move, and I was afraid he had

fainted again, and I tilted my head back enough to see that his eyes were still open. They were, even though his face was still pale, and I let him pull me back so he could rest his face back in my hair, hugging me tight. I cleared my throat, turning my head a smidge so I could speak to my parents directly. "I'm having triplets."

My parents sat there in shock as I told them everything the doctor had told us. Everything. All the way down to some of the horrible risks. My mom's face turned as pale as Daniil's at one point and Dad wrapped his arms around her, supporting her. We were almost to Daniil's house when I pulled the pictures out of the book I was given and handed the shots over to them.

Mom took one look at them and started bawling. Daniil came out of this comatose state, glancing at her, saying, "Please don't get those wet."

Dad quickly took them from Mom when she kept blubbering and studied the pictures, a small smile forming on his lips. "I know you're both worried about their livelihood, but Dr. Wisser said everything was fine right now, right?"

Daniil and I both slowly nodded.

Dad's smile increased, and he faced the shots toward us. "Then you shouldn't let it worry you right now when there's nothing but what-ifs. The future is full of those, anyway. And it's not healthy for either one of you. You should be thanking God that he's blessed you two with three babies when there are so many people out there who are unable to just have one." Dad's gaze turned straight to Daniil, and he smirked, an odd gleam in his eyes. "And at your age, too. You should be proud."

Mom tried to grab the strip from Dad, mumbling, "The first pictures of my grandbabies!" She sobbed. "Give them back, James!"

Daniil stiffened at what Dad said, and amazingly, his chest puffed up a little. His color returned. I couldn't believe it. Dad had just helped him in a way I hadn't been able to do.

"Not until you quit crying, Frankie," Dad said, after a quick, satisfied smile at Daniil. "I want copies of these without water spots on them." Dad beamed at the pictures. "Three! Three to spoil and love." He grinned at me. "You did good, sweetie. Real good."

I blinked. "Daniil had a little to do with it, too." Hell, he'd just said that. It was like a huge rollercoaster ride of emotions. And not mine. I was still shocked and scared while everyone around me went from shocked to proud and thrilled.

Mom waved her hand absently, drying her tears as fast as she could. "We know, sweetie." She grinned through more tears sliding down her face. "But triplets! Oh!" She actually leaned over and patted my leg, and then Daniil's leg—happily. "I was so worried when you came out of there…" She waved her hand. "Never mind. That doesn't matter. What does matter is the doctor said everything's fine right now. One day at a time, sweetie. And enjoy it while you can. Pregnancy isn't forever."

"Thank God," I muttered. I had been puking my

brains out non-stop for the past week, then eating everything in sight afterward. And now I knew I was about to balloon up even bigger than a normal pregnant woman does. Yeah, thank God it wasn't forever.

Daniil reached over and snagged the pics from my dad, staring down where he placed them over our legs. Yeah, we had enough kids in my belly for there to be that many. And that quickly, my vision blurred. I gulped, staring down at them, wide-eyed, whispering, "We did that."

Daniil nodded. "Yes. We did."

I turned my head to stare at him, seriously feeling faint. "Three, Daniil. I don't even have that many arms to hold them." I held said arms up.

His brown eyes turned to mine, his definitely looked better, his eyes crinkling ever so slowly as he smiled. A beautiful, truly happy smile. "Good thing you have mine. We'll have one spare arm to clean the spit up with."

I choked, seeing that he was serious. And happy about it. "Do you know how many poopy diapers that is?"

He nodded, his eyes staying locked on mine. "I'll buy more trashcans."

"Oh!" Mom exclaimed. "They have those Genie things now to help with the smell!"

"We'll need three car seats, and three strollers or an extra-large one, and three outfits of everything, three diaper bags, three bottles because I sure as heck am not going to breastfeed three children, and—" Daniil cut me off mid-mad-rant by placing his lips on mine. None-to-gently. I growled against his lips, "Daniil, I'm serious—" He kissed me again, even harder, smiling half the time against my lips, holding my cheeks so I couldn't move away.

Irritated, I bit his lip gently, and he chuckled but pulled back. Then he placed a hand over my mouth when I started to speak again, murmuring softly, "It will be all right. I have plenty of money for everything you mentioned…and think about it, Beth…*three babies to love*. Three of those tiny, perfect, beautiful gifts staring at you with unconditional love. You don't just get to see the first time they smile once. Or the first time they roll over once. Or the first time they say their first word once. Or take their first step once. You get to experience it three times. *You get to love three babies, my sweet.*"

I blinked…and started bawling, realizing I was a complete dufus worrying about materialist things when Daniil was right. We had three babies on the way to love. "We did that," I whispered, grinning through a sob, "three. And they're all right, right now."

Daniil grinned, wiping my tears away. "Yes. We did do that, and they are all right, right now." Daniil handed off the pictures to my dad when the tears wouldn't stop flowing and held me tight, kissing my forehead repeatedly, even though he pulled out his cell phone, dialing, and saying, "Grigori, call your brothers and sister and Kirill. I've got news and I want you all home for it." He hung up without saying anything else.

It was Monday in the middle of the day, so they would all have to be home if they were at work. Luckily, I had taken a half day, so I was in the clear. But I did manage to mumble, "Our cars are back there."

"Don't worry about it, my sweet," Daniil murmured against my hair. "It'll be taken care of."

And it was. Not even two hours later our cars were there, along with Daniil's kids, Kirill, Chloe, and Ember. Daniil and my parents were all having a glass of wine together—me with water—when everyone rushed into the study, looking frazzled, and more than a little worried. Daniil stood and grinned at them, walking over and hugging and kissing each of their cheeks, grinning like an idiot still. It was as if he couldn't lose the smile. I, on the other hand, was yawning and about ready to pass out since I had stuffed my face once we had arrived.

Everyone he embraced wore a dumbfounded expression, standing there with their mouths gaping as they stared at the overly proud man in front of them, and when the round of over exuberant greetings were done, Grigori asked, "Papa, what's going on?"

Daniil's smile somehow...well, it increased, and he walked over to me where I sat at the desk, trying to keep my head up. He grabbed the sonogram photos and brought them over to them, handing them to Grigori first. He thumped them as Grigori stared down at them. "They have pictures now inside the womb. It was amazing!"

Grigori looked at his father as if he was crazy, and I tried not to laugh, coming a little more awake. Ember hiccupped her way into a chuckle, leaning on Grigori, who asked, "Papa, you had us come home from work to show us pictures of the baby?"

Kirill was even starting to chuckle deeply, and Chloe was snorting a little.

Daniil nodded. "Yes. But that's not all."

They all stared at him, and his smile positively gleamed as he rubbed his chest proudly, then pointed at the pictures, just the way the doctor had done. "One. Two. Three." He beamed into their even further dumbfounded faced. "Triplets! We're having triplets!"

Predictably, everyone's jaw dropped. Then it was like the open gates as a racetrack as they all swarmed around Grigori, staring over his shoulder…or, in Eva's case, dropped to her knees in front of him, and squirmed her way to stare at the pictures an inch from her nose. She asked even as the rest started yelling at her, "Show us again! What's what? I never can tell with these things."

Grigori growled and pulled the pictures up a little so her head wasn't blocking the pictures. Daniil reached a hand over them and did the '*one, two, three*' thing again. And everyone stared.

"Three babies," Ember whispered into the quiet, and I was pretty sure her voice caught. She glanced over at me, clearing her throat, stating, "You don't know how blessed you are to be able to do that without fertility meds."

Staring at her, realization hitting me that she wanted more children, and God, by the shock on her face, maybe she was even just realizing it, too. Grigori blinked and glanced at her. She hadn't even noticed, her gaze back on the photos, a tiny smile lifting her lips. It almost matched the rest of the family's faces except for it was a desolate smile.

Right then and there, I knew I needed to say a small prayer. My dad, sadly, was right again. Apparently, in the real world, not everyone was blessed to be able to have children the good old-fashioned way. And here, Daniil and I were lucky enough to have three on the first go.

Daniil watched each of his children's faces, absolutely not missing the interaction between Grigori and Ember...or even Kirill and Chloe for that matter, both of them with glistening eyes and covertly glancing at the other.

Eva looked up at her dad, and her eyebrows puckered. "You may actually get a boy like you said. Another *brother*." She scowled.

Daniil turned to me. "What do you think they are?"

Everyone stopped breathing—at least, it seemed and stared. Yawning, because I couldn't help it, I murmured, "Healthy."

Daniil smiled softly, nodding. "Yes, I agree."

"What does that mean?" Chloe asked, turning her

attention from me to the photos, trying to edge her way in closer, and getting a gentle, but firm elbow in the gut from Artur, who had finally gotten in place beside Grigori.

Daniil's eyes turned serious, and he cleared his throat, gesturing at the couches were my parents were sitting. "Why don't we all have a seat?"

Just like that, everyone's expressions hooded and they all sat down, passing the photo's between them as Daniil sat on the edge of the desk, holding my free hand. I only heard a little of his speech, informing them what the doctor had said. Somewhere in there, I knew I murmured tiredly, "He pulled a knife on my doctor..." Right before my face hit the desk, and exhaustion took me under.

That evening, we all had dinner at the table—my parents included. Zane, Stash, Carl, and Anna joined our group, Grigori having called them to tell them the news. Everyone congratulated us, carefully staying on topic of a healthy pregnancy. I ate only healthy items, but sadly, plenty of them since I was starving again, and watched the reaction of our news.

Daniil was still grinning. Grigori was watching Ember covertly with pinched eyebrows. Ember kept glancing at the sonogram photos with a slightly wistful yet confused look on her face. Carl and Anna were giving each other eyes and the same as Kirill and Chloe. My parents were still thrilled, but they were back to watching Daniil and me closely. Artur, Eva, and Roman were all arguing about what the sex of the children should be. And Zane and Stash were taking bets of said sex of the babies.

It was a fun time had by all...until my phone rang.

I rifled through my pocket, happy I was still able to wear regular jeans for the time being and pulled it out, answering, "Hello?"

"Is this Elizabeth Forter?" asked a male with a heavy Russian accent who I didn't recognize.

"Yes. Who's this?" I put a finger in my free ear to hear better over the racket everyone was making.

The man chuckled. "So, this is the woman who got knocked up by Daniil."

I pulled my phone away from my ear, staring at the readout—unknown. Placing the phone back to my ear, I said, "I'm not sure what you're talking about. Who is this?"

"Oh, come on. Everyone's seen the coverage by now online," he purred. "Tell me. What's it like getting fucked by the big bad boss man."

I glanced at Daniil. He was talking with Grigori, but again, as if he could feel me staring, he glanced my way, doing a double take at my face, his conversation abruptly cut off. As calmly as I could, I said, "Again, I have no clue what you're talking about. And it's really not fair that I don't know your name since you know mine."

The table started quieting, seeing half of its occupants mute and staring at me. I licked my lips nervously and put the phone on speakerphone as everyone shut up sharply when Daniil snapped at them. The guy started talking again as I laid the phone on the table, "My name's not really important. What is important is that you're fucking Daniil, and supposedly carrying his child." Daniil glanced up at Artur, jerking his head, indicating something. "And, seriously, I have a few colleagues who are jealous of you and want to know if his cock's as big as what they've all heard. They say he can screw for hours. That he makes women scream until their hoarse from pleasure." He chuckled low again. "Is that what he does for you? Is that how he got a good little preacher's daughter in bed?"

I tried not to look at my parents at the end of the table, swallowing nervously, and I barely noticed when Artur had jumped out of this chair, obeying his dad's command, and raced out of the room. "If you're going to ask personal questions like that, I would really like your name."

Daniil's hand was gripping mine in a death grip, even as Artur flew back in the room, racing to me, and messing with my phone, hooking it up to some kind of silver device with a large touchscreen as the guy starting that sick purr again. "No denying it this time. So you are pregnant with his child. Interesting. He usually goes for the strong, beautiful type. Although, there are perks to the small, subtly pretty ones. You're so fragile. Easy to break."

Daniil grip was crushing mine, and he glanced at Artur, who shook his head, his fingers still flying across the touch screen. Daniil gritted his teeth but motioned for me to continue talking even though I really just wanted to hang up on this psycho.

I stated quietly, "I honestly have no clue what you're talking about."

Psycho snarled, going back to his favorite topic. "Does he tie you up like we've all heard? And pour hot wax on you when you're coming? Does he choke you to the point you almost pass out as he slams into you?"

I closed my eyes, wishing my parents seriously weren't in here for this. "You're sick."

The guy chuckled. "Ah. He doesn't do that to the good preacher's daughter, huh?" He paused. "I could do that for you. Give you that pleasure-pain feeling of release. Would you like that, Elizabeth? Have the real power of Moscow between your legs?"

My head snapped to Artur, way past done talking to this guy. Artur held up a finger, tapping a few more buttons...and then nodded. Daniil released my hand instantly, grabbing my phone, and taking it off speaker. He started growling in Russian into the receiver, his voice booming and explosive in the silent room. I jumped, and Eva put her arm around me, holding me as I stared wide-eyed at the table, a little freaked by the venom in his tone.

And then, it hit me. What the guy said. Something was surfacing online. I jumped from the table, shaking my head, and holding my arms out when people stood, and raced from the room even as Daniil threatened—he had to be doing that with his tone—the guy over the line. Apparently, the psycho actually stayed on to shoot the breeze. Trofim was at my heels as I slid into the study and grabbed my laptop I left here on my previous visit. I panted, my belly past full, as I raced back into the dining room where Daniil was pacing and slashing his hand through the air, still hissing threats into the phone…until he closed it and chucked it across the room into a wall. And there went my work phone, shattered into bits. I wasn't quite sure how I would explain that one, but I ignored it, sitting at the table and turning on my computer even as Daniil wrapped his arms around me from behind.

He kissed my cheek and temple repeatedly, and I slapped at his face when he started whispering things in Russian, too busy for this right now. "I don't know what you're saying, but I get it. You're sorry I had to put up with Psycho." I jerked my head at my parents. "Go tell them you're sorry. That kind of threat was really nothing new to me, but I'm sure they didn't like hearing it."

"If that was nothing new to you, you're quitting that damn job," my dad shouted from down the table.

I paused in mid-key stroke with everyone in the room doing the same, turning their attention to my dad who had just cursed and shouted at the same time.

He stood, pointing at me. "I should have made you quit that job when Katie's boyfriend beat you so badly you were in the hospital for two weeks."

Daniil straightened, clearing his throat, sounding a little more cheerful. "You may, or may not, like to know that gentleman met an unfortunate outcome while in jail a few weeks ago. I believe his funeral service was a few days later."

I blinked, turning around, and stared at Daniil. "You didn't."

He shook his head. "No. I didn't personally do it. A poppy seed did. Apparently, he was deathly allergic to them." He shrugged. "Who knew something so tiny could be so dangerous."

I heard my mom muttering at the end of the table, and my dad cocked his head, staring deadpan and saying, "That's terribly unfortunate. I'm sure he's enjoying his time in Hell."

I turned my gaping attention on my dad just like Mom had. "Dad!"

Dad raised his eyebrows slightly but changed the subject. "Sweetie, if those are the types of phone calls you get at that job, then you do need to quit. Your life is taking on a much more dangerous angle as it is," he gestured to where my phone was laying on the ground, "to need any more added worries, especially since you're relationship with Daniil, apparently, isn't so secret anymore."

Mom murmured quietly, sounding a little shell-shocked, "You always wanted to become an author growing up, sweetie. Maybe you should listen to your father and take another profession. Writing a book sounds much more preferable than getting obscene phone calls." She glanced at Daniil. "And I swear to God, if I ever hear about you pouring hot wax on my daughter or choking her, I will shoot you with your own gun."

I just about fainted. In fact, my eyes kind of crossed.

"I can assure you, Mrs. Forter, I have never poured hot wax or choked a woman for their pleasure or mine. And I don't plan on starting it in the future," Daniil stated smoothly, and then bent down whispering in my ear, "What did I tell you about the anti-gun coalition?"

I swatted his face away. "You and I are going to have a talk about poppy seeds," I mumbled, blinking at my computer and trying to focus.

He kissed my cheek and went to Artur, who had re-entered the room, leaving sometime before I arrived back in here, watching his son plug the silver device into the laptop he'd gone off to get. I ignored them and started typing up my name and Daniil's together, grabbing a piece of cheese from Daniil's plate and popping it in my mouth, waiting for the search engine to finish.

And finish it did. With too many damn hits.

"Shit," Eva muttered, leaning over watching what I was doing. She pointed. "Bring that one up."

I shook my head and scowled, clicking on the top one instead...the article was done by one Micah Olson. A picture of Daniil and I flashed on the screen. I gawked...because...it was of us on the golf course in Key West. It was dark, and you couldn't really tell it was me because Daniil's back was to the camera covering most of me, but you could tell he was locked in an embrace with my leg over his hip and hands in his hair. Jesus, Micah had been working this fucking story from the beginning.

The next shot was of us standing outside my resort's door, still in our obstacle course attire, and we were deep in a lip-lock with Daniil opening the door behind me, but his hair covered half of our faces—not the best picture. Then there was another shot of us, clearly me, staring blindly out the bus window, wrapped in Daniil's arms with his chin on my head, clearly him, also staring blindly out the window. Another shot of us on the dance floor, getting down and dirty, both of us wearing expressions like we'd rather be in bed. And the clincher—a picture of Daniil and I leaving the building today—only hours ago—with my parents on either side of us, helping us to the limo, while we wore shaken expressions…with the name of the obstetrician business practice in the background on the building.

"Oh, fuck," I muttered.

"Elizabeth," Mom scolded.

"No, Mom. This is definitely a fuck moment," I managed to say.

Eva nodded slowly, her eyes narrowing. "Papa, get over here. There's another situation."

Everyone at the table froze at the deadly tone in her voice, stopping whatever conversation they were having with Daniil and Artur about the phone call. Daniil came over and I showed him the pictures. His jaw was clenched, and he hissed, "Scroll down." He added, "Please."

I did, not really wanting to read the article. And...yeah...I really didn't want to read it. And I seriously hoped my parents didn't read it. I groaned a few times during it.

Micah apparently caught Daniil and my drunken walk from the bar to the elevator but didn't have his camera with him. That's when the story started. He gave an in-depth description of all of our comings and goings throughout the event, apparently following us. And I had to give it to him—he had patience, unlike any other reporter I've ever known, waiting for the prime story. Like I had done with Grigori. A story that would boost his career. Us, separately entering the OBGYN's office, and then the perfect picture of us leaving, leaving us all to come up with our own assumptions on why Daniil and I had looked so heart-stricken exiting the building.

"You were...under the table at the club?" Eva sputtered.

My lips pinched. Yeah, Micah had been very thorough. "Daniil, you done?"

"Yes," he growled, and I snapped the laptop closed.

He started pacing, and in the silence, I asked, "Mom. Dad. Are your cell phones still off?" They normally turned them off when they sat down for dinner, so they wouldn't be interrupted.

Both said, "Yes."

"I wouldn't turn them on anytime soon if I were you. There's an article running about Daniil and me from a reporter that was at the resort." I rubbed my temples, muttering dryly, "And he did a stellar job getting the story."

Dad sat forward, even as my mom's face went blank, and he asked calmly, "How bad is it?"

I whimpered. "Probably not something I would want you guys reading." Honesty was needed right now. Micah had followed so well, he indicated each time Daniil and I had gotten it on, and his numbers weren't wrong, or where it took place.

There was a pause, and my dad cleared his throat. "Okay," he cleared his throat again, "and there's reference to the babies?"

"Implied with a picture of the four of us leaving the OBGYN's office," I stated factually, trying to get control of myself.

Dad sat back silently, and Mom whispered, "Well, James. We knew this was a possibility." Mom stood abruptly and started pacing right along with Daniil. "I'll be fired for sure, but that'll give me the opportunity to stay by her side. Try to help her with the babies and keep her safe."

My heart sank. Mom loved her job. And they went into this because I had wanted to be with Daniil. Probably one of the worst people I could have picked for their professions—their livelihood. I started to tear up, and I mumbled shakily, "I can give up my apartment and move back home and help with the bills."

SCARLETT DAWN

Eva slapped a hand down on my thigh, her expression turned fierce. "Do you seriously think Papa is going to let you guys go poor?"

"Eva, hush," Daniil ordered, placing his hands on my shoulders. "She should know this already." He started massaging my shoulders gently and stated coldly to his children, "Get on the phone. We'll need more guards brought over. Enough for Mr. and Mrs. Forter. I want another three put on Elizabeth. And at least ten more for the house. Two more limos. And I want construction on a house started on the property to the west of us for Mr. and Mrs. Forter. Cancel Elizabeth's rental agreement on her apartment. Have all of her items brought here, along with some items from her parents' house for them." He paused. "And contact the Dr. Wisser and have him put Elizabeth's files in a secure location offsite." He released my stunned shoulder, barking, "Now, kids!"

My parents were sputtering, just like me. He ignored us and his children, who all were on their cell phones now. Daniil pointed at Kirill. "You're coming out of retirement. I'm going to need your services again." Kirill nodded instantly with hardness in his gaze I hadn't seen before, and Daniil muttered, "Hire Lion Security if needed." He jerked his head at Zane, Stash, and Carl. "I want the asshole who called her found, and I want him here, in front of me—alive, within twenty-four hours. And any of those colleagues he mentioned if you deem them threats. Artur's got the name and number. That'll give you a starting point."

247

Dad managed to state in the pause, "I can't accept what you're offering."

Daniil walked to him, and they stood, staring at one another, and I had to listen hard through the noise around the table to hear Daniil state softly, "You're giving Elizabeth and I a chance without interference. You and your wife are smart enough that you knew the consequences of our relationship. Take my hospitality and generosity. Elizabeth needs you. She loves you." He paused, and stated calmly, "And, honestly, after that article, if you want to stay alive, you need to take it. My enemies won't just come after her or me. If they see a weak point, they will strike there first. And you don't want to be the weak point, trust me. No matter what, your lives will never be the same now. But…you already know this."

Dad was silent for a full minute, my mom standing slightly behind him, waiting for his judgment as he just stared at Daniil. And then, he leaned in and whispered something to him.

Daniil's lips twitched as he listened to my dad, his eyes dancing to me and twinkling before Dad pulled away. And he nodded, saying something back just as quietly, his face turned serious when Dad could see him.

Dad ran a hand through his hair. "Well, I guess we can sell the house and stay here for a little while. But, whatever profits we get from it will go to whatever you're planning for us. I won't just let you give us a house."

Daniil nodded respectfully. "If that's what you want."

Mom sighed, apparently going along with whatever Dad agreed to. "James, the pews are going to be empty now."

Daniil chuckled. "I would imagine after that article, you're going to have a full house filled with interesting…individuals…although you may have lost some of the old. I would start preparing your sermon. Lots of lost souls will be entering your doors."

Dad actually beamed. "I love a challenge."

Daniil grinned, smacking him on the back…and Dad actually kept his footing. "There is light in the darkness."

Dad chuckled, shaking his head, stating, "Just keep my daughter and grandbabies alive, and leave the preaching to the professionals."

Daniil laughed, nodding

What. Had. Just. Happened?

"Daniil, can I speak with you?" I asked loudly over the noise.

He glanced at me, his face turning serious again, seeing my expression. "My study?"

"Yes," I nodded, grabbing another bit of cheese from his plate before walking out of the room, going directly toward his study…where we had spent a lot of our time working through our 'issues.' As soon as we entered, and he shut the door, I rounded on him, stating bluntly, "You didn't even ask me if I wanted to move in here. You just assumed it because the world knows I'm carrying your love child, and because of some idiot calling me. I understand you're freaked out. I understand I'm in danger and so are my parents. But, Daniil…you have to ask me instead of just going around barking demands like some damn alpha dog. The end result may be the same, but you still need to ask!" I heaved in a breath, having said that all in one go.

Daniil leaned against the door, giving me room, my instant pissed off fury filling the room around us. "Beth, my sweet—" Daniil started to say calmly and slowly, but I cut him off.

"Don't give me that 'my sweet' bullshit right now. I'm not going to be placated with simpering words. I want a damn apology and a promise you won't do that again. You can't just order me around! Hell, even if we did fall madly in love with one another and got married, I still wouldn't want you ordering me around. I've already told you, I'm not that type of woman!"

Daniil's nose crinkled, and his eyebrows snapped together. "I'm not going to apologize for keeping you and your family safe." There. At least, he was done with the endearment bullshit right now. We were getting somewhere.

"You will. And it's not for trying to keep us safe. It's for your damn domineering ways." I pointed at the ground. "Right now, you're going to apologize, or you can protect my ass from some other place. I won't put up with this. I'm not lower than you. I'm not less than you. If we're going to have a relationship when we're alone together, we're equal."

I wasn't stupid enough to think of myself as an equal to him in the public's eye…well, because I wasn't. Status, money, society…yeah, he had a lot more than me in every materialistic way. Sadly, there was a ladder in the world, and he was more than a few rungs higher than I was on it. But he was polite enough never to mention those things, and I knew he would never demean me in public. Hell, he was pissed when my parents had done it.

Daniil opened his mouth with that same damn look on his face, and I held up a hand, stating bluntly, "Think before whatever is about to come out of your mouth."

His mouth snapped shut and he tried glaring at me. Didn't really work as well as it used to. "If you keep that up, you're going to…" I pointed at my eyes and forehead, "…get wrinkles faster." I almost laughed when his expression immediately cleared. He was so vain.

He started pacing, his strides long and brisk. "We can compromise on this."

"Explain," I stated slowly since he sounded reasonable.

"First, I'm sorry for not asking you if you wanted to live here. I assumed that we," his hand gestured to me and then him, "had moved on to a deeper level this week. Apparently, I was wrong."

He sounded a little downhearted at that thought, and I told him honestly, "You aren't wrong on that. I agree. We have moved into a deeper relationship, but it just proves my point that if we keep going, I want you to ask, not assume."

Daniil nodded slowly. "Good. My apology stands." He stopped pacing and glanced at me. "Beth, would you please move in with me?"

I nodded once curtly. He had given me what I needed. "Yes, I will." Sleeping next to him every night? Seeing him every morning and night? Not really a hardship.

He started pacing again. "Now, for the always asking issue. I'm not really used to that."

Deciding to finally bring this up, I asked slowly, "Did your late wife really let you boss her around?" He never said anything about her. I didn't know how to take that. He had spent a large portion of his life with her, and not one word other than how she died had he ever said.

Daniil stilled. "You're nothing like her." I heard him mutter under his breath, *"Thank God."* And he started pacing again.

I didn't say anything then because I finally got my first clue, things weren't perfect between them. Not a subject I wanted to touch right now. It wasn't the time for that.

Daniil said slowly, "I will compromise that if your life is not in immediate danger, I will ask first about routine issues." He ran a hand through his hair. "I'm a born protector and leader, Beth. I always have been. That's who I am. I can't just stop that part of me." He stopped and faced me. "That's what I can give on the compromise."

He stared, and I nibbled at my lip, asking, "What about if I'm just threatened. Will you ask me what I want to have done to the person threatening me? The person would be coming for me, after all. I should have a say in their outcome." Poppy seeds were dancing in my mind. I sure as hell hadn't gotten a say in that.

Daniil scowled, and I didn't comment because it actually appeared he was thinking this through before barking out a *no*. He growled, "You want a say in their welfare?"

"Yes."

He actually bared his teeth.

I mumbled, "Wrinkles, Daniil."

His mouth snapped shut, and his face cleared. "So, when this asshole is brought to me tomorrow, what would you plan to do with him?"

My thoughts emptied. "I honestly have no clue." I didn't. What did someone do to someone else who threatened them obscenely, but knew they were probably capable of more?

He nodded. "You really don't know what you're asking for, Beth. You've never had to deal with this." He stated softly, "Just let me take care of these issues."

I shook my head. "No. They'll all end up dead if I do that."

His soft expression disappeared and turned fierce again, as he slashed a hand through the air, and he hissed furiously. "That fucker should be dead after I question him. Would you want to meet him in a back alley? Be drugged and raped? Have him choke you to death while he's doing it?" He took a step forward. "Because that's what he will do to you if he got you alone. What he said to you wasn't nearly as sick as what he said to me. He has plans for you. And it won't just stop with him now that the world knows about you." He then shouted, "Just let me handle these things! Without argument!"

I stood my ground. Barely. "When it comes to people coming after me, I want a say. I don't know what the hell I'm really doing, and you know this, but I want to try. Not everyone deserves to die."

He shouted, throwing his hands in the air, and resumed his pacing. I hoped he didn't get this angry with everyone. It couldn't be good for his heart.

"Fine!" he continued shouting. "I will let you in on those issues as long as you're not in immediate danger. But if you are, I have the right to blow the fucker's head off!" He glanced at me, utterly pissed. "Are we done here, my sweet?" Again with the endearment being used not so…sweetly.

"Yes, my dear," I stated back just as pissy as he had. Heh. Now he had an endearment I could use against him when I was mad. "That works for me." Hell, it wasn't really any different from a cop using lethal force when needed. Just not exactly legal…but better than the alternative…which would be everyone dead who looked at me crossways.

"Wonderful," he shouted, banging the door open and storming out of the room.

"Perfect," I hollered after him, quickly following on his heels.

Both of us erupted back into the dining room, practically banging shoulders as we went through the archway to see who got in the room first. Pretty childish really, but it was our first real argument where actual communication was used, neither one of us completely satisfied with the outcome.

Everyone kept talking, but covert glances were pointed our way, and Daniil growled a little at me, scowling before walking away, and I whispered after him, "Wrinkles." It was low enough where I was certain only he had heard, but I could have sworn Carl choked on his drink, staring at us.

He stopped in his tracks and glanced over his shoulder at me. Yeah, I was seeing some kind of threat there, but I pointed to my forehead and eyes, and gave him a saucy wink before I turned my back on him and marched stiffly over to my parents...and stole my dad's bread.

Mom's eyebrows rose as she sat back relaxed even knowing she was going to be fired. "First fight?"

I growled, sounding a lot like Daniil, and stayed mute chewing my bread and glaring at him across the room where he glared right back even as he talked to Grigori and Roman.

Mom chuckled. "Well, you're still breathing so he must have shown some restraint," I grunted, knowing he had, but not appreciating Mom's joke. "May I ask what it was about since there are so many things to choose from?"

I hissed, "Not funny."

"But no less true."

I chomped into the bread again, talking around it, "I had to put my foot down. He just can't assume I'm going to do what he says all the time." Mom nodded and Dad looked amused. "And there's the issue of him wanting to kill everyone who insults me. I don't want everyone with a bullet in their head."

Dad looked positively entertained, glancing quickly at Daniil and back to me. "How did that go over?"

"As long as I'm not in *immediate* danger, he won't blow," I used finger quotes, "*the fuckers head off*," I bit into the bread again, "and he'll talk to me to decide how I would like to handle it. If I am in immediate danger…well…I compromised and there might be some unattached heads."

My dad paused and turned and walked out of the room…and then I heard him start laughing out in the hallway.

Mom's lips twitched. "Well, that's a start, I guess."

"A biggie, really," Ember stated from where she was eavesdropping next to us, leaning against the table next to Zane.

"Butt out," I griped and went to bite into my bread…and saw it was missing a large section that I hadn't put there. I glared at the wicked redheaded bitch next to me. "I'm pregnant! With triplets! Quit stealing my food!"

She popped the bread into her mouth and grinned. God, I realized I was going to have to be around her even more often, too, since she had been staying over here, her children separating their time between here and Cole and Brent's house. I groaned, and she patted my cheek, grinning even more and then cheerfully saying, "Welcome to the family. *It'll be an experience unlike any you've ever known.*" She chuckled deep like Count Dracula.

"You're not funny," I stated bluntly, finishing off my bread before she could.

"That was funny."

"No. It wasn't."

CHAPTER 11

Being driven in an armored limo with bodyguards—three in the limo with me and three in a car behind me—I tried to ignore them on my way to work and figure out a way to end mine and Daniil's feud. I learned last night when we fight…well, we really fight. He doesn't like to change his ways and I didn't like changing mine. So, the battle of wills lasted all night.

My stuff was delivered close to nine o'clock, and I had unpacked my clothes in his closet—more like banged around, throwing stuff—while he scowled from his desk in his living room. At ten, I was tuckered out emotionally and psychically, and seeing him still there glaring at me, I closed the door and locked it, pushing his heavy as sin dresser in front of it.

He heard me grunting, and banged on the door and hollered for a while, but honestly, I hadn't wanted to sleep with the growling sourpuss. I set the alarm clock and lay on the bed. I knew there were no hidden staircases or hidden doors in his bedroom since he had shown me all of those the middle of last week. After about an hour of curses and Russian spouts, he shut up and left me alone.

I woke up to puke all by myself. Showered all by myself. Even ate breakfast without him since he was passed out on the couch with a tiny blanket over him. I felt like shit now, but I didn't really know how to end it. And the bad part was I knew I couldn't until after tonight with the guy who threatened me on the phone. I had to make sure Daniil saw I was serious. And...well, it sucked.

I sighed, lost in my own thoughts. I blinked when I recognized we had pulled up to my work. Daniil had growled through the door last night I would be having three guards with me at all times while the other three hung back.

Right now, I was grateful.

There was a mess of reporters—some I even worked with—in front of my office building and there were also news crews. God, I wasn't enjoying having a sure-to-be-fired conversation with my editor. I was pretty sure my mom wasn't the only one getting canned today.

I straightened my navy suit jacket, and pushed some curls behind my ear, and nodded to Trofim—the only guard I thought I'd had previously—and he spoke into an earpiece. The three guards who were driving behind us got out of their car and pushed some of the reporters back before Trofim got out in front of me, the other two, which I hadn't caught their names yet, following behind me.

I kept my head down as flashes went off and questions were zinged at me from everywhere. I was jostled, but it was only from the bodyguards keeping me on track to the front door, the other three doing a damn fine job of keeping the pushy reporters at bay. And then I heard Micah's voice as he shouted, "Is it a boy or a girl?"

I glanced in the direction of his voice, tapped Trofim's shoulder, and pointed to Micah. I wanted a word with him. Trofim made way for Micah, who quickly stepped beside me as we made our way into the building. The only reporters who followed were the ones I worked with.

I stayed silent, and so did Micah, until we got onto the elevator, squeezed between all six bodyguards, and that's when I stated, "I hope you're happy, Micah. I'm sure to lose my job today."

He cocked his head at me. "You don't need to worry about money with Daniil as your baby's daddy."

I turned toward him, pissed off, the bodyguards making room for me. "Don't even expect to get a word out of me to confirm your fucking article. And I don't want anyone's money. I love what I do. I wanted my damn job! I didn't do a thing wrong, and I'm about to lose it because some snot nosed little upstart decided to make his career from my personal life. I hadn't realized this before, but I do now. A little word of advice, Micah —not everything should be in print when you ruin someone's livelihood all because of who they might or might not be sleeping with." I shook my head at him. "You fucked up and you don't even realize it."

His eyebrows rose in a bored manner. "So, are you or are you not pregnant with Daniil's baby?" He completely ignored what I had just said.

And I was smart enough to know a thing or two. Glaring, I glanced over his shoulder at two of the guards before we hit my floor. Each of them grabbed one of his arms, and he started struggling, but I ignored that and reached inside his jacket pocket, pulling out a tape recorder that was running, recording our conversation. I clicked it off and dropped it to the ground, slamming my heel into it, shattering the thing all over the short gray carpet.

And then ground it in for good measure, hissing at him, "You can go fuck yourself and your damn article. Any possibilities of friendship or contact that we might have been able to start, you just ruined by not listening to someone with a helluva lot more experience than you have. You make friends with the people you write about, not act like they're an adolescent twit because that gets you nowhere. Get a fucking clue, you dipshit."

I glanced over his shoulder and nodded at the guards, thanking them for their efforts since he was pretty damn squirrelly in their holds. "Don't kill him, please." I had to make sure they knew I wasn't into that.

One smirked, but they both nodded. I wondered how much bodyguards talked and if they knew about Daniil's and my argument. They had been standing outside the door to the study like freaking sentinels.

Micah's eyes went wide at what I said, and I smirked, tapping my temple as the elevator dinged and opened. My three standing bodyguards moved out first and I followed, only one coming out behind me, the other two going to dispose of the 'trash' I assumed. My editor was leaning against the wall outside the elevator —not good—and cocked his head glancing through the bodyguards and me, more than likely seeing Micah being restrained inside the elevator.

His lips twitched and he stated, as the doors closed, "I never liked that little bugger. He actually applied here before taking his current position." His eyes twinkled at me, glancing around at the guards. "You've got some interesting friends, I see."

I cleared my throat. "Clifford, I can explain."

He nodded, crossing his arms and ankles.

"Can we go inside, perhaps?" I gestured toward the double glass door on our right where tons of activity was already in motion.

"Elizabeth. If we go in there, all of those reporters are going to surround you. You know this."

I bit my lip. "You aren't even going to let me clean my desk off, are you?"

He jerked his head to the right.

There, off to the side under a water fountain, was a box full of my personal effects. Feeling tears spring to my eyes, I lowered my head to hide them and stated, "I can work from home. Revise articles. Edit them."

Clifford snorted. "You're wonderful at reporting, but I always have to review your work before printing it. Your editing skills are not exactly up-to-par." I heard him sigh and saw him take a step forward, bending a little to see my face. "Look, Elizabeth, I'm not firing you. I'm just putting you on a temporary leave of absence. There's no way you can work effectively with this type of upheaval going on." He cleared his throat. "Things should cool down in a few months."

"I'll probably be on bed rest by then!" I snapped, feeling tears fall down my cheeks, utterly pissed and hurt that I was being 'temporarily' let go even though I knew it was more than likely coming. But, then again, knowing and doing are two completely different things. And then…I realized what I had said. I sucked in a breath, glancing up at him.

He wore a slightly crooked grin, his hands behind his back, rocking back and forth on his heels. "I think for your safety's sake and mine, I'm going to forget you ever said that…or even why you would have to be on bedrest. But I do need a particular timeframe of when you might be able to come back so I can get a temp in here."

I sucked in another harsh breath, realizing he was going to be quiet. This was the difference between a good reporter and a bad one—Clifford vs. Micah. I stated softly, "Thank you." He nodded, and I cleared my throat, wiping some of my tears away but fuck if they didn't keep coming. "I imagine I could come back to work in," I tried to do the math of what the doctor said on normal triplet births, "probably eight or nine months." That would give me a few months with my babies before entering the workforce again.

He nodded. "All right. Do you want me to carry the box down for you since your entourage might need their hands to manhandle another reporter?"

I shook my head and gave him a quick hug. "No. I've got it." I pointed at him. "I'm the best you have. Remember that." I stooped to pick up the box, realized it was heavy, and grunted a little, heaving it up.

He helped me steady it, and stated quietly, "Take care of yourself, Elizabeth. This is a whole other lifestyle you've gotten yourself into."

I nodded. "Yeah, I know."

He cleared his throat and said more loudly, "I'm only keeping your spot open since you are the best. Don't piss me off by waiting too long."

I smirked, nodding, sentimentally staring at the doorway where some of the reporters had started to congregate. "See ya, Clifford."

He nodded with a quick glance at my stomach before, going into the doors where I wasn't welcomed right now, herding the reporters away, and back to their desks. I told Trofim, "I want to go to my dad's church."

Leaving the building was just as hectic as entering. Micah was in the crowd scowling, so I knew he hadn't been killed. I was jostled even more than before as more reporters showed up with the news I was here. They got my walk of the unemployed on camera, box in hand, and head hanging so they wouldn't see the residual effect my tears on my face.

And on the way to church, I actually had paparazzi following me, making the journey there much more interesting since they were driving in ways guaranteed to get us in a wreck. I bumped against the door as our driver took a sharp right just as one of my bodyguards phone started ringing.

It was Trofim's and he answered it, then immediately handed it to me. It was Daniil. Sighing, I put it to my ear, trying to right myself after the driver swerved to miss one of the idiots with the cameras. "Hello?" My phone was no longer in existence, so this was the only way he could contact me.

"I just saw the footage of you leaving work," he stated, sounding worried. And that was all of ten minutes ago, which meant some of those cameras had been running live. "I could tell you had been crying. Are you all right?"

"I just lost my job. A job that I loved. What do you think?" I asked dryly and then grunted, hitting the door again.

"Your editor fired you," Daniil stated slowly. "Because of us."

It wasn't a question, but I stated, "Yes. I knew it would happen, but it doesn't make it any easier. I couldn't do my job properly with this much press hounding me…when I'm supposed to *be* the press."

There was a pause, and then I shouted, falling forward and onto the floor when the driver slammed on the breaks. The phone went flying out of my hand, and damn expertly, Trofim reached out a hand, catching it in mid-flight and helping me back into the seat. He handed the cell back to me, and Daniil was hollering over the line by the time I put it back to my ear. "I'm fine. Just some damn paparazzi bothering us."

"You just scared the shit out of me!" he shouted, breathing hard. "Just come home! You don't have work now. And I'll stay home today. We can have a day to ourselves. It would be nice, especially after last night."

It startled me, hearing him say 'home' like that. I sat there for a few moments a little stunned, and I heard his breath catch, and he shouted my name again. Christ, he was going to have a heart attack if he kept that up. "I'm here. I'm fine. I was going to go to my dad's church, but a day alone would be nice." I paused, remembering I was supposed to be sticking to my guns. "As long as you don't try to finagle a different outcome for tonight."

He sighed. "Just come home. I don't want to argue anymore." He snorted. "Besides, my back can't take another night on that couch. I never knew how uncomfortable it was."

"All right," I said hesitantly, wondering if there was a catch somewhere there. He was giving in too easily. "I'll tell the driver to turn around."

"Good," he cleared his throat and said quickly, "I miss you. Hurry up." And he hung up.

I pulled the phone away from my ear and stared at it. Had Daniil just shown a weakness to me? Stunned, I handed the phone back to Trofim, telling him we were changing course and going back 'home.' He relayed the information to the driver. I spent the ride home hanging on for dear life as the paparazzi hounded us the entire way.

Walking through the door completely frazzled, I was jumped by Daniil. I dropped my box, barely missing smashing our toes as he hauled me off my feet, carrying me across the foyer and up the square stairs. Breathless, I asked, "What are you doing?"

"Walking, Ms. Forter," he stated factually. And that was it.

"Daniil!" I squealed when he started a full out run down the hallways once we got to the top of the stairs. Amazingly, I was being jostled, but I was a little mystified. "Why are you running?"

"Makeup sex," Daniil murmured, not even out of breath. "I really don't like arguing with you. And I don't like being shut out of my own damn bed. But, if it's going to happen, there's going to be some fucking perks involved afterward."

Stunned, I stared up at his face. He was serious. About all of it. It seriously bothered him, us arguing. Maybe even more so than me—which surprised me since he did it so damn well.

I squeaked again when he tossed me lightly on the bed and started stripping. He wasn't wearing a suit jacket so his shirt was off in seconds, and he was kicking his dress shoes off and unbuckling his belt before I even had a chance to catch my breath. I had stared for all of a few seconds before I got with the program, quickly stripping off my own clothes.

We hadn't had sex since Key West, and I was more than hungry for him. Especially, since I wasn't tired or hungry right now. I had a feeling this was probably how it would feel after the babies were born, stealing moments here and there. And I was game.

Maybe thirty seconds later, we were naked and Daniil was on top of me. I could tell he was trying to keep his weight off me from below, but his chest was smashing my sensitive, swollen breasts, making me arch into him before his mouth even met mine. He groaned as our lips touched, and it happened…the fireworks. And I went a little wild. I wasn't sure if it was the hormones taking over, but within a minute, Daniil had my hands above my head after I scratched his back too hard.

"Easy," he murmured, kissing my neck. "The doctor said it has to be gentle. And I won't be gentle with you doing that."

I whimpered, arching under him, rubbing against him. I wanted him now.

He sucked hard on my throat, and I knew he was giving me a damn hickey, but I groaned, pushing into him, wanting more. He yanked my arms over my head, holding both of my wrists with one hand, and cupped one of my breasts even as he sucked. He was so damn gentle that I moaned, "Harder. It doesn't hurt."

And he squeezed firmer, both of us groaning.

Starting to wrap my legs around his waist, I tugged on my arms. I wanted to touch him. He growled, "Behave, my sweet, or I'll tie you up."

"Have you ever done that before?" That made me think of that phone call.

"I've done many things before," he moaned, grinding his hard cock against my core.

Instantly, I asked, "What about the wax thing? And choking?" I needed to know what I was dealing with here.

He lifted his head, his hair hanging around his face, his eyes practically pitch black. "Never to a woman. And never for pleasure."

My lips pinched as I watched him move down my body, watching me. Slowly, he bent his head, opened his perfect mouth, and gently bit down on my puckered nipple, eyes on me. I sucked in a harsh breath and automatically arched, needing it harder, but I managed to say, "Well, at least you didn't lie to my mom."

Daniil grinned around my nipple before lowering his eyes and sucking my breast into his mouth with just enough pressure to have me crying out his name. He continued while trailing his finger down my stomach, twirling circles around my belly button, making my stomach flutter and my hips rise of their own accord. He rested his hand on my lower stomach for a moment before letting it lower between my thighs.

Lifting his head from my well-loved breast, he watched me as he slid his finger between my folds, and his eyes hooded when he hit how wet I was. I really started panting and moaning as he coated his finger and started circling my clit slowly, then faster and faster. Not to be outdone, even as I rocked my hips against his talented fingers, I gripped his cock and immediately started stroking him as quickly as he was me.

Breath rushed past his lips against mine from where he hovered over me, and he groaned, instantly rocking his hips. He was so damn big it was hard to do, and as much as I loved what he was doing to me, I wanted him in my mouth. Quickly, I unhooked my legs from his waist, carefully placing them between his, and slid down the bed.

"Beth, what are you…" and he never finished his confused, surprised question, except to gasp as I opened my mouth and took him in. "Oh, shit! Fuck yes, my sweet." He reached down with one hand and grabbed the back of my head, gripping my hair as he started thrusting into my mouth, a little farther each time until he was groaning and bumping the back of my throat. "More, Beth. Please, more."

I smiled around him, my lips completely

stretched, totally understanding what I had only just discovered that night in the club, and grabbed his ass, pulling him down further. And I liked that he was begging. Please will get him a long way in bed.

And I swallowed. He shouted, his whole body quivering over me. My gag reflex surged, and I quickly swallowed again, pulling him more, knowing he wanted this. Once I got past that initial puke point—which was a definite possibility—it was fucking good. He tasted good. He smelled good. And he felt good.

I groaned, repeatedly swallowing as he thrust very gently into my throat, yelling my name out. His hand fisted in my hair, and he groaned low, "Just a little more, my sweet." He panted. "Please."

I hummed at him in agreement and swallowed again when he thrust. My lips hit the base of him. He shouted and started shaking over me, a string of Russian flying past his lips as I kept swallowing and let my fingers run over his hard ass…right to his anus. One of my previous boyfriends loved this, and I started gently playing with him.

He jerked, and stilled, "Beth?" He sounded hesitant and unsure. A great many things must not have included anal play.

I hummed and pressed a little harder on his tiny hole. And then swallowed again, right as I pressed the tip of my finger inside him. He shook so damn hard over me that I thought he was having a convulsion until I heard him mutter, "Jesus Christ. Fuck… That feels great."

I nodded as much as I could, and as he started thrusting gently, I pressed in farther, and he shouted so damn loud, I thought my eardrums would rupture.

I licked him hard and sucked, pressing my finger inside his ass…just so…hoping I remembered how to do this right.

Daniil gasped and slammed his hips harder down into my mouth, and he groaned, "Fuck…gonna…gonna…*Beth!*" He shuddered, and I repeatedly swallowed as suddenly his body really did convulse over me, his hot cum shooting down my throat, his hand brutal on the back of my head. I pressed just a little harder inside his ass. He jerked, shouting in pleasure again.

I swallowed all he gave me…and then I needed to breathe as his body started going limp over me, falling. I slapped his thigh lightly, and he groaned low and sated but pulled his hips back, his now semi-hard sliding from my throat and out of my mouth. He rolled onto his back and stayed there, his eyes closed and his breathing labored. Grinning at him, I started kissing his thigh where my head lay and rolling so I could kiss his slightly perspiring stomach, dipping my tongue into his navel and tasting him. God, he tasted great.

He jerked under my ministrations and his eyes slowly opened. "Where did you learn to do that?"

"I've done a great many things," I murmured deeply, mimicking him and smiling up at him, and his sated expression. "You like?"

He nodded, licking his lips. "Yeah. I like." He

groaned in contentment, and then a tiny smile lifted his lips. "Do you want to know what I know how to do?"

I nodded, rubbing my nose against his nipple, feeling it harden.

"Straddle my mouth," he purred and he grinned. "Please."

There was a special little gleam in his eye...and I stared at him just figuring something out.

He chuckled softly, saying, "Ah, my sweet. You don't think we've spent this much time together without me learning how to get my way, do you?" He ran his finger over my eyebrows that were pinched. "Please... that is a beautiful word, is it not?"

I bent down and bit his nipple. Hard.

He grunted but only arched into the touch.

Ah. Dammit. He liked it.

"Now, would you please straddle my face? I want to lick you up," he raised a leg between mine, pressing his thigh at my core. "You're wet. And I want to eat you."

Damn shark. "You don't have to manipulate me in bed, you know."

"I know. You would have done it anyway, but you like hearing me say it." He paused, rubbing his thigh against me. "So, will you please straddle my face?"

My eyes hooded because it was so damn good, restarting that damn fire in my belly. "All right." I crawled over him, and his hands instantly went to my breasts and squeezed them tightly, just as I liked it. I groaned, stopping over him, my head going dizzy as he lifted his face and took the breast that had been neglected earlier into his mouth and started sucking. I bucked on top of him, grinding myself against his semi-hard, feeling him grow against me.

And yeah…I couldn't wait. And we didn't need any fucking condoms anymore, so I altered my hips, and the crown of his cock slid inside me. His head fell back on the pillow as he gasped, and I shouted, pushing down farther. He grabbed my hips and stopped me, though. Hissing through clenched teeth, he said, "I said I wanted you straddling my face, not my cock." He growled and pulled me off him, and I was suddenly positioned exactly where he wanted me. Glancing down at him with my hands against the wall, I whimpered, "I want you in me, Daniil."

"I know," he stated hoarsely, staring at my core, "We'll get there."

He pulled my hips down, my core onto his mouth, his tongue immediately piercing into me. I groaned, throwing my head back, my nails digging into the wall as I rode his mouth. Fuck, this was amazing. He put two fingers inside me, the sudden intrusion breathtaking as I was stretched. He rubbed his tongue hard over my clit.

My orgasm came that quick, taking me up and away, my brain blown away in *ever after ecstasy*. It had never happened quite that fast and it shocked me as I screamed, pressing down harder on him. He moaned under me, pressing into that spot inside me that had me jerking on top of him, riding the waves.

As I came down, I panted and let my head fall against the wall, staring at him. He was watching me with crinkles around his eyes, which meant he was grinning...and he started again, murmuring quietly, "I've always heard pregnant women come faster."

That stopped me for a second, making me glance at him. His wife had been pregnant four times...so... wouldn't he know that instead of only 'hearing' about it?

Feeling me stop, his eyes slammed opened, and he stilled for a few seconds, then glanced at me. He tilted his head back, licking his lips, and stated in a cool voice, "I told you, you are nothing like how she was."

I nodded slowly. There was a story there. It was all in his eyes. But, I said, "Are you gonna show me what you can do?"

He stared at me a moment, his eyes darting all over my face until he nodded. Smirking slowly, he murmured, "You sure you can handle it?"

I raised my eyebrows in answer, and his grin grew...and then he went to work. Tongue, fingers, lips, chin, and even his nose, I think, rubbed against my clit at one point as his fingers worked like magic inside me, and then his tongue, and then his fingers, and then his tongue... And then he gently bit down on my clit, sucking as he pressed his fingers inside me.

It rocked me. Wholly and completely. Mid-pant slash moan, I screamed his name, arching so far I grabbed his thighs and ground against him. And came so damn hard I thought I was going to faint. My brain might have blown away before, but there wasn't a whole shit ton left in my mind as I floated, not even feeling it when I started to fall back on him except for his hands that caught me.

Through my hazed mind, I felt him entering me. I blinked open my eyes, staring up at him, seeing that our heads were on the opposite side of the bed from the pillows, the direction I had landed. Dark eyes stared down at me, and he thrust gently, groaning, "So fucking wet."

I was a little dazed, and not really able to move, which he seemed to understand, lifting my legs farther over his waist, murmuring, "I take it you liked."

I croaked something unintelligible but managed a nod.

His lips curled, and he pushed in farther, his overly huge cock spreading and stretching me so wide, there was a pleasure-pain there I didn't need any kinky shit to feel, unlike the fuck I would meet tonight. "Beth," he gasped, his lips kissing me lightly.

"Better without the condom?" I panted, kissing him back.

"Yeah. I can feel you," he moaned, driving in a little more. "It's going to be hard to be gentle."

"I'll tell you if it doesn't feel right," I pulled his head down and took his swollen mouth, tasting myself, but his too. I moaned against his tongue and he started short, quick thrust, pushing a little farther each time. "I want all of you."

"Do you?" he moaned. "Do you want all of me,

Beth?" He lifted his head, staring down at me, but kept moving his hips, making my eyes cross. "Beth, my sweet. Do you want all of me?"

I whimpered, the feeling so damn intense below, but I knew what he was asking. "Yes, but we have some major issues to work through first."

His eyes closed, and his mouth opened a little as he moaned. "We can work through them." He sounded determined even though his mind was stuck on pleasure. It was 'adorable' as he normally called me.

"Mmm-hmm." I nodded, touching his face.

He leaned into the touch, opening desire-filled eyes.

"This communication and compromise thing may be new to me and a royal pain in my ass," he murmured, thrusting slowly all the rest of the way in, "but the make-up sex is phenomenal."

I gasped, chuckling. "What are you going to do when the doc says no more sex, and we're still arguing?" Because that was more than likely going to happen.

He was still catching his breath, and he huffed, "Vodka."

I started laughing, and we both groaned. Then there were no more words. No words to describe what it was like having him so deep inside me, sliding so slowly and gently. I was a part of him. Like we were one individual bound together in pleasure and intimacy, our eyes never closing longer than a blink. Caught and tangled and thrust together against all other odds, two people somehow making one perfect unity.

I knew then that I wouldn't be able to walk away from him. Not because of the sex. Not because it was dangerous. Not because I was pregnant with his children. But, because of the look in his eye as we connected. It was all there. He got me. And he was beginning to fall in love with me. And I was beginning to fall in love with this overbearing, domineering, vain, violent man. We were… a match… somehow, someway… we were that one perfect harmony.

My breath caught as I got it, and Daniil smiled softly…and I remembered what he had said in that bathroom during my pregnancy test—*and that's the beautiful irony of it.* He may not have been falling in love with me then, but he had known. All along, he'd known. He may not have liked it at first, with the whole nose-crinkling thing, but he got it a lot faster than I had. His damn experience rearing its ugly—okay, perfect—head again.

"You knew," I mumbled, even as I shuddered.

He nodded slowly, kissing my lips, breathing against them, "Yes, I knew. But you only needed a little time to figure it out yourself."

"I'm falling for you," I whispered.

"And I'm falling for you," he answered, staring into my eyes. His dark orbs were a looking glass into his soul, showing me every dark place…and every light place.

I didn't hide myself after that. Not that I was

very good at that kind of thing in the first place, but every person holds a piece of themselves back, almost as a safety net. I didn't right here in this stolen moment for us. I let him see, just as he had gifted me. I knew he saw vulnerability there. And even a little fear of the unknown, everything I tried to mask and hide.

He blinked and held me tighter, kissing me just as softly as he was entering me, and I met each of his caresses with one of my own only for him. Together, with each thrust of his hips or a lift of mine, we eventually came together, our climaxes slow, explosive, and drawn out, a little earth shattering, I think, for both of us since I had never had a man love me so tenderly and thoroughly. I was fairly sure the experience was unique and new to Daniil, as well. Silent for some time afterward, we simply held one another. It was one of those perfect moments that everyone craves. And I memorized every bit of it, never to forget.

After a short nap, and I, ahem, had a 'little' lunch, we played basketball with a smidge of coaxing from me. It wasn't anything hard. We only played HORSE at first, since he was afraid I was going to trip or something. Hell, I had no clue really, but he was worried. So, I kept it simple so he would see I wasn't going to die right then and there now that we knew we were having triplets.

After he beat me in HORSE.

With a fucking granny shot.

I gently coaxed him into an easy game of one-on-one, using half the court. I didn't want to do full court, because I sure as hell wasn't in prime form for that against him. Never would be, but I didn't let on about it. He played light against me, pretty much playing grabass.

He beat me again. Asshole.

It was relaxing and fun. The simple side of him that just enjoyed life and being fit. I learned that he liked to rub in his wins just as much as I did. I would like to think I took it better. Although, since he fell on his ass laughing at me one point, I wasn't so positive.

While dinner was being prepared, no one home yet from work, we watched a movie in the living room that was weird as shit. It was Daniil's favorite from Russia. That gave me a chance for a little catnap. Which I woke up to him laughing—I seriously didn't get what was so funny with the show when I glanced over—and then rubbed my eyes and snuggled in closer to his chest, going back to sleep.

He whispered my name and nuzzled against my neck.

Mmm. Not really a bad way to wake up.

…and to the smell of meatloaf. *God, could it get any better?*

I rolled on top of him, not even caring I was still in my grimy shorts and shirt from basketball, or that he was either, and kissed him flat out, running my hands up under his shirt to his hot, hard pecs. He made a surprised sound, grabbing my hips, saying, "Beth... wait..."

"Yes, please wait," Eva said dryly from my left.

I yelped, my head shooting up in that direction.

The whole damn family standing there, ready to go into the dining room. Including my parents. And Nikki and Beth.

"Oh, Christ."

Dad crossed his arms. "You really need to quit saying His name in vain, sweetie."

"Mommy, what are they doing?" Nikki asked, pointing at us.

"Er...," Ember stuttered.

Nikki and Beth stared at her with wide innocent eyes.

"Wrestling," my mom interjected easily.

"Oh." Beth blinked, also pointing. "Is that how Elizabeth got that bruise on her neck?"

Nikki's mouth opened in a wide "O" and she said hurriedly, "That must be how mommy got hers on vacation." Beth dropped her arm, and they both looked up at Ember. Nikki continued, "Were you wrestling with Grigori when you got yours?"

Ember's mouth dropped and her cheeks pinked. She glanced at Grigori, who was also decidedly uncomfortable...I couldn't believe it...with flushing cheeks. He cleared his throat, running his hands through his hair, and then nodded to the girls. "Yes. She got it while we were wrestling."

Both girls scowled, crossing their arms.

Grigori froze like an ambush was coming.

Beth declared heatedly, "We never saw your bruise."

Daniil chuckled under me.

I quickly pulled my hands out from under his shirt and got off him, straightening my ponytail and shirt.

Both little girls were ready to pummel Grigori.

Daniil stood and moved to speak quietly with Kirill.

Grigori cleared his throat, moving an arm up really slow. He hesitated with it half up in the air when Nikki took a step closer to him, his other hand instantly going to his crotch protectively. He glanced at Ember, who was now looking entertained by this, and he sighed, lifting his hand up the rest of the way and pulling his gray t-shirt's collar to the side. Between his neck and shoulder was a fresh hickey. It was how my first one had appeared, with tiny teeth marks around it, but smaller…Ember size.

I bit my cheek to keep from laughing.

The girls oohed and awed over it, even giving each other high fives. Nikki cheered, "Mommy's lasted longer. She beat him."

Beth nodded, giving her mom a thumbs up. "Good job, Mommy."

Ember was positively tickled, her shoulders shaking. "Thanks, pumpkin."

Daniil clapped his hands. "And on that high note, let's eat."

Staring down at my meatloaf, macaroni, and fries, I debated my options. I wasn't sure which to start with first. My fork hovered over one, and then the other, pretty much going in a circle around my plate slowly. But…sniffing the air…my gaze shot to the right. There was…mmm… something good. I could smell it.

Standing, I walked down to the end of the table, taking delicate, covert sniffs until I stopped in front of my mom's plate. I stared. Oh! She had green bean casserole on her plate. My gaze went to my dad's plate. He had some, too. A quick, thorough scan of the table didn't show that sitting in the middle.

I stood there like a zombie. I stared at my mom and dad's plates. Considering the situation. Dad must have brought that home with him from church. Something left over from any given event there during the evenings. And since he hadn't put it out for then there must not be enough for everyone. It would be rude…

I pointed. "Can I have that?"

Fuck rude. The FOOD WAS SINGING TO ME.

I suddenly realized how quiet the room had gotten since I wasn't lost in my own thoughts. I wasn't sure how long they had been silent. I did know they were probably all staring at me, so I turned my back to the table, whispering to my parents, "The green bean casserole. Can I have it?"

My mom's mouth pinched and her chin started quivering, but she nodded. "Go get your plate, sweetie. I'll put it on there." She reached over, lowering my dad's hand where I stared since he had a bite paused right in front of his mouth…of the green bean casserole. Now *my* green bean casserole.

I gulped and nodded, walking back clear across the table. I kept my eyes averted from everyone and grabbed my plate, and quickly walked back over to my parents. I turned my back on the frigging silent table again as Mom scooped out both of their portions onto my plate, and I pointed when she missed some on hers. Her body started quivering, but she scraped her plate and added the little bit to mine.

"Thank you," I mumbled, my eyes glued to my plate as I walked back over to my seat. I don't remember my mom saying you're welcome because the green bean casserole was singing a soulful tune. It was saying *Mine! All mine!* And God, it smelled and looked great.

Licking my lips, I sat down and instantly grabbed my fork…and after that, things got a bit blurry.

I knew my fork was ripped out of my hands.

The soul tune screamed in displeasure.

And then, somehow I had a knife in my hand.

…and it was aimed at Daniil.

"Papa…I think she wants her fork back," Eva stated slowly.

I blinked into Daniil's clear eyes. And dropped the weapon, hearing it clatter to his plate.

"That needs to be tested," Daniil said calmly and slowly. "Then you can eat it."

Sucking in a harsh breath, I nodded.

Slowly, he took the plate, and I watched avidly as my green bean casserole was taken back into the kitchen.

"She's worse than I was," Ember stated cheerfully, and I glanced her. She toasted me with her wine glass. "Congrats. You take the cake for cracked preggos craver." She grinned, taking a sip. "And it's only just beginning."

I would have flipped her off, but her kids were sitting right there, and I had already pulled a knife on Daniil in front of them. Ember smiled at me evilly, but it changed as she looked down at Nikki and Beth, saying, "Elizabeth's pregnant. Sometimes pregnant women do crazy things around food." She glanced at me, and back at them. "So guard your cookies."

I watched Nikki and Beth each take their cookies off their plates and stuff them in their laps. I glared at her. *Thank you for that, bitch*, I told her with my eyes. And her eyes just laughed right back at me.

And then, I stilled, sniffing the air. And my gaze snapped to the left, past Daniil, who I couldn't quite bring myself to look at yet. I watched the door to the kitchen, and about three seconds later, it opened, and my plate was brought back out.

"Her nose is better than yours," Eva muttered to someone.

"It's just the hormones," Ember stated, sounding miffed. "I'd like to see her do that when she's not pregnant."

I stopped listening after that because my green bean casserole was placed back in front of me. I glanced around for my fork…and remembered Daniil had taken it. I actually debated eating with my fingers for a few moments, but I heard him softly clear his throat. Timidly, pathetically, I peeked up at him. I had held a damn knife to him. The man I was falling for. Ashamed didn't even begin to describe my emotions.

His eyebrows rose mockingly, and he twirled the fork between his fingers. I knew what he was doing, trying to get a rise out of me to pull me out of my funk, but I honestly didn't feel like it. I just wanted to erase that instance. I opened my mouth, but nothing came out, and I closed it clearing my throat, feeling my chin start to tremble as I whispered hoarsely, "I'm sorry."

His eyes instantly softened, and he bent over. "If you think having a knife pulled on me, which you seriously need to learn how to hold properly, hurt my feelings or scared me, then you need to pay better attention." He placed the fork down on my plate.

My hand went to it immediately, but I breathed through the soulful tune and looked back up at him. "I'm still sorry."

He kissed my crinkled forehead. "I know. Now eat." He grinned against my skin. "I'll make sure cook makes some of that every night, just in case."

I stabbed a green bean and watched myself hold it up to his mouth, my hand trembling a little with the action. "You first."

He shook his head slightly, his lips curling. "No."

I scowled at the trembling fork. "Take a bite or I'm going to have the cook put it down the garbage disposal." Dammit, this was a kind gesture; he had better damn well take it. This was better than a simple worded apology.

His eyes darted all over my face.

He opened his mouth and took my offering.

And his nose crinkled.

I shook my head. "Well, that means more for me." I dug in…and heavenly choirs sang. I groaned, and disregarded everyone as I inhaled each and every last bite of it. I eyed my plate when it was all gone, wondering if anyone would notice if I used my finger to get that last bit in the crevice of the china.

Ember started snorting on the other side of the table.

My eyes flashed to her.

She shut up abruptly with the laughing, but she mumbled, "Yeah. She takes the cake, all right."

Brent and Cole showed up right when dinner was being cleared out, apparently working late, to pick up the girls. It was an interesting scene when Nikki and Beth told them about the crazy pregnant lady and how they had to hide their cookies. That was a real special moment for me. They also told Cole and Brent all about the bruise Grigori had from him and Mommy wrestling—with Mommy being the victor. The girls talked so fast I could barely keep up, but Brent and Cole didn't have any issues understanding, holding the girls in their arms and glancing at Grigori.

The looks were not exactly friendly.

Grigori just nodded to them, trying to be cordial in front of the girls. But it didn't seem to help Brent and Cole. Behind the girls' heads, their heated glares even turned on Ember before they left. I was a little surprised since I had heard from Daniil, who seemed to keep up on everyone, how they'd been regular tomcats out on the town since that first dinner here and the resulting argument.

Ember was quiet in the face of their fury, her eyebrows pinched. Only a few seconds after they left the room, she quickly stood. "I'll be back in a second." She jerked her head at Ruslan. "Come with me, please."

Grigori's eyebrows snapped together. He stayed where he was, watching her hurry out of the room. Pretty much like the rest of us. My parents, quiet like the rest of the table's occupants, just watched.

We all heard Ember say loudly, "Brent. Cole. Hold up a second." A pause, and she said, "Ruslan, could you take the girls outside?"

We all stared at the doorway, hearing the girls retreating footsteps, although Ruslan was damn silent. The front door opened and shut.

"Why are you mad at me?" Ember asked, her voice shaking. "I've apologized so many damn times for what happened when you left. So what did I do now?"

The coffee mug in Grigori's hand shattered…and he didn't even seem to notice the hot liquid spilling over his hand or the fact that he had cut himself.

Cole growled, "You think we didn't see the look on your face today when everyone started talking about the triplets?"

"What?" she croaked.

"You want another baby, Ember. We aren't blind," Brent stated heatedly. "You think this is easy for us? You think we didn't fucking dream of having more children with you? All that time we were alone, praying for the fucking day we could come back to add to our family?"

It sounded like Ember choked.

"And now we're here. Our dreams are shattered. And when you have another child, it will be with *him*. Not us!" Cole practically shouted.

There was a heartbeat of silence, and it sounded like Ember was crying softly, quietly saying, "He's not ready for children."

Grigori stilled completely.

Cole laughed coldly. "So you've already talked to him about it. I should have known."

There was another silence, and Brent said quietly, "No. She hasn't talked to him about it. She read him."

"It doesn't matter how I know," Ember stated heatedly, her voice still hiccupping. "I won't be having any more children, so you two can quit with the damn looks, all right?"

Silence. For some time.

And then, Ember asked, "What? Why are you looking at me that way?"

Cole cleared his throat and said, "You want more kids. We want our damn family back together. If he's not going to give you what you want, we will."

"What?" Ember asked, sounding stunned.

"Come back to us. Quit being scared and open your heart again. And we'll give you what you want," Brent said softly. "I know what it's like to be frightened, Ember. But, we were good together once." He paused, chuckling. "No, twice. We can be good together again. And we all want more children. You read him. If you say he doesn't want children, then he doesn't. We do." He paused, his voice going even softer, a little wistful, "Christ. Another Beth or Nikki. I would love that."

Grigori was damn near panting, and sweat was breaking out on his forehead, but he still wasn't interrupting them. He sat there. Listening as if his life depended on it.

"I…I…" Ember stuttered.

"Sweetheart, you know we can be good together.

I can see it in your eyes, even through all that scared," Cole murmured quietly.

I wanted to smack Grigori as he sat there, and it looked like Daniil and most of the occupants at the table did, too.

His eyes closed, head still turned toward the door, and he started whispering so quietly, "Come on, kitten. Come on. Say it. Say it, kitten."

I glanced at Daniil worriedly. *Had his oldest lost his marbles?*

Daniil started rubbing his chest even as Grigori kept whispering toward the silent door.

And then we all heard it. Ember said clearly, "No. I love him. I can't do that. Even if he doesn't want children now, I'll just have to deal with it somehow. He's mine. My partner. My lover. My best friend. There's no way in hell I would do that. I want him."

Grigori's eyes flashed open, and he jumped up from his chair, startling all of us. He stalked out of the room, stuffing his hurt hand in his pants pocket, stating coolly, "If the two of you are done propositioning her, you can get the fuck out my home...or I'll help you out." There was a pause, no one making a sound. And then, Grigori said cheerfully, "All right. I've been waiting patiently to do this for some time."

And...we all heard the fight start.

"Shit," Daniil grumbled quietly, everyone flying out of their seats. He pointed at me. "Stay back."

I almost laughed. As if I was going to do that.

I followed discreetly as everyone rushed out of

the room, and I slid up the stairs a few steps, getting a better view of it all. Ember was shouting, standing against a wall, yelling at all of them to stop, her face clearly showing she had been crying since she wasn't one of those pretty tear shedders. No one was intervening yet, letting them duke it out, standing in a loose circle around them, standing far enough away just in case...well, like when...

Grigori was slammed against a wall, literally cracking it with his back from Brent's forceful shove. Grigori ducked his punch and raised his massive, scary-ass boot with tiny silver spikes all over it, and nailed Cole in the chest as he came up, sending him flying back through the air, and tumbling on the ground, almost to where Eva and Chloe stood.

Brent took advantage of that and swiped Grigori's feet out from underneath him, and he landed on his side but rolled right into Brent, taking him down. They both popped up to their feet quickly, but Grigori didn't see Cole get up and come at him, taking an elbow hard to his shoulder muscle. Grigori grunted, spinning, and suddenly, it was kind of like watching one of those martial arts movies where they seem like they're all moving in fast forward. Fists and legs flew from all of them, Brent and Cole working like a team just as well as Ember and Grigori had done in the sparring ring in Key West. Although Grigori held his own somehow, getting in just as many hits as they did on him.

They worked in a circle, staying contained in the area...and then, Brent and Cole charged him. Grigori

293

ducked one fist but caught the other in the face—I wasn't sure whose hand it was at this point—and his head shot back, his mouth bleeding. And…that's when it appeared he stopped playing nice even though I hadn't realized he had been. Every shot he landed on them had one of them groaning, and then they all started fighting just as dirty.

Cole almost landed a shot right at Grigori's crotch, but Grigori caught it and grinned, shaking his head before twisting his foot, and Cole with it, down to the floor. But that little move cost Grigori's kidneys when Brent got in a solid kick. Grigori gasped, spinning away, holding his back, and glaring at Brent.

And that's when Ember jumped in the middle, right when they were all going back in at one another. She held her hands up, screaming, "Stop it! Now!"

They didn't really listen so well, though. Dodging her, all three of them slammed into one another against another wall, making another crack in the foyer. Ember stalked up to them, and she yelled right next to their flying arms. "I swear to motherfucking God, Grigori, if you don't stop this now, I'm going to a damn hotel. And staying there indefinitely." She paused. "I said I wanted you. Isn't that enough?"

The fight continued, and Grigori groaned out when he got punched in the stomach. "They asked you to fucking leave me. And have a baby with them. In my own damn house!"

He shoved Cole up against the wall by the throat, but Cole somehow slipped out of his hold at the same time Grigori kicked backward nailing Brent, who was sneaking up on him, right in the gut.

Ember screeched through clenched teeth her hands in fists at her sides, "Fine. I'm leaving." She turned on her heel and started marching toward the front door.

Grigori sighed and spun, and suddenly, he had two guns in his hands, aimed at Brent and Cole's heads.

Ember stopped in her tracks, hearing the fighting come to a dead stop as Brent and Cole stood frozen, glowering at Grigori. She glanced over her shoulder, taking in the scene. Slowly turning around, she crossed her arms, asking coolly, "Is that really necessary?"

Grigori grinned with blood trickling from his eyebrow and lip. "You were going to leave. It's the quickest way to get them gone. Win-win."

"Grigori…" Ember said in warning.

Grigori heaved in a breath and blew it out slowly, playing with his tongue ring and staring at Brent and Cole. "Just get the fuck out like I asked before. Nikki and Beth would miss you too much if you died again." And…I think he was actually serious. Like the only thing keeping him from shooting them was the fact that their kids would miss them. He jerked his head at the door, stating calmly, "Now. Get the fuck out of my home. And the next time you come to pick up Nikki and Beth, stay outside. One of us will bring them to you."

They stared right back at him for a few moments

longer, and then both turned on their heel at the same time, walking toward the front door.

Ember stated to them as they passed her, "Just tell the girls you wrestled each other. They'll think you both won."

They didn't say anything, both storming out of the front door, not bothering to shut it. Grigori put his guns away, holding the back of his hand to the corner of his mouth where he was bleeding, staring at Ember as Ruslan came inside, shutting the door behind him and standing there quietly. Ember glared at Grigori, not moving from her spot, arms still crossed.

Grigori glanced at the back of his hand and wiped his mouth again, his eyes back on Ember. "All I have to say is one word…" He paused, leaning forward and stating, "Blue."

Ember's lips pinched. "That was nothing like this. I only dyed their skin blue. Not try to beat them to death and wave my damn gun around like it's a fucking measurement contest."

Grigori grinned, raising his eyebrows. "I don't need a measurement contest to know who's bigger. Your eyes said it all the first time you saw me."

"Not. The. Damn. Point," Ember hissed. She glared, and then waved a hand. "Never mind. If you don't get it, then you can sleep on the couch."

She turned and started marching up the stairs.

Daniil glanced at his oldest with sympathy.

I moved out of her way, plastering myself against the wall. She was in some kind of mood right now.

Grigori hollered, "Oh, come on. I'm bleeding just as much as they are."

I could hear Ember grumbling some pretty unflattering things about him under her breath as she kept moving up the stairs. I bit my cheek, trying not to laugh as Grigori watched her trek. He shouted, "Ember, honey. What would you have done?"

She stopped and glared at him over the railing, pointing at him. "That's the point. What would I have done if the situations were reversed?"

Grigori's eyebrows snapped together. "That doesn't really make a whole lot of sense to my question. I'm a man. See exhibit A," he pointed at his crotch, "I have a dick. Therefore, I can't really think from a female's viewpoint. That's why I asked." Daniil and my dad and Kirill all started chuckling softly and shaking their heads at him, but Grigori kept digging his hole deeper, stating, "See exhibit B," he pointed lower on his crotch, "I have balls. Big ones. You told them you didn't want them, and then I asked them to leave, but they didn't. I didn't have to grow a pair since I already have mine, so I helped them leave when they couldn't find theirs."

Ember gaped at him, her mouth slightly drooping, and she mumbled, "The couch, Grigori. In fact, make it in another room now."

He threw his arms wide when she started moving up the stairs again. "You didn't answer my damn question. What would you have done?"

"Figure it out yourself, *Mr. Dick and Balls*," she griped loudly.

"Ember, honey," Grigori stated loudly, his arms still wide. "You're acting unreasonable."

I shook my head at that, right along with Chloe and my mom.

"And you're impossible," she hissed over the balcony, now at the top. "Enjoy the damn couch."

"Ember!" Grigori shouted when she moved back, going into the hallway, most likely out of his line of vision. He paused and shouted again, "Ember!" I could see that she kept on moving, not turning around or stopping. Grigori's arms crossed for all of three seconds, scowling at where she had disappeared from his view before he mumbled, "Dammit," and dropped his arms, racing up the stairs. I plastered myself against the wall again since he seemed to have a one-track mind right now—and I could hear him mumbling different reasons under his breath, apparently trying to figure the best explanation why she was so pissed.

My eyebrows flew up at one of the reasons I heard him mumble, and I started chuckling, throwing a hand over my mouth. The man seriously didn't have a clue. Apparently, Daniil's un-reasoning skills passed on to him when he thought he was right. Glancing at Daniil, who was watching me with raised eyebrows, I shook my head. Grigori was going to fuck it up even more.

Daniil scowled, and barked, "Grigori! Wait!"

Grigori didn't seem to hear him at first, almost at

the top of the stairs, so Daniil shouted louder. That time Grigori stopped in his tracks, peering over his shoulder, his eyebrows together, but he kept glancing back to the hallway. Daniil stated in a hurry, obviously seeing his son's short attention span, "I need your help in my study."

Grigori scowled at Daniil, and then glanced down the hallway again before looking at his dad. "Papa, can't you ask someone else? I'm kinda busy."

Daniil shook his head. "No. I need you there."

I was confused, but Grigori sighed, glancing down the hallway one more time before nodding, and turning around. "All right. Let's go interrogate the bastard."

My jaw dropped, and I turned my attention to Daniil.

He shrugged when he saw my expression. "I wanted you to eat first before I told you he was here."

"Lord have mercy," my mom muttered, throwing her hands up in the air, and shaking her head as she started stomping out of the foyer, mumbling, "None of these men have a clue in this family."

"Agreed," I said dryly, scowling down at Daniil. He was holding someone—probably not nicely—in his study and had let us all eat dinner before going in to take care of business.

Daniil just shrugged, though. "You were hungry." He motioned for Grigori to come down the stairs, but kept talking to me. "We're going to question him first before you," his nose crinkled, "tell me what you want done with him."

I shook my head, hurrying to cut Grigori off and began racing down the stairs, taking them two at a time. "No. I want to be in there." Who knew what his 'questioning' would entail.

"Slow down!" Daniil barked so loudly everyone in the room froze from the obvious command in his voice.

I was no exception.

I halted, but slowly started taking the rest of the stairs down as he started marching to me. "Calm down. I'm not going to fall." Hell, his face was a mixture of furious energy and worry. "And quit snarling orders at me." If it weren't for the honest worry on his face, I would have finished running down them, but instead, I took them slow and steady, landing on the bottom step where he had stopped and stood glaring at me. Crinkled nose and all. My positioning put the top of my head at his nose level, so I didn't have to reach up as far to smooth the creases on his nose. "And I'm going in with you."

His teeth clenched. "You won't be able to understand us. We'll be speaking in Russian."

I shrugged. "Have Trofim come in with me to translate." Or not. Really, I didn't care about hearing what they said. I was sure Daniil would truthfully give me the details. I just wanted the man breathing.

He shook his head. "No. I don't want you seeing this. It's no place for you."

Exactly. Bluntly, I asked, "Do you plan to hurt him while you question him?"

His nostrils flared as he took a slow, deep breath in through his nose, eyes like granite. "Beth, I don't want to say anything unkind or rude to you right now, so I'm going to walk away, and you're going to go with your papa while Kirill, Grigori, and I go talk with this man." He paused, leaning down to eye level with me. "This is one of those times you need to be quiet and just do as I ask."

Time went hazy at the sound of his brutal, condescending tone.

Instant. Intense. Pissed. The. Fuck. Off. Fury. "I am not a fucking servant." I slammed his chest with my palms, ignoring that it didn't move him at all. "Or a goddamn child." I slammed him again. "Or a little fucking barefoot wife." Another slam. "I am a grown woman with her own damn mind and thoughts and ideas. I will do as I goddamn please without a fucking dictator ordering me around! This is fucking America if you've forgotten, and I have the fucking right to my free-fucking-will and free-fucking-dom. Do. You. Fucking. Get. Me?"

And...then...I burst into tears, which I really hoped it didn't ruin the effect of what I had just said.

Daniil...just...stared at me, looking a little surprised. Well, more than a little surprised I guess since his eyes were huge and his jaw had dropped a little.

"Sweetie, I'm going to ignore how many time you just dropped the f-bomb in your patriotic speech," Dad said quickly, walking up beside Daniil. He took my arm and pulling me down next to him, he wrapped his comforting arms around me as I continued to bawl. He whispered over my head, "I'm going to take her to her mom. She handles pregnant woman better than I do. And apparently, you, too."

I pushed out of his hold furious and upset all at once, yelling, "I'm not acting this way because I'm pregnant! I just want to be there to keep that man alive!"

Dad blinked, and then glanced over my shoulder worriedly. "Maybe I should go get Frankie."

Dad's obvious worry, well, it made me blink. And the hazy furious venom rushed out of me. And my breath caught. Unconsciously, I placed a hand on my lower stomach. And started bawling even more, making both Daniil and my dad look almost freaked out. Quickly, I started mumbling, "I'm sorry! I'm so sorry! Tonight, I've pulled a knife on you," I stepped forward and started patting Daniil's pecs were I had hit him, "and shoved you. I'm turning into a fucking crazy pregnant woman." I cried harder. "Pregnancy doesn't like me." I sobbed. It hurt my heart that I was acting this way.

"Beth…" Daniil purred softly, coming out of his stupor, his hands rising to my hips.

But my dad pulled me back putting his arm around my shoulder and began leading me away. "Come on, sweetie. Let's go talk to your mother." He pulled me in close, kissing the top of my head. "Daniil's right. Let him take care of this right now. Besides, he said you would have the final say," he glanced over our shoulders to where Daniil stood, "and I'm sure he will keep him alive so you can have it."

I hiccupped and nodded. Daniil wouldn't go back on his word. What was one punch or two to the man's face? Hell, I wouldn't mind doing that myself. "O-O-Okay." The tears wouldn't stop coming and Dad continued hushing me as he took me in the direction my mom had gone. I didn't even notice the others around us as. I knew they were there, but they were so silent, they didn't even register on my radar.

Dad led me to the kitchen, and I smelled fresh bread being made and heard the clang of dishes being cleaned from our dinner. Mom was sitting at the island bar flipping through a cookbook and taking notes when we entered. She looked like home to me sitting there making out lists to give to Ms. York, a new single mom at Dad's church who Mom was trying to teach to cook. For the past few months, Mom had been giving her simple recipes that would be cheap on the budget. It looked like she had raided their cooking books with at least six piled to the left of the one she was going through.

"Mom," I blubbered, pushing out of Dad's hold and rushing to her. Her head snapped up and she jumped from her chair, catching me against her. Motherly arms surrounded me, her hands immediately starting to rub my back soothingly. "I'm one of those scary pregnant freaks you see in the movies." I hiccupped, burying my wet face in her neck. "Forget Jekyll and Hyde. They've got nothing on me."

She crooned softly, hushing me, even as she managed to get the story from Dad of what happened in the short period of time since she had left. Petting my hair, she placed me on a bar stool when my sobs quieted. My damn contacts were horribly dry and scratchy now, and a little irritated. I took them out right then and there. I had worn them a week longer than I was supposed to anyway.

Staring down at the translucent spheres, watching them dry up on the counter, Mom ordered Dad to go find my glasses for me before sitting down next to me. She cleared her throat, and said, "When I was pregnant with you," she cleared her throat again, "I not-so-accidently rammed my car into the car of the woman who had cut me off in the check-out line at Walmart."

My head snapped up, and I gawked at my mom. My supposedly non-violent mom.

She grinned. And it looked satisfied. "I crunched her bumper *good*."

"Mom!" I gasped, completely dumbfounded.

Still smiling, she began wiping my face off, studying me. "You know, sweetie, there are some downfalls of pregnancy. Emotional disturbance is one of them." She paused, looking thoughtful. "And you're having triplets. I'm sure that's going to make it worse for you." My shoulders slumped as that reasoning made sense. She kept going, though. "But do you want to know a trick I learned after that whole bashing-the-wenches-car-thing?"

I nodded.

"The trick is when you start to feel," she paused, clicking her tongue, "*overly emotional*, like really sad or happy or furious…stop. Just stop whatever you're about to do or say. Close your eyes, think of a peaceful place and take in a deep calming breath, and then count to ten." She paused, chuckling. "Sometimes twenty." She brushed curls behind my ear that had escaped my ponytail. "When you open your eyes, try to think rationally and calmly. It won't always work because sometimes pregnancy tends to just take over, but it does help."

I nodded. That sounded reasonable. Something I could handle.

Mom cocked her head and said, "Now that you know how I got through my pregnancy, I want to ask you a question." I nodded again, staying mute, and she asked slowly, "I know your generation is different from mine, but personally, in here," Mom placed her hand over my heart, "who do you believe runs a household? The man or the woman?"

That gave me pause, and I thought about it while Mom took her hand back, patiently waiting for my answer. I was an extremely independent woman. I believed in women's lib, and all that. And ever since I had been on my own, a free adult so to speak, I had become even more independent. But…

Down deep, my family roots were buried in my

heart, not just in my head where the independent part of me lived strong. My parents had raised me with Christian values. I had grown up in a loving, truly happy home where my dad was the head, my mom the neck. That part of me was just too engrained to come up with anything different.

I stated, "The man." I held up my hand when Mom started to speak. "But I firmly believe it should be a partnership. Not one cowering behind the other. The man and woman should have the same say," I sighed, "but, in the end, I do believe the man is the protector and has the final say."

Mom's lips twitched. "Your generation has so many problems. And I believe this to be the starting point." She sighed. "Sweetie, in a nutshell, you can't have your cake and eat it, too." I blinked at her, and she placed a hand on my cheek. "A committed relationship, any type of committed relationship, is hard. It's constant work once those sweet feelings of first love vanish and reality sets in. You state the man is the head of the household but say you want a partnership." She tapped my forehead. "You're confusing yourself. Yes, a committed relationship is a partnership of sorts. The man and the woman should always have communication between them. And no one should ever cower behind the other, but you have to have a leader in the household. Be it man or woman, there has to be a leader. If you have two leaders constantly battling it out about everything, it doesn't make for a contented relationship. It just makes for a lot of small fights, which could possibly end up as one huge one."

I didn't totally agree with what she was saying. And she was probably right about why. My generation was *a lot* different from hers. "I can't agree with all that. I do believe the man should have the final say, yes, but that doesn't mean it has to be 'his' final say."

Mom's lips twitched. "No. It doesn't always have to be 'his' final say. But communication is the key. If you've made a good match, the man will see your side," she chuckled, "sometimes more times than not." She held up a finger. "As long as you know how to communicate properly, which doesn't include screaming at one another." She paused. "Although I'm woman enough to say sometimes it does come to that."

"How do I get someone like Daniil to listen to me without screaming at each other?"

She smiled, and it was a knowing smile. "Daniil is a very strong man. But he does have a weakness."

I waited patiently.

Her grin grew in my silence, appearing tickled by my confusion. "You, sweetie. His weakness is you as much as it pains me to say it." She chuckled, shaking her head. "Honestly, other than the knife issue and hitting him tonight, you've been doing wonderful from what I can tell. But your conflicting issues," she tapped my forehead, "got in the way tonight. From what your father said, Daniil actually said he was going to walk away from the situation before he said something rude.

That takes a lot for a man of his caliber to say something like that."

I blinked. Confusion bared down.

Mom sighed. "Elizabeth, you picked an older man used to getting what he wants. As much as you don't want to hear this, he does have more experience than you do. Do you know how hard it probably was for him to back away and not call your actions childish?"

My jaw set and my eyebrows snapped together, but Mom kept on. "You need to realize this is his life. He gave you his word…" she paused, clucking her tongue, "…how did you phrase it? Ah, yes. That you would have the final say in those who threaten you as long as you're not in immediate danger, which I actually agree with. And then, you act as if he isn't going to stand up to his word once he's—Daniil, the head of the Russian Mafia—already compromised, a major feet for him." She paused, cocking her head, stating slowly, "In other words, you threw a hissy fit when you didn't get your way. That's how he would see it."

Jaw still set and eyebrows still together, I hissed, "I just wanted to go in there and make sure he didn't —" I stopped, realizing I was about to say 'kill him.' Daniil had promised me previously he wouldn't do that. So…I had thrown a fit. I hadn't trusted him enough to take him at his word when he had never done anything to justify that from me. Instead, I had stomped down the stairs, gung-ho and ready for battle, to make sure it didn't happen. Though… "What was wrong with me just going in there to listen?"

Mom shook her head. "That's where the whole man-the-head-of-the-household thing comes into play. You, yourself, said the man should be the protector. Well, that's what he's doing. I imagine he's probably in there intimidating and scaring the crap out of that guy…which, again, I have no problem with." Her eyes unfocused. "I wouldn't mind having a few minutes alone with the man myself."

That look she had on her face freaked me out a little, so I stated, "Remember that trick, Mom. I think you need it."

She shook her head. "You'll understand when you're children are born." She sighed, shaking her head at me. "If you're going to continue this relationship with him, you have to understand who he is. You picked *him*. And again, *he* is an *older man* who is used to getting what he wants. Sometimes," she paused, leaning forward nose-to-nose with me, "you're just going to have to trust him and do what he says even though you don't understand. Because you will. In time. You will see what he already knew because sometimes explaining something to someone younger just doesn't give the life experience justice, and he's intelligent enough to know it." She sucked in a breath. "Of course, this wouldn't happen if you chose someone your own age."

"No. I pick him," I stated instantly, even though my mind was racing. I stuttered out, "Do you really think he thinks of me as a child?"

Mom snorted, glancing down at my stomach, stating dryly, "No. I don't believe so."

I waved my hand at that and then tapped my head. "You know what I meant. Up here."

Mom's lips pursed. "Do you sometimes think of him as an older man?"

I licked my lips and nodded slowly. Yeah, his age showed sometimes.

Mom nodded slowly, "Then, to be brutally honest, sweetie, I would have to say yes. He most likely does think that sometimes." She studied me as I tried to process that.

I really hated that. I despised feeling inferior.

Mom asked softly, "Is that a deal breaker?"

I glanced away from her. "I don't know." I paused, asking, "Does that mean he thinks I'm stupid?"

Mom pulled my chin around, staring me in the eyes, hers soft and loving. "He's a very intelligent man. More so than I can probably imagine with all the cunning he has to do having four strong-willed children as he has. So, with that said, no, he doesn't think that. He's smart enough to realize, it's just inexperience on your part, not ignorance."

"You think so?"

"I know so." She sighed, releasing my chin. "I still can't believe I'm helping him, but I've seen the respect and caring in his eyes when he looks at you when you're not watching him."

That startled me since I hadn't obviously seen it. I

thought through what she said before. "You said I was his weakness."

Mom nodded, a small smile lifting her lips. "I saw him lose it, protecting you in his gym, and then he kissed you like you were his singular sun." She nodded. "Yes, you're his weakness, sweetie."

We were both silent, and soon, my lips were smiling softly like hers. "The age difference isn't a deal breaker. It's just something I'll have to deal with better instead of ignoring it." Daniil had apparently been dealing with it already since he had tried to back away from me, seeing I wasn't going to understand before. It was time for me to take some responsibility and trust in the man I had chosen.

Mom patted my leg, and I asked her about her work since I hadn't gotten to that yet. Dad walked in, handing me my glasses, watching me carefully—almost making me laugh at him. Yeah, I was the big scary pregnant psycho. Sadly, Ember probably wasn't too far off the mark earlier. So, I listened to my mom tell me how she had been canned today, pretty much getting the same treatment I had gotten today.

Dad held her from behind, placing a small kiss on her forehead, seeing through her masked upset as I did. My parents were... Well, they were infuriating most of the time, but I couldn't ask for a more loving and unselfish pair. They were still making sacrifices for me. Just like I knew I would when I had my children. I sniffled a little and hugged them both, earning chuckles from them. And then, I sat back down and helped my mom and dad go through the recipe books—that looked new—and waited for Daniil to come and get me.

CHAPTER 12

The decision wasn't hard. Not at all.

I had thought it would be, but it wasn't.

Daniil walked into the kitchen, his fury barely in check. He stood rigid just inside the door and stated in a low voice, "Beth…" That was all he said. His fists were clenched, and his knuckles were red and almost raw—as if he had beaten someone with his fists.

I stood, and using my better judgment—opposed to how I had early—I walked over to him and followed him out of the kitchen. As soon as we were out of everyone's sight, I placed my hand on his elbow, gently turning him. And then I wrapped my arms up and around his neck, hugging him in what I hoped was a comforting embrace.

He shuddered hard and instantly wrapped his arms around me, pulling me in close. Dropping his head to my shoulder, he then began speaking softly, telling me what this man had planned. Apparently, he was working alone. Just an outright hater of Daniil and everything Daniil loved. He had been here for months trying to find a way to hurt him. And what he had planned...God, the man was sick.

Daniil held nothing back. Like normal. He told me that the man had planned to kidnap me, take me over to Russia, and place me in the dregs of the prostitution ring...like had happened to someone else Daniil had loved. He didn't tell me who, and I didn't ask, but he continued explaining what would have happened to me from the man's accounting. Oh, and the lovely kicker that I would have been cut a zillion times in the process until I eventually bled out.

I managed to stay strong through it since it appeared Daniil was not at this moment, and I was smart enough to know Daniil was also telling me all these details so I would let him kill the guy. But...the way Daniil recounted what the man said hit a certain 'vibe' with me.

So, I asked softly, "I know you don't want me to do this, but before I make any kind of a decision, I would like to meet him."

Daniil stiffened around me, and I continued in a hurry, "Just thirty seconds. That's all."

He stood there for a good two minutes, just breathing heavily against my neck before he finally stood. And nodded. "I understand."

I shook my head because I really didn't think he did. "It's not because I don't trust you. I believe everything you said. It's just that I've," I shook my head side to side slowly, "got this feeling from what you said. I want to see if I'm right."

Daniil's body visibly relaxed—some. "Okay." He paused, hesitating before saying, "He's a little bloody."

I tapped his knuckles. "I'm sure he is. And I'd hoped you wore gloves. Diseases are passed through blood, you know."

Daniil nodded, a small smile lifting his lips. "The leather rubbed my knuckles wrong."

I nodded once curtly. "All right." I gestured down the hallway, and we both began walking toward his study. "I'm sorry about earlier."

He placed his hand on the small of my back, his palm huge against it. "It's all right. I understand that, too."

"The pregnancy does things…," I trailed off but said after a small hesitation, "I also realize I was behaving a *little* childishly. I'll try to work on that."

He pulled me closer so our sides brushed as we walked. "Thank you." He paused, stating slowly, "And I'll also try to remember this is America. And you want your free-fucking-will and free-fucking-dom."

I couldn't help the embarrassed chuckled that escaped even as I elbowed him playfully in the ribs. "Leave me alone. That was inexperience and hormones talking."

He nodded, grinning softly. "It was a very impassioned speech. Not one I'll forget anytime soon. In fact, I may have you initiate any new bodyguards I have. You'll whip them right into shape." His eyes were crinkling down at me as I crinkled my nose up at him. "But I'll try not to be so overbearing. It'll take some time…if I can manage it."

I stood up on my tiptoes and hopped, kissing his cheek in mid-stride. "Thank you."

And then we were at the studies door. I sucked in a breath and reached out turning the door handle. I had mentally prepared myself for the worst. But when I viewed the man sitting in the center of the study in a lone chair with his hands and ankles tied to the arms and legs of it, I was a little shocked. Daniil had held back. Yes, the man was bloody, but not like I had expected.

He was a 'dirty' looking man with mud brown hair and brown eyes with a normal build and normal facial features, but he had a swelling cheek, blood running down a busted lip and nose, and…well, maybe his right leg was broken. But, all in all, he didn't look like he was pouring blood from anywhere significant like I had thought most likely with what Daniil had said. He had most definitely held back.

Walking into the room, I glanced around seeing a shit ton—more than I realized were here on Daniil's property—of bodyguards standing silently against the walls around the room. Grigori was standing off to the side looking decidedly pissed the fuck off, and Kirill stood next to him, watching the man with hard eyes. Slowly, I made my way to this man, Daniil following silently behind me. Daniil had kept his word, so I decided to keep mine and make this short and sweet.

The man smiled at me with blood covering his teeth. "Hello, Elizabeth Forter."

I stood in front of him, keeping a good four feet of space between us, before bending over and placing my hands on my knees, asking him simply, "Have you ever been diagnosed with a disorder?"

His smile faltered for the barest heartbeat, but he laughed his ass off, spitting blood all down the front of his shirt. "Would you like to be tied up like I am? But have me between your legs?"

I slapped my hands hard, saying loudly, "Focus! I'm asking you a question that will decide your damn fate!" I leaned in a little more and cocked my head, asking him bluntly and honestly, "Do you want to die? Because that's what's going to happen if you don't answer my damn question. Have you been diagnosed with a disorder of some sort? Gone off your meds maybe?"

He laughed again, staring at me hard. "Such a sweet preacher's daughter. How I wouldn't love to taste your pussy. Lick the heavens that are surely there."

"You. Are. Going. To. Die," I stated each word clearly. "Do you understand that? Death is scary. Even to the toughest assholes, death is frightening in the end."

He continued to cackle, spurting off obscenities, and I stood upright, turning to Daniil. Holding out my hand, I asked calmly, "Can I borrow your gun, please?"

He was furious, glaring at the man, but he blinked at my request, his head snapping to me. Staring at me, his eyebrows pulled together, but he nodded slowly, and even more slowly, reached around his back and withdrew his gun. He turned the safety off with a click, and gently placed it in my hand I was holding still—just barely.

I was nervous as hell, but this needed to be done. I gripped its heavy weight, making sure I didn't drop it and turned back to the man still spouting obscenities. Walking a few paces to his left, I moved in and when he could see me, I took a deep, calm breath and placed the gun to his temple.

"Do you understand death?" I asked quietly. "I know you understand I am the preacher's daughter. So, I have it on pretty good authority where you'll go when I pull this trigger. You will go to Hell. You will burn in agony. Burn for the rest of eternity. Every second, of every day, of every year, of every decade for the rest… of… your… life. You will burn. The most horrific pain you can imagine will be bestowed upon you. And you will begin to pray to a God, who won't answer your prayers because He won't be able to hear you. Because you made this choice. Here. On earth. Here and now. And you will *burn*." I paused, leaning in closer and pressing the gun harder into his temple, whispering, "So, I'll ask you again. Do you understand death?"

And…he laughed again. And more vulgar indecencies flew through the air at me.

And…that was my answer. Not to mention the tiny twitch of his smile in the beginning. And his recount of what he would do to me.

I leaned back and lowered the gun. "He's insane. Not just sane insane. But really insane." I glanced at Daniil, who was standing where I had left him, watching me silently with loosely crossed arms. "Check his records. I guarantee he's off some type of meds. This isn't his fault. Not really. Put him in some type of hospital of your choice. But, one that has permanent bars. He doesn't deserve to die because of a mental imbalance. He can live and try to find his way back to sanity from there."

Daniil stared at me long and hard, now cocking his head and listening to the man's taunts. Gradually, he nodded, apparently hearing what I said. The way the man rambled, his repeating words, mixed in with nonsense. "I know of a place. I can agree to that."

I nodded once. "Thank you." I walked over to him slowly, but quickly gave him his gun back. "Well, that was loads of fun."

His lips twitched as he put the safety back on and put his hands behind his back, leaning down and murmuring in my ear, "I am the preacher's daughter?" He chuckled. "Absolutely beautiful. And you would have scared the shit of me."

I bit my lip and glanced at him a little embarrassed. "I just needed to know if the lights were on up there."

He laughed outright, herding me out of the room, and away from the rambling man. "Go on. I need to finish up in here."

I nodded but stopped, asking, "This place you

have planned for him isn't like some third world jail, is it?"

He shook his head but stalled, glancing at the ceiling. "It's not the penthouse suite, but it's suitable."

"A bucket of water and straw for a bed?" I asked dryly.

He grinned. "It's a little nicer than that. And I'll check his history to find out what medication he needs. He'll be taken care of." His eyes hardened. "But you said permanently."

I crossed my arms but nodded. I didn't want that loony on the streets and going off his meds again. From what I could hear him still rambling about, he had already done enough deeds to have a man here in the States tried and convicted and put on death row. That was enough for me. "Definitely permanently."

"You're damn adorable." Daniil kissed my forehead, murmuring, "And sexy as hell with a gun in your hand," he touched my glasses, "even wearing those, covering up your kewpie doll face."

I pointed into the air, turning and walking away down the hallway. "I'm going to take that as a compliment." I glanced at him over my shoulder. "Don't take too long." I smiled at him, and yeah, it was blatantly carnal.

His jaw clenched, and his gaze roamed over me from behind. "I won't be."

...and he wasn't. Even though the night was long and full of heated, but carefully gentle lovemaking that turned me inside out and back again. And by Daniil's reactions, the feeling was mutual. After the day and night we had together, we were falling headlong into each other.

That Friday morning, I woke early having to pee.

And *not* puke.

Hurray for small favors!

After doing my business, I climbed back into bed, crawling on top of Daniil. He stirred, his arms instantly wrapping around me. His palms climbed up under the back of my simple white spaghetti strap pajama top and rested against my back. He held me tight but immediately fell back to sleep as I rested my forehead against his chest and listened to his heartbeat, strong and steady. His lungs filled and emptied with each relaxed breath.

I was content.

I roused to him running his hands up and down my back, grabbing my derriere firmly. He pressed against my little white shorts with an impressive morning erection. The sun was just filtering in through the windows…and it was tempting as hell…but my stomach growled. I leaned up, mumbling, "I'm hungry. Food first."

He blinked lazily, a soft smile lifting his lips. "Please."

My own lips curled. God, I loved it when he said that. But… "That's not fair."

He ground against me again. "Please, Beth. I need you."

I stalled, wondering if that were true in ways other than sexually. "Do you?"

Instant. "Yes."

"No." I undulated against him. "Not this way. I mean—"

He cut me off, placing one finger on my lips. "I know what you mean, my sweet. And the answer is yes."

My heart softened even more, and I grinned. I knew it was big and goofy, but I couldn't help it. "I think I like that."

His lips lifted more. "Think you can help me with something else I need you for?"

I chuckled. "Yeah. I think I can help with that." I looked at him sternly then. "But, you're going to feed me afterward."

His smile increased, and he had a special twinkle in his eye. "I think I can help with that."

I turned immediately suspicious as I started moving down his body, staring at him hard. "What are doing?" That look in his eye didn't bode well.

Daniil grinned. "Trying to make love, Ms. Forter."

"Uh-huh," I murmured, pulling his pajama bottoms—the sexy as hell ones—over his lean hips. "What else are you doing?"

"Loving you, Ms. Forter," he stated quietly.

I paused, my gaze meeting his. Those dilated brown eyes said it all. He loved me. Flat out loved me. And he wasn't hiding it. I sputtered the first thing that came to my mind, "Is it a little too early to for that?" I was falling in love with him…but…

He smiled, brushing his finger over my cheek. "Sometimes you just know."

My heart was damn near full, but… "I…I…I'm not…" I finished lamely, "quite there yet." I bit my lip. "I'm sorry."

His grin only improved. "I know."

I wasn't sure what to say, so I blubbered, "Thank you?"

He sputtered on a laugh. "Beth, my sweet, you're so adorable, it's precious." He pulled me up and kissed my lips lightly. And then proceeded to show me just how much he loved me. Twice.

We went down for breakfast, pretty much just throwing our night clothes back on because we were running late.

323

OBSIDIAN MASK

I pushed my glasses up on my nose, fumbling around with my hair as we walked down the stairs barefoot. It was surreal walking around his mansion dressed as we were. Like it really was home. And oddly, I was beginning to feel like it was. My parents had even settled in peacefully.

Over the days, since my mom and I had lost our jobs, we started looking online for baby room ideas. Daniil had offered my mom—Kirill and Artur, also— jobs doing some such thing, but she had turned them down politely, saying right now she was where she was needed. And then, Daniil gave her a black charge card of some sort—my mom's eyes had bulged—and he said to buy whatever we needed for the baby and ourselves. Neither one of us had bought anything for ourselves, but we were busy making plans for the babies' room.

Daniel disappeared during part of the day into his study, and even left to go with Roman to the new club that was under construction, so I only saw him in the mornings—I actually got up early to eat breakfast with him—or at lunch, and then the evenings. I knew I would get cabin fever eventually, but right now, I was doing all right. Plus, tonight we were supposed to be going out to dinner, and to my cousin, Mary's performance tonight. Along with art, Mary also sang in a small band. She was an artist all around.

It had taken some talking to Daniil about, but he had eventually agreed once he had the logistics of every location we were supposed to go. I was pretty sure he had the security down pat for our first venture out together. There would be paparazzi everywhere, I was sure, but we couldn't stay holed up in his house forever. So tonight was our first public outing.

I glanced at Daniil, fumbling with my own hair. "Maybe you should have put a shirt on." He hadn't even bothered to comb his hair. We look straight from the sack…which we were.

He met my gaze steadily. "This is my home. My children will just have to deal with it. I've given them long enough."

I sighed. He wasn't the one they would look at knowing I had just had sex with their dad. They were all fine with me…as long as they didn't see anything going toward the sexual. Then they all kind of backed off. "You're starting fires that don't need to be started."

"No," he shook his rumpled head. "I'm putting the fire out for good."

I kept my mouth shut. This was one of those instances over the past few days I didn't quite understand. But I had learned to just sit back and watch. And learn. He hadn't been wrong so far.

We entered the loud dining room where everyone was already seated and eating. Most were ready for the day, but some, like Kirill and Artur were in last night's clothes still, just getting home from work. And Nikki and Beth were with us for this last half of the week, so they sat in their pajamas—like Daniil and me—eating pancakes and dripping syrup down their chins looking adorable. Grigori and Ember were sitting side-by-side, but Grigori hadn't been able to repair the rift between them yet, so they were quiet next to each other.

And everyone's attentions turned toward us as we walked to our normal places. I tried my hardest to ignore my parents and everyone else's stares. It wasn't hard when I spied what was in front of my seat. There, on the table like a golden gift, were...donuts and a box of Fruity Pebbles. I stumbled and stopped to stare. My jaw gaped because I had been dreaming about food lately before waking. Those were the two main stars in my dreams.

I glanced at Daniil, my dropped jaw turning into a huge grin. "How did you know?"

He smiled softly, happily, his gaze darting all over my face, and bent down whispering in my ear, "You talk in your sleep sometimes."

"Seriously?" I gasped, and he nodded, standing straight again, watching me still. I didn't know I did that. Oh, well. It had worked in my favor. "Thank you!" I hadn't wanted to ask for anything special after that whole knife and green bean casserole issue. Especially because there was always a bowl full in front of me at dinner that no one else touched, and—ahem, somehow managed to be empty by the end of dinner. Yeah... well, anyway...

"You're welcome." He brushed me forward, pulling my chair out for me, glancing at everyone—snooping, and then stated, "You can all go back to eating."

I sat quickly, and ignored Eva muttering

something about clothes being needed at the table, and started scarfing down a pink iced donut with pretty sprinkles. I was so zoned into it, and the other three I ate, I didn't notice at first Nikki and Beth staring at my plate, but eventually, I took a breath and glanced up seeing the prettiest innocent...and scared...blue and green eyes staring at me and my plate. They had stopped eating but were sitting there silently just watching me.

I licked a little of the icing off my lips and glanced down at my plate. There were two left. Another pink one, and a sugar and cinnamon one. They looked really good, but I took a deep soothing breath, and stood up, leaning way over and down the table, firmly ignoring how they pushed back in their chair as I reached over, grabbing the tiny plates in front of the ones already filled with their messy pancakes. I proceeded to place one donut on each plate, and then put them in front of the girls.

Big, blue and green eyes darted from the plates to me, and I nodded, sitting back down in my seat. "Go ahead. There yours."

Both girls glanced at Ember, who was watching me with a small smile on her lips. "Go ahead, girls. It appears Elizabeth's morning activities have made her less...cranky."

I took a deep breath trying not to say anything offensive to her, and both girls grabbed their donuts and bit into them with relish, mumbling around mouthfuls, "Thank you."

I smiled and decided to try out something I had learned, saying clearly and distinctly in Russian, "You're welcome." Both girls looked at me funny, and I smiled, grabbing the box of Fruity Pebbles. "That means you're welcome in Russian." I paused with the box of cereal up and glanced at Daniil. "That does mean you're welcome, right?"

Everyone at the table who spoke Russian nodded, but Daniil was grinning like an idiot, and he asked, "You're learning my language?"

I shrugged, filling my bowl up. "I'm trying." I glanced at Ember under my eyelashes, seeing her frown, and stated, "I found a book and tapes to study when I went in search of that mousse I somehow lost on Wednesday."

Ember's scowl turned fierce.

I smiled at her.

I stated in Russian—because I had looked it up specifically, "You're a thief. You take mine and I'll take yours." Plus I had asked Trofim if I was pronouncing everything correctly. He had looked surprised but nodded, repeating what I had said in English.

Ember's scowl didn't falter, but her eyebrows puckered a little.

Daniil choked on his coffee, glancing back and forth between us...pretty much like everyone else at the table who spoke Russian. He coughed, saying, "How long have you had those books and tapes?"

I shrugged again. "A few days." My gaze was on Ember.

"*They really do work*," I heard him whisper to himself quietly, but I didn't think anyone else heard him.

Ember glanced at Grigori, her expression turning even more perplexed by the second, and she broke her silent treatment she had been giving him for the past few days to ask, "What did she just say? Something about kitchens?"

I blinked at her because…damn…those books had looked well read. A few places were even highlighted. Grigori cleared his throat carefully, glancing at me, and said, "She was wondering if you would get her more donuts from the kitchen."

My gaze immediately went to my bowl of cereal. Christ. I hadn't realized Ember wasn't picking up on the language. And that look Grigori had given me clearly stated I needed to back the fuck off.

Ember asked me, sounding flabbergasted, "You want me to get you donuts?"

I bit my lip and picked up my spoon. "You know, never mind. I'm good with this." I took a deep breath and glanced at her. "I want my mousse back, and I'll give you the books and tapes back."

She scowled again, but slowly nodded, appearing not to want to give me what I wanted. "Okay." She paused, her cheeks pinking. "Um…I'd really like them back."

I nodded and took a bite of my cereal, honestly not enjoying making her feel this embarrassed. "All right." I cleared my throat when the table started talking quietly, and I leaned forward on a whim, saying quietly to her, "You know, maybe we could work on learning it together. It's hard. And I'm having some trouble with it."

Ember's eyebrows pinched together, and she stated bluntly, "You're lying."

My own came together. *How the hell did she know that?* But, more to the point, who really cared? "And if I am?"

Grigori and Daniil sat quietly, stuck between us— Daniil at the head and Grigori directly across from me like normal—and watched us while they ate.

"Why are you lying?" she hissed, leaning across the table.

I glared. "Do you want to work together or not?"

Her nostrils flared. "No. Not if my life depended on it."

I whispered harshly—in Russian, "Fuck you."

She blinked.

And I smiled and stated clearly in English, "Your loss."

Sitting back in my chair, I pushed my glasses up and took another bite of my cereal. Daniil leaned over, wiping a bit of milk off my chin, his gaze hooded as he placed his lips to my ear, whispering in a purr, "I'm going to do something very special to you for learning my language. It sounds like sex rolling off your tongue. You have a natural talent for it."

I grinned around a mouthful of Fruity Pebbles and kissed his cheek, smearing milk on him.

He leaned back, chuckling and wiping his cheek off. "Thank you, my sweet."

"You're welcome, my dear," I mumbled, still grinning at him.

"Ugh," Eva muttered. "Isn't it enough that you two came in like that," she waved her hand up and down at us, "but now you're doing the whole mushy crap on top of it."

I quickly wiped my mouth off and asked her honestly, when Daniil's expression went stony, "Would you prefer us arguing? Your dad unhappy?"

Her lips thinned, and she glanced at her dad, but back to me, and slowly shook her head.

I shrugged. "Then let him be happy." That was pretty simple logic to me.

Her lips stayed thinned, but this time she slowly nodded. "You're right. I'm sorry."

"No biggie," I mumbled, holding my box of cereal out to her since I had seen her glancing at it. "Want some?"

She stared at me, and a slow, genuine smile lifted her lips. Not one placed there because her dad said to or because she found out I was pregnant. It was there because she wanted it there. "Yeah. Thanks." She took the box from me and filled her bowl, stating, "For a pregnant crazy, you're not bad."

I chuckled around my food. "Thanks. I think."

"What…Shit…*Wait!*" Grigori practically shouted across the table, snatching our attention. He was grabbing at something Ember had. "I gave you that yesterday! I thought you would open it in private!"

Ember held it at length. It was an envelope. She was giving him a stunned expression. And I could see why.

Grigori was frantic as he fumbled for the envelope.

She moved her arm, barely missing Grigori's swipe. "I didn't have time to open it yesterday."

And then she turned her back on him, ripping the envelope and opening what looked like a blank, red card. And suddenly the lyrics to *Everything* by Lifehouse blared over the silent table. Grigori stilled and closed his eyes. A quick blush stained his cheeks that Ember didn't see because she was staring down at the card with her back still turned to him.

Oh. Oh, my. Grigori had been trying to—again—make up for his blunder with Brent and Cole. And this one was pretty damn mushy. I had heard Artur and Roman talking about his previous attempts. From food to jewelry to flowers. But…this one…

I glanced at Daniil, who was sitting back, trying to keep from smiling. His gaze caught mine, and his eyes were twinkling at me before he got better control and took his coffee, sipping at it and watching Ember stare at the card—stiff—and Grigori in his chair—blushing and stiff. I, on the other hand, leaned over the table and peeked where she held the card, seeing what she saw.

Nikki, who sitting next to her, asked, "When did you have black hair, Mommy?"

I was wondering the same thing because there was a picture taped to the inside of the card. It had her and Grigori, sitting on what appeared to be a white couch, their heads tilted in together and both smiling like idiots for the camera. But Ember's hair was black and curly. Also, there was writing on the card that she appeared to be reading over and over again, but she glanced up, clearing her throat, saying to Nikki, "When you two were much smaller, I had black hair." She ruffled Nikki's hair. "You wouldn't remember, though."

Then, she turned slowly, staring at Grigori's flushed face—at least he had opened his eyes by now. They stared at one another, Grigori not looking away even though he was clearly embarrassed. Ember whispered, "Back at you." And then, she practically threw herself into his arms. He grunted but wrapped her up quickly enough in a tight embrace as Ember mumbled against his neck, "Where did you find that picture?"

Grigori tilted his face toward hers, puffing out a huge breath of air that had her straight, red hair shifting. It was like he inhaled her with his next breath in through his nose before he lowered his forehead to her hair, closing his eyes, his own hair falling down over his face, mumbling deeply, "I had everything brought to New York from Vegas a long time ago. I searched through some boxes and found it." He paused and then whispered so quietly I was pretty sure no one down at the other end of the table could hear him even though they were silent, "I'm sorry, honey. I won't do something that stupid again."

Ember nodded and stayed where she was, and I could have sworn I heard her sniffing him.

Nikki asked, "Can I play the song again?"

"Yeah! It's pretty!" Beth chimed in, sporting syrup and pink frosting around her mouth.

Grigori glanced over at them, shaking his head to get his hair out of his face, and again his cheeks pinked, but he shrugged. "Why not. Everyone's already heard it."

The girls squealed and grabbed the card from Ember's seat where she had dropped it, opening it back up, and the lyrics played again, and Grigori rushed to say, "Don't touch the photo with your sticky fingers."

Both quickly nodded, placing the card down on the table, and started dancing in their seats to the music.

I overlooked Ember and Grigori when she looked up from his neck, because I was pretty sure Grigori shouldn't be kissing her like that in front of the kiddos—hypocritical, maybe, but they were young. Even if he had tilted her away from them and his hair hung down around their faces. I continued eating my cereal, raising my eyebrows at Daniil.

He was positively entertained, his eyes glued on me—and not his oldest making out right next to him—while he sipped his coffee. Especially when he had to not only clear his throat once the song ended but also nudge them with his elbow to get them to separate.

They weren't exactly quiet and had finally caught the attention of Nikki and Beth.

Ember blinked rapidly at Grigori.

Both of their breathing was damn labored.

Beth asked, "Are you two gonna wrestle again?"

"Oh!" Nikki squealed. "I bet Mommy wins again!"

I had to slap a hand over my mouth to keep my food in, and it seemed like everyone at the table had the same issue, including my parents who didn't even try to keep from chuckling at the end of the table.

"Um…Ugh…There…Buh…," Ember muttered incoherently.

Grigori hadn't moved from where he was staring down at her, so Daniil sputtered, "Probably girls. Now why don't you go upstairs—" That was all he got out because…

…a huge older man, probably seventy to eighty years old with black hair with white streaks stormed into the room, pointing a cane he so obviously didn't need, right at Daniil, shouting harshly in Russian. I had never seen the man before and he scared the shit out of me. My heart kicked up more than a few notches and I squeaked as he, and what looked like some nasty-fatal bodyguards, stalked through the room right toward Daniil. I jumped out of my chair as everyone sprang from theirs, and I grabbed the only weapon I could find —a damn butter knife—and turned quickly, stepping between him and Daniil, but somehow managing to get the knife clear up to his throat.

He shut up then. And stopped moving.

My hand was shaking, but I yelled quickly, "Get the fuck out of our home!"

He blinked down at me with brown eyes that somehow seemed familiar, and Daniil's hand was instantly on my mine, grabbing the knife back. I sputtered, stumbling back and bumping into him, asking, "What…what the hell are you doing, Daniil?"

"Shh," Daniil tossed the knife on the table, rubbing my arms quickly, pulling my back flush to him. "Calm down, Beth. This is my papa."

My jaw dropped. Oh, Christ. I managed a squeak, "Your dad?"

"Yes, now, just calm down," he stated quietly, wrapping my trembling form in his arms from behind before he started to speak in Russian with…*shit*…his dad. The man I had just pulled a knife on. Albeit, a butter knife, but a damn knife, nonetheless.

I reached a hand out almost in a trance even as Daniil spoke, and I patted his dad's neck, mumbling quickly, "I'm very sorry about that."

His gaze flicked down to me even though he was obviously furious with his son about something, and ignoring Daniil completely, he bent down, right at eye level with me. And he stared. And then he plucked my glasses off my face and tossed them on the table. I blinked at him in surprise, and Daniil had even shut up, but his dad's attention was on me, his gaze darting around my face like Daniil's tended to do.

His gaze stuck on my curls, and he asked in

heavily accented English, "What is wrong with her hair?"

I bit my lip, and Daniil barked something at him in Russian, but I patted said hair, and stated honestly, "Everything. It's a pain in my behind. It seems to have a mind of its own."

His dad huffed out a breath and continued inspecting me, and he mumbled quietly, "Her eyes are pretty."

"Um…thank you," I stated slowly, realizing he really was inspecting me. Like a damn dog to buy.

His eyebrows puckered on his slightly wrinkly face. "She looks like those dolls…what are they called?" My breath caught as he said, "The ones with the pointy hair and rosy cheeks and button noses?"

Daniil stilled behind me, and I stated dryly, "Kewpie dolls."

He nodded once curtly. "Those are the ones." His eyebrows stayed puckered, and he asked bluntly, "How old are you?"

Daniil barked at him again in Russian, but I stated, "Twenty-eight."

"And do you know how old my son is?"

I nodded. "Forty-nine."

"And you do not have a problem being in bed with someone who's almost fifty?"

Pretty much everyone around the table made some kind of comment at that. Be it a groan, or a 'dedushka, please stop' to a snorted laugh—thank you, Ember.

"No," I told him just as bluntly, not backing down from this pissing contest.

Which he apparently got because he surprised me with his next action. His hand struck out damn fast for an older man, but even though it was fast, it landed gently on my lower stomach. I froze—as did everyone else—as he spread his fingers wide, encompassing all of my lower stomach, and getting close to an area he should definitely not be touching. I jerked back farther against Daniil, but he kept his hand there, and he asked harshly, "Do you have his child in here like the papers say?"

"Papa," Daniil stated sharply, swiping his dad's hand away, now speaking in English, "Leave her alone."

"Does she, Daniil?" Abruptly, his dad stood upright, glaring at his son. "Does she have your child in her womb?"

Daniil moved me behind him carefully, and I grabbed my glasses off the table to see better, peeking around him. This was apparently a touchy subject. One Daniil hadn't even discussed with his dad. He cleared his throat and nodded once curtly. "Yes. We're having triplets."

His dad's face froze. "Three?"

Daniil nodded once.

I watched as his dad's features strained…right before he started shouting in Russian at the top of his lungs at his son. Wow. I skittered backward and traveled so I was farther away from that meltdown, maneuvering behind Grigori, who pushed me farther behind him when I peeked out too far to watch. Grigori was stiff as a board, same as Artur, Roman, and Eva, but all of them, with the exception of Roman, wore shocked expressions.

Daniil and his dad went toe-to-toe hollering back and forth between the other in a damn language I had yet to learn, so all I could do was stand there and watch. And get death glares by his dad when he deigned to turn his furious face away from his son. At one point, his dad picked the knife up off the table I had held, and put it to his throat still spouting away furiously before throwing it back on the table. Thank God, Ember had been smart enough to get the girls out of here when the hollering had first begun.

And now, she was back, oddly, standing next to me like she was going to protect me by the way she hovered and watched everyone. And then, his dad turned a furiously pointed finger at Grigori. Grigori sucked in a breath and listened to whatever his granddad was hollering at him, turning his pointed finger in Ember's direction.

Grigori grabbed Ember's hand but shook his head, stating in English, "No. She's not pregnant."

Daniil growled and stepped in the way of his dad's bickering at his oldest, and interrupted with another ranting shout, slashing his hands through the air and hollering. Ember started to lean over and say something to Grigori, but he shook his head harshly before she could even voice whatever she was going to say. She kept quiet then and left her hand in his, still keeping a watchful eye on everyone new in the room.

About ten minutes after the shouting began, his dad pointed directly where I was peeking between Grigori and Ember, hollering in English, "You will go to Russia and marry my son!"

"Oh, fuck," I muttered quietly. Who the hell would have thought that was what this was about?

"Get over here!" he hollered. "You held a damn knife to my throat and now you cower? Get. Over. Here!" He was damn near breathless he was so furious.

"Papa!" Daniil yelled, getting right in his face, hollering again in Russian.

And, well, that's when I moved. His dad was going to harm himself if he kept yelling like that. I darted out from behind Grigori and Ember and rushed around the table, pushing between them. I wasn't sure they noticed at first, but I raised my hands and grabbed both their chins, yanking them down to look at me.

"Both of you need to take a minute to breathe." Both blinked at me, and I smiled up at them as calmly as I could. "We can talk about this rationally. And calmly."

"No! We can't!" Daniil barked, and I yelped as he whipped me around and hoisting me so high up in his arms, my waist was next to his face. He held me under the rear with one arm, and I gripped handfuls of his hair, trying to keep my breakfast down from being swung about. He pointed with his free hand at his dad as he backed away. "I won't marry again because of pregnancy. I spent a quarter of a century living in Hell, doing as you bid. It won't happen again. You won't ruin this time for me. So stay the fuck out of it, Papa."

"Daniil," his dad shook a fist in the air his son couldn't see because he was striding so quickly out of the room, me bouncing with each pounding step he took. "You will marry her! It is the right thing!"

Daniil spun, and I gripped his hair tighter, burping. He didn't seem to notice as he shouted, "You never knew the right thing for me where matters of the heart were concerned. I'm not sixteen anymore as you so tastelessly put it. I do not follow your damn rules anymore. And if you don't like it, then get the fuck out of my home!"

I could see my parent's blank faces as they watched this interaction. I thanked God, here and now, that I had parents like them. His dad was a real bear. A fucking grizzly bear from the way he stomped toward us after Daniil swiftly marched through dining room door.

Roman and Grigori blocked his path.

Oh, and his dad really didn't like that so much.

But he did take a deep breath and back away.

I hung on as he clomped up the stairs, jostling me the whole way, apparently not noticing my groans as he was so intent on getting me away from his dad. When we entered Daniil's room, he was grumbling harshly in Russian, talking to himself.

Yeah, I didn't interrupt.

Nor did I interrupt when he took us straight to

the bathroom and set me down and start stripping me, and then himself…still muttering things under his breath. I kept quiet as he turned the shower on and picked me back up, this time lower so I could wrap my legs around his waist and my arms around his throat. I stayed silent even when he placed my back against the wall and held me there under the spray with his head on my shoulder, still grumbling to himself.

I merely held him tight and closed my eyes against the spray—thankful that he had remembered to take my glasses off and rested my head against his. Gently, slowly, I started running my fingers through his thick, wet hair, getting the tangles out. Once that was done—his muttering getting quieter, I started massaging his shoulders, working the tight kinks out of his muscles, which was a long process. His mutterings turned into a whisper by this point, and I gently ran my fingers up and down his muscled back as far as I could reach until he stopped altogether.

Then I just held him until he started speaking again, still not moving, but telling me the tale of his life in English. And I listened. And kept quiet. Hearing his pain, feeling it radiating through his body as he started trembling.

He whispered, "When I was sixteen, I met a girl named Olya. She was beautiful and shy and quiet. And I may have even loved her some for a short time." He sucked in a breath and continued, "She became pregnant with my child. Her family was poor while mine was wealthy. And when Papa found out about her pregnancy, he ordered us to marry. It was the way it was done then, the way Papa still thinks. I'm also fairly sure her family got a nice payout from it, too.

"I was young and foolish, partially blinded by her looks to really see the person she was inside, and I didn't argue about the marriage. Neither did she, but later, I found out her family had some say in that, also. After the quick ceremony, she still lived with her parents. They wanted her to finish school and thought it best if she stayed with them to do so.

"She and I saw each other regularly, but after she found out she was pregnant, she wouldn't let me touch her. I still don't know the reasoning behind that. It may have been her parents doing or some fear she had of losing the child, but after our first few couplings, I didn't receive more than a kiss. Even when she was my wife.

"Grigori was born and it was the happiest day of my life. And even though, my wife was many unsavory things, she was a wonderful mother, being as young as we were. She wanted another child, so she allowed me back into her bed. Eva was conceived. I was booted back out of her bed...and the beginning stages of her life. She was quiet and didn't argue, and we didn't fight, but she started pulling back from me.

"This behavior continued even when we finished school and moved in together. Eva and Roman and then Artur were born. That's when she really started pulling back from me. I didn't realize until later I had been somewhat of a stud mare for her. She saw me as giving her healthy, strong children. Once she had all she wanted, she...she went to other's beds for her pleasure."

I sucked in a breath and stroked my fingers through his hair again, his trembling increasing.

He chuckled harshly against my neck. "The sad fucking thing was I didn't even figure it out until years later when I caught her in bed with someone who was supposedly my best friend. You see, she toyed with me, occasionally entering our own bed to keep me from getting suspicious. And I was furious with her. So fucking mad.

"I couldn't stand the sight of her... couldn't stand to be around her.... hearing her voice... smelling her perfume... none of it. I couldn't fucking stand it." His chest expanded against mine as he sucked in a large breath. "And yet...I had taken vows. I would never have done what she did to me. So I hoped to leave her, asking around, finding out my wife was a certified whore, practically sleeping with any of my friends who would have her, risking my wrath."

My heart broke for him. I bit my lip to keep from crying. He didn't want my sympathy. He just needed to tell me this and get it off his chest. This much I knew for certain, the way he spoke so quickly as if he wanted to get it over with as quickly as possible.

"I asked my father to help me leave her, and take the children with me...but he convinced me to stay with her. Told me I needed to learn how to pleasure my wife better and then she wouldn't be fucking everyone else." He laughed harshly. "As if I would ever touch her again after that…but, Papa made one good point during his rant. It was wrong to take the children away from their mother. As I said, she was many things, but she truly loved her children and they adored her.

"So I stayed with her. Through all her infidelities. Sharing a bed, but not really. There might as well have been an ocean between us. We never touched each other again—and I don't think she really wanted to touch me—and I never touched another woman. She may not have been loyal to me, but I would not break my vow to her. I have always kept my word."

He sighed. "She kept her affairs quiet per my request…but one day, years later, it wasn't me who walked in on her again. It was Roman." I stilled, understanding now why Roman's actions had been different from his brothers and sister since almost the beginning. "Roman…oh, God…he…" Daniil shook his head on my shoulder. "After that, I put my foot down. Olya agreed to stop, not arguing with me after what happened. And that's when my brother struck."

I was confused. "Why would your brother attack you then?"

"Because he was one my wife fucked on a regular basis."

Oh. My. God.

I held him tighter as he continued. "I truly think that's why he did what he did. He was in love with her. Everyone knew it. He didn't exactly hide his desire for her. He never had." He pressed me harder against the wall. "He killed her first. Classic spurned lover. And then, he came after me. Left me for dead. And then he…" His body shook so damn hard I was afraid he was going to fall. "He went after Grigori. What he did to him…"

His breath caught, and my mind raced trying to put it all together. The only thing that made sense was what that insane man had said about putting a person Daniil loved in the prostitution rings.

Oh, dear God. I might puke.

Daniil's voice boomed through the bathroom as he continued, "But Grigori got free and killed them all. Fucking all of them. Including my godforsaken brother."

I stilled, hearing the truth and venom in his voice…not to mention the pride. I didn't know what to think of that. It wasn't something I could reason through right now because…well, I believe in an eye-for-and-eye. If Grigori had gone through any of what that sick fuck said in Daniil's study, I was sure I could have condoned his actions.

"I lost my children when Grigori took them and ran away with them, protecting them from anyone who would come after him. You see, he was given false information about my welfare, and he didn't believe it safe to be at home. So he disappeared. With Eva, Roman, and Artur. For seven years. And I couldn't find them."

He hissed, "And this all happened over a fucking girl. My wife. Her whorish ways. My choices. The fact that I didn't stand up to Papa and his dictates. It all could have been stopped if I had just taken the kids and left her. But instead, I messed up. And my children were hurt because of it."

Gripping me tight, he stated, "That won't fucking happen again. If I ever choose to marry for a second time, it will be because I love the woman with all my heart and she loves me just as fiercely. I won't let anyone tell me what to do again. That's why I'm a harder boss than my father ever was even when he controlled everything. It was the only way I could be taken seriously with the wife I had. I do it now, I stay in power, because my children and I have too many enemies. If I were to give it all up, everyone I love would be taken out just for spite. Or, for some, revenge."

I sucked in a breath. "None of what happened to you or your kids is your fault. You didn't make your wife sleep around. You didn't tell your brother to try to kill and hurt everyone. They did that. Together, they did that. Not you."

Daniil stayed quiet.

I ran my fingers through his hair again. "But, you already know this. You're too smart not to. And yet, you still take the blame."

"I should have stopped her earlier. Taken the children."

"And who's to say your brother wouldn't have done what he did, anyway? He sounds like he was a very jealous man."

Daniil nodded against my shoulder. "He was always jealous of me."

I nodded with him. "You know better than to blame yourself. You're the smartest man I know. Do the math. It would have happened sometime." I stroked his hair. "You know it wasn't your fault. You sacrificed. Gave your kids what they needed growing up. And then, your brother took. You're not to blame." I sucked in a breath. "And, although your dad didn't do everything right, he wasn't to blame, either." That was the truth.

Daniil was silent for so long, I started to worry, leaning my head back to look at him. He gazed at me through the water and snorted...and then chuckled. I watched him warily, wondering if he was going to have another mini-breakdown. He asked through his soft laughing, "For someone so young and inexperienced, you give excellent advice."

I closed my eyes and rested my head back. "I just figure, no matter how old the parent, as long as they're of well mind and body, they're all a pain in the ass. But they mean well, even if they are a little misconstrued."

Daniil's body really started shaking as he laughed. "God, you're adorable. Smart. Beautiful. And fucking perfect." He kissed me lightly, saying against my lips, "How did I get so damn lucky to find you?"

I shrugged again, feeling better that I had helped him. "I am the preacher's daughter. God gave me to my best match."

Daniil grinned against my lips. "You really believe that."

Not a question, but I kissed him softly. "I do."

That night, after a harrowing day of avoiding Daniil's dad and Daniil talking with his kids—since most of them had thought their parents relationship perfect— and giving Ember her books and tapes back in exchange for my mousse, the entire lot of us were dressed pretty damn snazzy. We were going out to dinner. I wore a little black dress—that was a little snug around my belly since I had been eating so much—with the pearls Daniil gifted me. Daniil was in all black, matching me with wool pants, dress shoes, and a V-neck cashmere sweater. I was proud to say, my curls had been manageable, so my hair only looked halfway inhuman. I wore contacts, not because Daniil thought I looked better with them, but because I thought so with this outfit.

My parents were even along for the ride after a little persuasion from Daniil, pretty much guilting them into keeping his dad busy since he insisted on joining them. His kids were abnormally quiet. Ember, Chloe, and Kirill were trying to get them out of their funk they'd been in all day—they seriously didn't even go into work today after hearing the news about their mom…and the fact that they were upset with Roman because he hadn't told them…but he was even quieter than normal staring out a window silently.

It was Daniil's dad who was making the most racket, arguing—good Lord—with my dad about something in the Bible. It appeared his father knew his Bible verses and was going toe-to-toe with my dad trying to prove a point about whether or not it was all right to—ahem—take care of someone if they stole from you. Yeah, interesting conversation there.

Daniil actually looked a little amused, but he turned his attention from them, asking me loudly, "Beth, is Katie going to be at the restaurant?"

I blinked because we had already discussed this. In fact, he had specifically asked me to invite her to dinner with us. And…then…I noticed Artur's eyes zoning in and out, darting to us. I turned my attention to the side window, so he could see my expression, and said in a normal voice, "Yes. She'll be there." I paused and had a moment of worry, but shrugged it off. "She's bringing a friend of ours, Merc Farris, with her."

Daniil stiffened. "A friend of both of yours?"

"Mmm-hmm," I stated casually. Fuck, I hadn't even thought of that. Merc was handsome as hell. All golden skinned and dark hair and eyes. Not to mention a body to die for. "Just a really good friend of ours." But he wasn't what any of them was going to expect.

My dad's gaze darted to me, and then Daniil, stating, "They're really just friends. You don't need to kill him or anything. He's a good kid."

I tried not to gawk at my dad as he grinned at Daniil and then went back to arguing with Daniil's dad.

"What does he look like?" Ember asked, hitting the nail on the head.

I tried not to scowl at her. "Handsome."

"Is he single?" Eva asked, finally breaking her mold and paying attention.

I nodded slowly. "But he's not…er…" I sighed. "He wouldn't be interested in someone like you. Or me. Or anyone in this car for example."

Eva's eyebrows came together as the limo came to a stop in front of the restaurant. "And why not? Is he practicing to be a monk or something?"

I shook my head quickly, seeing the photographers all around the limo and a bodyguard getting ready to open our door. "No. But you'll see soon enough." I didn't have time to explain.

Daniil was looking at me with raised eyebrows, but bent over and kissed me gently right before the door opened. Then he was pulling me out of the car swiftly and tucking me in close to his side as flashes went off. Someone had tattled about our reservation. We were having Italian, which I was grateful since I was starving, and I was sure the dive we would be going to after this would only have greasy unhealthy—yummy—food, so I was going to fill up here first so I wouldn't be tempted to do so later on.

And again, amazingly, it was Micah's voice I heard over everyone else's who was shouting our name as we slowly made our way to the front door. He stuck his hand through the bodyguards when they were busy with others, and yelled, "Is it a boy or a girl, Elizabeth?"

And…I knew I shouldn't, but I snatched his tape recorder from him before his arm was thrown back and tossed it into my clutch. *Dick*.

Daniil's shoulders started shaking, and he stared down at me as the shouting changed from us to Grigori and Ember since they must have exited the limo behind us and then Eva and Artur. It was kind of nice to have some of the attention pulled off us, and Daniil leaned down, asking, "Was that really necessary. I know what you did to the poor man in the elevator."

I huffed. "I'm going to have a talk with Trofim."

He chuckled outright as we reached the front doors, and he hurried me inside to the main foyer where the photographers weren't allowed. We waited for the rest of our group, and once everyone was inside safely, the hostess took us back to a private room where Katie, Merc, and Mary would be waiting. We got more than a few stares from actual—in my opinion—celebrities who were eating in the restaurant as we followed along, Daniil's hand resting possessively on the small of my back.

I tried to ignore it, but it was a little unusual. Especially when one of the starlets of a new season hit, stopped us and gave me her phone number, asking if we could have lunch sometime. I was a little taken aback, and Daniil seemed to sense this, smiling charmingly at the girl right around my age, telling her I would call her. Yeah, thanks, Daniil. I had heard a few things about her, and she wasn't someone I really wanted to hang with. Hell, the way she smiled coyly at Daniil pretty much confirmed that, and I politely—er, yeah—stepped in front of him, handing back her card and tugged him along, earning another chuckle from him.

"That wasn't very nice," he murmured against my hair as we skirted another table of gawkers.

"Screw nice," I muttered, glancing back over my shoulder at Ms. Coy.

Daniil laughed at that, and everyone who hadn't been watching us before did so at the sound of his deep, infectious, booming laugh.

"Great. Now everyone's staring," I muttered, elbowing him, not helping the situation since it only made him laugh harder. "Quit that!"

He gurgled and tried to stop, staring down at me. "Were you jealous?"

"No." I sighed. "Yes."

Daniil pulled me tighter, stating calmly, cutting off his laughter, "I'm loyal. Don't ever think I'm not."

I rested my head against his shoulder, nodding. Yeah, I knew that. Especially, after what he told me today. But it still didn't mean I liked seeing women flirt with him. "Just try to keep the charm level down with the women who want to fuck you, all right?"

Daniil snickered again. "All right." The hostess opened a door to our private area, and Daniil stopped, seeing who was inside. It was Mary, Zane—surprise, Katie, and Merc. His eyes were glued to Merc, who stood, smiling at me, and Daniil growled, "Just a friend?"

Yep, Merc looked as hot as he normally did. "Yep. Just a friend." I glanced at Daniil and smiled at his furious face, making sure my curls covered my mouth. "But be careful because he can lip read."

Then I patted his chest and went and hugged my longtime friend. Merc picked me up and twirled me around, setting me down gently and placing a hand on my stomach, mouthing, "Pregnant?"

I nodded.

Merc was off and running, signing to me as he grinned away, flashing that beautiful smile of his. I knew Daniil had crept up behind me and stood there a moment in probably shock since he went stiff when Merc started signing.

I immediately started interpreting for Daniil, who was smart enough to know when someone is deaf, you look at the person signing, not the person interpreting. I said quickly, "Congratulations! How far along are you?"

I sighed back and said aloud, "Almost six weeks."

Merc stared at my stomach and his eyebrows pinched together. He signed, "Only six weeks?"

I said that last bit aloud for Daniil, but my jaw gaped.

I glanced down at my only slightly tight dress and shoved his shoulder. I signed and said aloud, "That's just rude! And what is it with everyone touching my stomach?" The damn servants in the house had even been doing it and then crooning to my stomach while they fondled my *flat* belly.

He touched my stomach again and smiled softly, and then signed, "It's a baby! All babies are precious."

I grinned. Signed and said, "Not one baby. I'm having triplets."

I was pretty sure his eyes couldn't get any bigger, and he glanced over my shoulder to Daniil and mouthed, "*Damn!*"

Daniil chuckled and moved next to me…and freaking started signing and speaking, "I'm Daniil. Father of the triplets. It's nice to meet you, Merc."

Merc glanced at me, winking. Approval was given.

They were off, signing, meeting, and greeting each other—along with the rest of his family—while Grigori, Daniil, Katie, or I interpreted for him.

When we sat down, I asked Daniil quietly, "Is there anything you don't know?"

He grinned at me, pointing at his menu. "Wine. I don't know squat about wine."

Well, neither did I—so that didn't help much.

His laugh increased and he leaned over kissing my forehead.

Eva had strategically placed herself next to Merc, and she kept glancing at him. Apparently, the deaf thing wasn't an issue for her, but her being a 'hearing' was a turn off for Merc. He didn't date anyone unless they were deaf. His parents had divorced because his mother was deaf and his father was hearing. The relationship had too many complications and he led by their lead. So he was politely ignoring her. The gentle brush off.

Daniil was watching this as he watched everything, so I took the opportunity to ask Mary, who sat beside me, "What's up with you and Zane?"

Mary grinned at me, throwing her arm around Zane's shoulders, stating, "We're having a torrid love affair. Sex all day and night."

"Mary…" my mom said disapprovingly, "language."

Zane chuckled outright, glancing at Mary where she clung to him.

Mary's eyes opened innocently behind her glances, "No. Really. He can go *all night long.*"

My mom rolled her eyes and averted her attention from them.

I stated dryly, "Now that you're done scandalizing my mom, what's up?"

Mary blinked at me. "What? I was telling the truth." She reached under the table and cupped his cock under the table, making Zane jump a little. "Seriously." She glanced up at Zane, puckering her lips. "Isn't that right, baby?"

Zane stared down into her eyes and said softly and deeply, "Oh, yeah. And tonight I'm gonna go *all night long* again." And…he bent his head down where she rested her head on his shoulder…and flat out kissed her.

I jerked back. Staring. Jaw dropped. Well, because there was some definite tongue action going on there.

Yep. Pretty much the whole table shut up and gawked right along with me.

The kiss didn't last all that long, but Mary and Zane parted, staring at each other, and Mary said in a deeply drawn out voice, "You're gonna have to do better than that tonight, stud." She took her hands off his junk and patted his leg.

And swear to God, they both started laughing.

Mary waved her hands at everyone. "We're just kidding. You guys can shut your mouths."

Zane snorted hard, pointing at Ember, whose jaw was only slowly closing. "Fuck, Ember. You gonna be all right?"

She stuck her tongue out at him. "You suck." Then she jerked her head at my dad. "There's a preacher at the table."

My dad stated dryly, "As if that stopped you this morning from playing tonsil hockey with Grigori."

Ember's cheeks pinked and she shut her mouth, managing to turn her glare on me somehow.

I ignored her, and pointed back and forth between Mary and Zane, asking my cousin, "So you two aren't…"

Mary bit into some bread before passing Zane a roll he started to butter. "No. Just hanging out at lunch." Her head cocked. "And we went to see a movie. Just friends, though."

She shrugged. Zane shrugged.

They were serious.

I guess there could be weirder things.

"You went to see…a movie?" Ember asked quietly, baffled by this.

"I know it's mundane stuff, Ember. But I do enjoy seeing a show that's not rated G every once in a while," Zane stated, just as dryly as my dad had to her.

Ember's mouth shut, and she said softly, "Well, I guess it's a good thing I moved out so the girls are only there half the time." She busied herself putting her napkin in her lap and grabbing a roll.

It dawned on me. Ember missed everyone in her old house.

Mary glanced at me, apparently noticing something was up…and she missed the roll that went flying through the air from Grigori, chucked right at Zane's head. Pegged him straight in the nose, too, when he was getting ready to take a bite. I stifled a laugh, watching as Zane managed to catch it on its rebound, and he turned scowling eyes on Grigori, who was in turn glaring at him and jerking his head at Ember, who was oblivious as she cut into her roll.

Mary caught the gist, though, and she elbowed Zane.

Zane's expression cleared, and I swear his eyes went soft seeing Ember's clear discomfort. He cleared his throat and asked, "Ember, maybe you and Grigori could come out with Mary and me to a movie or something sometime." He popped the bread into his mouth, saying around it when her—Jesus, slightly wet eyes glanced at him. "If it's not too mundane for you two."

Ember pounced, nodding quickly. "Yeah. We'd like that," she glanced at Grigori, looking hopeful, "Right?"

Grigori nodded slowly, staring at her. "Yeah. We'd like that."

Ember smiled great big, her shoulders actually lowered as if a weight had been lifted, and I was pretty sure her chin trembled for the barest heartbeat…and no one missed it before she looked back at Zane even though she played it off well. "Thank you. It'll be fun." She shrugged, playing it cool now. "Even if it is mundane."

Zane nodded, playing it just as cool, but watching her just as closely as Grigori. "Maybe we'll even go bowling." His eyes went wide. "Or maybe to an arcade. I haven't been to one of those in years."

"Dude, I'd so kick your ass in Golden Tee," Mary stated factually, popping her hand on the other and pushing forward with her palm like she was teeing off.

"What's Golden Tee?" Grigori, Ember, and Zane all said together.

I laughed outright, nudging Mary when her eyes went wide. "The beauty of hanging out with the older crowd."

She blinked and shrugged. "It'll make it easier to kick their asses."

I leaned over into Daniil and watched everyone enjoying their time together, and after a bit, I said to Daniil softly, "This is nice."

"What is, my sweet?" Daniil asked just as softly, sipping on vodka.

"This. My family. Your family. Just…it's peaceful. I never would have imagined that."

Daniil kissed my head and wrapped his arm around me.

It *was* peaceful, just like I had said.

Watching and listening to Mary sing was like a whole new insight into her. It was always a shock to the system when I saw her sing. It was beautiful…but eerily twisted. She sang songs you would normally pick during a break-up with a boyfriend. She sat in the middle of the stage in a chair with her band members behind her, a pianist, a guitarist, and a cello. The light shone down on just her with the other shaded in blue spotlights. And she wore black. All black—which was nothing like her normal crazy attire.

I sipped on my water and glanced around at our surroundings, wondering what Daniil thought of it. It wasn't exactly his four-star restaurant or even Crimson City or Obsidian City worthy. It was just a small dive, in a not so great part of town, catering to your normal average Joe New Yorker, which really wasn't saying much since half of them had purple or pink hair, and the other half wore flannel shirt and baseball caps. It really was a mix of the middle class.

The place had four walls and a roof, halfway clean tables that were only slightly sticky, and a decent sized dance floor that looked good and scuffed—well used and well loved by the way it still managed to shine through the couples slow dancing to Mary's music.

"Bored?" I asked Daniil softly. This was the type of place I would hang out with my family. Busy, but not too rowdy...and the drinks were inexpensive if I weren't pregnant.

He shook his head, staring at Mary. "No. Not at all." He glanced at me, his eyebrows puckering. "Do you want to leave? Are you getting tired?" He glanced at his watch.

I placed my hand over it and shook my head. "No. I don't want to leave. That was just my polite way of making sure you were all right with these surroundings."

Daniil glanced at me, and around at everyone in the club, and slowly, he turned his head back to me, a slow smile lifting his lips. "Be careful or I'll think you're calling me a snob."

I snorted. "You are." I pointed at his perfect feet. "You have your feet manicured, for God's sake."

Daniil's grin increased. "I'll have you know that this is the exact type of place I loved to go to in Moscow."

I blinked. "Seriously?" He looked like he was telling the truth.

He nodded, moving his head in closer to mine. "Yes. Seriously. I may know that an establishment like this doesn't make that much of a profit, so I would never open one myself, but do you want to know why I came to places like this when no one was around?"

I shook my head, mystified.

He kissed my lips softly. "Because it was easier to do this without anyone grumbling."

"To do what?"

He reached over, placing a hand on Roman's shoulder. "You'll see." He leaned over saying something against Roman's ear…who groaned but nodded. And they both stood up and started making their way across the dance floor, and stood at the edge of the tiny platform, waiting…*Jesus, what?*…they walked onto the stage when Mary stopped singing, and she glanced at them smiling.

Daniil bent down and asked her something, and her eyes widened, but she nodded. And then Daniil went and tapped the guy on the shoulder at the piano, the same as Roman was doing to the guy on the cello. And my jaw dropped when Daniil and Roman took their places.

"Oh, my God."

Grigori chuckled next to me. "Papa made all of us study an instrument growing up, but only Roman took after him and is able to play damn near any instrument."

I shook my head as I watched Daniil and Roman get comfortable. "Is there anything he doesn't know?"

Grigori was silent and then stated, "Wine. He doesn't understand the complexities of it."

I choked and nodded. Great. I had thought Daniil was halfway joking. Apparently not.

And then Daniil started playing the piano, and I realized it was *My Immortal* by Evanescence. Seriously one of the most beautiful songs ever written. I didn't even realize I had stood when Mary started to sing. I was now moving across the dance floor as Roman started playing the cello, letting my feet take me where I wanted to go—up the stairs to the stage.

I stood behind Daniil with my arms wrapped around his shoulders with my cheek pressed to his, watching his fingers fly over the keyboard to this heart-wrenching song. His cheek moved against mine as he smiled, and he turned and kissed my forehead even as he continued to play. I held him, but lightly, moving with his body wherever he needed to move on the board, slightly swaying with him. And my God, was he talented.

I had seen the music room in their house, full of all kinds of instruments, but never saw anyone using it, with the workout room and gym getting much more attention. But now I knew why he had it. He may be good at many things…but playing music…he seriously had a God-given talent. Roman did too. To go right along with Mary's soul-tearing voice.

As the song ended, and as his fingers played the last chord, I reached down, pulling them back slowly and kissed them gently. "That was beautiful."

He turned on the bench, peering up at me with honest, content eyes. "Thank you."

I licked my lips. "Can I see you play something else?"

He nodded slowly, a special twinkle in his eye. "I think I know the perfect song." Daniil took my hand quickly, pulling me over to Mary. Daniil asked her something quietly.

She laughed, nodding. "Last one. Otherwise, my guys will get jealous."

Daniil nodded and politely thanked her, snapping his finger at Roman and pointing to the piano. Roman even wore that look in his eye. The happy contented look. He nodded without argument moving from the cello to the piano, saying something to Mary as he passed her. She nodded, her grin huge, laughing.

Musicians just seem to have this bond.

Odd to me, but no less fact.

Daniil politely borrowed the guitar from the slightly disgruntled gentleman while Mary pushed her chair back, standing, and stating, "This is dedicated to…" She paused, walking over and putting the mic at Daniil's mouth as he sat down, tugging me on his lap. Daniil cleared his throat, his cheeks—sweet Jesus, how seriously adorable—pinking, but he stated clearly, "To Beth."

I bit my lip, not glancing out at the crowd, who cheered politely, this crowd not really knowing who we were. Daniil kissed my cheek quickly, situating me so he could play the guitar around me. It really wasn't a problem since his arms were so long and I was so small. I pushed his hair behind one ear so I could see his face without it hanging in the way, and then placed my arm over his shoulder and the other on my lap so they wouldn't get in the way.

Mary chuckled into the mic and she grinned out at the audience. "This isn't my normal slow stuff, so get ready to dance!"

She glanced at Daniil and Roman, and threw her hands in the air and started clapping them, saying loudly, "One, Two, Three, Four!"

Daniil started playing, and I stilled, realizing he had picked a completely cute and corny, but appropriate song. I smiled, and God, it actually hurt my cheeks I knew it was so big. They began playing *I'm A Believer* by Smash Mouth. Mary sang and Roman actually made up his own damn part, sounding perfect with the song, since I wasn't sure if there was an actual piano in the piece, and Daniil's eyes darted to mine, his cheeks turning pink again.

I kissed his burning cheek. "It's perfect."

He kept playing, but turned his head and flat out kissed me right there in front of everyone. I managed to not bump him as the dancing crowd cheered with good-natured jeers, and I laughed against his mouth. God, he was something else. He leaned back, his eyes on mine as he sang right along with Mary, who I was thrilled to say was better than he was…but, sadly, not by much since he was actually pretty damn good at that, too.

OBSIDIAN MASK

I couldn't decide between watching his hands or his eyes and mouth while he played and sang. I improvised, glancing back and forth between the two. Mary stuck the mic in front of his mouth, and he grinned at me, singing into it as his cheeks went even pinker.

Mary smirked at me, and pulled the mic back and started bopping to the music again as she sang...yeah... and I couldn't look away from Daniil after that. He was seriously laying it all out there. No holds barred, push back all of my defenses, take no prisoners, full frontal assault. And my God, it was working like a charm. Because, at that moment, as the great head of the Russian Mafia sang to me in front of everyone...well, fuck...I didn't know anyone who wouldn't have fallen in love with him...

I fell over the edge I had been so carefully holding myself back from—and it must have shown because Daniil's eyes crinkled as he grinned so damn happily. I placed my palms on his cheeks as he stopped playing, the song ending. I leaned down, whispering, "Yeah. I'm in love with you. Now stop grinning and kiss me."

He chuckled, but placed the guitar on the ground and engulfed me in his arms, and stroked my lips with adoration. Deeply. Happily. With tongue right in front of everyone. The fireworks went off right along with the cheering crowd.

Mary was the one to interrupt us, nudging my

shoulder, stating calmly at my ear, "Your parents are in the crowd, you know."

I leaned back, placing a finger on Daniil's lips when he followed almost drunkenly…which I got completely, except for Mary had said the magic words —my parents. That brings anyone down. "Thanks, Mary."

"No prob." She patted Daniil arm. "Welcome to the family, by the way. You and Roman are welcome to play anytime while I'm singing…just not now since my guys are seriously getting pissed."

Daniil blinked, his eyes slowly moving away from my mouth to Mary's face. "Huh?"

Mary's shoulders shook, and she glanced at me. "He's not so scary right now."

I chuckled, slapping his shoulder. "Come on. We need to move."

He cleared his throat and stood…with me still in his arms. "I want to dance." He glanced at Mary, his eyebrows snapping together, ordering sternly, "Sing something slow if you can handle that."

Mary snorted. "Funny man."

His lips twitched, but his gaze was back on mine as he moved, carrying me off the stage and down the stairs to the dance floor. His gaze was heated and possessive, and no one got in his way. As soon as my feet hit the floor, his lips were on mine, and I barely noticed when the music began and we started moving. It was one hell of a kiss.

The night wasn't even ruined when some jackass

from the audience, apparently the one person knowing who we were, videoed the entire stage performance and even some of our dancing, and then plastered it all over YouTube before we even got home. And honestly, other than the fact that there were actually reporters waiting outside Daniil's home for a week straight didn't even bother me. I took the opportunity given, and asked Artur to help me take some still shots of the performance online, and print them out. He was even kind enough to buy a frame for me since I stayed around the house instead of going out into the mess.

I handed over my gift to Daniil late one night when he was up working late. He stared at the photo of me wrapped around him from behind on the piano. The one of us smiling at each other as I sat on his lap while he played the guitar. And, the final one in the triangle of us kissing on the dance floor.

He got up wordlessly and moved into the bedroom, placing the frame smack on the top of his bare dresser. And then he wordlessly threw me on the bed and followed down right on top of me, murmuring how much he loved me. Yeah, in darkness, there's always a light somewhere. You just have to find it. And we did. Very much so.

CHAPTER 13

Nothing could beat that night when I realized I was in love with Daniil. The very same day he had professed his love for me. Every day thereafter had been damn near perfect as my mom and I worked throughout the day trying to decide what to do with the babies' room and fixing that picture for Daniil…but there was a day that beat it.

Daniil held my hand but leaned over me again as I lay on the doctor's table while Dr. Wisser moved that weird contraption around on my stomach again and we all stared avidly at the screen. I was officially seven weeks pregnant, and Dr. Wisser said we might hear the babies' heartbeats today. At least, he said it was a possibility.

"Anything?" Daniil asked gruffly, clearing his throat hard.

"Just a second. I'm measuring first." He moved the contraption around, thumping on the keyboard. "You'll be pleased to know you can keep having intercourse until I say otherwise. The babies are positioned fine for it. But, keep it gentle like I said before."

Daniil's hand was actually a little clammy, and he had mine in a death grip, but I didn't mind. I was probably cutting off his circulation, too. Daniil nodded at the doctor's comment, sparing me a glance to grin with a come-to-papa expression. I snorted and went back to watching the screen.

The doctor flipped a switch of some sort, and suddenly, there were red and blue colors on the top of the screen, and he studied them, and hit another button, stating, "Here's Baby One."

Whooshoo-whooshoo-whooshoo.

I closed my eyes, hearing the most beautiful sound in the world.

Daniil asked suddenly, "That's the heartbeat?" I glanced up at him, smiling, but he looked worried when the doctor nodded. "It's too fast, isn't it?"

"No. That's normal." He paused hitting another button on the screen. "It's actually a very nice strong heartbeat for only seven weeks."

Daniil breath rushed past his lips, and he abruptly leaned down, kissing my neck. "Hear that?"

"Mmm-hmm," I murmured, closing my eyes again.

"It's beautiful," he whispered, breathing heavily. I was afraid he was going to pass out again, so I didn't tell him his chin was killing my collarbone. The man was seriously tough as shit but put him in a doctor's room, talking about his babies, and he was a nervous wreck. I'd never told anyone he passed out before, and I didn't want a repeat performance and have to call one of his kids to tell them we were going to the hospital. It had freaked me out too badly the last time.

"Okay, let's see if we can find baby—" the doctor stopped moving the little contraption and chuckled. "Well, that was easy. Here's Baby Two."

And we heard another little fast-paced w*hooshoo-whooshoo-whooshoo.*

Still against my neck, Daniil breathed in heavily and out slowly.

I just lay there and started petting his hair, silently listening to my baby's heart and feeling the sweetest glow and warmth start in my chest. And I recognized the feeling like it was inert—just a simple part of me.

Love. Unconditional love for the little ones inside me. But, also a possessive feeling, which I thought odd until Daniil murmured quietly, "Those are our babies. Yours and mine, my sweet." His gaze was so forcefully, I understood he was feeling it, too. It wasn't just a connection of two people joining together…but…a parental connection. It was new and surprising, but I welcomed it nonetheless and let it in without a fight. We were going to be parents for these babies together. Two people working and loving as one unit for these babies.

"Okay, on to Baby Three," Dr. Wisser murmured, moving the contraption up and slightly tilted. He moved it around for forever. Daniil and I both knew the odds. Having three was more than risky.

Daniil's frame stiffened as one minute passed.

Two minutes.

Dr. Wisser said, "Here's Baby Three."

The sweet *whoohshoo-whooshoo-whooshoo* filled the air.

I choked, tears streaming down my cheeks. Happy, so damn deliriously happy, tears ran freely.

Daniil, on the other hand, took the news and sound of our third child's heartbeat differently. He jumped away from me, straight into the air, shouting, "Fuck yes! Those are my damn babies!"

I jumped. The doctor jumped. Hell, I even heard a thump outside in the hallway at his victorious holler.

He pumped his fists in the air, grinning like a fool, whooping pretty damn loudly. Again.

The doctor paused with his hands over me, just staring, but I laughed after my initial startle and stated, "Hush, Daniil, or the bodyguards are going to come in."

He blinked and his chest rose. And all that went through my mind was, *oh, shit*. And suddenly, he was yanking the door open, shouting at the guards to get in the room and hear his "fucking babies' heartbeats!" Christ. I seriously had to open my mouth.

He surveyed me, quickly pulling the blanket up over any exposed areas so the doctor's hand was under the blanket…yeah…right before nine damn bodyguards squeezed into the small room. That wasn't awkward or anything.

But Daniil motioned for Dr. Wisser—who was shocked silly—to continue, and then started talking a mile a minute in Russian to the guards whom I barely saw him ever speak with. Dr. Wisser blinked—kind of like me—and turned back to the screen and found a heartbeat. And a round of cheers went up in the room pretty much scaring both the doctor and me. There were just too much scary ugly and guns in the room for me, and I glanced at Daniil.

On a positive note, it only took one look from me before he shooed them back out into the hallway.

After shutting the door, Daniil started dialing on his phone and stated, "Grigori, are you around your brothers and sister?" Daniil nodded. "Put your cell on speaker phone." He waited, and said, "Sorry to interrupt your work, children, but you've got to hear this." He put his own phone on speaker phone and I could hear them talking quietly to each other, asking one another what the hell was going on. Daniil jerked the phone to the doc. "Put this by the speaker and do it again."

Dr. Wisser's eyes looked like they were going to cross, but he sucked it up, placing the phone by the speaker, and Daniil barked loudly, "Be quiet and listen." And amazingly, I heard all his kids shut up. The doc's eyebrows rose, but he placed the contraption back on my belly, and within thirty seconds, the *whooshoo-whooshoo-whooshoo* was heard again.

"What the hell's that?" I heard Eva state.

"The baby's heartbeat," Grigori mumbled, "Shut up!"

"What's going on in here?" I heard Ember's voice from far away, and then a very un-Ember-like squeal. "Is that the baby's heartbeat?"

"Hush!" Artur piped up. And then…silence.

Daniil pointed at my belly, commanding, "Find all of them again. I want them to hear." I bit my lip as the doctor took a deep breath in and started moving the *thing*—I was going to call it the *thing* from now on—around my belly again, and Daniil stated loudly and clearly into the silence, "That was brother number one. Dr. Wisser will find brother number two in a moment."

My jaw gaped. "We have no damn clue if it's a boy or a girl!"

Daniil leaned over me, stating solemnly, "We know their healthy and alive. And that was most definitely a boy."

"What are you? A damn Native American medicine man?" I griped. "You. Have. No. Clue." I glanced at the doctor, stating sternly, "And we don't want to know. When the babies come out, then we'll know."

"Oh! Oh! We want to know as soon as we can," Daniil countered quickly, pulling out his wallet.

"Put your fucking wallet away," I griped harshly. Shit, I couldn't compete with that.

"Be still," he told me quietly and then asked the

doctor bluntly, starting to count his wad-o-cash, "How much to know for certain they're all boys?"

"Daniil!" I stated, *hmm*, a little shrilly. "I don't want to know!"

He glared at me and started counting again.

Pissed, I grabbed the cash from his wallet and tossed it across the room. In retrospect, that probably would have been a great time to implore my mother's neat trick. But, I do remember her stating it didn't work all the time. And this was one of those times for me.

The doctor's hands paused over me as we all watched the green bills flutter throughout the room, silhouetted against the sunshine coming in through the window. Daniil growled, "I cannot believe you just threw forty thousand dollars across the fucking room. Do you know how long that will take to pick up?"

The doctor's jaw gaped at the still falling money, but I sputtered, "What type of person carries around that much cash?"

"The kind that can afford to," Daniil griped, moving across the room to pick up his money. But, he stopped and pointed at the floor, stating bluntly to Dr. Wisser, "The monies all yours if you pick it up and promise to tell me their sexes as soon as possible."

I heard a whistle over the line that I had forgotten about and heard Anna state, "Man, she can't compete with that." I hadn't even realized she was there. Honestly, the whole fucking work was probably listening in. And sadly, I couldn't agree with her more... except...

"The couch, Daniil. Long…cold…lonely fucking nights on your lumpy couch," I stated slowly, meaning it fully. If he was going to use his arsenal to its fullest and ignore my wishes, then I needed to fight fire with fire. And this was the only fire I could think of on such short notice.

Daniil stilled, glancing at me. "You wouldn't."

"Just like you wouldn't offer my doctor forty G's to give you information about babies in *my* stomach after I *already* said *no!*"

The doctor was still staring at the money on the ground, and I tried to ignore that and keep my game face on.

Daniil smirked, his grin knowing. "I could seduce you like that," he snapped his fingers, "and you know it."

I smirked right back. "Not if I sleep in my parents' room."

His mouth thinned, and he looked positively pained, asking the doctor, "How many more months until she has the babies?"

I pointed at him. "You know what, *my dear*, you're sleeping on the damn couch tonight for even considering it!"

He rolled his shoulders, and glared at me, but bent down and started picking up his money, muttering in Russian under his breath. I snapped my fingers at the doctor, stating, "That's his way of giving me what I want. Now hurry up, so *everyone* on the line can get back to work."

"That was impressive," Zane stated clearly over the line. "You're learning."

I snorted as the doc finally yanked his gaze away from the money, a little downhearted and went back to work. "I hope I've learned something by now."

Daniil muttered loudly in Russian, and most of the men on the other end of the line laughed. I decided to let that one pass. He was ticked and venting.

"Baby Two," Dr. Wisser stated…and there was silence as everyone listened to the heartbeat. Daniil even stopped moving to look up at me from his squat on the floor. Though he was still upset, his lips lifted in the tiniest of smiles and dark eyes softening instantly. My heart melted, irritation gone that fast, remembering —knowing—that our babies were alive and well, growing as they should be.

Daniil dropped the money in his hand to the floor and stood, walking on all those bills to come to my side. He took my hand and placed my fingers to his lips, and kept them there, staring down at me with so much love in his eyes, I knew he wouldn't be sleeping on the couch tonight. By the time Dr. Wisser found our third child's heartbeat again, Daniil and I both heard a few sniffles over the line.

I heard Anna state softly, "I want one."

"Then let's go make one," Carl stated instantly, his voice a hell of a lot rougher than it normally was, and we all heard another squeal that had to have been Anna.

Daniil chuckled, his gaze on Dr. Wisser, "You may have a referral soon."

That night after dinner, I headed in the direction of the music room where Daniil had promised he would play the piano for me. He had been too busy earlier and I had been asleep by the time he was free. Peace and happy, the last thing I wanted to see was Ember staring silently out of a window in the front room. It was late, and most everyone had gone to bed by now.

I sighed and stopped. Dammit!

She seemed so fucking lost standing there with her arms wrapped around herself, the darkness of the room like a blanket around her.

Over the past week, I had noticed little things that I had missed before. Her confused looks that she tried to mask when everyone around her started speaking Russian. Her careful expressions when Brent or Cole was around because of Nikki and Beth. The way she chattered non-stop with Zane about the occupants of the mansion across the street. Where she was staring now as if she could see it. It wasn't possible even in the daytime. And then, there were her furtive glances at my stomach.

Pretty much, Ember was a mess.

I felt for her. I had begun to like the redheaded

bitch…because I knew she had a soft heart that she obviously tried so hard to shelter and protect. I took a deep breath and walked into the dark room, standing by her side and staring out the window. I ignored how she stiffened.

She didn't move away, though.

I asked, "Wanna talk? I'm actually a pretty good listener." *Duh.* I was a reporter…er…would be again once the babies were born and my boss let me have my job back. Like Ember, I didn't have a lot of friends here to talk with where the information wouldn't make its way back to the men we were hiding our issues from. Sometimes I might need to speak with someone. And fuck, if she wasn't the only one around here to do it with.

Ember snorted. "Duh."

It was best not to let her know how entwined that was to my thoughts. So…I waited.

And waited a little more.

My feet tingled with numbness.

She murmured, "This is going to sound awful… but…do you know how badly Brent and Cole's return screwed everything up?"

Blunt. "No. I don't." Because, really I didn't.

Ember nodded. "Honestly, there are so many fucking things…" She made a frustrated sound in her throat. "I don't even know where to begin."

When she didn't say anything else, I shrugged. "Start at the beginning."

And...fuck me...if she didn't start at the beginning.

The *very* beginning.

Like from when she was a little girl first meeting Brent. Her relationship with Brent and a woman named Ally. Abuse from her father. Her ability to read people from said abuse. When she ran from her home to New York, hoping and praying Brent still wanted her. How she met Cole. Then when she fell in love with Brent and Cole. Her run from them.

Meeting Daniil's kids, which she called the *Donnallys*. Her instant friendship with Grigori. The twin's birth. The time she spent with them—three years —on the outskirts of Vegas. Then, Brent and Cole finding her and bringing her back to New York.

And then...Jesus...her and Zane's kidnapping.

What had happened to her...

Brent and Cole rescuing her. Her recovery back to sanity. Brent and Cole leaving for a mission. And dying.

Her heart with them.

How she and Grigori had first started seeing one another privately. The friendship. The bond. Their connection.

Someone from Brent, Cole, Zane, and Stash's past resurfaced...which I found out I had been used as a pawn by this individual with four stories I had written. And the 'numbness'—like my feet—that she had experienced when Grigori left her to protect his brothers and sister. But he had come back...and everything had been all right again, the numbness gone.

She told me of the harm my articles had caused revealing Grigori. I didn't say anything as she spoke factually, almost as if she didn't want to hurt my feelings but sensed it needed to be said. It was a part of her life's story. Grigori being hurt in Russia when he left to take care of some *business*. And the utter fear that had consumed her when no one told her anything.

"I thought I had lost him," her voice cracked. "I..." She sucked in a sharp breath. "But he was fine. He came home to New York. Everything was wonderful. Life was peaceful. A real first for me. Ever." She cleared her throat. "Then Brent and Cole came back. From the *dead*. Just walked into the house as if their initials were still on the door instead of Stash, Zane, and mine. And everything went to shit," a rapid head shake, "and I didn't know what to do. So, I did the only logical thing I could. I began seeing them again, the fathers of my children. The men I had loved with all of my heart, ending my time with Grigori the day they came back." Her voice cracked. "Shit. It was all fucking shit."

I stayed silent—more than a little shocked that she was sharing all this, but understanding it nonetheless—while she continued, her words getting more heated as she went. "It's stupid because I see them almost every day at work, but I miss all of my friends over there. All that's there is some grass and concrete—and maybe a gate or two—between this house and that one, but it feels like so much more. Like the big fucking divide. Them vs. Us. When, before Cole and Brent came back, we all got along great, but instead, we can't even have fucking dinner together without fighting and people leaving. Instead of that being my haven, it's now off limits to me."

She shook her head. "I love Grigori. I do. But before, when we all lived together in Vegas, none of them ever spoke Russian. And now, they do it all the time. I can't understand them. At all. It's like watching one of those foreign films without the subtitles. If I weren't as good at reading people as I am, then I probably wouldn't understand a damn thing." She shook her head, glancing at me. "I have no clue how you do it." Her expression turned a little sheepish. "I may need some help, so I wouldn't mind sharing my books with you if you would help me. I would ask Grigori, but I don't want him..." She trailed off, but I got it. She wasn't the weak sort, and she didn't want him to think she was.

I nodded. "Yeah. I'd actually like that."

Her gaze went a little freaky...and God, I realized that she was reading me...and she nodded once. "Thank you." She sucked in a big breath and glanced back out the window. "And then, there was the time I spent dating Brent and Cole, do you know what I realized?" I shook my head, and she stated, "That Cole, the man I thought I had loved—which I had loved, seriously didn't know a damn thing about me. He may have at one point, but he doesn't get me now. Whether it was the fact he's changed or I have, we just didn't work together anymore." She rested her hands on the windowpane, staring blindly out the window. "But Brent...Brent was...is...a different story. He and I have so much history together. And, to tell you the fucking truth of the matter, it still bothers me knowing he's out there fucking someone else. Liar or not. He and I have the same roots."

She swung an arm behind her, gesturing blindly at the room. "This. All of this pompous shit, I don't give a fuck about. Yes, I grew up with money, but to tell you the truth, I've always hated it." She pointed across the way. "And Brent still does. Like me. He may own a mansion, but he did so because he and his best friends wanted to live together and a pretentious house was needed for their business." She sucked in a breath. "But Grigori...he's rich...very, filthy fucking rich. Not as rich as Daniil." She glanced at me. "Daniil's damn near a billionaire, by the way." I blinked, my head swimming at that little bomb, but she kept on. "And he didn't tell me he was rich until recently. And the fact that he likes it. Likes having the best of everything." She shook her head, stating, "His fucking showerhead and faucets are gold! Real fucking solid gold! Who the hell needs that?"

She growled a little, her hands fisting on the windowpane. "I should have known. I should have read it. But I didn't. Somehow, that fucking little detail skipped me." She growled again. "And now, I want a fucking baby."

I didn't think she should be doing anything so

soon because she was so damn confused, and there was a part in her rant that had surprised me, so I asked, clarifying, "You picked Grigori, right?"

She nodded.

"So why does it bother you that Brent's having sex with someone else?"

Her lips pursed, but she stated quietly, "Feelings and emotions just don't disappear when you've known someone as long as he and I have known each other."

Uh-oh. "Do you still love him?"

She nodded slowly. "I probably always will."

My own lips pursed. "Does Grigori know this?"

Ember snorted, stating heatedly, "Let me tell you something about Grigori. He loved someone when he was young and lost him. The great love of his life died right in front of him with a horrible, painful death. And Grigori's heart went with him." She sounded fucking pissed. "So, to answer your question, Grigori's not stupid. He knows that it will take some time for me to be over Brent completely. But, I knew who I wanted to be with. In the time Brent and Cole were 'dead,' I picked Grigori. And when they came back, despite all that I would have to give up and have to put up with now, I still picked Grigori."

She thumped the glass, her voice getting a little shrill the faster she spoke, words just spewing out of her. "But who the fuck would he pick if his first love came back from the dead?" She shook her head rapidly. "I sure as fuck don't think it would be me." Her voice cracked, stating, "Jesus, I want to have his fucking baby, and anytime I even think about talking to him about it, it's like he knows and he," her hand motioned all over her face, "breaks out in a sweat and he looks like he's going to puke. He doesn't want to have kids with me. Do you," she stopped mid-rant, sucking in a breath and glancing at me, "do you think it's because it's me...and not *him*? Or just that he doesn't want kids? I know I'm a little fucking weird, but I'm not that bad. He's just as screwed up as I am."

You've got that right. I was kind of—okay, I was—wishing I hadn't come in here at all since she was asking me this. I cleared my throat delicately but did what I did best, "Ember, I'd like to have a 'come to Jesus talk' with you. It'll be blunt and to the point because, honestly, that's how I do this best. Think you can handle it? The truth of the matter?"

Her eyes darted from each of my eyes, and her mouth thinned, but she nodded.

"Good," I pointed at her, "and just hear me out without screaming or hitting me." Her eyebrows puckered, but she nodded, so I stated bluntly, "Like I said, I'm a good listener. That makes me a great reporter. And I have the inside scoop that you seem to be missing."

I paused, then stated slowly, "You've had a shit ton happen in your life. It's been constant hell without much peace. But, almost all of your adult life, you know what I heard as your constant? Your rock?" I paused for a moment. "Grigori. That's who. I get that you still love Brent, and I understand why you don't love Cole anymore, since in reality...in the real world...you only knew him for a very short period of time. And I understand you miss everyone over there..." I pointed at the window in the direction of her old house, "... because they were the loving, caring family you never had. Give it time for everyone to adjust and you'll have them again.

"But," I cleared my throat, just putting it out there, "Grigori loves you and you love him. And sometimes, in a relationship, it takes more time for one of the partners to adjust to wanting a baby. That's a huge leap. And you and Grigori are just finally coming out together publicly. I would give him some time. Talk to him, yes, let him know what you want, but then give him time and space to figure out what he really wants. And, to answer your question, no, I don't think he's holding back from having children because you're not his first love. First loves are a dime a dozen. He wants you. He's made that abundantly clear. So, just give him some time...and yourself time for your life to calm down some. Both of you will feel better about whatever decision you make together." I had decided at the last moment to keep my mouth shut about both of them being 'in love' with one another, remembering what Daniil and my mom had said about sometimes it's best that people figure things out on their own. She would have probably started screaming at me, anyway, if I had mentioned it.

Her cupid's bow mouth was thinned so badly, I could barely see it, and I added softly, "And you can't say that Grigori wouldn't pick you over his first love if he were to come waltzing in those doors miraculously from the dead. You picked him over your first loves. Who's to say he wouldn't pick you, too? You're only creating issues in your head that don't need to be there. He wants you now. In this lifetime, Grigori has picked you. Understand?"

Ember stared silently for almost five minutes straight.

I stayed silent. Rotated my ankles a few times.

Her breath caught. "Thank you, Elizabeth. I—" She glanced down at her feet. "I needed someone to talk with."

I smiled. "We all do sometimes. Someone that won't judge and look at it from an outsider's viewpoint. I'm here anytime you need me."

She grinned softly back at me. "You're a lot like your father even though you may not think so."

I chuckled. She wasn't the first to tell me that. I started walking backward, pointing at her. "Now I'm going to listen to the love of my life play music. In the meantime, get your shit together, and figure out a way to let Grigori know—without a doubt—what you want. Got it?"

Her arms crossed. "I was only confused."

"And now you see the light." I gestured grandly, then pointed at myself, grinning, "I. AM. THE. PREACHER'S. DAUGHTER. I know these things." I pulled an Ember, laughing like Count Dracula.

She snorted. "Not funny."

I laughed. "Oh, that was better than when you did it."

I turned on my heel when she opened her mouth again and exited quickly, enjoying getting the last word in. I almost ran smack into Daniil where he rested against the wall a few feet from the doorway. Eavesdropping.

His eyebrows rose and his lips quirked, enjoying seeing me startled.

I scowled. That only made his lips turn into a sexy smirk.

Dammit.

He whispered, "First, I'd like to say that was beautifully put." His head cocked. "And second, can you imagine what a kewpie doll would look like if they made one trying to glare?" My lips pinched because I got a visual of that and was pretty ridiculous. His grin increased, and he stepped forward, backing me up and down the hallway as he continued moving, and I tried to keep some distance between us. "It's adorable as you can imagine. When you do that it makes me want to make you do it more."

Predictably, my scowl increased.

He licked his lips still coming at me. "Yes. Like that. But now, you're lips are all puckered up, and all I want to do now is taste them." He didn't hesitate. He lunged at me.

I squeaked and turned tail, running.

This was...us.

I ran as hard as I could. Straight toward the music

room, hearing him chuckling behind, taking chase. Oh, he could catch me easily, but that would take away all the fun. So, as I sprinted, he jogged lightly behind me.

And then I turned the corner…*Oomph!*…grunting, I grabbed whatever I had just run into. Warm, hard arms enveloped me as my face rebounded off the hard chest I'd slammed into. Daniil cursed behind me, running into my back, pressing me even harder into…I tilted my head up…and blinked a little in confusion, thinking I had hit my head too hard and was seeing double. Until I noticed the pink streaks.

Ah. Grigori. I'd just run into a half-naked Grigori.

"Papa, what are you doing to poor Elizabeth?" Grigori asked dryly, a little smirk on his face.

Daniil wrapped his arm around me under my breasts and stepped back from Grigori, taking me with him, Grigori's arms dropping even as his shoulders started to shake. I glanced up and saw why. Daniil's cheeks were beginning to pink. He cleared his throat and stated sternly, in a practiced fatherly voice, "That's none of your business."

Grigori grinned outright and started to play with his tongue ring, making it peek out between his teeth. "Sure." He snickered, shaking his head, but asked, "Have you seen Ember? She hasn't come to bed yet."

Daniil was edging us around Grigori, apparently set on finishing our game out because he slapped me on the ass, pushing me forward a few paces, stating, "Front room last time I saw her." Then he glanced at me, his hair blocking his face from Grigori and mouthed, "I'll give you a head start."

I laughed, ignored Grigori's amused look, and raced off.

"You're going to give me nightmares, Papa," Grigori said from behind me, teasing his dad.

I ran flat out and heard Daniil laugh, and it sounded cocky as hell. "If this gives you nightmares, then you better stay the hell out of the music room tonight." Then, he shouted, "That's all the head start you're getting, my sweet!"

And even though he was silent, I knew he had taken chase as I darted down another hallway because I heard Grigori groan loudly and dramatically, "Too much info, Papa."

"More like fair warning!" Daniil shouted, and he sounded damn close.

I squealed and made my feet move even faster.

And he caught me, anyway. Right when I entered the music room, slamming the door shut behind us. Yeah…well…I was pretty much naked in less than five seconds and had a death's angel with shark eyes ready to devour me. But, instead of doing it instantly—as I was more than game for, he placed me on top of the piano and played me that song he'd promised me… before me made the keys bang in passion. Oh, yeah. I really liked the music room.

CHAPTER 14

Munching on my Fruity Pebbles the next morning, I stared at Ember's pancakes. On top of them, as she played with her food in fidgety movements, was a glob of whip cream and strawberries. I had already eaten about five strawberries so that wasn't what held my attention. It was that fluffy, sugar white goodness sitting on top of the crisp brown pancake.

I swallowed my mouthful and scanned the table, spying the can of whip cream in front of Chloe. It held my attention as I took another mouthful and chewed. I dropped my spoon, standing and chewing, walking down the table. Again, my feet just moved me as I leaned between her and Kirill, bumping them only slightly and snatching it. Holding it protectively to my chest, I made my way back to my chair and swallowed down my mouthful.

After sitting back down, I spooned up a big bite of cereal and then squirted a portion about the same size as my spoonful on top of the cereal in my spoon, then put the can back to my chest and licked my lips, staring at the heaven on a spoon I held.

I groaned, opened my mouth extra wide, and took it in. And groaned again, closing my eyes. *Heaven.*

"Jesus. I didn't know her mouth could open that wide," Eva muttered next to me, bringing me out of my food coma, and my eyes snapped open as I chewed.

"I did," Daniil whispered quietly, and I almost choked on my cereal, but luckily, only Grigori and I heard him because Grigori choked on his coffee and Eva didn't puke right there on the spot.

Daniil was eyeing my mouth with a gaze that needed to stay in the bedroom. We hadn't done anything this morning because I had been sicker than a dog, puking my guts up, but it appeared Daniil was contemplating ways to fix our lack of fun this morning. Like right now.

I cleared my throat and mumbled around a mouthful of heaven, "Daniil..." My parents didn't need to see that.

Daniil's lips quirked and his gaze met mine. I could see the humor there even through his heated brown eyes. He thought I was being 'adorable' again. How nice for him.

I started to scowl but stopped when Roman stated, "Papa, I think we need to have the piano tuned. I couldn't sleep last night and went down to play, but it's all off. It sounds horrible."

I blinked slowly.

Daniil's lips quivered.

Oops. Looks like we messed it up a bit.

Ember stated in choppy words, "That's probably because someone was banging on it. I walked past there last night, and it sounded like a two-year-old was taking a sledgehammer to the keys."

Grigori made an odd gurgling noise.

Daniil quickly glanced away from me, breaking the hold he'd suddenly had on my eyes. I quickly stuffed another bite in my mouth without whip cream this time. Daniil picked up his coffee cup, stating, "I'll have to talk with the servants. Sounds like someone was trying to learn to play. I'll call someone to have it tuned."

He sipped his coffee, looking calm and collected, and Grigori made that odd gurgling sound again. I glanced at him and willed him to keep it together. He looked like he was about to bust up, staring at his dad with wide eyes.

Roman held his hands up about twenty inches apart, stating, "About this much of it is jacked. I don't know if it can be fixed, but having it tuned will tell."

I was the one that stared wide-eyed now.

My ass wasn't that big...

Was it?

I glanced down at my lap, studying my hips.

Christ. I didn't think it was, but... I calmly and coolly—hopefully—set the whipped cream far, *far* away from me. And the rest of the box of cereal. Pure sugar. I didn't need all that.

Grigori lost it then, he was laughing so hard.

Daniil's hand landed on my knee under the table

as everyone stared at Grigori like he was deranged. Daniil leaned over the table putting the box of cereal and whip cream back in front of me, giving me a look that clearly stated he didn't think my ass was that huge. But still, I really didn't need to eat all that. Er…my gaze got caught on the whip cream. Maybe just a little more wouldn't hurt.

Grigori bumped Ember in his hilarity, breaking my train of thought…because she was the only one not staring…and she jumped. Literally squeaked, too. Oh, Jesus. She was freaked.

Grigori's laughter cut off abruptly at her reaction, his face snapping to her. "Did I hurt you?"

"No," Ember squeaked again. "I'm good."

Grigori's eyebrows slammed together, and he growled, "What's wrong? You've been jumpy since you *finally* came to bed last night. I don't even think you slept when you did."

Ember stuffed her mouth full of pancake, mumbling almost incoherently around her food, "Nothing's wrong."

He lifted his hand and took hold of her chin, turning her face to his. She continued to chew calmly, but her hands were shaking next to her plate and she wouldn't meet his gaze. She stared firmly at his nose— and it flared.

Any conversation that had begun to slowly take place around the table, everyone multitasking with their eavesdropping, abruptly cut off when Grigori shook her chin—head—a little, hissing, "What the fuck is wrong? You're acting scared shitless."

Ember's fingers clenched on her silverware, which did stop the shaking, but pretty much confirmed his statement.

As the seconds passed in silence, little sweat beads broke out of his face. "Are you going back to *them*?"

Ember stopped chewing.

Come on Ember. Be smart. See what was in front of you, dammit. The man loves you completely. And I knew why she was scared, too. She was planning on having that talk with him about making babies. That would freak anyone out.

For the first time ever, there was hope in her expression as she swallowed heavily. Her regard relocated from his nose to all over his perspiring, but carefully neutral, face. "No. And don't ask me that again, please. You should know by now I'm not going back to them." She glanced up into his eyes, but she quickly dropped them when his eyebrows pulled together. "And you're right. I didn't sleep well. It's making me jumpy."

Silently, Grigori sucked in a breath and he nodded, running his hand over her jaw to her throat, and back behind her neck. He leaned down and kissed her lips gently, whispering, "I won't ask again."

Grigori was missing something. Something big that he couldn't see from his elevated height. Ember's eyes were hooded as she kissed him back just as gently, but I could see. Ember was getting ready to take the plunge by the set determination slowly filling her eyes. She cleared her throat, placing her silverware down, and turned in her chair to look directly at Grigori.

He blinked, probably because he saw Ember's face was serious. Like somebody died, serious.

She took his hand and cleared her throat. "Grigori. You mean the world to me." The table went silent. "I won't ever leave you. No matter your answer to what I have to say."

She licked her lips in a nervous action, but she threw her shoulders back and kept going. "You're the strongest, most incredible man I've ever known. That I ever want to know. You're all I could ever want in a man." She smiled softly, and it was timid and sweet, making my heart melt for her.

Her cheeks pinked a little, and she hesitated, her breath hitching. She glanced down at where she held his hand, but she gradually looked back up at him. Her voice was strong when she stated, "I want to have a baby with you. And even though this is a typical girl comment, I'm going to use it because it's true. I'm not getting any younger, and I would love for us to be parents together."

Grigori's face was so damn blank, I wanted to hit him.

She was trying. Really, really trying. Being honest. And she looked so damn hopeful...and sweet.

Ember shut her mouth and waited to hear what he had to say. She was trembling. Yep, she was pretty damn scared. I probably would be too if I had just made that speech in front of everyone.

Grigori breathed evenly for at least thirty seconds, staring into her eyes, and said gradually, in a deep voice, "I'm honored, honey, but I need a little time to figure out if that's what I want, too. Children are such a huge step and so much responsibility. And, me being a father, I—" he licked his bottom lip, his expression breaking from his careful control, appearing decidedly nervous, "I'm not positive I'm ready for that." He leaned down, touching the tip of his nose to hers. "But, if I did decide I want children, you would be who I'd choose to have them with. I love you, honey."

Ember's cheeks stayed pink, and she nodded. "Okay. I understand you need time." She cleared her throat, fidgeting with his fingers. "Just…um…think about it, will you?"

Grigori's lips twitched slightly until it turned into a soft smile. "I have been. Ever since Papa told us they were having triplets, and I realized you wanted more." He kissed her lips. "Just a little time. That's all I'm asking for to figure this out."

Ember's mouth opened a little in shock, fully realizing Grigori had already been thinking about it. But danced away and a small, secretive smile played on her lips as she murmured softly, "Remember, it could be fun making those babies."

He grinned full out.

I glanced away because there was just too much of Daniil in that carnal look he gave Ember. It weirded me out a little. I wasn't sure I would ever get used to it. And it looked like, out of the corner of my eye, he leaned down, whispering something against her ear that I didn't catch. Which I was happy for since Ember giggled.

Daniil's dad broke in, stating gruffly, "I think I need to stay here a bit longer, Daniil."

I heard Daniil growl a little under his breath, but he said calmly, "You are welcome here as long as you like, Papa." He leaned on the table. "As long as you understand the rules of my home."

Daniil told me that he had spoken to his dad. He hadn't gone into detail about what the discussion was about, but it hadn't taken a rocket scientist to figure it out. Daniil had laid down the law. And his dad didn't take it well, but he was behaving for the most part.

At least, in front of Daniil.

Now, when Daniil *wasn't* around, I still had to practically hide from the man since he was like a fucking bloodhound, tracking me down...to talk. And talk. And talk. Never-ending discussions about how the proper way things were done. Very—extremely—old and strict ways that he grew up with. They weren't chats I wanted to have...or, from the way he was eyeing Ember...would put on anyone else.

So, I asked her, "Ember, would you like to help me after work today at my dad's church. Katie, Mary, and I are putting together a party for a couple celebrating their sixtieth wedding anniversary there this evening. We could use the extra hands." I knew she got off around noon.

Ember glanced at me in surprise, and I jerked my head slightly at Daniil's dad. She took the hint fast enough and nodded slowly. "Sure. I think I can do that."

"I don't have work. I could help, too," Artur stated.

Yeah. Mention Katie, and of course, he could. He paid attention to everything I said about her.

"I could help, too," Roman stated, wiping his mouth off. "Artur and I are both tall. We can help with things you women can't reach since you're all so damn short."

I glanced at Daniil, and he was staring at his coffee cup, but his lips were twitching. Had I missed something?

"Okay," I stated sluggishly. "Thank you. If you guys could be there around one o'clock, it would be great."

Artur and Roman nodded.

And then, we all got a surprise.

Zane and Stash entered the dining room. I hadn't even heard anyone enter the house. But...they weren't dressed in their usual suits they wore for work. They were dressed in all black cargos and long sleeved t-shirts. And were armed.

The conversation cut off abruptly, and Zane stated quietly, "Ember. Grigori. Can we talk to you in private for a moment?"

Ember and Grigori went motionless, but Ember's eyes went all freaky. She shook her head, slowly standing up. "No. *No, no, no, no, no.*"

Stash's face was calm as he walked toward her. I was so damn confused that I looked to Daniil for a little assistance. *What the hell was happening?* He shook his head slightly, indicating for me to stay quiet.

Stash took Ember's arm and gently herded her out of the room while Zane stayed mute. Ember broke Stash's hold, and her hands started fluttering about... and God...tears flooded down her cheeks, freaking me the hell out.

Had someone died?

"No! You can't be leaving! No!" Ember practically yelled. "It's been so long! They can't do this now!"

"It's our last one," Stash stated quietly, trying to calm her, but it wasn't working. She was so overwrought.

Grigori took three long strides and picked her up like an infant, holding her tightly against his chest. She clung to him and balled against his neck while Zane and Stash watched her worriedly. Grigori ordered gruffly, "Papa's study. Now."

And they left to go to Daniil's study.

I waited a beat and glanced down the table at my parents, who were leaning and ogling the four of them as they walked away since they had the better view. When they relaxed—nothing more to see, I turned to Daniil and asked, "What the hell was that about?"

He cleared his throat, and opened his mouth, but shut it. He looked like he wanted to tell me something, but he didn't. Very fucking frustrating.

Luckily, Eva didn't have any such compunction and stated dryly, "You know how Brent and Cole went off to do that damn hero shit, and supposedly died?"

I nodded.

She jerked her head toward the doorway. "Zane and Stash are going to go do it, too. Same affiliation. Same stakes. Different mission. Different time." Her lips thinned. "Ember's scared they'll end up the same way, but really dead." She didn't look too happy about it, either.

"Oh," I murmured, placing a hand over hers since she was really upset. It would be like having a family member I loved going off to war and doing the most dangerous missions. I had gotten that much from Cole and Brent's heroic story, even though they hadn't said much. And really, their silence had said it all. "Well, maybe some time at my dad's church will help today." Dad smiled at me, but Eva gave me an odd look. I shrugged, adding, "It always helped me when I needed it. There's solace in something so pure and loving. It's… um…peaceful."

Daniil's dad nodded. "I've always found peace in the church."

I tried not to look as shocked as I was. I imagined the only time he ever entered a church to ask forgiveness for the most recent person he had killed. But, I guess it was never too late to repent. For anyone.

He added, "Especially, weddings. They're so lovely and peaceful. Don't you agree, Daniil?" Maybe he didn't repent so much, just making more troubles that pushed people to seek solace in church. My dad should be grateful.

The morning was shot to hell. No one was in a good mood after Zane and Stash left the house, pretty much getting hugs from everyone. Including my parents. My mom, who supposedly hated violence, told them, "Kill the bastards and make sure you come home safe and sound." Yeah, she was surprising me all around. Apparently, she had a patriot streak in her I had never noticed before.

Ember was mute. She wasn't crying anymore, but her face was all puffy and splotched and her bloodshot eyes were cold. Very, very cold. I didn't even look into her eyes once after seeing her expression, but I did talk her into going to the church early. Roman and Artur came along for the ride after I hurried to get ready. No fun times for Daniil and I, sadly. But he seemed to understand.

"Try to have some fun." Daniil kissed my lips none-to-gently right in front of his kids, apparently done with hiding our affection for each other. "I'll see you later tonight."

SCARLETT DAWN

I nodded, a little breathless, and wobbled out to our limo, Ember, Artur, Roman, and bodyguards tagging along. Ruslan sat in the limo with us along with my normal three guards, while the other three rode in a non-descriptive sedan behind us. Like normal.

On the way there, in the silence that fell on us, I called Katie and Mary to let them know we were going early. Katie agreed to meet us there, but Mary sounded a little distracted—painting, apparently—and said she would be there as soon as she could. This time, I watched for a reaction from Roman when I told them the news. There was the briefest flick of interest when I mentioned Mary.

Oh, boy. I had no idea how I had missed that one, but it all came back to me. I realized that even though I had missed it, Daniil hadn't. He had paired them against each other in basketball. Always had them sitting close to one another during any meals, but never too close. Asking him to go on stage and play the instruments. The way he had been watching Mary. Huh. Damn, I had been clueless on that one.

The paparazzi were out in full force again. They were lined up outside the gates—like normal—and reporters and photographers pretty much gave chase right off the bat. I fumbled around for a bit, trying to stay in my seat from all the swerving. Now, Artur and Roman, on the other hand, looked like they just wanted to shoot out their tires. And Ember just stared out the window as if she just wanted to shoot the person driving.

Artur grunted when I started to fall for the third time, and moved to sit next to me, placing his arm around my waist.

It shocked me, and I stared at him wide-eyed. "What are you doing?"

He held me tighter against him. "Keeping you safe."

"Oh," I stated stupidly, and the limo jerked again...but this time, I didn't fly around as Artur braced his legs, taking the impact and held me in place. Ah. Got it. He was my seatbelt. "Thank you."

And the car jerked the other way...dislodging both of us. We landed sideways on the seat with him on top of me, and I grunted under him. "Maybe I should have said no thanks." Christ, he was as heavy as his dad was.

Roman muttered something in Russian to Artur, who was helping me up, and then moved sitting on the other side of me. He didn't say anything. He wasn't a man of many words, but he placed his long leg in front of both of mine, reminding me of a safety bar in an amusement park ride...and I was safe, never falling at any of the jerks and swerves, both of them keeping me firmly in place.

"Where do you want the gold streamers to go?" Roman

asked, standing on the top of a ladder, done taping it to the ceiling fan in the cafeteria.

I twirled my finger, stating, "Twist it lightly, and tape it periodically to the ceiling so it drapes every so often all the way to that corner." I pointed to the opposite corner. God, I loved having tall people around to help. Even with the ladder, none of us girls would have been able to pull that off. And I seriously doubted any of the bodyguards, who were standing still and mute around the room, would have helped.

Roman looked like he was having as much fun as a tough guy could in a situation like this, but his gaze flicked behind me…and his eyes quickly hooded…but not before heat flared in their depths.

"I'm here!" Mary stated from behind me.

The door shut after her.

Trying to keep the smirk off my face, I turned and watched to see if my young cousin had any of the same attraction that Roman seemed to have for her. I hugged her in greeting…and wished I hadn't since she had on a pair of old overalls that still had wet paint on them to go along with all of the old paint marks. She sure as hell wasn't wearing her sexiest attire, although her tank under the overalls did reveal a bit of flesh from her small chest. None of us in the family was blessed with large breasts.

I rubbed at her cheek, under her pink glasses, where a streak of green paint was. But she gave me a look. I stopped and moved out of her way, letting her see the room. Or, more or less, who was in the room.

She stretched her back, glancing around and nodding approvingly at the amount of work we had done.

And then, her gaze halted. Roman had gotten off the ladder and moved it to the next place he would have to tape the streamer to the ceiling, but he was squatting down and picking up another roll of tape. His dark shirt—the man never wore color like most of this group—had raised a little on his back, and between it and his low dark jeans, there was a sliver of his lean, tan hips showing. That and his ass was exactly where Mary's gaze landed. Pretty much staying there until he stood back up and started climbing the ladder.

She cleared her throat and looked away, her gaze resuming its progress around the room.

I seriously had no idea how I had missed that. Like I was blind or something. Now I hadn't missed Artur's interaction with Katie. In fact, he seemed to have come out of his shell, and was flirting wholeheartedly with her today, seeming to take Katie by surprise—pleasantly by surprise based on the looks she was giving him as they chatted by the table they were setting up for gifts.

"I think I'll go help Ember," Mary murmured, rubbing at her cheek over the green mark, quickly going to the far corner where Ember was tying off gold and silver balloons. The exact opposite corner where Roman was headed. I squashed a laugh quickly, telling her I'd help Roman. Mary may be out there sometimes, but she was still young. And by the looks of it, a little shy. She wasn't always the tough woman. Sometimes, she was just a girl learning her way.

An hour later, the streamers were up and Roman had brought in drinks for all of us from the kitchen. I sipped on my water, listening to Ember tell Mary that Zane and Stash left this morning on a 'job' and they would be back in a month or so. But, it appeared Mary already knew this, taking a soda from Roman quietly and then telling Ember that Zane had already called her this morning.

Artur and Katie were taking a break, and Artur changed the subject quickly when Ember's face started to pucker up a little. Mary didn't miss it, and quickly went along, seeing Ember's obvious worry, telling Ember that even though Zane wasn't around, they could still go out and do 'mundane' things. That got a smile out of Ember, and we all talked quietly, enjoying our break.

Katie was hungry, so she went to raid the fridge, but when she came back, she held a pink package in her hands along with a turkey sandwich. She brought it over to me and chewing around her food, she said, "This was by the door when I came back. It's got your name on it."

I took it and stared at the nametag. It said, "To Elizabeth. From The Church."

Apparently, Dad's congregation was already starting to hand off baby gifts since this one had little orange giraffes all over the pink paper. I grinned like an idiot. "I bet it's those cute little onesies." I laughed shaking my head and tearing off the paper. "Hope they put three in here, though."

Katie chuckled, staring over my shoulder as everyone watched me open my first baby gift. Handing the paper to Katie, I opened the box, also handing her the lid, which she quickly stuffed under her arm, still munching on her sandwich. Gently, I lifted the pink tissue paper aside.

And stared.

It wasn't what I had thought. At all.

With a shaky hand, I lifted the note off what appeared to be some kind of black mask, and read aloud, "Put this on now, if you don't want any harm to come to your babies."

Katie was already unmoving behind me, but the group sitting on the ground relaxing in front of me froze.

All hell broke loose.

Ember was instantly on her phone, calling Grigori. Artur and Roman jumped up to their feet to see what I held. Two men I didn't know ran into the room, slamming the doors behind them, guns drawn and shouting to Ruslan.

Artur and Roman's faces turned damn frightening when they saw these two men, but they didn't attack them as I thought they would. I was stationary, my feet not moving as Roman started shouting in Russian to all the bodyguards, who all quickly drew their weapons.

Ember's voice penetrated my numbness. "I think we're about to be attacked. Two men that know

Ruslan," she paused when Roman shouted their names to her, "all right, a man named Abram and Vadim have just come in. They're guarding the door, guns drawn." She paused, and I could hear Grigori shouting over the line. "I know. I love you, too. I'll kill them all." She hung up. Calm as could be.

Mary and Katie hugged me, but I stared down at the mask. It all came from the mask. A gift left for me. I stared at the mask hard, my heart in my throat as I realized what it was…too late.

"Get out! Everyone get out!" I screamed, interrupting a call Artur was having with someone on his phone, his gun drawn in his other hand. "It's a fucking gas mask! They're going to gas everyone!" I held up said mask. I had no clue who the hell was coming, but they weren't coming in with guns. They were smarter than that.

The new guys, Vadim and Abram, stared at what I held for all of a beat before they lunged at the doors.

Just as a hissing echoed in the room above our heads.

"Put the mask on," Artur demanded sharply, coming to stand in front of me. Vadim and Abram aimed at the door when it wouldn't open—even though they had just come through it. He held the phone up to my ear. "It's Papa."

I stared into Artur's calm, but fierce eyes.

Over the line, Daniil said, "Beth, put the mask on. Put it on now. Stay alive for me, my sweet. Stay. Alive."

OBSIDIAN MASK

I choked, and the world went a little blurry.

Artur stumbled but put his gun away, taking the mask out of the package. He placed it up to my face. I ripped it away long enough to say, "I love you, Daniil."

He was so calm. "I love you, too. Now put on the mask."

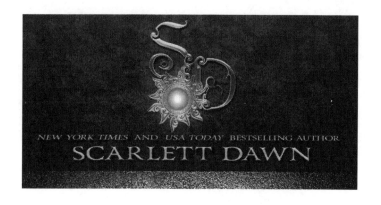

NEW YORK TIMES AND USA TODAY BESTSELLING AUTHOR

SCARLETT DAWN

Thank you so much for reading Obsidian Mask. I hope you enjoyed it!

All honest reviews are appreciated.

Sign up for Scarlett's newsletter to stay updated on her new releases: Eepurl.com/4X1rv

About the Author

Scarlett Dawn is drawn to all things quirky and off-beat. She believes there are no boundaries for an imaginative soul. Her love of the written word started from at an early age, when her grandmother would take her to bookstores every weekend. Dreams came alive within the books she found there, and now, she is thrilled to share her stories with others who have fallen under the spell of taking fantastical journeys. Scarlett resides in the Midwest with her family.

Where to find Scarlett:
Facebook.com/AuthorScarlettDawn
Twitter.com/ScarlettDawnUSA
Scarlettdawn.net

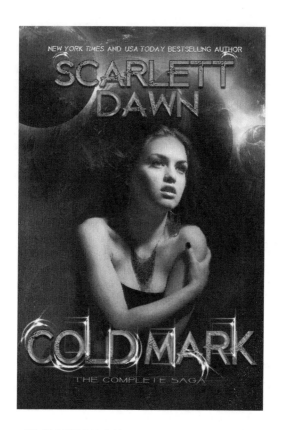

*"MY WORLD WAS FOREVER
CHANGED."*

FALL

Thrown head first into a barbaric world she knows
nothing of, Braita Valorn must adapt to a dark life as a
slave of the Mian society--her existence depends on it.

SINK

Danger lurks, and Braita's lack of knowledge of the
planet, Triaz, is now abundantly clear. On a mission to

find her best friend, Jax, she must infiltrate the Crank Pit, a brutal complex where Mian enter, only to leave absent a heartbeat.

STOP

Braita Valorn is stuck. She has no real freedom, her existence dependent on what the men of Triaz decide. But she desperately wants it to be, and will do anything to capture it.

RISE

Judgments are made, an archaic stand within Mian laws, and Braita finds herself charged with treason. But never one to sit during a battle, she risks her last chance of release with blackmail.

SOAR

Braita Valorn is a disaster walking. One mistake after another on the planet Triaz has landed her in trouble time and again. Will Braita obtain her freedom? Or will she finally accept a life she never asked for?

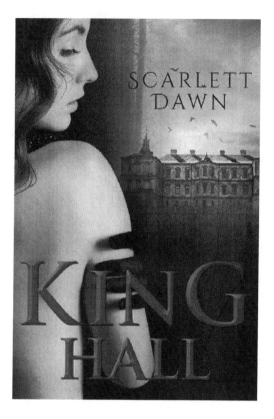

A fresh, meaty, sink-your-teeth-in-and-hold-on-tight new adult fantasy series kicks off with King Hall...

King Hall — where the Mysticals go to learn their craft, get their degrees, and transition into adulthood. And where four new Rulers will rise and meet their destinies.

Lily Ruckler is adept at one thing: survival. Born a Mystical hybrid, her mere existence is forbidden, but her nightmare is only about to start. Fluke, happenstance, and a deep personal loss finds Lily deeply entrenched with those who would destroy her simply for existing — The Mystical Kings. Being named future Queen of the Shifters shoves Lily into the spotlight, making her one of the most visible Mysticals in the world. But with risk comes a certain solace — her burgeoning friendships with the other three Prodigies: a wicked Vampire, a wild-child Mage, and a playboy Elemental. Backed by their faith and trust, Lily begins to relax into her new life.

Then chaos erupts as the fragile peace between Commoners and Mysticals is broken, and suddenly Lily realizes the greatest threat was never from within, and her fear takes on a new name: the revolution.

Made in the USA
Lexington, KY
22 November 2015